Praise for John Love's *Faith:*

"Succeeds both as a purely visceral, exciti
on the place of humanity in the universe...There is a kind of passionate
wonder on display here that makes *Faith* exhilarating to read, a novel
that demands and rewards the reader's attention from the first sentence
to the last."

—Katherine Farmar, *Strange Horizons*

"A science fiction debut of the highest order. It has fascinating, well-
rounded characters who will remain with you for a long time. [...] A
novel I maybe would have expected from the mind of Iain M. Banks—
and if that isn't a compliment for an SF debut, I don't know what is...
I'm already sure this novel will end up on my list of 2012 favourites."

—Stefan Raets, *Tor.com*

"A huge widescreen premise...The perfect mix of space battles and
politics."

—Charlie Jane Anders, *io9.com*

"Sophisticated, inventive and beautifully written, *Faith* is a cut above
the rest. John Love has made an excellent debut."

—Allen Steele, author of *Oceanspace* and
The Coyote Chronicles

"The beautiful, brutal bastard of Iain M Banks and Peter Watts—absolutely brilliant."

—Sean Williams, author of *The Resurrected Man*
and *The Grand Conjunction*

"Gripping and original."

—David Moles, Theodore Sturgeon Memorial
Award-winning author

"Tremendous science fiction that blends literary traditions with space
opera and all the various subgenres therein...John Love's debut is on
par with Dan Simmons's *Hyperion* in its quest to pose questions and
attempt to answer them."

—Justin Landon, *Staffers Book Review*

"A genius bit of writing, and an absolute home run for first-timer John
Love."

—SteveSkojec.com

Also by John Love:
Faith

EVENSONG

JOHN LOVE

Perry and Martin :
thank you for your
friendship, and I
hope you like my
second book.

John

28. 6. 15

NIGHT SHADE BOOKS
NEW YORK

Night Shade books may be purchased in bulk at special discounts for sales promotion, corporate gifts, fund-raising, or educational purposes. Special editions can also be created to specifications. For details, contact the Special Sales Department, Night Shade Books, 307 West 36th Street, 11th Floor, New York, NY 10018 or info@skyhorsepublishing.com.

Night Shade Books™ is a trademark of Skyhorse Publishing, Inc.®, a Delaware corporation.

Visit our website at www.nightshadebooks.com.

10 9 8 7 6 5 4 3 2 1

Library of Congress Cataloging-in-Publication Data is available on file.

Cover design by Claudia Noble

ISBN: 978-1-59780-552-0

Printed in the United States of America

For Sandra, Helen and Ian

JUNE 2061

They'd wish her dead if they knew what she'd done. But they are only a congregation, mostly elderly and infirm, and they know nothing about her.

Some of them look round as she enters. This is the third consecutive Sunday that Olivia has come to Evensong at Rochester Cathedral, and they are beginning to notice her. She is shabbily dressed, her blonde hair lank and greasy. She looks like someone they would once have recognised.

Habit makes her glance round every few minutes, though she doesn't expect to see those hunting her. Not yet. It normally takes them a few weeks, but they always find her—after what she did, they'll never give up—and then the cycle begins again: flight, to another rundown flat, in another rundown neighbourhood. She thinks, *Anwar would have handled the last few months much better,* but *Anwar is long gone.*

The choir is singing the evening's first psalm. She recognises the words from other Evensongs at other churches.

For he shall deliver thee from the snare of the hunter.
He shall defend thee under his wings,
And thou shalt be safe...

It is a pleasant summer evening. The sunlight is the colour of burnished copper; it deepens and enriches the red-brown of the pews and puts alternate light and dark bands across the aisle. Above her the Cathedral is vaulted and groined, with stone Gothic arches curving up into a dark wooden ceiling. Twilight floats there, bobbing against the ceiling like a helium balloon after a party, waiting to float down and become night.

Lord, now lettest thou thy servant depart in peace...

The words of the Nunc Dimittis always sound to her like they should be the closing words, but Evensong doesn't finish there; there are some responses and collects, a short sermon, and a hymn. Then they file out through the West Door into the Cathedral precincts: College Yard, with lawns and park benches, magnolias, and a huge spreading catalpa tree hundreds of years old. Something still remains of the copper evening sunlight, and there are some refectory tables in the courtyard and around the trees, where some of the congregation have stopped for coffee.

She avoids eye contact and hurries past them. She has lost many things in the last few months, including her need for companionship. And her capacity to return it.

Lord, now lettest thou thy servant depart in peace...

Olivia's flat is only a few minutes' walk from the Cathedral, at the other end of the old High Street. It is above a computer repair shop, a low-rent business in a low-rent area: only poor people need to repair computers, and her landlord, who owns the business, is only marginally better off than she is.

The walls of the stairway and landing are painted dark green and cream. The landing smells of damp. So does her flat, when she opens the door, but it also smells more strongly of something else: nonhuman urine.

"Fuck you" is the ginger cat's probable meaning as it meows at her indignantly; not for the first time, she's forgotten to put down its litter tray. She cleans up the mess (leaving a few more dark patches on the carpet, as though an old map had suddenly grown some new continents) and

goes through to her bedroom. In there is the only genuine souvenir of the old days.

Anwar had once torn a page out of one of his books (an impulsive act, for someone who valued books as he did) and had left it on her bed. She has kept it ever since. It contains the first four lines of a Shakespeare sonnet: his favourite Shakespeare sonnet, and now he is as long gone as its author.

Let me not to the marriage of true minds
Admit impediments. Love is not love
Which alters when it alteration finds,
Or bends with the remover to remove.

ONE: SEPTEMBER 2060

1

Anwar sat in a formal garden in northern Malaysia on a pleasant September afternoon, reading. *The Moving Finger writes; and, having writ, Moves on...*He liked FitzGerald's translation of Omar Khayyam, but felt it took liberties with the text; he preferred the original, in the cadences of twelfth-century Persian.

It was 4:00 p.m.: time. He closed the book and retreated back under the roof of his verandah, just as the afternoon rain began with its usual promptness and intensity. While he watched it he performed one of his standard exercises: using the fingers of his right hand to break, one by one, the fingers of his left hand. The core of the exercise was not to blank out the pain—though his abilities were such that he could have done that, too—but to feel the pain and still not react to it, either by noise or by movement, as each finger was bent back beyond the vertical and snapped. It was a familiar exercise and he finished it satisfactorily.

The rain stopped, as promptly and suddenly as it had begun. He leaned back, breathing in the scent of wet leaves and grass. A brief gust of wind shook rain from the trees, so that it sounded, for a few seconds, like another downpour beginning. He cupped his right hand round his left, easing his fingers back to their normal position, and waited for the bones to set and regenerate; it would take about an hour.

It was not unheard-of for a VSTOL from the UN to land on the formal lawn at the centre of his garden, but it was not something which happened often. This was one of their latest, silent and silvered and almost alien. A door melted open in its side and a dark-haired young woman got out and walked across the lawn towards Anwar. She was Arden Bierce, one of Rafiq's personal staff, and they smiled a greeting at each other.

"Rafiq wants you." She handed him a letter. He studied Rafiq's neat italic handwriting, not unlike his own, and the courteously phrased request and personal signature. When Rafiq made this kind of request, he did so by pen and ink and personal meeting. Never remotely, and never electronically.

"I should go now." He was telling her, not asking her. She nodded and turned back to the waiting VSTOL. Anwar Abbas stood up, stretched, and walked after her. He was as powerful as a tiger, as quiet as the flame of a candle.

Offer and Acceptance. The VSTOL would take him south to the UN complex outside Kuala Lumpur, where Laurens Rafiq, the Controller-General, would formally offer him a mission and request his acceptance. Anwar Abbas had received such requests before from Rafiq, but this one would be different. It would lead him to two people, one of them his beginning and the other his end.

2

Anwar liked the VSTOL, almost to the point of kinship; it was quiet, did exactly what it was supposed to do, and did it supremely well. It was even superior to America's Area 51 planes, and their Chinese and European equivalents.

There was a growing concern in some quarters that the UN was developing better hardware than its members. Another example, Anwar reflected, of the Rafiq Effect.

The northern highlands of Malaysia hurtled past underneath. They were heavily wooded, and seemed to be smoking without flames; vapour from the last downpour, hanging above treetop level. He clenched and unclenched his left hand.

"Is it healed?" Arden Bierce asked him.

He smiled. "The Moving Finger breaks, and having broke, resets itself."

"Don't you mean 'broken'?"

"Wouldn't scan."

He liked her; she had this ability to make people feel comfortable around her. She was very attractive, but seemed genuinely unaware of it. Most people born with looks like that would be shaped by them; would probably be cynical or manipulative. She was neither. Perceptive and clever in her dealings with people, but also pleasant and companionable.

Anwar had never done any more than flirt mildly with her. He was awkward socially, the result of having a normal circle of acquaintances but few close friends. Only about thirty people in the world knew what he was.

He leaned back and watched the shapes and colours moving just under the silvered surfaces of the walls and furniture of the VSTOL's lounge. It would be a short flight. The UN complex outside Kuala Lumpur would soon appear.

The UN had adapted to the increasing complexity and volatility of the world order. It had a Secretary-General (political) and a Controller-General (executive). As it gradually took on more executive functions, the Controller-General became more important, at the expense of the Secretary-General. The Controller-General was Laurens Rafiq.

The old UN in New York still remained, but Rafiq's UNEX (UN Executive) in Kuala Lumpur was overtaking it—restructuring the major agencies like UNESCO, UNICEF, UNIDO, and transforming them. Policy was still in the hands of the old UN, but it was becoming apparent that policy was meaningless without executive rigour. The medium was overtaking the message.

Rafiq had acquired many assets at UNEX. Not only the agencies, but also some independent military capacity—not enough to make the UN more powerful than any of its individual members, but enough to settle some of the increasing conflicts over resources, energy, borders, and trade. Often Rafiq's UNEX would take pre-emptive action which later the political UN had to ratify—had to, because the action worked.

One of the smaller and more mysterious components of Rafiq's UNEX was something he called The Consultancy, known colloquially (and inaccurately) as The Dead. Its members did things for him which mere Special Forces could never do. Outside UNEX, nobody knew exactly how many Consultants Rafiq had, but it was only a handful. This was because only a handful could survive the induction process, and because only a handful was all that even Rafiq could afford. Their training, and the physical and neurological enhancements which made them unique, were uniquely expensive.

Anwar Abbas was a Consultant: one of The Dead.

Dusk fell quickly and was short-lived, turning abruptly to darkness in the few minutes' duration of the flight. Anwar got only a glimpse of the lights of the UN complex before the silvered plane dropped vertically and landed—or, rather, hovered politely one inch above the ground while they stepped out through the door that had rippled open for them. What enabled it to hover was something to do with room-temperature semiconductors, the Holy Grail of frictionless motion: not fully achieved yet, but getting closer.

The plane slid noiselessly up into the night. For the second time, Anwar found himself following Arden Bierce across a lawn. This lawn was part of the park which formed the centre of the UN complex.

Ringing the park were some tall buildings, each a different shape and colour: ziggurats, pyramids, cones, ovoids. Each stood in its own smaller piece of manicured parkland, and was festooned with greenery hanging from walls and windows and balconies. The overall effect was pleasing, without the pomp of the old UN buildings in New York and Geneva; more like the commercial district of any reasonably prosperous city. Kuala Lumpur, a few miles south, was similar but larger-scale.

The central parkland had lawns and woods, landscaped low hills and a river, over which was cantilevered the Controller-General's house, Fallingwater. It was based on Frank Lloyd Wright's design, scaled up, but still house-sized. The security around this building, of all the buildings in the complex, appeared to be nonexistent, the way Rafiq had personally designed it to appear. They simply walked up to the front door and rang the doorbell. The door opened into a large reception area.

"I'll go and tell him you're here," said Arden Bierce as she went through an adjoining door, usually known as *the* door because it led to Rafiq's inner office.

Anwar looked around him. He knew Fallingwater well, and found it calming. The interior of the house was larger than Wright's original, but furnished and decorated in the same style: comfortable and understated, a mix of regular and organic shapes, of autumn browns and ochres and earth tones. Large areas of the floor were open expanses of polished wood, with seating areas formed by clusters of plain stone-white sofas and armchairs. Several people were there, talking quietly. They were all members of Rafiq's personal staff, like Arden Bierce, but only a few of them looked up as he entered. The rest paid him no attention.

Except for Miles Levin. He and Anwar had known each other for years, and they exchanged their usual greeting.

"Muslim filth."

"Jewish scum."

Their Muslim and Jewish origins, if any, were no longer important. They had taken their present names, along with their present identities, when they became Consultants. Which they had done at the same time, seven years ago.

Levin was six feet five, nearly three inches taller than Anwar, and more powerfully built. He looked generally younger and stronger, and was—for a Consultant—louder and more outgoing. Anwar was thin-faced, with a hook nose. Levin's face was broader and more open. Both were dark-haired and wore their hair long.

"Waiting to see him?" Anwar asked.

"I've seen him. Offer and Acceptance. I was just leaving."

Normally they'd have had a lot to talk about, but not this time. They couldn't discuss missions, that simply wasn't done; and also, Anwar noted a strangeness in Levin's manner, a kind of preoccupation. So he just nodded briefly at him, and Levin turned to go.

"Take care," something prompted Anwar to whisper.

Levin heard. "You too." He did not look back.

"Scum."

"Filth." The door closed softly behind him.

Another door—*the* door—opened. Arden Bierce came out. "He'll see you now."

3

Laurens Rafiq was of Dutch and Moroccan parentage. He was a small, neat man, quiet-spoken like Anwar. He was not the UN's first Controller-General, but was by far its most

effective. Even the enemies he had made during his ascend-
ancy conceded that.

"Thank you for coming so promptly, Mr. Abbas." Rafiq
motioned to a chair, and Anwar sat down. "I want to offer you
a mission. May I describe it?"

"Please."

"First, I should tell you this. It involves bodyguard duties."

Anwar spoke carefully, to mask his surprise. "We don't
usually do that, Mr. Rafiq. Even for you."

"This isn't for me, it's for someone else."

His surprise turned to anger. *For someone else?* Playing
for time, and trying to compose himself, Anwar gazed round
Rafiq's office. Like the original Fallingwater, and the reception outside, it was spacious and understated and restful. But
it didn't relax him. *This is wrong,* he thought. *Special Forces,
mere Special Forces, do bodyguard duties. Not us. Asking a
Consultant to do that is like...*

"It must be like asking Shakespeare to write greeting card
verses," Rafiq said. "I know how you feel.

"But there's a UN resources summit next month. Several
member states attending have been, or still are, at war with
each other over water rights. A volatile subject, and security
will be a concern. Also, the usual venues might offend political
sensibilities. So the New Anglicans have offered us the conference centre attached to their Cathedral in Brighton, on the
south coast of England."

"I know where Brighton is, Mr. Rafiq," Anwar said. "I go
to bookfairs there."

"Yes, I'd forgotten." He hadn't. He wanted to give Anwar
a minor point now, to help the dynamics later. "So. The New
Anglicans' offer is tempting. Their Cathedral complex, with
conference centre and hotels, is large and well-equipped. And,
most important for security, it's at the end of a two-mile-long
ocean pier. But there's a price."

Rafiq paused, not for dramatic effect but because what he said next could lead to something unprecedented, a Consultant refusing a mission.

"Olivia del Sarto has asked for a Consultant to attend her during the nine days of the summit, starting October 15. Apparently she's always wanted one of The Dead—" he spoke the phrase with distaste "—as her personal bodyguard."

Olivia del Sarto, thought Anwar, still somehow masking his feelings. *Archbishop of the New Anglicans. And Archbitch: brilliant and offensive, with her hidden political and financial backers and her sexual appetites and her foul ginger cat.* The sexual appetites and the cat were familiar parts of her media persona. She consistently refused to tone down the former, or to have the latter castrated. He'd seen her, again and again, on the news channels. *This is wrong. One of* us, *as a fashion accessory for* her?

"She's asked you for something you shouldn't give. We only do things for *you.* For the Controller-General."

Rafiq said nothing, just waited for Anwar to continue. He knew when to pause and when to press. So did Anwar, but with Anwar it came from enhancement and training. With Rafiq it came naturally.

"It's the heart of the compact. Any mission you offer us must be impossible for anyone else. And only for *you.* This doesn't qualify on either count."

Again Rafiq waited.

Anwar stood up suddenly, shockingly fast, and glared down at Rafiq. "Occasionally, *very* occasionally, if there was exceptional risk, we'd do bodyguard duties for you or the Secretary-General. This is different! You want me to nurse that—that person, because you've done a deal with her for a conference venue?"

With Anwar still towering above him Rafiq thought, *I'm alone with one of The Dead, and I've seriously annoyed him.*

Be careful with this one, he's obsessive. Likes everything just so. But still he said nothing.

"You negotiated with her? You let her have one of *us*, as a fashion accessory?"

Still Rafiq said nothing.

Anwar added, "And she must have security people of her own."

Got him. Rafiq smiled. "She has. Mere Special Forces, as you would say, but they're good. I doubt whether you'll either add to her safety, or uncover anything her people may have missed. Also, she's not a participant in the summit, only the host. The national leaders and UN officials are more likely to be targets, and they too will have their own security."

"Including you?"

"I won't be there. This is political, not executive, so the Secretary-General will go." Rafiq rarely referred to the Secretary-General by name; he had already outlasted three of them.

Something's threatening her, Anwar thought suddenly. *Something beyond the abilities of her own security people, so she wants one of us. And whatever it is, it's specific to the summit, because she only wants me for the nine days.*

"You've just assigned Miles Levin. Are our missions connected?"

"You know I can't answer that." Rafiq knew that they genuinely weren't connected, but even if he'd said so he doubted that Anwar would believe him. Anwar had a tendency to look for pockets of darkness in everything.

In fact, Anwar had only asked about Levin to buy some time while he tried to think it through. *She isn't asking this as a whim, and Rafiq doesn't grant whims. He must owe her. Or the New Anglicans, or their political and financial network. And for a lot more than just a conference venue. Do I cite the compact and refuse? Or find out what it is?*

"Why did you ask *me* to do this?"

"I really don't know. I just had an instinct that you would be the right one."

Pause.

"I need Offer and Acceptance. Will you do it?"

"Yes." As he spoke, Anwar heard a succession of doors closing, and others opening, all the way to England.

TWO: SEPTEMBER 2060

In seven years Levin had carried out fifteen missions for Rafiq. None of them compared, even remotely, to this. It was why he'd been preoccupied when he met Anwar. *If only I could have told him*...It was heaven's gate. It would take him to Croatia to locate Parvin Marek, the only person ever to evade The Dead.

"I don't aim to destroy society," Marek once wrote, after one of his atrocities, "but to demonstrate that it has already destroyed itself."

Rafiq had given him a detailed briefing, but Levin already knew most of it. The case had always affected him deeply, particularly its later events.

Ten years ago Parvin Marek led a terrorist movement called Black Dawn. It wasn't a mass movement, and had no interest in becoming one. It wasn't religious, or even conventionally political. It was nihilist. It had no goals or aims, only methods; its slogan, sprayed over derelict buildings, was "Justify Nothing." The group consisted of Marek and seven others, who operated as one-person cells. They rarely met or even talked to each other, and had long ago cut all ties to family and friends. The Croatian authorities knew who they were but not where, which made them almost unstoppable.

Marek himself was quiet and withdrawn, an absence of all qualities except action. He didn't shout, threaten, exhort, or inspire. He only *did*. What drove him was the Marxist dialectic seen through the dead eyes of nihilism. Society was an illusion, a mere theatre: religion, culture, values, art, politics, all merely a mask for economic forces. Destroy the economic forces? Impractical. But destroy the mask, and the economic forces will be uncovered and die.

Black Dawn attacked random civilian targets: stores, airports, stations, even schools and hospitals. They took no hostages because they had no demands. They were unique, not because of the numbers they killed, but the nature of their killing. Religious fundamentalists killed more people; but they had reasons, however insane, and would say so. Black Dawn had none, and said nothing.

The culmination came in 2050 when Marek bombed the UN Embassy in Zagreb, killing twenty Embassy staff and seven passersby. Before leaving, Marek went back and shot dead two people lying on the pavement who, he noticed, were still alive. Later he issued a statement saying that the bomb had been designed to explode outwards as well as inwards, to kill passersby as well as Embassy staff. Justify Nothing, his statement concluded.

The Croatian authorities formally requested UN assistance. They had never been able to locate Marek and the other seven, but UN Intelligence did. Two Consultants (not Levin or Anwar; this was before their time) accepted a mission from Rafiq. In one night they took the seven, alive, and gave them to the authorities. Marek, remarkably, evaded them, but Black Dawn was broken.

It still wasn't enough.

The Dead hardly ever did bodyguard duties: that was the province of, in Anwar's words, "mere Special Forces." So, six months later, three mere Special Forces bodyguards were on duty when Rafiq's wife and two children, a boy of seven and a girl of five, were shot dead by Marek. The family had just arrived at a marquee on the lawn in front of Fallingwater for the boy's birthday party; Rafiq was on his way to join them. After shooting them, and the bodyguards, Marek turned back: the boy, he noticed, was still alive. Marek shot him again, twice in the head. From his wristcom he detonated a couple of bombs nearby. He didn't know, or care, if they'd killed or injured anyone. They were a diversion, allowing him to walk— not run—away. Again he proved untraceable; this time, not for six months but ten years.

After it happened Rafiq became isolated and solitary, though no less effective. His only public statement was, "Marek has killed more people than just my family. For all of them, this is unfinished business."

The family wing at Fallingwater was closed and sealed.

And now, ten years later, the UN had a possible lead.

"Not a direct lead to Marek," Rafiq had told Levin, when he summoned him to Fallingwater a day earlier, "but to someone who might be prepared to sell him: Slovan Soldo, a distant relative. Soldo lives in Opatija, a seaside resort on the northern coast of Croatia. He's facing arrest on rape charges, and probably looking for a deal."

"How good is the lead?" Levin asked, trying to mask his elation.

"It's from UN Intelligence. It's good, but it's tenuous, and we don't want it compromised. Whoever we send to follow it can have no surveillance or backup."

So, Levin thought, *this mission satisfies the compact. It's impossible for anyone except a Consultant, and it's specifically for Rafiq. More so than any other mission.*

I was right to choose him, Rafiq thought. *He really wants it.*

"I'm formally offering you this mission. I want you to contact Soldo, and locate Marek. But if you accept," he added, "you'll need to move within a day. Soldo won't wait around. Will you do it?"

"Yes." Levin had enough good taste—but only just enough—not to show Rafiq his genuine delight. If he'd punched the air, as he originally wanted, he'd probably have knocked it unconscious.

Marek would now be in his early to middle forties. What little information there was showed him to be a dark-haired man of average height and stocky build, running slightly to fat. Softly spoken, like Anwar. Physically unremarkable, except for his hands. They were broad, almost spadelike, giving a large lateral spread. But the fingers were long and slender, like a concert pianist's. Ideal for the manipulation of devices.

Levin's imagination was racing. He'd seen possible Mareks all through the flight, and was seeing more of them now he'd landed. Every third or fourth adult male Croatian seemed to be stocky and fortyish with unusual hands. The Croatian national basketball team had been on his flight. Most of them were in their twenties and nearly seven feet tall, but Levin still caught himself double-checking them for hidden resemblances to Marek.

Levin carried no luggage, not even a briefcase. He was alone and unarmed. He had travelled by scheduled flight to Rijeka, where he was to be met and driven to a villa near Opatija.

Rijeka Airport, Zracna Luca Rijeka, was nondescript when it was built and had not improved with age. Its minor buildings and outbuildings were like architectural acne. It did have a new terminal, built on a part of the runway that was no longer needed since the advent of blended-wing VSTOL airliners, but it wasn't much better than the 1960s building it replaced. It was flyblown and fluorescent, and smelled of stewed coffee and styrofoam. Levin walked quickly through it and out to the main entrance. A car eventually pulled up alongside him. It wasn't battery-driven, like most of those around it, but a newer hydrogen fuel cell model. The window opened.

"I'm here to meet Slovan Soldo," Levin said, in Croatian.

"I know," said the driver. "Get in, please." He was dark-haired, stocky, fortyish. *This mission,* Levin thought. *Mareks everywhere. Mareks, Mareks everywhere, and none of them are real. Anwar would have said,* Nor any one is real, *to follow Coleridges's original wording. But Anwar's got his head up his ass.*

They took the main road out of Rijeka, a journey of about thirty miles and twenty-five minutes. By the time they reached the town centre of Opatija it was still only late afternoon, a good time of day to see the town. In the nineteenth century, when Croatia was part of the Austro-Hungarian Empire, the Hapsburgs had used Opatija as a holiday resort. Levin, whose other identity in the real world was founding partner of a large architectural practice, studied the ornate and elegant Hapsburg buildings. He thought of the long slow circlings of history: in the late nineteenth and early twentieth centuries, the Hapsburgs had been targets for nihilist groups like Black Dawn.

They continued for a few minutes along the palm-lined main boulevard until they reached the gates of the Villa Angiolina Park. From there they turned left and up into the foothills of Mount Ucka, the national park to the north of Opatija. Roadside buildings fell away as they climbed higher, and were replaced by dense laurel woods and cypresses. The smell of their leaves and resin hung in the air. It was still only late afternoon.

The villa stood in a clearing in the laurel woods. It was surrounded by cypresses, dark verticals to the villa's white horizontal, and it looked large and expensive. Levin thought, *Does Slovan Soldo own this? Rape pays well here.*

The car stopped, and the driver—they had not exchanged a word since Rijeka—stayed put. Levin got out, walked up to the front door and rang the bell. It opened, apparently automatically, into a large reception room. He walked in, immediately killing his shock and smiling a greeting at those inside. *Never look surprised* was one of his maxims. As if they shared it, those inside smiled back.

2

Anwar was back at his house in northern Malaysia. He'd activated an immersion hologram in his living room, making it a dark and dripping alley. It was an expensively detailed hologram: smells of wet pavement and urine, sounds of running water and rodent scurryings. It suited his mood.

Do I have to guard her cat as well?

Arden Bierce had given him the usual crystal bead containing Rafiq's detailed briefing. He could have played it at Fallingwater, but preferred to take it back home. He pulled up a chair—in reality it was a black and silver Bauhaus original, but in the hologram it was a damp stained mattress—and settled down. He pressed the bead into his wrist implant, and watched the headup display resolve on the inner surface of his retina, a simple full-face shot of Rafiq.

"Thirty years ago," Rafiq said, "this summit would have been about fossil fuels—oil, gas, maybe coal and shale. But alternative energy sources are now commercially viable: wind, sun, tides, high-atmosphere turbulence, nuclear fusion, hydrogen cells, even continental drift." (*Yes,* Anwar thought, *and I know how much you've made the UN invest in them. You always play long.*) "This summit is about something much more basic, ever-present but ever-scarce where it's most needed: water. It will be difficult. Some of the member states going to Brighton have been, or still are, at war over water rights."

A tramp was pissing copiously against the wall of the alley. It steamed and frothed on the mouldering brickwork. All the tramps who came and went in this hologram were different, Anwar noted approvingly. It never quite repeated itself.

He liked immersion holograms. He had once turned his family living room (and later, his school gym) into the UN Security Council Chamber, complete with all the then members, except that he made them naked. He enjoyed imagining what they were like under their clothes. He gave them liver spots, varicose veins, pimples on buttocks, local accretions of fat. And he made them carry on debating exactly as if they'd been clothed. In his hologram they were debating water rights—then, as now, a big issue.

He switched his attention back to the inner surface of his retina. Rafiq had been listing some more details of the summit, its proceedings and participants, then turned to the subject of its location.

"Brighton Cathedral...your friend Levin would like this. It's a full-size replica of Brighton's Royal Pavilion, one of Europe's most eccentric buildings. The New Anglicans' parish churches are all new designs, commissioned from contemporary architects—Levin's partnership designed two of them— but they decided that their Cathedral should echo the style of Brighton's greatest symbol.

"The original was built in the eighteenth century by the Prince Regent, but the New Anglicans have built theirs at the end of a two-mile-long ocean pier. The Cathedral is surrounded by other buildings, architecturally matching, to house conference facilities, hotels, function suites, and media centres. There are also commercial offices, studios, shops, restaurants. The ocean pier has maglevs running up and down its length; and, of course, it's easy to defend. The New Anglicans make a lot of money from it. It's a world-class commercial centre."

Transcripts of Rafiq's speeches showed that he spoke exactly as a good writer would write. They were like passages from William Hazlitt. Measured sentences of meticulous construction. Grammar like precision engineering.

"So: our hosts, the New Anglicans…" Anwar touched his wrist implant and paused the briefing. At his gesture the hologram died and his living room reappeared. He walked around the black and grey and silver Bauhaus interior, playing the last Tournament on a wallscreen. It hadn't gone well, and he wanted another look at it.

It had taken place two weeks ago, in a large dojo in the UN complex near Kuala Lumpur. It was a six-monthly event, Rafiq's idea. Sometimes Consultants needed actual combat between missions, to supplement their standard exercises. It was open to all comers, inside or outside the UN: Special Forces, mercenaries, martial artists, and anyone else who could satisfy the exacting criteria. The kind of opponents they would most likely encounter on actual missions.

Each Consultant was assigned six opponents by lottery, and had to face them simultaneously and unarmed. Opponents were allowed any weapons except firearms, and could kill or injure, or try to. The Consultant couldn't; he or she could only disable.

Tournament fees were large, with bonuses for every member of a group who killed or injured a Consultant. Stories circulated from time to time about injuries inflicted and bonuses paid—all untrue, but Rafiq found them useful urban myths. Reality was different. It was proven, in real missions, that a Consultant had a near-100 percent chance of defeating six proficient opponents, even if one or more had a gun. Tournaments, however, remained oversubscribed.

Anwar fast-forwarded to the replay of his own combat. He was addressing his six opponents. His voice sounded strange because of the effect on his face of the Idmask, a nanobot injection which altered the configuration and proportions of his features. The alteration lasted only two hours, enough to mask him during a Tournament, and was random and different each time.

"You must genuinely try to kill or injure me. If I think you haven't," he kept his face straight, partly out of a liking for deadpan remarks and partly an effect of the Idmask, "Rafiq will do something worse than I ever could. Sue you for material nonperformance of contract."

A couple of them smiled briefly, then it began.

A lot was written, some of it pretentious, about martial arts being a mirror for life. Anwar's fighting style, however, exactly mirrored his life. It was cautious, measured, contained. He liked counterattack. He liked to come out of safety, strike, and return to safety—a pattern which characterized all his missions, and all his relationships such as they were. His maxim was to do nothing risky or unexpected—at least, by Consultancy standards, though to ordinary opponents he was frightening, inhumanly fast, and strong. Like most of The Dead, when he fought he stayed silent.

Original martial arts moves were transformed by The Dead into moves that were impossible for anyone without enhancements. Over the years The Dead had given these moves new names, often ironic or obscure, sometimes obscene. Like The Penumbra for Shadowless Kick, The Circumnavigator for Roundhouse Kick, The Flying Fuck for Heart Kite. And others, for which no previous equivalent move existed: The Verb, The Compliment, The Gratuity, The Abseiling Pope.

Unusually, the six opponents Anwar had drawn were all armed: a katana, a quarterstaff (Anwar's own favourite weapon), various knives, even a flail. He circled among them.

His first instinct was to analyse them, to assess what they were; and it was wrong. His first instinct should have been to attack and disable them, because whatever they were, he outmatched them.

To any observer, he was a blur while they moved normally. To himself, seen through his own ramped-up senses, he moved normally while they were stationary or wading through treacle, expressions of shock at what he could do forming like geological processes on their faces, exclamations at his speed and strength oozing out of their mouths in low bass notes. But he'd only been starting cautiously, waiting to assess and counterattack.

Use speed first, his enhancement maxims told him. With speed, everything else is possible. The other "S" categories— strength, stamina, even skill—are secondary. But he didn't follow the maxims. His speed was actually quite good, approaching that of the highest-performing Consultants, but his instinct was always to step back and take stock; it was why his rating was merely average. Still, it was enough to leave his opponents aghast.

He dodged the katana and knife-blades and quarterstaff by hundredths of an inch, which his retinal headups could measure and display if he wanted while he was still in motion. He didn't want; he'd assessed their weapons skills to his satisfaction. The other weapon, the flail, was hardly worth his attention: fearsome to look at and dangerous if it connected, but slow and clumsy and telegraphed.

His private nickname for such opponents was Meatslabs, and it was always like this when he fought them. He could see, hear, smell, touch, and taste their inadequacy. And their shock, when he decided to let the one with the flail land a blow. The flail was a six-foot cluster of segmented black metal whips, glistening like a tangle of liquorice. He let it land without apparently noticing. A good tactic: it set them wondering what he must be made of, inside. But it wouldn't have impressed Levin or the others.

He tried some cautious counterattacks. His hands and feet, fingertips and toes (he fought barefoot) flickered out at nerve clusters and pressure points. Not yet to touch, but to see how well they defended. Quietly, carefully, he was assembling a kinetic dossier on each of them.

But he still couldn't take full advantage. Something went wrong. One of his opponents, the one with the quarterstaff, suffered a broken collarbone: Anwar had mistimed a fingertip touch to a nerve-centre, and had to turn it at the last moment into a shuto strike to avoid killing him. The other five were on Anwar immediately, fired up by what he had done, and he wasted seconds adjusting to the new dynamic—slowing down to assess it, rather than using it to his own advantage. Then his speed reasserted itself, and he did to them what he'd failed to do to their colleague with the quarterstaff: landed precise fingertip touches to nerve centres and pressure points, enough to disable and immobilise, but no more. He finished them in thirty-six seconds.

There were nineteen Consultants. Fourteen took part in this Tournament. The other five were on, or recovering from, active missions. Of the fourteen, only Anwar suffered the indignity of injuring rather than disabling an opponent. It was a notable Tournament. The previous record was twenty seconds, broken first by Miles Levin (nineteen seconds) and then by Chulo Asika (seventeen). Asika's display even outshone Levin's. Asika, in the real world, designed and built theatre sets.

Anwar's time was tenth out of fourteen. Even without his mistake, it would probably have been no better than seventh. Levin came up to him afterwards and clapped him on the shoulder. "I'm Miles ahead of you, Anwar," he said, as usual.

Levin was full of such remarks. Anwar privately nicknamed them Levin's Levities. He often thought of good rejoinders, but only when it was too late. At Fallingwater, for instance, he could have said, "Don't look so preoccupied. You don't have the attention span." He thought, *How can two people so dissimilar develop a friendship?* He smiled, as he knew Levin would do every time he asked himself the same question. The question contained the answer.

But he couldn't distance himself from the mistake. He'd been replaying it obsessively for days. It mortified him.

3

The door opened, apparently automatically, into a large reception room. Levin walked in, immediately killing his shock and smiling a greeting at those inside.

His shock was caused by the room: a replica of the reception at Fallingwater. *They know what I am.* He parked the thought, and concentrated on the eight men waiting in the reception. They hadn't surprised him at all.

Their suits were immaculate, almost as expensive as his. He could tell, by the drape of the jackets and trousers, where guns and knives and other weapons were variously stowed in shoulder and ankle holsters, forearm and wrist implants. He could tell by details of stance and mannerism where they had served: SAS, Green Berets, Spetsnaz, and so on. At least three of them looked vaguely like Marek. Not their build, just their faces.

Eight. Normally this would not have been outside his competence—any one of The Dead would be certain of taking six such people, and almost certain of taking eight. But they had an *ease* about them. They knew, as well as he did, that he could defeat them. But their ease suggested they had something else.

Among his enhancements was a sensitivity to changes in ambient air pressure, replicating that of seabirds and spiders. It worked, but it didn't help him.

He felt a shift in the air behind him, and realised that the eight were a diversion for the ninth man, who shot him quickly with a tranquiliser gun, then disappeared. He caught a glimpse of him: stocky, dark-haired. About mid-forties? Running to fat? No, he was seeing Mareks everywhere, and it didn't matter because something else was happening which was impossible: the tranquiliser was actually working. It was a new compound, and slid easily past his molecular defences, which were designed to be infallible. He felt it taking hold of his motor functions. His molecular defences gathered and regrouped, then collapsed utterly.

Does Rafiq know about these people? was his closing thought as he crumpled to the ground. *He has to. Rafiq knows everything.*

4

Anwar settled back into his black and silver chair and pressed his wrist implant. Rafiq's face reappeared on the inner surface of his retina.

"...our hosts, the New Anglicans. When an environment changes, omnivores, not specialists, adapt best. The New Anglicans are omnivores, feeding over a broad spectrum, from religious near-fundamentalists to secular near-atheists. They've taken spectacular advantage of a changing political, spiritual, cultural, and economic environment.

"The New Anglican Church was founded in 2025 as a counterweight to fundamentalist Islam, although by the time it appeared the need for it was already disappearing; mainstream Islam had effectively disowned fundamentalism. The New Anglicans flourished, however, because of their omnivorous robustness: their creeds and teachings could sound like all things to all people.

"Also, they were exceptionally well-run, with gifted and charismatic leaders. And still are. The current leader and Archbishop (unlike the Old Anglicans, they have only one Archbishop) is Olivia del Sarto."

There was some more about her, much of which he already knew from the news channels: her abilities and background, her organisational skills, her likely allies and enemies. And her spectacular success in her five years as Archbishop, causing upheavals in religious fundamentalism. Anwar, because of his own intense dislike of fundamentalism, knew this part particularly well.

Fundamentalists would never completely go away. The Islamists were marginalised but still powerful, and (because marginalised) harder to trace. Fundamentalist Christian sects were well-entrenched political lobbies, with good networks. So were the fundamentalist single-issue movements, like those against abortion or birth control, or those in favour of Creationism or faith-based education. Frighteningly, some of them were setting aside their historical differences to make common cause against what they perceived as a more serious threat from the New Anglicans—a scabrous courtship between extremists, like earlier courtships between Nazis and Communists. Olivia del Sarto called it the Batoth'Daa: the Back to the Dark Ages Alliance. *Like one of my private nick-names,* Anwar thought approvingly. It put them on the back foot, always having to deny it.

"So," Rafiq's briefing continued, "Olivia del Sarto rein-vented the New Anglicans as a centre of rationalism, confi-dent and assertive because they didn't have the baggage of older churches like the Catholics or Old Anglicans. They could choose which doctrines to discard, which to keep. They became more like a political movement crossed with a socially-aware business corporation."

Anwar paused the briefing as a thought returned to him, one that wouldn't go away. It was related to the Tournament.

He'd carried out thirteen missions for Rafiq in seven years, and had killed only once, and then almost by accident: a bodyguard with an unsuspected heart condition, sent into massive shock by Anwar's blurring speed. Speed was the key. Consultants had a 90 percent advantage in speed over most opponents. In the other three "S" categories their advantage was 30 to 60 percent, but speed was the key. It made everything else possible.

The details of their enhancement and training were overwhelming—musculature, bone structure, internal organs, neurological processes, sensory abilities, all transformed—but the outcome was simple. They were beyond black belt, or its equivalent, in all the main martial arts, armed or unarmed. As a by-product, they were also beyond Olympic standard in most athletic and field disciplines.

And the thought which had made him pause: *there are only eighteen others like me in the world, and nine or ten of them are better than me.* It nagged him and picked at him and obsessed him. Even more so since the Tournament.

Ironically, the shuto strike which broke his opponent's collarbone had been a good one, well-executed and with just the right weight. He remembered the feel of the collarbone shearing—not shattering, but shearing cleanly—under the edge of his hand. His hands and feet, and elbows and knees, and any other striking surfaces of his body, could—if he willed them to—become strengthened locally at the molecular level at the point of impact, acquiring the density of close-grain hardwood. Most of his abilities were powered by enhanced organic processes, not by metal or machinery or electronics.

So, a good shuto strike: if he'd got it wrong, it would have continued through his opponent's body and out at the shoulder-blade. But it was the result of an earlier mistake.

And it left him with a lousy Tournament time. Which in turn left him with a mission involving mere bodyguard duties.

Except that this time, there was something different.

He gestured, and another immersion hologram, one he'd programmed himself, replaced his living room: the reception at Fallingwater. The colours and textures always relaxed him, and he needed relaxing. There was something ominous about this mission...*No, not now. Later.*

5

When Levin woke the reception room was still there. So was the Fallingwater decor. It wasn't a hologram, he decided. The textures and colours, the weave of the stone-white fabric covering the sofas, seemed too tangible. No quivering round the edges. A real replica. And—the architect part of him kicked in automatically—not of Frank Lloyd Wright's original, but larger. Scaled up, like Rafiq's house. And the eight who'd been waiting for him (eight, not nine; the other one had gone) were lounging among the groups of sofas like Rafiq's staff had been lounging when he'd last been at the real Fallingwater. No, the real *replica* Fallingwater. So this wasn't a hologram, but a genuine replica, of Rafiq's original replica. His head hurt, not because of any violence done to him, but with the strain of following his own thoughts.

He remembered that Anwar liked this interior. He, Levin, didn't particularly: he thought interiors should be one thing or the other, either grandiose or minimalist, and this was neither.

He was sitting in one of the impeccable Frank Lloyd Wright armchairs. He had no choice. His wrists and ankles were tied.

Also his forearms. Also his thighs. Also his torso. And his neck. The fact of being restrained neither surprised nor disturbed him, but the fact that he'd been restrained with monofilament disturbed him very much. As did the fact that even if it hadn't been monofilament—even if it had been something he could break or loosen, like industrial cable or steel hawsers—whoever had tied it had done so with an obvious knowledge of how he might try to break free. There were blocks and local strengthenings in all the right places.

This seemed an incongruous place for torture—a cellar, though rather obvious, was the usual preferred location—but the prospect of torture didn't disturb him. He could shut out his pain receptors, even wind down to death if irreparably damaged.

One of the eight people lounging on the sofas turned to him. "We know you have inbuilt defences against torture. You won't need them. We have no plans to torture you."

After which they continued conversing among themselves.

It wasn't acting. They were genuinely behaving as if he wasn't there. Two of them got up and walked past him, and he caught a snatch of their conversation.

"A hundred years from now, none of this will matter."

"No. A thousand maybe, but not a hundred."

The *ease* of their manner, as before. Talking to each other as if he wasn't there. *These people can't be involved with someone like Marek.* The conversation of the two sitting closest to him gradually resolved itself above the murmur of the other conversations, none of which seemed to have anything to do with him.

"My talk at the Johnsonian Society. Are you still coming?"

"Yes, I'm looking forward to it. What title did you finally decide?"

"'Mask: The Nature Of Individual Identity In Postmodern Literature.'"

"Hmm."

"Yes, I know. Pretentious. It needs something to liven it up, maybe a witty opening. Something like 'What happened to the I in Identity?'"

"Hmm...How about this? A man invents time travel. He goes forward to a minute after his death, so he can have sex with his own corpse."

"Why only a minute?"

"So he'd still be warm. You could leave that bit out if you want, but the rest of it addresses your theme about the self-referential nature of Identity."

"Self-referential, yes. And the time-travel motif gives it a dimension of circularity."

"Literally a dimension."

One of the others detached himself from a group of two or three and strolled over to Levin.

"Sorry to cause you this discomfort, but we'll release you when our colleagues get here. If you'd like anything to eat or drink, we'll have to feed it to you. I know that's a bit undignified...you may prefer to wait until our colleagues get here."

"You don't know what you've done," Levin said.

"You're right, I don't. But our colleagues do. You'll soon be meeting them."

He'd never been in a situation like this before, never in fifteen missions. They'd done it so easily. *When I get out of here,* he told himself—it didn't occur to him to say *if* rather than *when*—*I can track at least two of them from their references to the Johnsonian Society. Anwar would be incandescent at this. Mere Special Forces, casually strolling into Doctor Johnson's sacred territory of literary criticism?*

But their *ease.* If he'd been free of the monofilaments, he could defeat them all. Not kill, just defeat. The Dead very rarely killed; with their abilities, they didn't have to. But he *wasn't* free of the monofilaments. And the tranquiliser, and the way they knew how to fasten the restraints. *Who are these people? Does Rafiq know about them? He has to, Rafiq knows everything. In which case...No. Don't go there.*

6

Anwar pressed his wrist implant and Rafiq returned to the inside of his retina.

"The Church's founders come straight out of urban mythology. The Bilderberg Group, the Trilateral Commission, the Atlanticists, and others who won't identify themselves. But the New Anglican Church has moved beyond them. It still takes their money, but it's also very rich in its own right—because it's well-led, commercially successful, and has a wide offer.

"Among the founders, Olivia del Sarto has friends and enemies. Her friends support her because she's charismatic and gifted and has made the New Anglicans rich and powerful. Her enemies distrust her for the same reasons. Even her own personal staff and security staff, as you will find, are split along similar lines."

So. A successful leader of a successful organisation apparently fears for her life, and this is a simple bodyguard mission?

In fact, it was. Rafiq could have said so, but chose to observe protocol. First, Anwar's mission was genuinely unconnected to Levin's. Second, Rafiq didn't have some secret deal with the New Anglicans, though he did want them in his debt because he judged he could use their connections: political, not financial. Anwar didn't know any of this, and it was in his nature to look for complications; for pockets of darkness. *So why did Rafiq choose me?*

The Dead were not secret agents, just uniquely gifted functionaries. After UN Intelligence—the real secret agents—had done their work, it all boiled down to a highly-guarded object which had to be stolen or sabotaged, or a highly-guarded individual who had to be abducted or disabled or subverted: specific in/out missions, impossible for anyone else. Bodyguard duties were different. They involved prolonged interaction with people and their staff, requiring new faces and identities—with the inconvenience of surgical and IT processes—afterwards. Also, bodyguard duties carried the taint of low status: Rafiq would tend to assign a lower-rated Consultant rather than tie up one of the top four or five. *One like me. Who can't dispose of six Meatslabs in under thirty-six seconds.*

In the real world, Anwar was an antiquarian book dealer. He owned shops in London and New York. He was comfortably wealthy; his business was doing well, and his Consultancy pay was extremely high. He was a good antiquarian book dealer but a better Consultant. Levin, of course, was "Miles ahead": an outstanding architect and an outstanding Consultant.

The Consultancy wasn't interested in psychopaths or sociopaths. Its members had to be personable and well-adjusted (Anwar scored lower on that than Levin, but still passed) and had to have lives and identities in the outside world, however illusory they might be. Also, they had to be people with few connections so that their deaths could be faked, and new identities added, on databases worldwide. The UN had people who did this; people who moved easily through the electronic landscape.

All Consultants had genuine occupations outside: usually one-person businesses, operated anonymously online. The online world, at least the higher end of it, was virtually unhackable. Terminals, whether desktop or wristcom-sized, were peculiar to their operator. Their processors were not silicon chips but cloned neurons and synapses from the operator: keyed to his or her DNA, with security scanners reading lifesigns and doing further retinal and fingerprint scans. Anwar, Levin, and the others all did their book deals or architectural designs remotely worldwide with no personal interaction. Older silicon-chip computers still remained, but those who could afford the new type—wealthier individuals and businesses—did so. Even though engagement with the outside world was encouraged, Consultants' contracts still stipulated they should not appear personally in a business capacity, even under an assumed name. Those working in Anwar's bookshops, or in Levin's studios, had never met or seen their ultimate employer.

Their personal contact with the real world outside was different. It was merely social, a network of shifting relationships of limited duration. They never stayed long in one place. They had different identities in different cities, and cover stories involving frequent travel. Their relationships formed and unravelled, grew and died.

Anwar turned his attention back to the inside of his retina. Rafiq was finishing up. "So, that's the New Anglicans. To anticipate your question, and purely for completeness, a brief word about the Old Anglicans. They're the original Church of England. They still have their great cathedrals, like Rochester and Canterbury, and their parish churches, but they're in gentle decline. Even in the cathedrals, congregations are small and aging. But they're generally a force for good, or at least not a force for harm. Some attitudes towards them may be dismissive, but very few people actually hate them."

There were no closing salutations. Rafiq's face was replaced by Further Material Follows. That would be a mass of supporting documents and images and recordings. Anwar decided he'd speed-read it later.

He touched his wrist, and the image on his retina disappeared. He gestured, and Fallingwater's reception disappeared. He remained sitting in his living room. He actually felt more at home in the Fallingwater hologram, among the natural colours and shapes and textures. His Bauhaus interior, black and silver and grey, reflected his taste but didn't feel like home.

7

Olivia del Sarto: a theatrical-sounding name, but quite genuine.

Anwar checked the UN databases, the most detailed in the world. He found nothing he didn't already know, or which wasn't already covered in the supporting documentation to Rafiq's briefing, but he always liked to check for himself before a mission.

There had been one earlier attempt on her life, three years ago, as she was leaving the BBC after her famous Reith Lecture, popularly known as the "Room For God" broadcast. It was not significant, Anwar decided. It was a spur-of-the-moment affair, carried out by a handful of zealots, enraged at what she had said that night. Their rage was a neat way of proving her point, so neat she might almost have staged it herself. Her security people dealt with it efficiently, keeping her safe and not hurting anyone. Anwar liked the way they conducted themselves.

She came from a wealthy London family of fourth-generation Italian immigrants. Her mother was a noted food journalist and broadcaster, and her father owned several restaurants. From them she acquired her ease with all branches of the media, and her prodigious appetite for food. Her equally prodigious sexual appetites were acquired later. A previous partner once said that if you were a half-presentable male she hadn't seen before, she'd be into your trousers like a rat up a drainpipe.

She didn't share her family's traditional Catholicism. She felt closer to the Old Anglicans, though she never joined them; she decided, reluctantly, that they weren't going anywhere.

When she found the New Anglicans, it was as if they were made for each other.

Rafiq had included among his briefing documents a recording of her "Room For God" broadcast. Anwar already knew it well, but something told him he should watch it again before leaving for Brighton. He put it on the wallscreen in his living room, and settled back.

She was onstage in the main theatre in BBC Broadcasting House in London, a small slender figure in an immaculate long dress of dark velvet. She was on her own, facing an invited audience of three hundred, representing all the major faiths. There were ayatollahs and immams, Archbishops and Bishops, European Orthodox priests, various questionable TV evangelists, and self-styled religious scholars; an impressive array of costumes and hairstyles and beards and dentistry, with only a small scattering of women and Old Anglicans.

Nearly all of them were hostile to her. It came off the screen in waves. This broadcast was three years old, and she had now taken the New Anglicans a long way down the road she'd described, but people still replayed it. It showed so much about her: the presentation, the preparation, the confrontation. She always had an instinct for aggression, even when massively outnumbered.

A distinguished BBC news presenter briefly introduced her to the audience. There was the barest scattering of applause.

"I'd like to thank the BBC for inviting me to give this year's Reith Lecture. As you know from the extensive way it's been trailed—" (*especially by you*, Anwar thought) "—I'll be talking about a set of projects which will define the future direction of the New Anglican Church. The Room For God projects. I know this audience will be familiar with them, but for the sake of the wider broadcast audience I'll outline them briefly. Later I'll describe them in more detail.

"The Room For God projects are part of the core business of the New Anglican Church. Whether you look through a telescope or a microscope, you see that science uncovers more and more about the universe. But the more it uncovers, the more that remains unknown—and the more room it creates for God. So the New Anglican Church will encourage, *and* finance, scientific research which other churches may find threatening. Medical research, too. We'll support campaigns for birth control. We'll attack bigotry wherever we find it. Religious bigotry. Homophobia. Subjugation of women. We'll fund independent research into the behind-closed-doors conclaves in which the Bible was put together: what was included and what was left out, by whom and why. And we'll finance campaigns against fundamentalism and Creationism, and in favour of secular education and secular politics. We'll even fight the tax-exempt status of religious cults. We'll shine our light everywhere! We'll..."

She paused. There were mutterings in the audience. "Oh, come on! People should come to a Church—any Church, ours or yours—as grownups! They should come from choice, not from being spoonfed by some ghastly priest caste who won't *let* them grow up!"

"Arrogant! You're arrogant and self-regarding!" someone in the audience roared. "This is just a PR event for you. You take an inordinate pride, young woman, in parading your anger!"

"Pride and Anger," she said. "Two of the Seven Deadly Sins. I use a mnemonic to remember them: SPAGLEG. Sloth, Pride, Anger, Greed, Lust, Envy, Gluttony."

"Yes," said another voice, "and you've shown two of them tonight, and all of them in your private life!" (Laughter, turning to applause.)

"Well," she replied, leaning forward on the lectern, "four or five of them are not so bad, in moderation. For rational people. For people wanting self-respect instead of self-loathing, or aspiration instead of guilt, or just some physical comfort." (Silence, turning to uproar.)

From there, the Reith Lecture ceased to be a lecture, and became a war: an audience against one person. All the protocols went out the window. Longboom mikes were swung out over the audience. Producers reordered schedules. This would be something unheard of in modern broadcasting: a major live event which erupted, in real time, before a worldwide audience of tens of millions. With any ordinary broadcast, corporate middle-managers might have killed the live feed and gone to a stock documentary on meerkats or modelmaking, but this was the Reith Lecture. Nobody dared kill it.

As if she sensed all this, she gathered up her sheaf of notes from the lectern and flung it, rather theatrically, to the floor. She glared down at them from the stage, awaiting their attacks.

"Even homosexuality," said a voice from the audience. The longboom mike immediately swung over to him. "Anything offensive to normality and decency, *you'll* be sniffing around it for its money. Even," sneeringly, "the love that dare not speak its name."

She smiled unpleasantly. "In Brighton they call it the love that dare not speak its name because its mouth is full." (Indrawn breaths.) "Try a mouthful. It cures all afflictions. Even fundamentalism."

Anwar was aghast at her aggression. And yet: just one of her, against all of them. She was like a small creature baring its teeth and refusing to back down. Ever. Against anyone.

"This is your new fascism! Anyone who disagrees with you, you call them afflicted! Brand them as fundamentalists! Turn them into hate figures!"

"I don't hate fundamentalists. I just think that 99 percent of them give the other 1 percent a bad name."

"Most of the people you brand with that—that offensive word, are legitimate religious scholars."

"Scholars who know more and more about less and less. And *religious scholars*," she hissed, "were put on Earth by God for *me* to offend them. Real scholars are scholars of a body of knowledge. You're scholars of a body of unproven and unprovable belief. You belong in the Dark Ages. What conversations you must have in your own heads!" (More uproar.)

"You're not an Archbishop, you're an Arch*business woman*!"

"And," someone else shouted, "an atheist!"

"I'm not an atheist. But I won't buy what *you're* selling. I want something better."

"Something *better?* You want God in your own image?"

"I want us in God's image. Does God want us ignorant and superstitious?"

"How dare you presume to say what God should want us to be!"

"It's what your priests have been doing for generations, and claiming it's God speaking through you. Our God's out-grown that. Evolved, perhaps. And if your God hasn't, then I and my Church have the right not to believe in him. Or her. Or it."

"Do you even believe in the New Anglicans' God?"

"Not just believe. *Approve.*"

There was more of this; a lot more. After it had finished, the New Anglicans' ratings soared. The rest was history. In the following three years she implemented most of the Room

For God projects, and the New Anglicans became the world's fastest-growing major Church.

Anwar sat in his living room for some time after the recording finished, repeating it to himself while the shadows lengthened around him. He knew it word for word. And he knew that inside it was something he needed. Something which would help him understand her, and this mission. He couldn't see it yet, but he would if he reflected on it carefully. That was how he liked to work: carefully, and reflectively.

He was born an American citizen. His pre-Consultancy name was Rashad Khan. His family were third-generation Pakistani immigrants, living in Bay Ridge, New York. His parents were both successful lawyers. He spent a comfortable childhood in a large nineteenth-century brownstone house on Ridge Boulevard. He had brothers and sisters with whom he exchanged normal affection. His family were not particularly religious, and neither was he.

His parents feared he might be mildly autistic. He wasn't, but he had some of the outward signs: a certain social awkwardness, and a liking for routine, for having everything in its fixed place, tidy and orderly. And he liked to see inside things—how they worked, what they were really like under the surface.

He probably saw more of the UN Headquarters Building in New York then, when he lived not far from it, than he did when he became a Consultant. He'd often look at it from across the East River, or at closer quarters from East 42nd or East 48th Street. It was an archetypal mid-twentieth-century building: clean and bright and optimistic when built, but now tastes had changed and made it ugly. Levin, when they met several years later, would never tire of telling Anwar about UNHQ's ugliness, and what it signified. "Architecture," he would say, "was once described as frozen music. It is. But it's also frozen hope."

Frozen hope. Anwar considered himself, and considered her. He knew which one the phrase fitted. *And that's what this mission's about.*

He always preferred UNEX to the old UN. UNEX had a closeness of form and function: its outside accurately reflected its inside. It was an engineer's construction, designed for results rather than idealism. The old UN was the opposite, a philosopher's construction. Its membership was a microcosm of the entire world's grudges and prejudices and conflicts. Its Charters and Declarations were impossible even before the ink had dried on them. UNEX's aims were less ambitious but more achievable. Something like Make Things Better, Or At Least Less Bad. It didn't compress easily into a slogan like Marek's Justify Nothing, but it meant as much to Anwar as, presumably, Marek's meant to Marek.

So, despite the fact that the old UN was practically in his backyard, he joined UNEX. By that time Rafiq was Controller-General, and the difference between the two parts of the UN was becoming clear. He felt he'd chosen correctly. He had a hope, then, that UNEX really could make things better—a hope which had now become frozen in him. He'd carried on doing the specialised work for which he was frighteningly well qualified, but these days he did it automatically. Without pride. Without passion or mission or meaning.

As the shadows continued to lengthen around him, he knew he'd at last found what he'd been looking for. It concerned her. *She's always out there.* Always at the sharp end, putting herself up to be judged, fighting her case. Often viciously, but always openly.

And it concerned him, too. He was her opposite: standing apart, coming out of his comfort zone to make simple in/out strikes (for which he was guaranteed success, against out-matched opponents), and then going back.

He'd taken the easier, stealthier way. Looking back on it now, it carried almost a flavor of cowardice. She had more risk, more *genuine* risk, in any seven days of her life than he'd known in his seven years with the Consultancy.

I've actually been like Marek, he thought. Marek's comfort zone was the darkness of nihilism—he reached out of it to strike, then went back into it. *I'm anonymous, like him. Marek and me at one extreme, Olivia del Sarto at the other. And Rafiq too, he's like her—willing to try and do something, and be judged on it.*

Most of her life has been like that broadcast. Mine's been arid, hers is real. I got this bodyguard assignment because I'm less valuable than people like Levin or Asika. And that's all. But he shook his head violently, partly to clear it and partly to deny the thought. No, he wasn't inventing pockets of darkness. Every instinct told him there was something more to this mission. She didn't just want a Consultant as a personal fashion accessory to parade at the summit. Something was genuinely threatening her. Something beyond even the abilities of her own security people. She wanted a Consultant because nothing else could protect her.

He would go to Brighton early. He would prepare and acclimatise. *Her life is more valuable than mine. Hers has actually amounted to something.*

THREE: SEPTEMBER 2060

1

Anwar was not entirely unacquainted with Brighton.

One of the UN's VSTOLs had flown him from Fallingwater to a small private airfield on the Downs, where he was met by a car that took him into Brighton. The car dropped him on Marine Parade, at the gateway to the New West Pier at the end of which, two miles into the ocean, stood Brighton Cathedral. It was late September and the summit was more than two weeks away: October 15, for nine days. He'd spend the two weeks in briefings with Archbishop del Sarto and her staff. But today—it was early afternoon—he wanted some time to himself.

The New West Pier stood near the site of the original West Pier, which had mysteriously burnt down last century. Less than a mile away along the beach stood another old pier, which still survived: the Palace Pier, a traditional structure of wooden pilings and dark wrought-iron Victorian filigree, totally unlike the swooping white New West Pier, which dwarfed it.

The New Anglicans were originally going to have traditional pier entertainments (gambling arcades, fairground rides, a musical theatre) halfway along their New West Pier. They decided against it, not because it was inappropriate—they liked the fusion of Church and Mammon—but because it would take trade away from the Palace Pier, owned by a local family. The New Anglicans knew when to step lightly.

Brighton Cathedral was a full-size replica of the Royal Pavilion, standing at the end of the New West Pier. Around the Cathedral was a complex of other buildings, architecturally matching, which housed conference facilities, hotels, function suites, and media centres; also commercial offices, studios, shops, restaurants. The Cathedral and its matching complex was pearlescent white, unlike the buff-coloured mixture of stucco and Bath sandstone which made up the original Royal Pavilion. It was the best, and most expensive, business address in Europe.

The New West Pier stretched out to sea on elegant arching supports. It was made of metallic/ceramic composites, reinforced internally by carbon nanotubes. At its far end two miles away, it rose high and widened out massively to accommodate the Cathedral complex, which soared above the Pier and faced back to the shore. Maglevs ran its entire length, with a station at the Pier's gateway and another at the far end.

The Pier looked beautiful by day, with its clean white lines and swooping arches. *But at night,* Anwar thought, *when it was lit...*

He was standing on Marine Parade, the main road running parallel to the beach. He wore a light grey linen suit, with a darker grey shirt, the colour almost of the ocean. On the other side of Marine Parade was Regency Square Gardens. Eighteenth and nineteenth-century buildings made an elegant frontage to the road, including the Grand and Metropole Hotels. There was also one newer development, standing on the shoreline near the gateway to the New West Pier: the i-360 Tower, built about 2015. It had a large observation pod, in the shape of a ring doughnut, going up and down the central spike of the five-hundred-foot tower.

He decided to walk along the foreshore. His luggage had gone on ahead of him, to the suite the New Anglicans had reserved for him in the nine-star New Grand Hotel in the

Cathedral complex at the far end of the New West Pier. So much was called New, but Newness could be a mask. *There you go again, looking for pockets of darkness.*

The foreshore and beach were almost unchanged from last century. Marine Parade was on an embankment about twenty feet above the level of the foreshore. Staircases were set at intervals along the embankment, their railings painted green, with rust spots bubbling underneath.

He had been to Brighton a few times before, and remembered it for the sounds of conversation and music, and the smells of things being cooked and substances being smoked. His previous visits had been in summer months, and this was late September, with fewer people around; but something of that atmosphere still remained. The beach was pebbles, not sand. As the ocean drew them back and rolled them forward, then back and forward again and again, they made a bubbling clatter, like applause.

Set into the embankment was a series of arches, housing a mixture of small businesses: craft and souvenir shops, painting and pottery studios, cafes, fishing/sailing lockups. A couple of arches housed the Brighton Sailing Club. The larger and more opulent private yachts were berthed in marinas up and down the coast. The boats here were small sailing boats, small enough to be drawn up on the beach near where Anwar walked. The wind blowing in from the pewter-coloured ocean set their ropes ringing against the metal masts.

The embankment was mouldering brick and weathered concrete, in various shades of black and khaki, randomly cracked and randomly repaired. Weeds grew at the joints of concrete and brickwork. There were occasional pedestrian underpasses, leading to the other side of Marine Parade. They were walled with stained white tiles, like old public toilets (which they sometimes became).

It reminded him of his favourite immersion hologram.

He stopped about halfway between the two piers, and looked back at the New West Pier. His eyes, if he willed them to, could have adjusted to show him the Cathedral complex in fine granular detail, so he could compare it inch by inch with what he remembered of the original Royal Pavilion. He decided not to ramp up his vision. He kept his senses at normal most of the time, especially sight and hearing. To amplify them too much might betray his identity. He was looking forward to seeing the Cathedral close-up, however.

Time. He started walking back towards the New West Pier.

He flipped open his wristcom and told it the number he'd been given. The number answered promptly.

"Anwar Abbas, to see Archbishop del Sarto."

"Yes, Mr. Abbas. Please go through the main gate and wait in the maglev concourse. Someone will meet you."

Parked along Marine Parade were some heavy multi-wheeled vehicles. "Patel & Co, Builders. You've tried the cowboys, now try the Indians." The slogan was nearly ninety years old, and on the back of it Patel Construction had become a major concern. They were here to refurbish a suite in the conference centre which would be used for the formal signing of agreements at the conclusion of the summit on October 23, assuming agreements would be reached. They wouldn't, not entirely, but something would be cobbled together. Probably.

He passed through the security and identity checks at the main gate without problems: as far as they could define it, he was unarmed and had an identity. The main gate opened out immediately into Gateway Station. It was the full width of the Pier, and echoed its style: pearlescent white arches supported the glass roof, like a giant inverted ribcage. There were four platforms, and the maglevs simply travelled back and forth the two miles from Gateway Station to Cathedral Station. They were fully-configured bullet trains, white and streamlined, with all the internal appointments. In view of the shortness of the journey something less elaborate would have done, but the New Anglicans wanted real trains, not a fairground ride.

Anwar stayed in the station concourse, as requested. One maglev was just arriving at Platform 1, not an unusual occurrence considering there were four of them and their two-mile journey took ninety seconds. Among the people disembarking was a tall man who made straight for Anwar. He wore a casual but expensive light grey suit and dark shirt, an outfit not unlike Anwar's. His hair was dark, cut short, and receding. His build and gait was one Anwar recognised. *Shoulder holster,* he noted from the drape of the well-cut jacket, *and a flat knife carried in an implant on the left forearm, under the sleeve.* Slim build, like Anwar, but slightly taller. Thin face, high cheekbones. *Meatslab.*

"Mr. Abbas? I'm Gaetano Vecchio, the Archbishop's head of security."

They shook hands.

"So this is what a Consultant looks like. I don't think I've met one before."

"Ah...and who else has the Archbishop told?"

"Just me and her personal staff."

Anwar didn't push it, for now.

They eyed each other. Each of them knew the other's abilities, and each of them knew that Anwar was in a different league altogether.

"She's the one who wanted you here," Gaetano added, "not me. But that's a conversation for another time. For now, she's anxious to meet you."

Ninety seconds later they disembarked at Cathedral Station and rode the glass lift to the Cathedral complex.

Anwar recalled his previous visits to the original Royal Pavilion: a deeply eccentric building, the definitive example of eighteenth-century European chinoiserie, swamped with flamboyant detail and surface ornamentation. In front of him was an exact replica, but clad in the same white ceramic/ metallic material as the Pier, and surrounded by other buildings, architecturally matching, forming the Cathedral complex. Everywhere were domes and minarets; stone latticeworks, balconies, arches, and spires; turrets, buttresses, crenellations. Even in the September afternoon light they gleamed.

The original Royal Pavilion stood in its own Garden, a small park of lawns and shrubbery and old spreading trees, with a main gate—the Indian Gate—commemorating the soldiers wounded in the First World War who were hospitalised in the Pavilion. This part of the New West Pier, widened and elevated, allowed space for a full replica of the Garden. It followed the year-round planting scheme of the original. Even in late September, trees and shrubs were in flower: hydrangeas, fuchsia, witch hazel, yellow broom, goldenrod. But there was no replica of the Indian Gate; again, the New Anglicans knew when to tread lightly. They'd decided that to replicate a memorial would be disrespectful and commercially unwise.

They walked through the Garden and into the Cathedral. In the original Royal Pavilion, the inside was even more heavily ornamented than the outside: the Octagon Hall, the Long Gallery, the Banqueting Hall, the King's Apartments. Here, however, the resemblance ended. None of the interior had been reproduced. Most of the ground floor was the Cathedral proper, a large light open space of minimalist white and grey and silver, with pews of unadorned pale wood and no stained glass anywhere. No service was in progress, and there were only a few groups of visitors and worshippers present. Instead of the usual smell of old incense there was a trace of perfume: an expensive perfume with fresh citrus notes, breathed out softly through the climate-conditioning.

Leading off the open space in front of the altar—also unadorned pale wood with a simple silver cross—was a wide staircase. They took it and came out on the first floor, where the Cathedral offices were housed. The landing was long and wide, walled and floored in white and silver. Gaetano pointed to a floor-to-ceiling door of plain pale wood at the far end.

"She's waiting for you in the Boardroom."

2

Levin was gone.

He'd been sent to Opatija alone and unarmed, with all his tracking and monitoring implants deactivated—essential for this particular mission. Now, five days later, they remained deactivated. Nobody had seen or heard from him.

Rafiq was writing another of his neat, courteous letters. He handed it to Arden Bierce.

"Please go to Chulo Asika's house in Lagos and ask him if he'll come here."

Arden Bierce brought Asika in another of the UN's beautiful silvered VSTOLs. He was offered missions frequently, and she was familiar with the journey: VSTOL to and from the UN Embassy in Lagos, taxi to and from his house. (Anwar lived near enough to the UN to pass as a senior employee who occasionally got flown to Kuala Lumpur, but generally it was considered less than discreet to land a VSTOL on a Consultant's lawn.) Asika nicknamed her Charon because she ferried The Dead. She liked him but didn't like the nickname.

Asika's company was designing and building the set for an upcoming production of "Six Characters in Search of an Author" at the National Theatre in Iganmu, Lagos. Asika's wife had been one of The Dead. When she became pregnant,

seven years earlier, she retired and they married. She now had
her own career, as well as two children, and they lived in their
family house in Lagos from which Asika ran his business—and,
unlike the others, ran it personally rather than online. He had
an elaborate system of cover stories to explain his occasional
absences, most of them centred on work he did for UNICEF.
There was a theoretical risk that his identity would be discovered, but Rafiq had decided, this once, to bend the rules.

The VSTOL settled an inch above the lawn. A door rippled open in its side. Arden Bierce got out and walked across
the lawn towards Fallingwater. Chulo Asika followed her. She
rang the doorbell, and they entered the reception area.

"I'll tell him you're here," she said, and went through the
door to Rafiq's inner office.

Asika waited. As usual, several members of Rafiq's personal staff were there, talking quietly among clusters of plain
stone-white sofas and armchairs. A couple of them looked up
as he entered.

A few minutes later, Arden Bierce came out.

"He'll see you now."

"Thank you for coming so promptly, Mr. Asika. I understand you had to postpone some business to come here."

"You trump everything, Mr. Rafiq. Even the National
Theatre."

"Still, I'm grateful. I hope your work won't be disrupted."

Asika smiled. He was a gentle man, who smiled often. He
was about the same height and build as Anwar. Along with
Levin, he was one of the four or five consistently highest-
scoring Consultants. Despite his abilities, or perhaps because
of them, Rafiq always felt comfortable in his company. More
so than with any of the other eighteen.

"My work? No, my colleagues are used to my occasional
absences. So is my family."

Rafiq had a poker face that he deployed automatically when anyone mentioned their family. Most people didn't notice when he deployed it. "I'd like to offer you a mission. May I describe it?"

"Please."

Rafiq briefed Asika: the tenuous lead to Parvin Marek, Levin's journey to Opatija and subsequent disappearance, and the villa north of Opatija which, according to the Croatian authorities, was now empty and deserted. When he spoke of Levin's disappearance, Rafiq was carefully dispassionate. So was Asika.

"And you want me to find out what happened to Levin?"

"Yes."

"And Marek?"

"Secondary. The priority is Levin. Will you do it?"

"Yes. Of course."

3

When he first saw her she was at the top of a stepladder, scooping a dead fish out of a floor-to-ceiling ornamental tank at the far end of the Boardroom. She had her back to him. Her bottom was wobbling interestingly under a long, voluminous velvet skirt.

"Sorry," she said without turning round, "I'll be right with you. I just noticed one of these angelfish had died."

"Do they die very often?"

"No, only once."

She turned to look at him, and he realised that all the stories about her were true. Coming off her in waves was a clean and simple lust, uncomplicated by any other motives.

He immediately reciprocated. He could feel the reciprocation growing, between his legs.

He watched her descend the stepladder. She was wearing a high-necked, long-sleeved dress of dark red velvet, like a ball-gown, with a fitted bodice and a full, floor-length skirt. New Anglican Archbishops didn't wear traditional robes, but chose something which suited them personally while also looking formal. The velvet dresses were her particular choice.

She walked over to him. She was smaller than she appeared (or contrived to appear) in the newscasts.

"So this is what a Consultant looks like. I thought you'd be seven feet tall."

He thought, *I only need another ten inches*, but didn't say it. He already knew her well enough to imagine her reply. So he smiled and shrugged, and muttered "I was, but I haven't been well."

Behind him, he heard Gaetano laugh softly.

"Don't smile and shrug like that, it makes you look gorm-less. Not good for a guardian angel."

She tossed back her blonde hair. Her face was small and almost delicate. Perhaps rather sharp-featured, but softened by the way she did her hair. Her movements and moods appeared quick and birdlike. Her expression was hard to read, and seemed permanently on the verge of changing. She was a little younger than him; middle thirties, he estimated. She really was quite slightly built.

Her eyes were dark violet. They missed nothing, including his reciprocation when he first saw her. It was now tenting the front of his well-cut trousers.

And there, rubbing against her ankles, was the famous ginger cat, brawny of body and wide of whisker. It glowered at him.

Fuck You it meowed.

"It doesn't seem to like me."

"It doesn't like anyone, except me. And It is a He."

As at Fallingwater, he tried to mask his feelings by taking stock of his surroundings.

The Boardroom was large, mainly white and silver; with its adjoining anterooms it covered nearly a quarter of the area of the Cathedral's first floor. It had a long table of light wood set for twenty people. There were windows floor to ceiling down two walls, looking back along the length of the Pier to the beach and the i-360 Tower, and looking to the left over the pearlescent domes and spires and arches of the Cathedral complex. The third wall was lined with comms and screens, and the fourth wall, at the far end, with the tropical fish tank.

There were clusters of armchairs around the room's perimeter, occupied by people who were obviously the Archbishop's personal staff. They reminded him of Rafiq's staff: competent and well-groomed, like Arden Bierce. They'd all stopped talking as he entered. They were still silent now.

He sensed a compression in the air behind him, and turned to see Gaetano approaching. *Going to make me put on a show for her.*

Gaetano carried a quarterstaff, and held it like he knew how to use it. Anwar reached out, blurringly fast, and took it. He broke it in two, then in four, then in eight, and handed the pieces back to him.

"Please," he said, "I don't have time."

He had done most of this without taking his eyes off her. Many of her staff had gasped as he did it, but she remained silent.

She studied him, his thin face and hook nose and dark eyes. *For he shall deliver thee from the snare of the hunter. He shall defend thee under his wings.*

He looked back at her. *Into your trousers like a rat up a drainpipe,* his eidetic memory helpfully reminded him.

"Leave us," she said to her staff, hoarsely. "Give us this room."

They left, with an alacrity which suggested this was not an unusual occurrence. After a moment's pause, Gaetano followed them out.

It happened on the Boardoom table, noisily and untidily. There was no foreplay, just an abrupt transition from the vertical to the horizontal. He fumbled with her long voluminous skirt, she with his jacket and trousers, and each of them with each other's underwear. They scattered the table settings. Normally he disliked making tidy things untidy, whether table settings or female clothing, but not now.

The ginger cat retreated to a corner of the room, and became absorbed in licking its private parts.

Because it was simple physical lust and nothing more, it came and went easily. There was little to be said afterwards. They sat on opposite sides of the long Boardroom table. It was a few minutes before either of them spoke.

"We'll dine tonight," she said, smoothing down her skirt, "and I'll brief you. Gaetano will take you to your suite, and he'll come for you at nine."

"And you?"

She smiled. Her lips were dark red, like her dress. "I have an organisation to run."

He turned to go.

"Wait," she added. "I'll walk back with you."

Outside the door, Gaetano was waiting.

"Quarterstaff," Anwar murmured. "Good choice."

Gaetano smiled but did not answer.

They walked back along the silver and white corridor, down the wide staircase, and into the silver and white Cathedral.

Anwar felt something wrong in the air. Too much stillness. All the Cathedral doors were closed.

It was almost deserted. Just eight people, two together and the others singly. The two stood facing them, in the large open space before the altar. The other six were sitting in pews, apparently at random. Anwar was already calculating distances, probable routes of approach. Vectors. Lines of sight. Estimating, from their posture and the drape of their clothes, what weapons they carried.

The two facing them approached Gaetano. Strangely, they hadn't even glanced at Anwar or Olivia, and didn't now. One of them was built like Levin. The other was smaller, stocky and dark-haired. With unusual hands.

The larger man went to speak to Gaetano. He made eye contact, smiled, and opened his mouth to begin a sound like "Erm..." on a rising note, as if about to air some routine matter. Then he delivered a huge kick to the testicles. Gaetano was lifted bodily, and landed doubled up and vomiting. The second man made for Olivia with a knife which came, as Anwar expected, from a forearm sheath. A specialist's knife, with a blade combining points and tines and serrations. Anwar decided to take the blow himself.

The knife was aimed at his heart, and he turned at the last moment to take it in his side. But his timing was fractionally off, making the knife penetrate deeper than he'd expected. He felt a surge of anger—*how many times must I mistime?*—but he killed it. Geared it down to something colder, something he could use.

Olivia had seen Anwar's mistiming and was shouting obscenities, mostly at Anwar. Quite unreasonably, he felt. *But she's genuinely afraid. And she's not supposed to be afraid of anything.*

He'd taken the knife-blow without apparently noticing. The blood it should have drawn was already clotting. He'd willed it to. The knifeman was starting another attack, but Anwar didn't care. He moved liquidly, almost accidentally. Then a shuto strike to the collarbone, this time intentional. He felt the molecules in his hand aligning to hardness, felt the collarbone give. He pulled back before his hand could actually penetrate and shear it.

While the knifeman dropped unconscious, he was turning to the second man, the one built like Levin, and struck him. This time only a light fingertip to a pressure point on the temple, to put him out for a few seconds. Anwar very much wanted him for later.

"Gaetano!" Olivia screamed. But he wasn't listening. He was still doubled up and vomiting. The kick had hit him like an express train. "Gaetano!"

"Shut up," Anwar told her, softly and precisely.

The six men sitting in the pews had looked convincingly shocked while all this was happening, but that was then. Now they were suddenly encircling Anwar and Olivia.

"Don't," he told them.

"Why, what will you do, surround us?"

"Yes." The word hung in the air behind him. He was already moving.

He really did surround them. He orbited the tight circle they'd made around her, attacking it from outside, silently and with frightening speed and from every angle and with every striking surface, so they couldn't face her but had to face outwards. And it still wasn't enough for them.

He fought them the way he should have fought in the last Tournament. Taking the initiative. They tried their best moves on him but he flicked them away, unnoticing. To him, their moves were slowed to near-torpor, and their martial arts yells to a hoglike bass. As usual, he fought in silence. That, and his speed, terrified them. They were good, better than his last six Tournament opponents, but still Meatslabs. He flickered in and out of them in a glissade, bestowing Compliments and Gratuities—all watered-down versions, enough to immobilise but not to injure or kill.

He was shockingly fast, and frighteningly silent. He thought, *This is everything I am, it's what makes me extraordinary. But even now, when I'm doing it better than I did in the Tournament, it doesn't mean much. My opponents are always outmatched, and half of the Consultants will always outmatch me. When will Everything I Am mean something?*

It was never going to be a bloodbath. His abilities were too considerable, and too precise, for that. But it was almost an anticlimax. His inbuilt timer told him he'd finished them in twenty-two seconds.

He could have just stayed by her side and defeated them. Waited for them to attack, and countered. Instead, for once, he'd done it differently. *Why? Because of her?* He had enough time, now, to ask himself this and reflect on the answer. *No. Because they weren't the real thing.* They weren't the threat which had made her persuade Rafiq to give her a Consultant. They weren't good enough.

He turned back to the Levin lookalike, who'd floored Gaetano and was now getting to his feet, smiling mockingly. Anwar indulged himself a little, and gave him a Verb. It was an openhand strike to the throat, fingers and thumb unusually splayed, the molecules hardening them into five striking surfaces. One of his favourite moves. A full-strength version would decapitate, but Anwar used only a powered-down version (an Adverb?) which didn't penetrate flesh. He did it because the man looked like the real Levin, even down to the smile (*I'm Miles ahead of you, Anwar*) and it was the closest Anwar would get to wiping the smile off Levin's face. The man fell, unconscious before he could cry out.

Anwar looked round. All prostrate, but neatly so. No groans or blood or writhing, except for Gaetano. All inert.

"Are you alright?" Olivia asked.

He opened his mouth to answer, but she was looking past him. At Gaetano.

"Not yet," Gaetano said, between coughs, "but I will be. Thank you, Archbishop."

Anwar turned to her. "Are *you* alright?"

She glared at him, but nodded.

"You were frightened when they surrounded you."

"No I wasn't."

"Yes you were, but not of them. You were frightened I wouldn't be good enough."

"You aren't," she sneered. "You mistimed, I saw it. I needed the best, and Rafiq sent me *you*. A fucking autistic retard!"

"My knife wound is healing quite nicely, thank you."

"Our appointment tonight," she said, "is for nine o'clock. Don't mistime *that*."

She flounced off, back up the wide staircase, almost tripping over her long skirt. Fury came off in waves from her small retreating figure. Anwar assumed she was going back to the Boardroom. She did, after all, have an organisation to run.

A couple of minutes passed. The eight were still inert. Gaetano was kneeling and coughing.

"Try to get up now," Anwar told him. "But take it slowly. I know the kick was genuine, and I know you weren't wearing protection."

"Couldn't. You'd have spotted it."

"Yes. You really are suffering for your art."

"We still have unfinished business." His breathing was growing less laboured. "I didn't want you here, *she* did. Because she thinks that her own security won't stop whatever's threatening her."

"Like it didn't stop me...And I didn't want to be here either."

"And yet, here you are, taking my men apart like they were nothing...My deputies, Luc Bayard and Arban Proskar." Gaetano waved his hand to indicate the two men, still unconscious, who'd approached them first.

Anwar glanced down at them. Bayard: like Levin, large build and smile and not entirely unfriendly mockery. But a Meatslab, not another Levin. And Proskar: stocky, dark-haired, fortyish. Unimpressive physically except for his hands, broad and long-fingered, like the hands of a concert pianist.

Gaetano watched Anwar studying them, and said, "What, you thought your trick in the Boardroom would be enough?"

"No, of course not. I recognised your two deputies from my briefing. Also at least four of the others."

"Yes, Rafiq's briefings. Always thorough. But *she* wouldn't know that. So," he added, "I gave you another opportunity to impress her."

"She didn't seem impressed...And it could have been real, not staged. Rafiq's briefing said some of her security staff can't be trusted; maybe helping whoever's threatening her. I just followed his briefing. You appreciate," he added, in a tone not calculated to make Gaetano feel any better, "that I could hardly have done anything else."

They left the Cathedral through the now-open doors and walked across the Garden to the New Grand Hotel, a large pearlescent building which, from the outside, matched the size and style of the Cathedral.

Gaetano, who was now beginning to walk less painfully, took his leave of Anwar in the hotel's large lobby. Like the Cathedral, and like most interiors on the New West Pier, there was a discreet smell of citrus.

"I'll come for you at nine."

The reception staff showed him to his suite, where his luggage waited. It was a large and well-appointed suite, with a view over the domes and spires of the Cathedral complex. The sun was setting. He walked out on to the balcony and watched it.

When he'd first entered the New West Pier, everything was sleek and serene and silver and white. Then the mask fell away and he glimpsed the soul of the New Anglicans. Joining them was like joining a pack of wild animals. *Fucking autistic retard,* she'd called him—their own Archbishop, in her own Cathedral, right in front of the altar. He thought *What are they? Are they still a Church? Or a corporation? Or a political movement? Have the last two identities consumed the first?* They had the wealth and slickness of a religious cult, but their teachings weren't so silly. The wealth and slickness of a major business corporation, but they practiced social responsibility. The wealth and slickness of a crime syndicate, but they stood for things rather more worthwhile.

He mentally shrugged. *Containers and contents. Surface and substance.* In the next few days he'd learn more about what was really inside them. For now, he knew for certain that everything about them, their very organisation and culture, was different to any other Church. They were to other Churches what Rafiq's UNEX was to the old UN.

He continued to watch the sunset, and listen to the sea and the noises from the Brighton shoreline, two miles away; and the cries of the gulls, riding the air currents above the skyline of the Cathedral complex. He reflected on what had happened. He'd fought differently, with less caution, and it had worked. Twenty-two seconds wasn't bad. And then there was Gaetano. And Bayard, and Proskar and the others. And something else, which made all the rest seem commonplace.

"Christ!" he whispered. "I've just fucked an Archbishop!"

FOUR: SEPTEMBER 2060

1

Many unusual things arrived daily at Fallingwater, but the object which arrived one morning in late September, two days after Chulo Asika had agreed to find Levin, was particularly unusual. It was a handwritten letter, ink on paper, addressed to Rafiq. Postage was a niche product, used mostly to make a fashion statement or as irony, and this letter had actually been sent through the post. There was an envelope, with a handwritten address, and even a postage stamp and post-mark. Opatija, Croatia. REDGOD: Recorded Express Delivery Guaranteed One Day.

Rafiq was told of its arrival, but it was exhaustively ana-lysed before he even saw it. Unsurprisingly it revealed no DNA, fingerprints or other residual traces, other than those belonging to postal staff. The paper on which it was written was expensive, but not exclusively so. Obtainable at better-class stationery retailers worldwide. So was the envelope, whose weave matched that of the paper; it was self-sealing and bore no trace of saliva at the seal. Whoever had written and sent it had touched neither envelope nor paper with an ungloved hand. The person who had signed the Recorded Delivery forms at the post office in Opatija had paid cash and given a false name and address. He left no traces on the forms he signed. Staff remembered a stockily built male, for-tyish, with no unusual features. The post office's CCTV wasn't working.

The ink, like the paper, was of superior but not exclusive quality. The nib of the pen used to write it was italic, and electron scans revealed traces of its metals: a high quality but not unusual mixture. The handwriting was regular and neat, and found no exact matches on any database, though it was not so unusual as to find no approximate matches. In fact there were thousands, all inconclusive. One of the closer matches, ironically, was Rafiq's own handwriting. One of the others was Anwar's.

When the letter was finally set before Rafiq, he had already been told what it said:

The villa north of Opatija is no longer empty.

At about the time Anwar Abbas met Olivia del Sarto for the first time, Arden Bierce was making another journey in another silvered VSTOL. This journey was less leisurely. The VSTOL took one hour from the lawn in front of Fallingwater to the grounds of the villa north of Opatija, where it hovered while a door rippled open and she got out. It waited for her.

The whole area was cordoned, drenched with arclights, and full of Croatian police and UN Embassy people from Zagreb. She was waved through the front door and into the reception. It was empty. Just the polished wood floor (which reminded her of Fallingwater) and the remains of Chulo Asika.

It looked like he'd been hit by a maglev bullet train. Something made of stuff like stainless steel and carbon fibre and monofilament. Something streamlined and frictionless, and so enormous and fast that it wrecked him without leaving any trace of itself. Without noticing him, if noticing was something it did. Every major bone in his body was broken, and hadn't had time, before he died, to set or regenerate. The note placed on his chest read *One character no longer in search of an author*. Neat italic handwriting, like

Rafiq's. And, like the letter he'd received, they'd analyse it but it would reveal nothing.

Whoever did this to him could have done so much more, but more would have been less. They could have torn him apart, left him in separate places around the room. They could have stuffed his penis and testicles in his mouth, torn off his fingers and poked them into his eyes. She'd been a field officer in UN Intelligence before her promotion to Rafiq's staff, and she'd seen such things before, usually done to civilian corpses by fundamentalist militias. But not here. This wasn't gratuitous or vicious, just clean, functional annihilation.

Neck broken, back broken, arms broken. Arden Bierce felt instinctively what the forensics would later verify: whoever did this to Asika left no traces of any kind on his body. No blood, DNA, saliva, fibre, fingerprints, flesh particles. *Look under his fingernails,* she was going to tell the forensic analysts, and stopped herself just in time. They'd have done that already, and all the other things which she was in no state to think of now.

Consultants had been injured, even killed, but never like this. By firearms usually. Not in combat, unless they were massively outnumbered. Chulo Asika had been wrecked on an industrial scale, but she didn't think he'd been massively outnumbered. *This,* she thought with a certainty which horrified her, *was done by a single opponent.* By something which had just gone through Asika on its way to somewhere else.

Neck broken, back broken, arms broken. She hoped, but doubted, that all this had been done to him after his death. *Is this what happened to Levin? Who are these people? Does Rafiq know about them? He has to. Rafiq knows everything.*

If this was done by a single opponent, then she knew of only four or five people in the world who could have done it. Four or five out of eighteen. And they were all accounted for, except Levin. But Levin couldn't have done *this* without leaving traces. Levin probably couldn't have done this at all, not to Asika. But Levin was unaccounted for. Either this had happened to him too, or he'd turned.

No. None of The Dead had ever turned. It was unthinkable. Their enhancements weren't only physical but psychological. Even moral. Necessary when giving them such abilities. Then maybe there was another explanation. Maybe, whether or not Levin had turned, they had something else which did this to Asika. And probably to Levin too.

Something that kills Consultants. Something like Consultants, but better.

As chilling as this was, it also suggested an organisation, which in turn suggested lines of enquiry: how and where they did it, who they paid, how much it cost. *Who are these people?* She couldn't imagine how they'd been unknown to Rafiq before now. But if there was an organisation, UN Intelligence would find it. She'd been whispering all this into her wrist implant as she picked her way around the villa. It would form her report to Rafiq, and she wouldn't edit it, even the *Rafiq knows everything* remark. A bit stream-of-consciousness, maybe, but Rafiq trusted her first impressions.

Strange to say this about someone with his abilities, but Asika had always seemed to her like a gentle man. Quiet, courteous. His laughter was soft and reflective; never loud, and never aimed at a target. People felt comfortable around him. It wasn't strange, of course. His abilities were exactly why he could be like that. To her knowledge he'd never killed or seriously injured anyone. In twenty-seven successful missions over nine years. He'd have retired soon.

No traces on his body. Maybe whoever did this wore frictionless material. Or was made *of frictionless material. Or I'm over-imagining. Trying to draw conclusions, not from evidence but from the absence of evidence.* She parked it for later, when she'd be able to consider it more dispassionately.

Anwar's mission will be simple, compared to this. She liked Anwar. He'd never actually made a move for her, though he did sometimes flirt mildly. Asika was married and had never made any move. Levin had, occasionally. The last time was two years ago, at a retirement party, coincidentally for one of the two Consultants who'd broken Black Dawn. She'd reciprocated (Offer and Acceptance) and found herself over a table, where he took her lavishly and thunderously.

Table. *Tables, sofas, chairs.* She tried to look at the polished wood floor without looking at Asika's body, to find the ghosting of furniture-shapes where the light hadn't been able to touch the wood. She thought she saw ghostings in clusters, like the stone-white sofas and armchairs at Fallingwater, but in her present state she could be over-imagining. *Still, this place must have had furniture of some sort. Where did it go, and when?* Something else to be parked for now.

"One character no longer in search of an author." If they knew Asika's identity in the real world, how many other Consultants' identities did they know? All of them, if Levin had turned and told them. And if Levin hadn't turned and told them, if Levin was dead somewhere, how did they know Asika's identity? Maybe Rafiq's decision to let him run his business in person, rather than anonymously online, had backfired. She'd warned Rafiq at the time that it was ill-advised. Asika's cover stories, involving absences to work on UNICEF projects, were painstaking and thorough; Rafiq had thought there were enough failsafes to conceal what he really did, but perhaps there weren't.

She parked that too. Pointless going there now. She had her report to complete; and then, in two days, a more pressing duty.

She was the member of Rafiq's personal staff with particular responsibility for the Consultancy, just as others had particular responsibilities for law, finance, and the UN Agencies.

So, two days later, she went to Lagos for Chulo Asika's funeral. She travelled by scheduled flight and took the identity of a middle-ranking UNESCO official who'd had dealings with his theatrical company.

Rafiq himself didn't attend; a Consultant's identity couldn't be overtly acknowledged, even posthumously. None of the other Consultants were there, partly for the same reason and partly by custom. On the rare occasions that something like this happened, their preference was to mark it privately.

Adeola Chukwu-Asika was a playwright and actress at the National Theatre. She knew who Arden Bierce was, though the rest of her family didn't. She lined up with her children after the funeral, to thank the departing guests. There were two children, a boy of seven and a girl of five, the same ages as Rafiq's when...*Something else to park,* Arden thought. *Lots of things to park.* She took both of Adeola's hands in hers (the maximum show of sympathy consistent with her assumed identity) and whispered, "I'm so sorry. I don't have words."

"There aren't words," Adeola said. "Except," glancing behind her at the gravestone, "those."

Chulo Asika 2022-2060
Loved a woman
Made a family with her

2

At exactly nine, as arranged, Gaetano arrived at Anwar's suite and took him to Olivia's private dining room. It was not a long journey. Her apartment, together with her offices and meeting rooms and quarters for security staff, took up the entire top floor of the New Grand, the floor immediately above his.

Her dining room was yet another interior of silver and white. The floor-to-ceiling windows looked back towards the foreshore, where Brighton's seafront lights flickered through the gathering dusk.

Gaetano left them to each other, and she began.

"You're not good enough. I'm telling Rafiq to send someone better."

Anwar laughed in her face; it surprised both of them. "Nobody *tells* Rafiq, ever. And he wouldn't send anyone else. I'm all you've got." He wasn't sure of this, but some instinct made him gamble. "Don't overestimate your importance. You're providing a conference venue, that's all. Venues can be changed, even at two weeks' notice. Not ideal, but Rafiq could do it. His concern isn't your safety, it's getting a venue. Yours is the preferred choice, but there are others."

He stared her down, and knew his gamble had won. *Why did I do that? Why do I want this mission so much?*

"Fuck you." She sounded like her cat, which as always was orbiting in her vicinity. "Nobody laughs in my face. Who the hell do you think you are?"

"I'm the designer product you rented for your protection. When this is over I'll stop and we can each go our separate ways. I won't even look like this any more."

A couple of minutes passed in silence.

"Why did you want this mission?" she asked.

"I didn't."

"You did. Rafiq *asked* you. I know how it works: Offer and Acceptance."

"I accepted, but I didn't want it."

"Do you want it now?"

"Yes."

"And if I decide to keep you on, will you—" she saw him about to laugh at her again, and hurried on "—will you honour the deal I did with Rafiq? Will you protect me during the summit?"

"No, I won't. I'll protect you before, during, and after. Until I'm sure it's over." He stared her down again. "So, against all the odds, you got Rafiq to lend you a Consultant. Now tell me why I'm here."

She paused. "To protect me from the snare of the hunter."

"What?"

"It's a phrase from Evensong."

"Even what?"

"Evensong. A service I attended once at Rochester Cathedral. That's the *Old* Anglicans. I paid them an official visit five years ago, when I became Archbishop. Do you know anything about the Old Anglicans?"

"They're the original Church of England." His memory, a substrate of his other enhancements, supplied the required text. "They're in gentle decline. Even in the cathedrals, congregations are small and aging. Nevertheless, they're generally a force for good (or at least, not a force for harm). Some attitudes towards them may be dismissive, but very few people actually hate them."

She looked at him curiously.

"That didn't sound like you. It sounded more like Rafiq."

"It was. Part of his briefing."

"Well, as usual he got it right...You know, on the way back from Rochester some of my staff were actually sniggering. They thought the Old Anglicans were ineffective and crumbling and outmoded: all the things *we're* not. One of them said that even their Advent Calendars have boarded-up windows. I didn't like them sniggering like that. The Old Anglicans are good people."

In a far corner of the room, the ginger cat meowed softly in its sleep.

"And that's where *he* got his name. Nunc. Short for Nunc Dimittis. Part of the Evensong service. Of course, nobody except me uses his name. They all think of him as an It, not a He."

Yes, thought Anwar, *me too. Alien, beyond gender.* "So who's threatening you? And why?"

"What do you know about our founders?"

Again his memory flicked up the pattern of words. "The Church's founders come straight out of urban mythology. The Bilderberg Group, the Trilateral Commission, the Atlanticists, and others who won't identify themselves. But the New Anglican Church has moved beyond them. It still takes their money but it's also very rich in its own right—because it's well-led, commercially successful and has a wide offer."

"It's them. Not the Bilderbergers and the rest, they're just the public face. It's the others, the ones who won't identify themselves. And Rafiq knows nothing about them."

"Yes he does. Rafiq knows everything."

A sideways glance. "He doesn't know about *them*. But he will."

"Rafiq had some more to say, about you. He said that among the founders, you've got friends and enemies. Your friends support you because you've made the New Anglicans rich and powerful. Your enemies distrust you for the same reasons."

"Yes. They don't like the direction the Church has taken. They originally set it up to be something else. They wanted to pull its strings, write its scripts, send it out on stage, and eventually I said No. I decided to reinvent it. Rafiq's briefing probably covered that."

"And only a Consultant can protect you from them?"

"Yes."

"Why? And why only during the summit?"

"Because that's when they'll move. Probably at the signing. At the end of the summit, when everyone is looking at the politicians, when they're all signing whatever they've cobbled together. The move won't be at them, but at the host. Live, and in public. And when they come for me, it'll be with something beyond even Gaetano. Something unstoppable. It's how they work. Stay hidden, then emerge once or twice in a generation to give history a nudge."

"How do you know these people will move for you?"

"I know how they think. And they aren't people."

Before he could ask her what she meant, the food arrived. It was brought in personally, on white porcelain and silver dishes, by Gaetano and Luc Bayard. They set it out on the table, efficiently and tidily. Anwar knew without asking that Gaetano would have been present while it was cooked, and wouldn't have let it out of his sight.

Bayard still bore the red abrasion at his throat caused by Anwar's Verb. Or Adverb. "How's Proskar?" Anwar asked him. He'd meant it genuinely, but Bayard didn't take it that way. As he left with Gaetano he murmured to Olivia, while smiling at Anwar, "Inferior. Only the inferior ones get bodyguard duties, and they don't like it."

There were several dishes, all Thai. Including Anwar's particular favourite, a Thai green curry. It had a thin consistency, like dishwater. It didn't look appetising, but when cooked properly, as this was, it had a delicate aromatic taste.

"How did you know I like Thai food?"

"I asked Rafiq. Or rather, I got my staff to ask his staff."

They finished the meal quickly, and without much conversation. He watched her while they were eating. She was small and immaculate. Her dress was similar to the one she wore earlier: like a ball gown, with a fitted bodice and floor-length bell skirt. This one was also velvet, but purple. Perhaps in deference to the occasion, she wore evening gloves.

And she ate like a starving tramp: far more, and far more voraciously, than he did. *Her appetites,* he remembered. *She must be one of those irritating people who never seem to put on weight.*

"Mm, I do like food."

"Yes," he said, "I think it's here to stay...Why did you say they aren't people?"

"The same reason you aren't. You were made like you are, you never had to work at it. And you move in and out of the world, with an ID that isn't your real one."

"Wasn't this evening supposed to be a briefing about them?"

"It was, but I changed my mind. You're scheduled to see Gaetano tomorrow at nine. He'll brief you. Until then, I've told you enough."

He shot her an irritated glance.

"Don't worry, there's time. We have more than two weeks before the summit. And whoever-they-are won't do whatever-it-is until the final day."

He didn't like her tone, and told her so.

"I don't like yours. What, you thought this was going to be simple and tidy? In and out, like your other missions?"

"I hope Gaetano will be more informative than you..."

"He usually is."

"...because I have trouble buying what you've said. Dark forces threatening you? So dark that even Rafiq doesn't know about them? So threatening that you question whether a Consultant can protect you? And then you describe them as if they don't really exist. As 'whoever-they-are.' As if you don't need protection at all."

"Why don't you like being a bodyguard?" she asked, as if she hadn't been listening.

He wanted to press the point, but decided not to; he'd rely on Gaetano's briefing. "Because we're seen by the person we're protecting, and by others around them. It compromises our identity in the outside world."

Another sideways look. Her next expression began to form, like a delayed echo, and he guessed it correctly. Mocking. "And what is your Identity In The Outside World?"

"Antiquarian book dealer. When this is over I may need to change it, or change my appearance. Another reason we don't like bodyguard duties."

"Antiquarian..."

"Book dealer, yes. Tomorrow, after I've seen Gaetano, I'm going into Brighton to pick up a book."

"Ah. Then I think I'll go with you."

"Why?" He was genuinely surprised, and immediately wary.

"Every time I go into Brighton, Gaetano insists on surrounding me with his people. In the next few days it'll be even worse. Tomorrow will probably be the last chance I'll get just to walk around Brighton without being surrounded. After all, I'll have a Consultant...Relax," she added, as he shot her a suspicious glance, "that's *all* it is. Sometimes things really are no more than they appear on the surface."

She was looking at him differently, as if she actually noticed him. Not as a person, he suddenly understood, but as the latest implement to scratch an itch which had begun somewhere in her velvet darkness.

Her other set of appetites. They do come round quickly. He started to get up.

Just then, they were interrupted.

3

At 10:00 p.m. in Brighton, it was 5:00 a.m. in Kuala Lumpur; the morning of the following day. Rafiq stood on the lawn in front of Fallingwater. He sometimes came there to watch the sunrise, when he had things to think about. He was apparently alone, but his security was all around him at a discreet distance.

Apart from his concerns over Asika and Levin, he also had an organisation to run. Today would be a big day. He was in the final stage of his restructuring of UNIDO. It was a brutal restructuring; Yuri Zaitsev, the Secretary-General, had openly questioned it. Also, Rafiq had precipitated a crisis by refusing to sign UNESCO's year-end operating statement until more rigorous performance goals were set. Both issues would produce internal conflicts which, although he would win them, were likely to be bloody.

He took out a cigarette. As nobody else smoked indoors neither did he, even in his inner office. Where, he remembered, he'd left his lighter. Arden Bierce, who had also been at a discreet distance, came up to him and gave him hers. She didn't smoke, but always carried a lighter when she was with him.

He watched the sunrise. *Dawn. Black Dawn.* He remembered the marquee which had stood here ten years ago. *It wasn't just my family. It was others. Empty places at other tables, empty halves of other beds. And it's still unfinished business.*

"Thanks for the light. And thank you for attending the funeral."

"Thank you for not asking how it went."

He saw she was doing that thing which people do to stop crying: clenching the face, compressing the lips, breathing in through the nose, looking upwards as if gravity might slow the tears. To his relief, she succeeded.

He lit his cigarette and handed back her lighter. He inhaled. A filthy and antisocial habit, he knew, but he never smoked more than one or two a day, and he wasn't a lifelong smoker; he'd started only ten years ago.

"I told Chulo he should wait until he retired before having a family, but... You know, of all of them Chulo was the only one I really felt comfortable with."

She nodded but said nothing.

"I listened to your report," he added.

Still she said nothing, for a while. Then it all came. *"Who are they?* Why would they do this? And how could they do it, to Chulo? And where's Levin?"

"I think," he said slowly, "that maybe they were just trying out. Maybe they killed Levin to get us to send someone even better...We'll get the rest of it, Arden. Our forensics and intelligence are the best in the world, just as the Consultancy is the best executive arm in the world. They're chasing down those questions you asked, and dozens more like them. We will get the rest of it."

She nodded. She knew he'd come out here to think about Asika and Levin and UNIDO and UNESCO, but she knew he'd also been remembering his family. Now even more people had died trying to catch the man responsible, and he had sent them. She could read it in his face. She didn't often see him like this, and it distressed her.

Rafiq was ruthless and cunning, but he inspired personal loyalty. People who worked for him—those he hadn't discarded or ruined—knew that within the constraints of his labyrinthine political agendas he still, usually, tried to make things better. Not perfect, but better. His compact with The Dead stated that they should serve the office of the Controller-General: not the individual, but the office. In reality, they served the individual. And now the nineteen deadliest people in the world (*No*, she thought, *eighteen. Or is it seventeen?*) were facing a new and apparently unknown opponent. One which had already done something unthinkable.

She again remembered the note. *One character no longer in search of an author.*

"They know so much about us. You think this might be Zaitsev? Or some other part of the old UN in New York?"

Rafiq almost laughed. "No, they don't have the imagination. Maybe the resources, but not the imagination. No, this is an attack on the *whole* UN, mine and Zaitsev's. And it comes from outside."

After she'd gone, Rafiq thought, *Only part of that is right, and I'm not sure which part. For once, maybe I don't know everything.*

4

The interruption was Gaetano, carrying a large folder.

"Sorry, Archbishop, but you asked to see this as soon as it was ready."

She turned to Anwar. "It's our year-end financial statement. I need to check it now."

"Should I leave?"

"No, this is just the first draft, it won't take long."

Gaetano stood silently by her side as she studied the documents. She took only a couple of minutes to absorb them (something which, like Rafiq, she did without enhancements).

She glanced up at Gaetano. "See what they've tried to do?"

"Yes. Notes 19 and 36 on the non-recurring and below-the-line items. I told them you'd never agree."

"So why did they do it?"

"To hide the real cost of some of the Room For God projects. They think that if the media find out what a *Church* is spending on campaigns against Creationism and blasphemy laws..."

"Why do they keep doing that? Thinking? Why is it that my head of security knows more about proper financial reporting than my Finance Director and his three Deputies? We had this last year, when they..."

"When they tried to hide the cost of commissioning independent research into the Bible conclaves. I reminded them of that."

"Alright, Gaetano, remind them of this: those items are our core business. I will not have them hidden. I want them where they belong, in the main Income and Expenditure accounts. I'm throwing out their draft. And remind them not to try this again."

"You could also," Gaetano suggested drily, "tell me to remind them about their appraisals."

"Yes, they're due in four weeks, aren't they? If I'm alive by then...Just checking you're still awake," she told Anwar, as both he and Gaetano looked at her sharply.

This is like her Room For God broadcast, Anwar thought. *Every day she fights real battles. More than I've done in seven years.*

"As the Archbishop," she explained to Anwar, after Gaetano left, "I'm a mix of Chairman and Chief Executive. Like," she looked sideways at him, "the UN Secretary-General and Controller-General rolled together into one."

Anwar thought of Yuri Zaitsev, the jowly and heavyset Secretary-General, and Rafiq. The idea of them rolling together into one was not something he could easily imagine.

"Back to who's threatening you. Why not fundamentalists? Your Batoth'Daa?"

This time, she laughed in his face. "Never! They don't have the imagination, or the intellect. Their religion sucks it out of them. Makes them turn unanswerable questions into unquestionable answers...That's not original. Someone else said it, I can't remember who."

"It was an Art Gecko slogan."

"What? Oh, of course. You and your old books."

"It wasn't a book..." he began, then left it. She'd already forgotten, and was busy pouring herself some wine.

"No thanks," he said as she started to pour a glass for him. "I don't drink alcohol."

"Oh, your name...Are you a Muslim?"

"No. Worse."

"Atheist?"

"Worse still. Agnostic."

"A *lapsed* atheist. Do you also bet each way at Brighton Racecourse?"

"I like to think it's rational," he said, rather pompously.

She scented blood and went for him. "Having blind faith in reason is not the same as being rational."

"You're a walking dictionary of one-liners."

"One-liners are useful for religious leaders. Martin Luther had ninety-five of them. His Ninety-Five Theses were good. But if he'd nailed the Ninety-Five *Faeces* to the Church door at Wittenburg..."

Anwar laughed out loud, something he rarely did. But she didn't notice. She was already busy clearing the table.

Later they stood at the window looking out at the lights of Brighton's shoreline and seafront. They were naked. They hadn't been naked while on the table. *Fully clothed, like the first time,* she'd said. *It's better when you act like it's spontaneous.*

Normally Anwar preferred the feel of a woman's naked body against his. But he was getting to like it her way. Disarranging her clothes was like unwrapping a gift. Seeing what was inside. And, if he still had to satisfy his obsession not to make tidy things untidy, he found he could disarrange her clothes carefully and slowly. She didn't seem to mind.

She'd taken him into herself even more greedily than last time. *I'm almost wiping her kidneys,* he thought incredulously, amid the swelter. They went again and again. *Her greed, for food* and *for sex. It's unbelievable. Where does she put all that food? And all that sperm?*

They kept stealing looks at each other. Naked, she was exactly as he'd imagined when he'd seen her for the first time: lithe, slender, and toned. He wasn't quite as she'd imagined. His musculature was impressive and defined, but somehow not entirely right. On Brighton beach, a few people might have looked twice at him.

It was modelled on the musculature of big cats. All cats had a higher ratio of muscle to body-weight than other mammals, and so did Anwar. He wasn't a cyborg or robot, but a living thing, with enhancements replicating other living things, in specific areas where they were better than human.

She didn't know that, but she knew the Dead were somehow *made*. His muscles didn't bulge unnaturally like those of a bodybuilder, but they rippled. Everywhere. She'd felt them moving, under his skin and under the touch of her greedy grabbing hands. They were living tissue. Not mechanical or metallic or electronic.

But still not entirely right. As if he'd been taken apart and somehow put back together according to slightly different principles. Which was, she realised, probably the case: millions must have been put into him. Tens of millions. She thought, *Can he protect me from what they'll send?*

As in the Boardroom, there was an easy silence between them: fitting for the simple slaking of simple lust. *Literally in and out,* he thought, *with no baggage. Tidy and self-contained. Even better than the best prostitutes.* And he could afford the best.

They looked out at the i-360 Tower on the seafront two miles away, at the bright lights of its main structure and the illuminated observation pod, a large ring-doughnut going up and down the Tower's shaft.

"I know an architect," said Anwar, "a good friend of mine, who would have seriously considered redesigning that doughnut as a hand."

She looked at him in puzzlement for a moment, then burst out laughing. But by the time he'd decided to join her (he normally preferred to smile quietly rather than laugh out loud) she'd already stopped and was thinking about something else.

1

The following day, promptly at 9:00 a.m., Anwar started work. It was an easy commute. Gaetano's apartment and offices were on the same floor as Olivia's. She had left three hours earlier on Church business.

Gaetano's office, like every interior he had seen—though he hadn't seen hers, yet—was nacreous white and silver. It was tidy and sparse, as Anwar had expected.

"You're early," Gaetano said.

"No. It's exactly nine, as we arranged."

"I meant for your stay here. September isn't over yet and the summit isn't for two weeks. A young woman named Arden Bierce called us last week and said you wanted to come here early. A very nice young woman."

"Yes, people like Arden. She has a way about her."

"Well, it made her suspicious."

"The Archbishop? Why?"

"It was different from what she got Rafiq to agree...She really does feel threatened. You may not think she acts or sounds like it, but she does."

"Last night she was supposed to give me a briefing about who's threatening her, but she changed her mind halfway through. Apparently I'm now getting it from you."

"She was in a strange mood last night...What did she tell you?"

"Only that the people threatening her are the people who really run the Church's original founders: the ones who aren't named, even in conspiracy theories, and they don't like her having moved the Church beyond their control. Is there any truth in that? Do *you* believe it?"

"Yes, I do."

"Then why didn't she say more? If she wants me to protect her, why didn't she say exactly who she wants protection from? Do *you* know who they are? Where they are? Why they're threatening her?"

"I can tell you some of that, but sometimes she's less than honest with me, too, and I don't know why. Sometimes she tries to conceal how frightened she is by talking about them lightly, or ambiguously. But I believe she's genuinely frightened. I can tell you the rest of what she was going to say last night, and I'll add some ideas of my own that might help you, although my own enquiries haven't uncovered much."

"Alright. But if I don't think it's enough, I'll walk away." *No you won't,* he thought, *not from this. Not now.*

"She doesn't know their individual names and locations," Gaetano continued, as if he hadn't heard Anwar. "They aren't even members of the Bilderbergers or the Atlanticists and the rest. They just work through them indirectly, when it suits them. They have larger agendas. Maybe Zaitsev's one of them. Or the presidents of some UN members. Or you, or me, playing a double or triple game. And they stay..."

"Stay dormant for years, then come out once or twice in every generation to give history a nudge. I know, she told me. But why are they suddenly a threat? And why at the summit? How does she know?"

"She's been dealing with them since she became Archbishop five years ago. She must sense their long-term plans. And they don't attend our Boards or Assemblies. They communicate only with her, by messages given to Board members. Handwritten messages in sealed envelopes, passed through a network of couriers and proxies which soon disappears if you try to trace it back. I've tried."

"The UN will have to check all this, I don't have the resources, and personally I don't buy it," Anwar said. "A conspiracy inside bodies which are themselves the subject of conspiracy theories. A shadowy cell that manipulates the manipulators. Handwritten notes. I don't buy it." But privately he was just beginning to. It fitted some of the observed data, and it felt right. "I really don't buy it," he repeated, as if the repetition would drive the uncertainty out of his voice. It didn't. "And this is what she was going to tell me last night?"

"Part of it. But you need to hear the rest."

2

I shouldn't really have come here this morning, Richard Carne thought. *But they didn't tell me not to, so they must have suspected I might. And I'm glad I did. It's quite striking. Really singular.*

It had been an easy journey from London, and only a short detour from where he was headed, to reach Brighton. And an easy journey of ninety seconds from Gateway to Cathedral, in a sleek white-and-silver maglev, to see the Conference Centre at the end of the New West Pier.

Those who employed him were unknown to him. He only dealt with them indirectly, through several layers of proxies and cutouts, but even the little he'd seen of what they could do was deeply impressive. They'd be doing more things between now and the summit, but the summit—here, in two weeks— was where it would really kick off. And what would happen at this Conference Centre would be only a small part of it.

What they could do, he reflected, was quite diverting and singular. He was a relatively minor functionary, but he'd seen and heard enough. There was what they'd done to Asika. And what they'd done to Levin, which was worse. And Levin's *face*, when he'd realised he couldn't defend himself. Now, he thought, let's have a look at that extraordinary Cathedral, and then a longer look at the equally extraordinary Conference Centre. That was where it would all really begin. The thing which would kill her was quite singular, quite diverting. It might already be here, in this beautiful silver and white building where the summit would begin on October 15.

If not, it would be on its way.

3

"Half a percent of the world's population," Gaetano said, "owns 40 percent of the world's wealth. Four million people. The ones threatening her are a few random and apparently unconnected individuals, out of four million."

"Individuals running the founders' organisations?"

"Yes, but indirectly, not as members. They operate through networks of proxies and subsidiaries, the way they operate their shareholdings and finances. And they don't have a secret underground HQ in Antarctica, or a hollowed-out mountain in the Himalayas. They have something much better: their corporations. When they want a task done, or an object made, they divide it down to its smallest components and farm it out to subsidiaries and sub-subsidiaries." When Anwar stayed silent, Gaetano added, "Maybe Rafiq's one of them."

"No. He's rich, but not that rich. He has millions, but the people you're talking about have billions. Or trillions." But Anwar was thinking, *Currency isn't only money, it's also power and knowledge,* and there Rafiq must be in their league. This was beginning to worry him. His mind was racing, but he

kept his face a mask. *If this is real, it's the worst combination
of threats: a cell, like Black Dawn, but with trillions. I must
talk to Arden.*

Gaetano waited politely for Anwar to digest this—he hadn't
been convinced by Anwar's convincing poker face—before he
continued. "I think they're putting together something intricate and far-reaching, and her death is only a part of it. But...
a handful of people, unconnected, not even members of the
founders' organisations. Out of four million. I don't think you
can easily locate or identify them."

"UN Intelligence can."

"Probably not in time."

"They've done nothing to invade our space yet."

"They will...And if you can't locate them pre-emptively, all
that's left is the inferior option: just wait for them to move
at the summit, and hope you can stop them." When Anwar
didn't reply, Gaetano got up. "Think about it, while I go and
make us some coffee. Vietnamese, yes?"

"How did you...Oh, of course. Her people asked Rafiq's
people." He watched Gaetano set the two glasses down. There
was a layer of condensed milk at the bottom of each glass, on
top of which the dark coffee floated without mixing. It looked
like an upside-down Guinness.

"So how did you come to work for her?"

"Isn't it in Rafiq's briefing?"

"Tell me anyway."

"I'm a mercenary. It was interesting—far more than
guarding politicians or business people or criminals—and it
paid well."

"And now?"

"I'm still a mercenary. It's still more interesting than
guarding politicians or business people or criminals, and
it still pays well. I'm a permanent employee with a job
description and a contract. But if I wasn't, I'd still go out

and die for her." The last sentence was spoken without any change of voice.

"She told me you'll be providing a two-day briefing on the summit. Do you want to take me through it?"

Yes, Gaetano did want. He would give Anwar a first look at the Conference Centre, where the summit would take place. Then he would detail the security arrangements for the summit, in the following order:

One, descriptions of each delegate and his/her entourage, especially security.

Two, liaison protocols with delegates' security staff.

Three, the currently-agreed version of the summit Agenda, which would be subject to last-minute changes.

Four, the arrangements on the first day of the summit: the delegates' arrival, and the style and content of the opening ceremony. "Despite what she believes," Gaetano said, "the threat could come on the first day, as well as the last. It'll be just as public, and just as high-profile. She'll be there as host, and she'll make the welcoming speech, all about the love that dare not speak its name because its mouth is full." Anwar looked up sharply. They locked eyes for a moment, then Anwar smiled faintly. Each of them thought, *Maybe he hasn't got his head as far up his ass as I'd feared.*

Five, the arrangements for each day: seating plans, meals, coffee breaks, break-out sessions, evening social events.

Six, the disposition of security people, translators, support staff, catering staff.

Seven, provisions for attack from sea and air.

"... And that's what I'll take you through this morning."

"Do I need to know it in such detail?" Anwar asked. "I'm here for her security only."

"She's the host. As well as speaking at the opening and closing ceremonies, she's expected to make appearances from time to time at the summit sessions. And when she does, you should know what's all around her."

"Yes, that's reasonable." *But you still haven't mentioned the important part.*

"And," Gaetano added, "you need to know it in detail because—this is the important part—she wants you to review all the arrangements and make any recommendations you see fit."

"And what do you think of that?"

"Not much, initially. But if it protects her better..."

"Good. Then let's not talk in code. If I see something wrong with any of your arrangements, I'll say so. If I think they're good, or very good, or mediocre, or sloppy, I'll say so. And can you put it all on an implant bead?"

"I already have. You can download it and study it over-night. And tomorrow, I'll take you through the Archbishop's engagements from now to the end of the summit."

"She has one this afternoon which she may not have mentioned."

"Going into town with you to collect a book?"

"Yes."

"I'll have some people follow you, but only at a discreet dis-tance. You understand that you'll be her primary protection?"

"Yes."

"And please, get her back here before four. She has several meetings."

"OK. And the briefing tomorrow?"

"We'll cover the detailed security arrangements for the Archbishop—how they operate now and how they'll be ramped up for the summit. I'll give you backgrounds and credentials for all my people. And I'll put it all on an implant bead, so you can..."

"Study it overnight. Thank you."

A short silence grew between them. Anwar noticed—for the first time, despite his enhancements and training—the signs of strain on Gaetano's face: sleeplessness around the eyes, tense-ness in the jaw. Signs of the inevitable and mounting pressure of the approaching summit and the threats to Olivia.

Gaetano, as if he sensed what Anwar was thinking, said, "You know, this is only about a tenth of what the summit involves. She has departments dealing with the PR and political aspects. And the legal. And the financial. Especially the financial. There are daily accounts for every item of expenditure connected to the summit. This meeting will be costed down to the last minute, and she'll see the costing tonight. She doesn't give any obvious appearance of micromanagement, in fact she professes a huge dislike of it. But she misses nothing."

Like Rafiq, Anwar thought. *When Arden and I deal with him, it's like we're the only thing he has in front of him. But there's legal, and financial, and political, and PR, and intelligence, and the conventional military, and the Agencies. Rafiq and Olivia del Sarto. Different characters, but similar styles of working.*

Anwar said none of this out loud, so Gaetano continued. "And what about you? I thought you people didn't like bodyguard work, because..."

"That's how I felt at first." He remembered what he'd thought, back at his home in northern Malaysia, after watching her Room For God lecture. *Frozen hope. My life has been arid, hers is real.* "But I feel differently now."

4

For two hours Gaetano took him through the security arrangements for the summit. The initial wary courtesy between them had developed into something slightly less guarded. Gaetano went through the briefing in the order he'd outlined and, as promised, gave him the implant bead. Anwar acknowledged politely and promised his detailed comments the following morning. Already he knew there would not be many; Gaetano's arrangements were characteristically thorough.

They walked out of the New Grand and across the Garden. It was a bright pleasant day for late September, like yesterday when he'd arrived. The domes and spires and latticeworks of the Cathedral complex were lustrous in the sunlight. The Garden showed blues and reds from hydrangeas, gradations of yellow and gold from witch hazel and broom. The trees and shrubs were swaying in the wind from the ocean.

Ahead was the Conference Centre. Anwar noticed some people wheeling luggage trunks.

"Contractors, from Patel. They're doing building work on the room where the signing will take place," Gaetano explained. "The UN wanted a replica of the Press Suite in New York. Nineteen-sixties décor and furniture."

"They don't look much like contractors."

"She insisted they shouldn't. They have to use containers that resemble luggage and are small enough to go in the luggage section of a maglev. She wouldn't allow anything to be dropped by VSTOL or by sea to the end of the Pier. It all has to go through Gateway Station to Cathedral Station, then up and along here, no matter how many journeys it takes. It means their equipment is disassembled in the vehicles parked on Marine Parade, and reassembled on site in the Conference Centre. It's taken weeks. And when they travel up here and back, they must wear normal civilian clothes, and change on site. And the site must be closed and soundproofed."

"She's very particular about appearances," Anwar said.

"She is, but it's also about security. Shall we go in?"

I could get here, Anwar thought, *through all the detectors. In a luggage trunk. I could dislocate my joints to bend into it. I'd go to near-death. A timed hibernation. No body-heat detectors would find me: surface temperature would be the same as my immediate surroundings. No heartbeat or breath detectors would find me: pulse and breathing would be almost nonexistent, and random. No scanners or imagers or DNA detectors would find me: my body would echo the texture and shape of its immediate surroundings.*

Enough of that for now. I'll add it to my overnight comments.

"Shall we go in?" Gaetano repeated.

The Main Hall, on the ground floor of the Conference Centre, was an interior space as large as that of the Cathedral. Anwar was transfixed. He'd expected a vast white and silver interior, with clean swooping lines, and that was exactly what it was. But the sheer scale was deeply impressive. And its style couldn't have been more different from the UN General Assembly Hall in New York. As with the Cathedral, and the rest of the New West Pier complex, the inside contradicted the outside.

The Main Hall was where the scheduled sessions of the summit would be held. There were adjoining smaller rooms for spin-off sessions, coffee shops and bars, translators' booths. Actually, the Conference Centre was bigger inside than the Cathedral, because there was no full upper floor, only a mezzanine: a balcony running round the entire circumference, with doors leading off. These opened into further anterooms for breakout sessions, and included the large room being refurbished for the signing ceremony. The contractors could be neither seen nor heard.

Anwar stood for a moment, memorising the lines of sight and tying them in with Gaetano's briefing.

"Let's go back to the New Grand. She'll be waiting. And please make sure she gets back by four. She cancelled several meetings to do this."

"She cancelled meetings?" Anwar asked in surprise. "Just to go into Brighton with me and collect a book?"

"I hope you don't misinterpret what's passed between you."

"No. I know about her appetites. Everybody does. And," he added, "don't misinterpret my accepting this mission. It's because of what she stands for, not her personally."

5

Olivia was waiting in the reception of the New Grand.

Gaetano had suggested she didn't wear her normal clothes. Not really a disguise, he'd said, just dress differently so your identity isn't so obvious. She did, and it totally altered her.

She wore flat loafers instead of her customary heels, so she appeared even smaller than usual. She had on very little makeup. She wore a sweater and jeans—though the jeans were black and expensively cut—and her famously-coiffed blonde hair, which normally she wore so it softened the slight sharpness of her features, was pulled back off her face and tied in a ponytail.

Anwar thought she looked too natural. He preferred her in her structured and tailored and madeup mode: her Formal Normal look, as he'd privately taken to describing it. Also, she made him feel overdressed. He was wearing another of his expensive linen-blend suits, with a contrasting shirt of dark woven silk.

They took the maglev from Cathedral to Gateway—nobody appeared to give them a second glance—and walked out of the Pier onto Marine Parade, from where they descended the steps to the seafront.

"Do you know," she asked suddenly as they walked along the shore, "how many Churches and religious centres there are within walking distance of where we are now?"

"Unaccountably, Rafiq's briefing didn't include that."

"Loads of them," she went on, as though she hadn't heard him. "There's St Paul's, West Street—Old Anglican. St. Mary's, Preston Park—Catholic. The Middle Street Synagogue. The Buddhist Centre in North Laine. The Quakers' hall in Meeting House Lane. The Al Quds mosque in Seven Dials." She turned and looked up at him, straight-faced. "I like to know where they all are. If they go fundamentalist, I can tell them I know where they live."

"If you add all of them together and multiply them by ten, they still wouldn't be a tenth of what your Church done—" he looked back at the New West Pier "—over there."

"Yes," she said simply, and unhelpfully. She knew where he was going, but she wasn't going to help him get there.

"The money for this..."

"I told you. Originally the founders. But now the Church has moved beyond needing their money. It has plenty of its own. And they don't like it."

They walked along the seafront. The mast-rigging of the small boats drawn up on the beach thrummed in the wind. They walked past the arches Anwar had walked past yesterday, and past some arcades with games. There was one where things popped up and you had to knock them down with a rubber mallet, only for others to pop up, also to be knocked down. She watched it for a while.

"Remind you of fundamentalists?"

"*Yes,*" she hissed, "and they're filth! Scum! I hate their beliefs more than I love mine."

"I only meant," he said mildly, "how they pop up somewhere else if you..."

"Theocrats, creationists, racists, homophobes, all of them! The death of dialogue. 'If you don't agree with me, you're better off dead.' Knock them down in one place, they pop up somewhere else."

"I don't like their beliefs either, though it may not matter to you. But they're not all filth. Or scum." The words had a strange echo for him, of the greeting he would sometimes exchange with Levin. "Some of them just want certainty."

"You're right. It doesn't matter to me."

" Don't hate them so much. It makes you ugly."

"If I didn't hate them so much, I wouldn't be who I am! And what business is it of yours if something makes me ugly?"

"You're right, it isn't. But if you hated them less and understood them more, maybe even more people would support you. Including some of them."

She looked up at him sharply. "I didn't expect that. I thought you were just a Consultant."

They climbed a stairway up the embankment to road level, just before the old Palace Pier. They walked across Marine Parade and into East Street, which led upwards, away from the seafront. It was busy and crowded, a mix of shops and restaurants, mostly upmarket. There was the usual doppler effect of approaching and receding conversations, and the usual mix of smells: things being cooked, substances being smoked. Still nobody appeared to give them a second glance.

He spotted Gaetano's people. He liked how they worked: discreetly, keeping a distance, constantly changing their patterns. She didn't seem to see them, but he knew she'd assume they were there somewhere.

Ahead they could now see the original Royal Pavilion in Pavilion Gardens with the Indian Gate. The New Anglicans, careful as always, had made sure the original Royal Pavilion and the New West Pier were never in direct sight of each other.

Leading off East Street on the left was the Lanes district, with small esoteric shops selling bespoke interiors, designer clothes, antiques and curios and books. It was an area of narrow alleyways, sometimes called twittens and catcreeps.

The walls were patchworks of old brick, flint, cobblestone, and stucco. The Lanes had been the original fishing village of Brighthelmstone.

Anwar took them to Ramsden's Bookshop, in Meeting House Lane. The proprietor nodded, apparently casually, but somehow giving the impression that he remembered Anwar from his last visit, two years ago. It was a small musty shop, but carried a good stock of Shakespeares, including the one Anwar had reserved online for collection: a replica of the 1609 Chalmers-Bridgewater edition of Shakespeare's Sonnets. So much, these days, was a replica, but this was a very good one. It wasn't cheap. Even replicas could be valuable in their own right.

They continued along Meeting House Lane.

"There," she said. "Frobisher's Tea Rooms. Come on, I'm buying."

Where Ramsden's had been genuinely old and musty, Frobisher's was a modern copy of age and mustiness. None of the darkwood wall panelling or furniture had ever been part of, or even near, a real tree.

It was more utilitarian than its outside appearance suggested, or than Anwar guessed she was used to. It was crowded, and she joined the queue at the counter.

"Self-service for the self-serving," she muttered. She got a pot of English breakfast tea for both of them, and a selection of cakes for herself.

"Fifty-five euros forty." The cashier pronounced it with a rising note of accomplishment on forty, as if it was the culmination of a trick he'd done. She'd forgotten she was buying, and took the tray to a table. Anwar paid and joined her.

"So you got your book."

"Yes, it's a nice edition."

"A replica?"

"Partly. It reproduces the typesetting and font of the original, but puts each sonnet on a separate page."

"May I look?"

"Of course." He slid the book across the table to her. "Sonnet 116 is my favourite. Especially the first four lines." He watched her turn to it, and said the words to himself as he watched her reading them.

Let me not to the marriage of true minds
Admit impediments. Love is not love
Which alters when it alteration finds,
Or bends with the remover to remove.

"Each phrase," she said, "has at least three or four possible meanings. Is that what he intended?"

"I think so."

"Didn't he write the sonnets to a mysterious Dark Lady?"

"Some of them, yes. But some might also have been written to a man."

"Oh."

Just then her wristcom buzzed. She flipped it open, listened briefly.

"It's Gaetano. He says they've detained a possible suspect on the Pier."

6

In the Cathedral complex, a thief had been tempted by an obviously wealthy-looking tourist. But this wasn't just any tourist.

"The thief," Gaetano said, "is a twelve-year-old boy, known to police. Dysfunctional parents. The social services put him in Care."

Care, Anwar thought. *A dismal word, smug and liberal. The boy was doomed.*

"He does petty crime," Gaetano continued. "Steals purses, wallets, briefcases, anything that looks valuable. Whizzes past on powered rollerblades, snatches and escapes. This man had just taken out his wallet, and the kid flew past and took it. The man ran—*ran*—after him and caught him. Kept kicking him, even after he'd knocked him down. Broke his arm and collarbone and three ribs."

"Where did this happen?" Anwar asked.

"Just outside, in the Garden. We detained him—" (*a simple phrase,* Anwar thought, considering what he'd done) "—until you could speak to him. The boy's in the Royal Sussex County Hospital."

Anwar, Gaetano, and Olivia were in the Boardroom. She was eating a cake that she'd managed to scoop up in their hasty departure from Frobisher's. In between mouthfuls, she asked Gaetano, "Were you already watching this man when it happened?"

"Yes. He'd been looking around the Conference Centre."

"Is that all? You don't think they've already got architects' plans and computer models?"

"Probably. But this man had the look of a professional. We had a feeling about him." Gaetano turned to Anwar. "I wish we'd got there before he caught the boy."

Anwar nodded. "How long can we detain him?" He saw Olivia glance at him, possibly because he'd said *We*, not *You*.

"If we invoke the summit, which I've done, the local police will let us hold him for twenty-four hours. He's in there." Gaetano pointed to the closed door of one of the Boardroom's adjoining rooms.

"Is he restrained?"

"Of course. Except for his conversation."

"What do we know about him?"

"We have his papers, and we checked his DNA, fingerprints, and retinas. His name is Richard Carne."

I used to have a name that sounded like that.

"He's ex-SAS. No currently known employer. Various jobs in the past, some legal and some not. Unpleasant habits. There's this thing he does with bread." Gaetano paused, and added, "And he's a member of something called the Johnsonian Society. He was carrying the text of a talk he gave in London a couple of days ago."

Anwar stood up. "Thank you," he said to Gaetano."I think I'll go and see him."

"And something else: we found two poison implants in his teeth. We've removed them. But..."

"Yes," Anwar said, "there'll be others. And there isn't time to locate them all. I must speak to him now."

"He'll trip them and kill himself, if the interrogation goes wrong...Look, maybe I should do this, I've done it before."

"No, I'll do it...Gaetano, does the Pier have a medical centre?"

"No. It has a fully-equipped hospital."

"Could you please ask one of your people to go there and bring me up a medical trolley with a tray of surgical instruments?"

There was an *ease* about Richard Carne. An air of insouciance.

The restraints which held him in his chair were not mono-filament, just extruded kevlar, but they'd been expertly tied. He couldn't move. But he still managed to give the impression of lounging.

He had straw-coloured hair, brushed flamboyantly back. Slightly pouty lips. Pale blue eyes. A large man, with an obvious Special Forces kind of build. His clothes were expensive: a dark blue jacket, sand-coloured slacks and cream shirt, and jaunty two-tone shoes in blue and cream. Even matching blue and cream socks.

"Do you know who I am?" Anwar asked him.

"I know what you are. Only a few like you in the world."

Anwar did not reply.

"And now *she's* got one of you, for the summit. It won't be enough, not against what they'll send."

"What you did was cowardly. That kid was totally out-matched. Why not take on someone who can fight back?"

"Like you? I'd be as outmatched as the kid. And you'd be as cowardly as me. In fact you already are. All you ever do is defeat outmatched opponents."

Two-nil to him. Anwar pulled up a chair, and sat facing him. For a while he said nothing, a tactic which didn't even slightly unsettle Carne. *Three-nil.*

He knew Carne was right. The Dead had it easy. Intelligence did all the hard work, before and after. Before, their work was to identify targets: dictators, oligarchs, criminals, political or religious fanatics. Then The Dead came in, to abduct or dis-able them. Usually abduct, in which case they were handed over to UN Intelligence. Information or compliance would be tricked or blackmailed out of them, or bullied out of them with threats of lifelong litigation or financial ruin.

The Dead had the most simple and self-contained part of the process, though it was physically impossible for anyone else. The parts before and after were more complex, less clear-cut, and didn't end. The people who undertook them couldn't go back into a comfort zone afterwards.

"Forty-love to me, I think," Carne murmured.

But this time, Anwar would have to do the before and after parts himself. He couldn't just guard her reactively. He had to identify and locate those who threatened her. And here was one of their minor functionaries. Clever and self-assured, and more experienced at this than Anwar; but there might be a way. When the instruments came. Until then...

"So you're a member of the Johnsonian Society."

"Yes."

"So am I."

"Really?" Carne was mildly, but genuinely, surprised. "I haven't seen you at any functions."

"I don't often get to London, but I've been a member for years. I keep all the Society's newsletters."

"You'll have seen my articles, then."

"Yes, that's where I remembered your name...What makes you a Johnsonian?"

"Oh, that's easy. He had an opinion about everything. His own, original opinion."

"Exactly," Anwar said, nodding enthusiastically. "Always an original opinion. He was High Church, High Tory, but anti-slavery. Risky, in those times. For a man of his class and profession."

Carne was now genuinely excited. "Did you hear about my talk the other day? It was called..."

'Mask: The Nature Of Individual Identity In Postmodern Literature.' Yes, I saw it advertised in the newsletter. No offence, but I thought it sounded rather pretentious."

"None taken. I was never really happy about the title."

"Also," Anwar continued, "it didn't sound like the kind of literary criticism Doctor Johnson would have recognised...Ah, here are the things I asked for."

He turned as Gaetano wheeled in a hospital trolley full of surgical instruments.

"What is it she usually says?" he asked Gaetano. "Leave us. Give us this room."

Carne was looking at the surgical instruments, almost as dispassionately and appraisingly as Anwar.

"Let's save time," Anwar told him. "I'm supposed to ask who you're working for, and you're supposed to say nothing.

So let's assume we've had that conversation. Now we move to the part where I help you."

Gaetano had arranged a good selection of laser scalpels on the surgical trolley.

"Never mind these things here. I promise I won't kill you, and I won't cause you pain. I do have the necessary surgical skills..."

There were even some antique stainless steel scalpels. All arranged neatly.

"...and before I start using these things, I'll give you a local anaesthetic. So. No death and no pain. This is what I'm going to do.

"I'll trap you, permanently, inside your own head. No light, or sound, or touch, or words, or communication of any kind. I'll give you to yourself. You'll inhabit yourself, and nothing else.

"How will I do that, Mr. Carne? Your Eyes. Eardrums. Tongue. Hands. Feet. I'll surgically remove them all. I'll leave your eyes to last, so you can see everything I'm doing."

Carne said nothing. His expression hadn't changed.

"I could leave you in some stinking twitten or catcreep in the Lanes," Anwar went on, "but I won't. I'll leave you near a hospital, where people will find you and care for you. But you'll never be able to communicate with them. Or with anyone, except yourself."

Carne spoke at last. "You know, I've actually done things like that; but I bet you haven't. You've only read about them." He smiled. "I must read the same books you do."

Anwar had thought that would be his ace. He'd remembered it from a biography of Parvin Marek, who'd used the threat very successfully in interrogations. And Carne had just batted it back.

"And you couldn't do it," Carne added. "You can keep me for twenty-four hours, then you have to place me in the custody of the local police. They'd probably notice if you'd removed my—what was it?—hands, feet, tongue, eardrums and eyes."

"Then we'd ship you by VSTOL to Kuala Lumpur and do it there."

"No you wouldn't. Even Rafiq wouldn't sanction it."

"The Controller-General wouldn't know." Anwar didn't like the ease with which Rafiq's name rolled off the other man's tongue.

"Yes he would. Rafiq knows everything. Or you think he does. Actually, about now Rafiq is probably beginning to realize he doesn't know everything."

Anwar's turn not to answer.

"I know what you are," Carne added conversationally. "Only a few like you in the world."

"Yes, I heard the first time."

"Two less, now."

"What? What did you say?"

Carne smiled but didn't reply. Still, he hadn't tripped any poison implants yet.

Desperately, Anwar ramped it up. "There are surgical techniques to restore some of what I'll do to you. New eyes and eardrums and tongue. Prosthetic hands and feet. But they're expensive. When the hospital identifies you from your DNA, they'll check your bank accounts, but the UN will have emptied them."

Still Carne smiled but said nothing.

Anwar pushed again, inexpertly, trying to amplify the threat but still speaking quietly. "So that leaves your employers, and they won't want to be identified. For the rest of your life, the whole world will be a darkness the size of the interior of your head."

The quiet voice was intended to sound menacing, but Carne wasn't buying it.

"Oh, behave," he said languidly. "We both know I'll activate the poison before you get anything useful. Your ham acting threatens to sully the dignity of my passing." He paused for a moment, then added, "Two less, now. They annihilated Levin. Then Rafiq sent Asika, and they annihilated him too."

Anwar wanted to cry out, but he didn't. Not yet.

"Who are they? Where are they? How did they do it?"

"They're even more subtle and ruthless than Rafiq. They've been there since before he was born, and they'll be there after he dies. They work in long cycles, longer than his lifetime." His voice was modulated and mocking. "Doctor Johnson used to say that the prospect of imminent death concentrates the mind wonderfully...You're not very good at this, are you? At what comes before and after the easy bits that you do? Everything I am, I worked for. You, you were just made."

Anwar moved in a blur to grab the man by his coat. "Who are they? Why did you come here?!"

Carne let out a long breath, and Anwar knew he had finally tripped the poison.

"You wouldn't *believe* what they can do. I'm just a minor functionary of theirs. And you're just a minor functionary of Rafiq. So our lives have both been pointless, but you're still living yours."

There was a dark stain spreading over the front of Carne's trousers: the final effect of the poison, a slackening of his bladder. Urine, which he'd never spilt through any of Anwar's attempts to scare him, now poured out.

Anwar turned away. *The second person I've killed. And both of them by mistake.*

When he needed to mask his feelings, as he did now, he could reach somewhere inside himself and find the ability to do it. He made his features neutral and static, as if he was a shrouded actor in a formal codified Noh drama. It was a minor piece of stagecraft, like the Idmask he used for

Tournaments; but it came internally, and didn't disguise his features, just covered his feelings. Normally he could hold it for hours, but after what he'd just discovered he calculated it wouldn't last long; maybe long enough to get him through the next few minutes and into his suite where he could call Arden Bierce.

The door opened and Anwar stepped out into the Boardroom, followed by a waft of urine. His manner seemed strangely normal.

"Anwar! What did you do to him?"

"Nothing." *The first time she's used my name.* "I threatened him with something, and he said something. Then he tripped his poison implants. Gaetano, I'd like his body kept securely here until the UN come for it."

"Bodyguard duties," Gaetano muttered. "I told you to leave the questioning to me."

"What did he tell you?" Olivia asked.

"Something I need to check first with the UN... And I need permission for a VSTOL to land on the pad at the end of the Pier. They'll want his body." Without waiting for her answer, he turned to Gaetano. "I want you to put it around that he's alive and being held here until the summit finishes. Someone might come for him."

"What did you threaten him with?" Olivia asked.

He told her.

She stared. "Would you have done that?"

"Of course not. But the threat works." *Just not for me.*

"Did...did *you* think it up?"

"No, Parvin Marek did. Remember Parvin Marek? About ten years ago he..."

"Yes, I know who he was."

"Is. He's still out there. And don't gape like that, it makes you look gormless. Eat a cake or something."

Somehow, Anwar made it back to his suite. He sent Arden Bierce a report through his wristcom, including word-by-word accounts of his interrogation of Richard Carne and his conversations with Olivia and Gaetano, and waited.

After ten minutes, about the time he estimated it would take her to digest his report, her call came.

His wristcom could project a small image on to the air a few inches in front of it, or a larger high-definition image on to a wall or other convenient flat surface. He chose the wall.

Normally, it would have been good to see her again. Her face was regular and open (unlike Olivia's, with its sharp small features and changing expressions) and he knew it genuinely reflected what was inside her—including, this time, a look of preoccupation which closely echoed his own.

"Anwar, I..."

"Levin was assigned to find Marek, wasn't he?"

"Yes. There was a possible lead, but it..."

"And when were you planning to tell me about Levin?"

"Until your call, I had no idea of any connection between his mission and yours."

He let the silence grow between them.

"I'm sorry. But we don't have his body. Maybe he's not dead."

"Annihilated, Carne said. Like Asika. Did you see Chulo's body?"

"Yes."

"And?"

She told him.

"Miles...and Chulo."

"We don't know for certain about Miles. His body hasn't been found."

"Yes; you said that." He studied her face. The distress was genuine enough. "But you'd say that if his body had been found. You want me functional. You're just beginning to see what's in this mission, aren't you?"

"Anwar, listen. Whatever did that to Chulo, when it comes for her, do you think you can stop it?"

"Find them, Arden. Find who they are and where they are."

"You heard what Gaetano said. A handful of people out of millions, connected informally. What does that remind you of?"

"You tell me."

"The Dead. Moving in and out of the real world, back to a comfort zone where nobody can touch them."

"You're wrong. They're a cell. Like Black Dawn, random and untraceable, but in every other way the opposite of Black Dawn. A cell with trillions. Which doesn't publicise itself, which plays long and patient, which operates through proxies and cutoffs, and uses corporations and conglomerates and shareholdings and banks and networks of subsidiaries." *The* exact *opposite of Black Dawn. White Dusk,* he named them privately.

"This is bigger than even Rafiq knows." She was unaccustomed to saying such things, and it showed in her face. "I spoke to him this morning. It's beginning to worry him."

"What did he say?"

"He didn't, I did. But he didn't argue. An enemy who hasn't been around for years, and now is. And knows all about us. And when they kill her, it will only be the first move of something larger."

"I think you meant *If*, not *When*."

She didn't seem to hear him. "It's not her, Rafiq doesn't particularly care about her, but it's what they do afterwards..." She took a breath, and made her voice louder. "And there's something else. Rafiq's concerned you're having to do what UN Intelligence usually does. You don't have the experience."

"Oh, I see. First the Archbishop, now the Controller-General, telling me I'm not good enough."

"What? No, that's not what I..."

But Anwar wasn't listening. "And her guard, Proskar: you're sure he isn't Marek?"

"Of course I'm sure."

"But you'll check again?"

"Of course."

"He's Croatian. Fortyish. And those hands."

"I *said,* we'll check again. We already checked, before you even took this mission—the surface resemblance was obvious. But nothing else matches—DNA, fingerprints, retinal scans, dentition, nothing. And his database ID is genuine."

"But you'll still..."

"...check again. Yes."

"Because if he is Marek, tell me and I'll kill him." Anwar had never intentionally killed, or offered to kill, anyone. It must be the mask slipping, he could feel it. Dissolving. Corroded by the feelings he'd kept underneath it.

"Well, *say* something."

"Anwar, listen. Maybe she was right. Maybe Rafiq should send someone else."

"You bring in anyone else, I'll kill them. I'll come back and kill Rafiq too, right in front of Fallingwater where Marek..." He stopped, horrified. *What made me say that? I've never said anything like that.* "Arden, listen to me! I want this mission, but not for her, she's appalling. I want it for what she stands for." It might have been his voice, but it sounded to both of them like rambling.

Embarrassed, she changed the subject. "So why this summit? Why now?"

"It's not about the summit. The summit is only important because it's live and public and gives them the perfect stage to make their move for her."

They both let it hang there for a while, and went on to safer things: when they'd pick up Carne's body by VSTOL from the Pier, how they'd pretend he was still alive (to see who might come for him), and how they'd fake his death later. Fake death was easy, real death wasn't. When Anwar joined the Consultancy, they faked his passing as thoroughly as they always did. The UN databases thrummed with his exhaustively-documented death from a virulent strain of flu. They sometimes did car/plane/boat accidents, but that involved corroborating wreckage: not impossible, but more troublesome. His new identity, later, was slipped into the world's electronic landscape as if it had always been there.

Carne was genuinely dead, but they'd still have to fake it. After they did all the things they needed to do with his body.

"Will you be aboard the VSTOL?"

"No. I need to stay here and brief Rafiq on what Carne told you."

She went to say something else, then cut the connection. Anwar stared for a while at the empty projected rectangle on the wall. His mask, now he was alone, collapsed.

Arden Bierce replayed Anwar's report and started making notes. Like Anwar, she worked quietly and reflectively, and worked best on her own.

She hadn't looked at Anwar's earlier files, when he was Rashad Khan, for some time. She did now. Most of them she already knew well, but she found something she'd almost forgotten, tucked away in a subfile: The Story of Arnold the Wart. It was Anwar's (then Rashad's) entry for a short story competition at his school, written at the age of twelve.

Hubert had a large wart on his head. It was growing larger every day. Hubert grew attached to it, in every sense of the word, and after living with it for a while he decided to give it a name. He called it Arnold.

Hubert and Arnold went through life comfortably together, but Arnold grew bigger and bigger. Eventually he got so big that Hubert became a wart on Arnold, and Arnold's friends kept saying to him "Arnold, why don't you cut off that ugly wart?" So he did.

Rashad's teachers told him that the Arnold story was cold and careless and brutal. It needed more work, particularly on Arnold's and Hubert's relationship to each other and their social interaction with their peer groups. Rashad went away and thought about it, then came back with a new ending.

... Arnold's friends kept saying to him "Arnold, why don't you cut off that ugly wart?" So he did, and they both died.

Not only did the story not win the competition, but it led—after a series of worried meetings with educational psychologists—to the school principal asking for a conference with Rashad's parents. The outcome was inconclusive.

The principal referred to Rashad's well-known skill with immersion holgrams. Indeed, Rashad had many impressive qualities, but (his parents sensed the "but" coming) the holograms often showed a kind of quiet disrespect for authority figures. They also showed a compulsive curiosity about how things worked and what was hidden inside them—the tension between containers and contents, surface and substance. None of these were in themselves bad things, but they gave him a quality of *apartness*. A quality further emphasised by the Arnold story. There wasn't just a quietly cruel humour hiding in there, there was a private dread of relationships and commitment: the idea that getting close to another person could kill you.

She pondered Anwar's exact, word-for-word report on his interrogation of Richard Carne, and remembered Annihilate. *I used that word myself, in the villa.* Asika was annihilated, and so was Levin. Both of them, long gone.

And she remembered what she'd been about to ask him before she'd cut the connection: would he really have done those things to Carne? She knew what he'd told Olivia when she asked the same thing—he'd included a verbatim report on that conversation, too—and knew that if she, Arden, was to ask him, he'd simply have referred her to that answer. She'd have to settle for that. But she remembered his outburst just now, and thought, *What is this mission doing to him?*

Dissolution. Corrosion. Collapse.

Anwar snapped his wristcom shut. The empty projected rectangle faded from the wall. Something was going to happen, *here*, live and in public, in two weeks. Whatever they would send, it wouldn't be some Meatslab. It wouldn't be just another outmatched opponent. It would be whatever killed Levin and Asika. Only about thirty people in the world knew what he was, and eighteen of them were others like him. Sixteen now. *How can they make things that kill Consultants? Who are they? How can Rafiq not know about them? Am I out of my league? Is Rafiq out of his?*

For the first time he actually feared for his own life, never mind hers. No, he *did* mind hers. Olivia was offensive, but this was his mission. Very offensive, but this was still his mission. Monumentally offensive, so that he could almost imagine killing her himself, but he wouldn't let *them* kill her, who-ever they were. Because of what she stood for. Bigots multi-plied everywhere and made the world ugly. Only a few people stood for things which made it less ugly: Rafiq, certainly, and maybe her, at least publicly, no matter how offensive she was privately.

So this was still his mission. The one he was made for. But his lifelong comfort zone was gradually, detail by detail, collapsing.

A VSTOL landed on the pad at the end of the Pier. *For the first time,* Anwar thought, *a VSTOL comes without Arden.* Another detail, changed. It contained people from UN Intelligence. Also some doctors, in case anyone was watching. Carne's body was stretchered aboard, an IV bag attached to his arm, busily and uselessly pumping fluid into a dead man.

Anwar watched the VSTOL lift off silently and flicker into the dusk, then he returned to his suite. He walked out onto the balcony, and for the second time saw the sun setting over the Cathedral complex. September was about to become October, with the summit only two weeks away. He cried out for Asika, and for his friend Levin.

A floor above, Olivia heard him. She too was crying, but silently, and for a reason of her own. It was a quite specific reason, almost a detail, but if she told Anwar now it would change everything. She would tell him after the summit, if they were both alive then.

SIX: SEPTEMBER / OCTOBER 2060

On the last day of September, the weather over southern England was pleasant. It was a warm autumn evening in Brighton when Anwar cried out over the deaths of Asika and Levin; and also in Rochester, as an Evensong service began in the Cathedral.

For he shall deliver thee from the snare of the hunter.
He shall defend thee under his wings,
And thou shalt be safe...

The congregation was small, and mostly elderly. The service took place in the Nave, the part of the Cathedral where the West Door opened out onto College Yard.

The Nave was divided from the rest of the Cathedral by the organ, and to either side of it by the Pilgrim Steps and the stairs to the Crypt. A small altar stood in front of the organ. This divison was known as the Crossing.

Thou shalt not be afraid for any terror by night...
For he shall give his angels charge over thee,
To keep thee in all thy ways.

There was traffic noise outside. Rochester had become down at heel now that the southeast coast and Thames Estuary areas had seen massive new developments. The main road from the new bridges over the River Medway ran parallel to the old High Street, taking traffic past Rochester on the way to and from the new retail centres and business parks, some of them financed by the New Anglicans. They were places as alien to, and as different from, an old conventional town like Rochester as the New Anglicans were to the Old Anglicans. Rochester was dwarfed by them, and left in their wake.

There were only seven people in the choir, and less than fifty in the congregation. The Nave had enough space for many more, but they were almost huddled together in a few pews close to the front. The service was conducted by Michael Taber, Dean of the Cathedral. The Bishop of Rochester was not present.

The service moved on. After Psalm 91, the choir sang the Magnificat.

For he that is mighty hath magnified me,
And holy is his name.
He hath showed strength with his arm:
He hath scattered the proud in the imagination of their
hearts.

At the back of the Nave, the opposite end from the organ and altar, was the West Door. Walled off from the Nave, to the right of the organ and altar, was the Lady Chapel. Two other doors, the North and South Doors, were behind the altar, the other side of the Crossing.

On the organ pipes there were painted Gothic patterns, making them look like the spines of books on a Victorian bookshelf. The ceiling was vaulted and groined, made of dark carved wood, with stone Gothic arches supporting it. The pews were also dark wood, glowing with evening sunlight that accentuated the swirl of their grain.

The five figures who, by now, had completed several circuits of the outside of the Cathedral, moved to the West, North, and South doors. At a prearranged time they entered simultaneously, leaving large packages inside each door as they closed it. They bent to make adjustments to control panels on the packages. They unslung their weapons, but kept them concealed, and waited for the next prearranged time to come round.

Those who entered by the West Door made almost no noise, despite the heavy weaponry and packages they were lugging. A couple of the congregation glanced round, but the people who had entered looked official. There was a uniformity about their clothing, and they wore identity badges.

There was a short Bible reading by Michael Taber, then the congregation stood as the choir sung the Nunc Dimittis.

Lord, now lettest thou thy servant depart in peace,
According to thy word...

The next prearranged time came round. From the North door, the South door, and the West door, the figures stepped simultaneously into the light. They took up positions at the front of the Nave, to either side of the altar, and at the rear, to either side of the West door, now showing their weapons openly, just as the choir stopped singing.

"Dean Taber, ladies and gentlemen: We have control of the Cathedral. You are hostages. We've rigged the entrances and exits: There are explosive devices with motion sensors at every door. In a moment my colleagues will rig more of them at every window. The Cathedral will be irreparably damaged if anyone tries to enter or leave. So will you."

There were shouts and a few screams from some members of the congregation. Michael Taber stepped forward, arms raised, to calm them. There was something about his bearing that actually did calm them, and most of them fell silent.

Michael Taber looked like a caricature of a patrician: tall, handsome, well-groomed, with grey hair brushed back from a high forehead, and with a natural courtesy towards everyone, even intruders. "You are welcome here," he said, "but your weapons aren't."

There was a brief nod from the one standing closest to him at the altar, who appeared to be their leader. His identity badge said, in large letters, Jones. He was dark-haired and heavily built, perhaps running to fat. Taber didn't remember the events of ten years ago clearly enough, but if he had, he might have thought the man looked a bit like Parvin Marek. But Marek, if he was still alive, would have been slightly older. And Marek's face had had a deadness about it which this man's didn't, somehow.

"Who are you? What do you want?"

"We'll come to that. For now, some housekeeping matters. We know your congregation is elderly. We expect that what we've come here to do will take all night." (More shouts.) "So we've brought chemical toilets. We'll set them up in the Lady Chapel, where people can use them in privacy. And one of us is a qualified doctor, and carries a field medical kit.

"As to who we are: Smith, Jones, Brown, Patel, and Khan." Addressing the congregation, he added "See? We have name-badges. Mine says Jones. Not our real names, of course. One of us really is called Jones, but it isn't me. And the two called Patel and Khan aren't Asian, as you can see..."

His mouth turned down at the corners, and there were fixed frown-lines where his eyebrows met. It was the face of someone who didn't really want to be doing this; someone who felt out of his depth. But he still brandished a gun, levelly and with precision. They all did.

He turned back to Taber. "We're mercenaries. We were handpicked for this. Our employers wanted us for a particular reason: we all have terminal illnesses. So we'll carry this through to the death."

Taber was horrified, but somehow managed to conceal it. They probably didn't expect to live beyond the morning, but until then they were invulnerable.

"Why are you doing this?" Taber asked. He thought he already knew the answer but he was playing for time, while he sought a way to establish some rapport.

"To provide for our families. We all have wives and families. Including—" pointing to Patel, "—her. She has a wife. And adopted children. And only the New Anglicans would give her and her partner a proper Church wedding."

"We would, too," Taber said. "Since 2035."

"Yes, but not willingly. Your Church held out against it for years. The New Anglicans embraced it without being asked."

Taber didn't press the point. "So what happens next?"

"I'm going to call the authorities and describe to them what we're going to do here. When you hear what it is, remember this: We'll kill people if necessary, but if we get what we want there's a high chance that your congregation will all leave here alive."

"You're not wearing masks. That means that *you* don't expect to leave here alive."

"Not at all," he answered, a little too quickly. "When this is all concluded satisfactorily, we'll surrender."

Taber didn't believe him. Taber wasn't as easy to convince as his appearance might have suggested. He was a good Dean, but many other things besides. Those who knew him well, knew that he possessed a set of sharp perceptions which he usually kept sheathed like claws.

Jones flipped open his wristcom and told it a number. His call went through to Rani Desai, Director of Counter-Terrorism at the Home Office. She listened without interruption or comment, and without asking how he'd got her direct number, and promised to call back in five minutes with confirmation that she had the Home Secretary's authority to deal with them.

By the time she did so—in four minutes, not five—more packages had been lugged in and fixed underneath the stained-glass windows of the Nave.

"I'm now authorized to negotiate with you," Rani Desai said. "So what do we have to do to make you stop?"

Jones watched his colleagues fixing floor sensors, threading their way through the congregation and occasionally muttering, "Excuse me." They released crawlers, self-programming sensor devices like spiders, which scuttled over the walls and ceiling, positioning themselves at optimum intervals.

"I said," Rani Desai repeated, "what do we have to do to make you stop?"

He told her. There would be a drip-feed of demands. Ransoms, paid to charities. Relatively modest amounts: one million euros each. Jones would announce each charity, one at a time. Rani Desai would call the CEO or equivalent to get formal agreement that the money would be accepted. She would then call him personally to confirm that the Government had electronically transferred the money to the charity. The relevant bank screen, showing the transaction, would be sent to Jones' wristcom. A maximum of one hour would be allowed for each charity. There would be eleven, announced one by one through the night by Jones.

"So," he concluded, when Rani Desai didn't answer, "easily affordable, easily doable, and some good causes benefit. Complying seems better than a firefight, and a live congregation seems better than a dead one. Doesn't it?"

"If we comply, you won't harm anyone?"

"If you comply, of course we won't. Who do you think we are, Black Dawn?"

She didn't answer.

"Come on, I need to know."

"No, I don't think you're Black Dawn."

"I mean, I need to know if you'll comply."

"Yes, we will."

"Good. Now, before we get to the details of our demands, there are some administrative matters I need to take you through.

"First, we all have a military background. The explosive devices rigged at each door and window aren't homemade, they're of military origin. We have other devices, also of military origin, to detect attempts to enter through the walls, floor, or ceiling. They'll trigger the explosives, as will any attempt to enter or exit through the doors or windows. The explosives will probably kill everyone here and damage the Cathedral irreparably.

"Second, we know you'll be deploying people around the Cathedral. I would; it's only reasonable. But when you deploy them, and when you give them their orders, remember what I've said. Only eleven million euros, and it'll be over by tomorrow morning, and then we'll surrender."

"You'll surrender?" she sounded genuinely surprised.

"Yes, surrender…Why, what's wrong?"

"Why not give us your whole list now, all eleven? Why do it one at a time? I've already said we'll pay."

"No. This is how we *want* it."

Taber, who'd been listening carefully, knew then that they wouldn't surrender. He suspected also that there was something different about number eleven.

"Eleven. One at a time," Jones went on, "an hour for each, and we should be through by early tomorrow morning, and fifty-seven people—Dean Taber, the choir and congregation— will be free to go."

"What if one takes more than an hour?"

"Then fifty-six people will be free to go. An hour's a reasonable time. It's not exactly complicated." Jones paused, as if he felt the need to soften what he'd said. He did seem out of his depth. "If there's some genuine reason why you can't do it, we have a reserve list. So, Number One: Cancer Research UK. Time now is 10:17 p.m. You have one hour."

"I'll call you back," said Rani Desai.

The charities will probably reflect what they're suffering from, Taber thought. Cancer. And maybe heart conditions. Or neurological diseases. He'd know them one at a time, through the night. It was a line of investigation Rani Desai would be pursuing, and hardly a difficult one.

Within thirty minutes, VSTOLs were hovering outside the Cathedral (though not as silently as the UN's would have hovered). College Yard and Boley Hill were lit up. There was the sound of boots on cobblestones. Muffled shouts from the lawns, under the spreading trees. Jones, true to his word, did not appear surprised or angry.

Cancer Research UK took a little longer than expected—the CEO was not at the address, or with the partner, that Rani Desai's staff had been told—but it was still completed inside the hour. Rani Desai obtained his acceptance, made the electronic transfer, and sent Jones' wristcom the bank screen showing the transaction.

"Good," said Jones. "One down, ten to go. Number Two is the British Heart Foundation. It's now…11:05 p.m. You have one hour."

The explosives and sensors were set. The congregation, perhaps because of Jones' manner and how smoothly the operation promised to go, were a little more relaxed. Even the sound of boots and muffled shouts from outside had dwindled slightly.

A few minutes later, Jones started stealing glances at Taber. Taber was initially too polite to mention it—especially as he wasn't the one with the gun—but after a while he turned to Jones and asked, "Can I help you with anything?"

"No, but you can tell me something."

Unconsciously—he never used his famous charm cynically—Taber put on his I'm Listening face. "If I can. What is it?"

"Your faith." Jones hefted his rifle angrily. "I've never had a faith, either before or after I was diagnosed. Why do you?"

"The answer's in the question. It's my faith. It's what I believe."

Jones snorted derisively and was about to turn away without replying, but something in the way Taber returned his gaze—maybe the charm was starting to work—made him respond. "Alright, so it's what you believe. So does God give you certainty?"

Surprisingly, Taber laughed out loud. "That's the last thing God gives me. God shows me some wonderful unexpectedness." Despite the tension, some members of the congregation rolled their eyes. They'd heard this one before.

But Jones hadn't. "Unexpectedness?"

"Yes, unexpectedness. Let me tell you a story..."

"A true story?"

"Not yet. This is set in the distant future. Humanity has at last found the actual, physical location of God. It is at the edge of the known universe, billions of light-years away. No human could survive the journey, so they send a robotic probe. Even with faster-than-light travel, the journey takes years, and tension mounts over the centuries: What will the probe find? Eventually it completes the journey, and its robot voice calls back, from the edge of the universe, telling them that it has found God. That it now knows God's nature and identity.

"And do you know what it said, in answer to all their questions? *She's black. And an atheist.*"

Some of the congregation, the minority who hadn't heard it before, laughed. So did Jones and a couple of his colleagues.

Taber decided to leave it there for now. A small bit of rapport gained, but better not to overdo it.

The British Heart Foundation was more difficult. The CEO refused to take individual responsibility for the money, and insisted on contacting Board members, despite Rani Desai muttering darkly about having a heart attack herself. Eventually the necessary acceptances were obtained, and still within an hour, though the process had threatened to overrun. Rani Desai made the electronic transfer, and sent Jones' wristcom the screen showing the transaction.

"Good," said Jones. "You see, that's why we need a generous time allowance. Things like this are bound to happen... And we didn't look like we were going to start shooting hostages, did we?"

"No." She wanted to point out that there was no question of shooting anyway, as the hour hadn't been exceeded, but felt it was best to let him have that one. She didn't think he'd react irrationally if provoked, but she wasn't sure.

"And you'll remember what I said about those people outside, won't you?"

"Yes. As long as the hostages are unharmed."

"Then I think we have a reasonable working arrangement. Now...two down, nine to go. Number Three is the Multiple Sclerosis Research Trust. It's now...ah, nearly midnight: 11:57 p.m. You have one hour."

"Turn yourself in," Taber said suddenly to Jones, a couple of minutes later.

"Don't be ridiculous."

"If you won't turn yourself in, turn yourself into someone else. Do this some other way. Don't threaten innocent people."

"Don't be ridiculous."

"Why not tell them all the eleven on your list now?"

"Because we're the ones with the guns, and this is how we want to do it."

"You mean how your employers want you to do it. You're no terrorists. They hired you to make some point for them. What is it? And who are they?"

Jones didn't answer. The cathedral clock chimed. The last September night became the first October morning.

"Number eleven is different, isn't it?" Taber continued. "We'll hit number eleven about eight in the morning, when the other ten have been done. When everyone will be getting up, and will hear it on the news."

"You're quite smart."

"So is Rani Desai. You think she hasn't come to the same conclusion?"

"Doesn't matter. They won't come in as long as we have the explosives rigged, and as long as we haven't killed anyone. They'll play it out rather than risk lives, because our demands are so easy. Exactly the way we pitched them."

"'Play it out' is right."

"What do you mean by that?"

"Watching you and the others here, all this feels staged. Like a performance. And maybe I'd have the same feeling if I could see Rani Desai and her people. Maybe they're acting, too."

Jones smiled ruefully. "You're wasted here, Dean Taber. But you're only half right. It's real enough for them outside."

Other charities followed. They included The Alzheimers Society, The Brain Tumour Trust, The Muscular Dystrophy Research Campaign, and The British Neurological Research Trust. By seven in the morning, the first morning of October, they reached number ten on the list: The Society of Friends.

"That was my idea," Jones told Taber proudly, after he'd got Rani Desai to call them. "I'm not religious, or a pacifist, but I admire the Quakers. They always stuck to what they believed in, even when it cost them. Like opposing slavery. Or refusing to fight."

"Yes," Taber murmured, "you'd never see them pointing guns at people." Jones shot him, but only with an irritated glance, which Taber answered with a disarming smile. He'd almost overplayed his reliance on that small piece of rapport.

And the Quakers continued to stick to what they believed in. When Rani Desai finally contacted them (a difficult process, since they didn't have a conventional leader, and certainly not a CEO) they refused absolutely. They would not, they told her, accept money obtained at gunpoint.

"This is ridiculous," Jones told Rani Desai. "I want you to pay all eleven, you've agreed to pay all eleven, you've already paid nine, and Number Ten says No. What should I do? Kill a hostage?"

"You're asking me what you should do?"

"Yes. No. Alright, I'm not asking you. I need to think. Go back and try them again."

"I can tell you, they won't budge."

"Try them again!"

Jones snapped his wristcom shut, a little too forcefully. The hostages, who had been close to lounging, now snapped to attention. Jones turned to Michael Taber and spat, "I thought this might happen! Ridiculous, isn't it? Everything works more or less sensibly until you add a religion."

"But the Quakers were your idea."

"Yes, yes...You know, I was going to suggest Rochester Cathedral itself as number ten on the list. Now that really *would* have been ridiculous..."

"We'd refuse, for the same reason as the Quakers."

"...to kill someone in your Cathedral because your Cathedral refused to accept money we'd earned for it."

"Earned?" Taber asked.

Jones shot him another irritated glance. "Yes, earned! For some good causes. And for our families. You might not like it, but to us and them it's earned!"

Taber was not perturbed. "Why not just go to your reserve list?"

"I don't like to."

"But you said you had a reserve list."

"I don't *like* to. I don't like it when things don't go how I said they should."

Taber looked at Jones, appraisingly. "You're making too much of this. It's uncharacteristic."

"What do you mean?"

"This really is all theatre, isn't it? The delay on number ten..."

Jones was quiet. Then he leaned in so only Taber could hear him. The parishioners held their breath. "*Shut it.* You're too smart for your own good."

"...and the unveiling of number eleven. Exactly when you want it unveiled."

"Shut it. This is the last day of my life. Don't make it the last day of yours."

Just then Rani Desai called back. She had tried again, but the Quakers absolutely would not budge.

2

Anwar arrived at Gaetano's office at exactly 7:00 a.m., as arranged. Gaetano was there but didn't expect him, in view of yesterday's events.

"Yesterday's events?" Anwar asked.

"Come on. You know what I mean."

Better than you think, thought Anwar. He'd told them nothing, of course, about Asika or Levin. They'd know if they had CCTV of his interrogation of Carne, but he wasn't going to tell them. He'd go on acting as if they didn't know, though it hardly mattered now. They were both dead.

"Of course I know what you mean. But there's nowhere for me to go now, except into the details of this mission. So I did some work last night. I've added my comments to the implant bead you gave me yesterday. Here it is."

Gaetano pressed the bead into his wristcom, and projected it onto a bare white wall. It resolved into a simple full face recording of Anwar, listing his comments. Gaetano listened for a couple of minutes. It didn't take any longer than that; Anwar spoke quickly and precisely, and didn't have much to say. Most of his points were minor, with only one of substance: the building work in the Conference Centre.

"I'd like to look over it personally," Anwar explained, when Gaetano asked him to amplify.

"Of course, but what are you looking for?"

"Remember I said those detectors wouldn't stop me getting through?"

"Yes, but..."

"You'll have to put probes in the Signing Room. Needle-probes in every bit of work they've done there. And you'll have checked all the Patel employees here?"

"Yes."

"I'd like to see the results. And I suggest..."

"That we check them again?"

"Yes. And I'll get the UN to double-check."

"You think I might have missed something?"

"Yes. Like I missed how to get answers out of Carne, where you would probably have done better. This isn't point-scoring."

There was a wall screen in Gaetano's office, playing a newscast. A kidnapping somewhere. The sound was muted, but occasional words and phrases were audible. "Explosives rigged...hostages...list of eleven charities...modest amounts, only a million euros per item..." Anwar blanked it out, concentrated on Gaetano's briefing. He paused at the oddness of the kidnappers announcing each item one at a time, but he only half-heard it and it didn't concern him. He left it behind in the detail of what Gaetano was saying, about Olivia.

She had already gone. She'd left the floor at 5:00 that morning, to catch up on meetings cancelled yesterday. Just one day and the media were already sniffing around: when she cancelled meetings to go with Anwar into Brighton, and cancelled more in the afternoon, rumours started.

The media were also asking about the man who'd been detained. Only precautionary, had been the line taken by the New Anglicans' press and PR people, while inquiries continue.

"And something else," Gaetano added. "She wants to establish an Outreach Foundation for people sucked into fundamentalist cults. She's got our corporate people doing mission statements, business plans, budgets, everything. She said she wanted their hearts as well as their heads. That she's running a Church as well as a business. Was that you?"

"Maybe."

Gaetano looked askance at him, but did not press it.

"And," Anwar said, "after yesterday I need to know about all your people. What ones I can trust when I'm not around. And she can't go off like today, not in future. Not without me knowing."

"Are *you* going to tell her that?"

"Yes."

"Well, I've got the details of my people. Here, I've made an implant bead."

"Thanks, but I need your advice on each of them—who I can trust, who I can't."

"That's there too. I've added it, name by name." Gaetano had ninety staff. About half were frontline ex-Special Forces, and the others were support: analysts, forensics, intelligence, admin, IT. "You might," Gaetano added drily, as Anwar seemed about to play it there and then, "prefer to read it in detail later. Most of us are loyal to her, including my deputy Arban Proskar and the six people you fought yesterday in the Cathedral. My other deputy, Luc Bayard..."

"Yes?"

"He's more ambiguous. He isn't someone you can trust like me."

"That's ambiguous too."

Gaetano smiled briefly, but said, "I'm serious."

Anwar nodded, and reviewed what he knew about Bayard. He'd done wet work for one of the more obscure of the several agencies attached to the French COS. Large, like Levin. Talkative. Loud. "Quite unlike you," he added.

"Except," Gaetano said, straightfaced, "that he makes you uncomfortable. And he also has something in common with *you*. He detests her cat."

"I don't..."

"Rafiq's briefing," Gaetano went on, "probably has most of these details about my people, but not the notes of their loyalties. I've never put stuff like that on record for anyone before."

"What made you do it now?"

"If you're the only one with a chance of protecting her, I decided I had to work with you. And if I have to work with you, I'll do it properly."

"I'm grateful."

"Don't be. We both want to protect her, whatever our reasons."

"She wanted to replace me. You know what she thinks of my ability to protect her."

"And I know what you think of bodyguard duties...But *this is different*." The sudden edge to Gaetano's voice caught Anwar unawares. "Whoever you've had to guard in the past—" ("I haven't," Anwar said, but Gaetano didn't hear him) "—they weren't as important as her. If you protect her, I'll owe you. If you don't, you'll owe me. And I'll collect."

Long before he became Anwar Abbas, he'd been fascinated by the difference between containers and their contents. He'd liked to see into things, and people, and catalogue how their exteriors and interiors differed. Gaetano was not unlike him: haunted inside by thoughts that he was good, very good, but not the best. So he understood Gaetano, even the implied threat. Gaetano was only a Meatslab, but Anwar knew that he'd always carry out a threat. Assiduously, intelligently, and persistently. He'd never give up. And, having finally decided they should work together, Gaetano would never give up on that either. He'd do it properly.

All this time the wallscreen had been murmuring more reports about the kidnapping, reports to which Anwar only paid partial attention. Then he heard a mention of Rochester Cathedral, and froze.

"It's *them,* Gaetano! Where is she? Where did she go?"

The Quakers still wouldn't budge.

"It's nearly seven in the morning," said Rani Desai. "We've been at this all night. You must be as tired as the hostages. Why not just go to your reserve list?"

"What do you mean, I must be as tired as the hostages?"

"Oh, come on. We know who you are," Rani Desai said. "All of you. And your medical conditions. Come on, we all want this to end. Your hostages are elderly people. Go to your reserve list, we'll do number ten, then we can move to number eleven and they can all go home."

Jones paused. "Alright. The first name on our reserve list is the Chronic Disease Research Foundation."

It took less time than expected—the CEO was an acquaintance of Rani Desai—and was completed well inside the hour. Rani Desai obtained the charity's acceptance, made the electronic transfer, and sent Jones' wristcom the page showing the transaction.

"Good," said Jones. "Ten down, one to go. And Number Eleven is good news: it's non-financial, so you're done with paying. It finished at ten million, not eleven. But this one may take all of an hour." He paused for effect, and glanced at Michael Taber. "You must get Olivia del Sarto to cancel the New Anglicans' hosting of the UN Resources Summit at Brighton."

There was a long silence, both from his wristcom and in the Cathedral.

"Go on," he told her. "Do it."

Rani Desai broke the connection.

The silence persisted in the Cathedral. Some of the congregation had relaxed again after the outburst over the Quakers and had even been starting to talk among themselves and with the kidnappers. Now all that ended.

Taber smiled bleakly. "This was always about Number Eleven, wasn't it?"

"Yes." Jones made a show of checking his gun, and wouldn't look at Taber. "We took the Cathedral last night because it was easier in darkness, and then we had to spin it out until now, so Number Eleven would get morning coverage. We were going too quickly, until the Quakers helped us. That's another reason I chose them, though I wish they'd taken the money. Still, we got ten million for some other good causes."

"Yes, but now it gets serious."

"I told you. This is the last day of my life."

Gaetano and Anwar burst into the Boardroom.

The news had erupted around her. She had cancelled her meetings before they'd begun and was already at the wall of screens, dealing with Rani Desai and the media and kidnappers and her own staff. Dealing with several screens simultaneously, like Rafiq would have done. Like Anwar could also have done, but he had enhancements. Olivia and Rafiq didn't.

The motives were obvious. The New Anglicans' original founders were probably employing the kidnappers. They wanted Olivia to give up her high political profile, of which the UN summit was the latest example. Originally they wanted the Church made rich and powerful, but she'd done it on her terms, not theirs. Originally they wanted the Church to run like a business or political organization, and she'd done that too; but on her terms, not theirs. So they wanted her dead, and until they could arrange that, they wanted her quiet.

Except that Anwar didn't believe any of it, either now or when she'd first told him, over the dinner which should have been a briefing but wasn't. There was more. Not necessarily something larger, but something more specific and detailed: perhaps only a single fact, but one which would overturn all the others. And she wasn't telling him.

And this pantomime at Rochester: too obviously staged and too obviously contrived. She might submit and lose face, or refuse to submit and cause the hostages to die. Either way it would be a PR problem, but not an insurmountable one; the New Anglicans' popularity, and their formidable PR machine, would see to that. But whatever she did, summit or no summit, they'd still kill her.

It was in Anwar's nature to look for pockets of darkness, and he'd found them. A whole billiard table of them.

Since Olivia was occupied—she hadn't even glanced round when he and Gaetano entered, and was busy dealing simultaneously with three screens and her wristcom, as well as her staff—Anwar took the opportunity to tell Gaetano all this. "So," he concluded, "Rochester is all an act. It isn't real. They never expected her to give in."

"It looks real enough to me," said Gaetano. "You heard their eleventh demand."

"She'll refuse. And when she does, they won't move again until the summit. This was just a try-on. If she really did stop the summit it would be less convenient for them, because she'd have to be killed later. Their preferred option is to kill her at the summit." *Publicly, in a way that gives history a nudge.*

One of Olivia's screens had a CCTV replay of the kidnappers stepping into the Cathedral last night and announcing themselves. Anwar studied them. Assessed their height, size, movement. *Not the real thing. Two weeks before the summit is too early. And those five are not good enough. A grade or two below Meatslabs, nothing special.* Except that he sensed they were carrying something inside them. He wished he could go there and see them face to face. He'd know what it was.

Rani Desai had gone quickly to Rochester by VSTOL, and had taken charge of negotiations and operational matters. By about number three on Jones' list she was speaking to him not from London but from an operations vehicle in the Cathedral precincts.

She had Special Forces in position around the Cathedral, but she wouldn't send them in unless negotiations failed. And, before number eleven was announced, negotiations had been going well, even despite the Quakers. Now all that was changed.

On her own set of screens, Rani Desai was watching. Body heat scanners picked out the congregation and the kidnappers. There were three figures standing separately at the front of the Nave by the altar (one of them Taber?), and others moving among the congregation and choir. She didn't know how many there were. She guessed five or six, maybe more; five, said her analysts, who had studied the body language of all those in the Nave, as revealed by the scanners, and had noted that five of them carried themselves differently.

Other scanners confirmed the location of the explosive devices. Sometimes you could deep-scan them, disable them remotely with motive beams, but their casings were impenetrable and they had beam-scramblers. They really were military ordnance.

Yet more scanners got snatches of conversation from the hostages. Before number eleven their relations with the kidnappers had not been particularly unfriendly, but now conversation had all but ceased. Would Jones kill them all if the

Archbishop didn't acquiesce? Or was he, as she suspected, out of his depth? The conclusion was still the same for Rani Desai: go in only if gunshots were heard.

There was a continuing commotion outside the Cathedral: helicopters and VSTOLs, operations vehicles gunning their engines, figures striding back and forth across College Yard and Boley Hill, under the spreading trees. Jones and the others watched them calmly.

"What are those trees?" Jones asked Taber.

"Magnolias. And the big one's a Catalpa—American Indian Bean Tree. It's more than two hundred years old...I met her once, you know. Olivia del Sarto. She came here as our guest, at an Evensong service like tonight's, five years ago when she became Archbishop. She won't give in."

"You know her?"

"No, I just met her that one time. But that was enough. She won't give in."

"Then, as you said, things will get serious."

Rani Desai said, "Archbishop, their leader wants to speak to you."

"Is this being broadcast?"

"No, it's a secure link. Only him and you."

"Put him on."

Jones appeared on one of the screens in the Boardroom. Now that number eleven was known, he was in no mood to waste time. "You know what we want."

"Yes. And you can't have it."

"Unless you comply," he said, "we'll execute them."

"I won't comply, and you won't execute them."

"Don't be ridiculous. Of course we'll execute them."

"No," Olivia replied, "you won't. Not execute. You'll murder them. And I won't comply. The summit will save more lives than you can take. So, murder or slaughter or kill or whatever, but don't call it Execute. Don't give yourself a fake judicial authority. You'll murder them. So No, I'll decline your invitation. And Fuck You."

She cut the connection, and the screen died, then relit with Rani Desai. She was dark-haired and well-groomed, a slightly older and plumper version of Arden Bierce.

"That wasn't smart," she hissed at Olivia.

"Look, I know you've been trying to handle this all night, but—"

"No, I meant it wasn't *smart.* The summit isn't yours to proceed with or call off. It's the Government's."

"And the UN's."

"Yes, and the UN's. But—"

"If the kidnappers were serious about getting the summit called off, they wouldn't go to minor players like you and me, or even to your Government, they'd go to Rafiq. He's the real authority. He could switch venues if he wanted. It wouldn't be ideal," she glanced at Anwar as she said this, "not at short notice, but Rafiq could do it. Except, of course, that he never would. They know the summit's never going to be called off, and you know they aren't going to murder anyone if the summit proceeds. At least," another glance at Anwar, "not anyone in Rochester Cathedral. It's all a performance." She killed the screen, and swiveled to face Anwar. "So what's your problem?"

"Most of it will keep for later...But you're right, this is a UN matter. Rafiq would send in someone like me, it's exactly that kind of mission. But the Government would have to ask him."

"What, and have one of The Dead running around Rochester Cathedral? I don't think so." She smiled at him; it was like a rat baring its teeth. "The thing about Governments asking Rafiq for help is that he usually succeeds, and then they owe him, and his prices are high." When Anwar didn't press the point—she'd expected he wouldn't—she went on. "This drip-feed leading up to the last demand. They wanted it to break now, when the whole country's woken up. But why didn't they demand more money?"

"You know why," said Anwar, with a trace of impatience. "To get it to proceed amicably through the night. To get to where we are now. So you mustn't—"

"I have no intention of complying. You heard me."

"Yes. It's better that you don't, because then they'll come for you at the summit. If you did comply, they'd still come for you, but we wouldn't know where or when. And I don't intend on living here indefinitely."

She looked up at him sharply; one of the occasions when she actually seemed to notice him.

From one of the screens, showing the exterior of Rochester Cathedral, came the sound of gunfire.

"The Archbishop's refused number eleven," Jones told Taber, "as we expected. So we have our orders." He put down his rifle and drew a sidearm. He spoke a few words in his wristcom to Rani Desai, snapped it shut, and smiled ruefully. "You're a good man, Dean Taber, and a perceptive one. I wish I'd known you better." When he and his four companions shot themselves, they made no formal leave-taking of each other. They'd probably done that before they even entered the Cathedral. It must always have seemed inevitable to them.

"Time for us to die," Jones had told Rani Desai, in his final call to her. "You'll hear our five gunshots. If you trust me, send in your people. The hostages are safe and the bombs are fake."

Rani Desai ordered the Special Forces to go in the moment she heard the first shots. They found the hostages safe and unharmed, as Jones had promised, and the kidnappers all dead. Subsequent checks confirmed what Rani Desai had figured out. They were mercenaries—not in Richard Carne's league, but like him they had no known current employers. They all had terminal illnesses. *That's what they were carrying,* Anwar thought when it came out later.

Also as Jones had promised, the bombs at the Cathedral entrances and windows were fake: casings only, with nothing inside them. The sensors on the floor, walls and ceiling were all genuine and active, so their operation would be detected, but the explosive devices weren't. They were just empty containers.

The congregation and choir and Dean Taber were all physically unhurt, but traumatized. Even at the end, after the announcement of number eleven, they couldn't bring themselves to hate Jones and the others. They were grief-stricken, not at having been held hostage, but at having to watch five people who they didn't hate and in some ways had grown to like, putting pistols to their heads.

As the wall of screens relit, Arban Proskar burst into the Boardroom. Burst awkwardly, because his left shoulder and collarbone were still heavily strapped. Anwar again noted the hands, broad and long-fingered.

He was breathless. "We've taken another one. Like Richard Carne. We think he was checking whether Carne was still here, after we put out the story that we were holding him. This one's called Taylor Hines. Similar CV to Carne. He's trussed up in a private room in the hospital. Says he wants to see you."

"I'm a little busy," Olivia snapped, as one of her staff pointed to a screen where Rani Desai's image had reappeared.

"No," Proskar was looking at Anwar, "you."

Taylor Hines looked more formidable than Carne, though he'd let them take him easily. As if it didn't matter. He was tall, dark-haired, and sinewy. Slim to the point of cadaverousness. His thin face, over whose bones the skin was almost shrinkwrapped, radiated the same ease and insouciance as Carne. Even manacled and chained in a hospital bed, he still looked like he was lounging.

"Another one like Richard Carne," Anwar muttered to himself, but Hines heard.

"Yes, Richard was another one like me."

Anwar noted *Was.*

"And," Hines went on, "the answer is No. I won't tell you who I'm working for, where they are, or how they'll kill her."

Physically, Taylor Hines wasn't like Carne at all. There was no fleshiness, just sinew. He was all sinew. His shirt was tightly buttoned up to the top, as if to conceal his thin lizard-like throat. But even so, there was a gap between his throat and the shirt. A gap which, when he spoke, opened and closed like a second mouth.

"Especially not how they'll kill her, though you wouldn't believe it if I did...And don't," he drawled, "try that thing about disabling all my senses, one by one, and leaving the eyes till last. You don't have time, and you wouldn't do it anyway. Even Marek didn't actually do it."

How the hell did he know about that? thought Anwar, without bothering to ask or show any reaction. Not that Hines was particularly looking for a reaction.

Anwar studied him. They both knew he'd be tripping a poison implant soon. His employers had sent him here to die, merely for tactical reasons: not to find out about Carne, but probably just to create another level of uncertainty. There was nothing of value he could learn. Not now. Hines really *was* one of the dead.

"My employers are still perfecting body enhancements. You'll see when your people do the usual autopsy on me, as they've probably already done on Richard. They don't do enhancements as clever as yours. Not yet."

"What..."

"But they're unbelievably challenging. They do other things much better."

He tripped the poison. Anwar looked away.

3

Back in his suite, Anwar called Arden Bierce. He gave her another verbatim report of another interrogation, and made arrangements for another body to be taken at night by another VSTOL from Brighton to Kuala Lumpur. Then he asked her about Carne's autopsy.

"Yes," she said, "it revealed some physical enhancements. But they're crude; just bits of metal and circuitry and servo-mechanisms. Nothing organic. Hines will probably be the same. Your enhancements are far more sophisticated."

Anwar nodded, remembering. *They do other things much better.*

That was the housekeeping part of their conversation, and was concluded satisfactorily. The rest of it was more difficult.

"And Proskar..." he began.

"No," said Arden Bierce yet again, "he isn't Marek. I know, he's Croatian, he's the right build, he's the right age, and..."

"He's got those hands."

"Anwar, *he isn't.*"

Anwar looked away. Proskar had done nothing remotely questionable, and Gaetano had listed him as one of those to be trusted. But all that would be true if he really was Marek. *Better kill him anyway?* Fortunately, Anwar managed to dismiss that thought without showing on his face the surprise it caused him. *Where did that come from? What's this mission doing to me?*

Arden Bierce cleared her throat. "Anwar...Rafiq wants you back at Kuala Lumpur."

"I told you before, I'm not leaving."

"I remember what you told me before."

"I don't know what made me say those things, Arden..."

"Neither do I."

"...but I won't leave. I mean it. I will not give up on this mission!"

"He's not taking you off the mission.You have my word, and his. He wants to talk face to face about who's behind this."

"Face to face?"

"Imagine," she went on, "I've just stepped out of a VSTOL on your lawn, carrying one of his letters. You'll be back in Brighton by tomorrow morning."

"Did you get that car I ordered?"

"How can you think of that now?"

"Because I'll need it now. It is where I wanted, isn't it?"

"*Yes*. In the underground lockup garage in Regency Square. I made all the arrangements, just like you said. I can't believe what it cost."

"I'm good for it. If Rafiq wants to see me I'll drive to the airfield. You can send a VSTOL there."

"Why not just..."

"*No*. Not the one you send for Hines' body. Send me one of my own. You have plenty."

"It'll be at the airfield on the Downs in ninety minutes. And Anwar: I'll be with Rafiq when you arrive. You won't be alone."

Anwar left his suite and walked up to the floor above. *Her* floor. Proskar was lounging on a sofa—stone white, the colour of those at Fallingwater, but more angular—just outside the door leading to her section of the floor. Anwar nodded politely, and Proskar, politely but awkwardly. Anwar did not go in, however. He walked past her door to Gaetano's office.

"Rafiq's ordered me back to Kuala Lumpur," he said. He'd deliberately phrased it like that so he could assess Gaetano's reaction, and he was gratified to see an initial approval replaced immediately by concern, both of them genuine.

"Rafiq's standing you down? Why?"

Anwar assessed his body language: facial muscles, voice inflexions, hand movements, moisture on skin. Gaetano's initial approval stemmed from his first reluctance to have Anwar there at all, but the concern which replaced it came from his decision to work properly with Anwar. *All the things which are right in him are often wrong in her when I look for them.*

"No, he's not standing me down. I understand he has some new information about who's trying to kill her, and he wants to talk it through face to face."

"Face to face?"

"Yes, he prefers face to face meetings. If he's got something of substance."

Gaetano's relief was as genuine as his earlier reactions. "It's about time we had something of substance. Both of us."

"I'll be back by tomorrow morning."

"Then you must be getting one of Rafiq's VSTOLs."

"Yes. Not the one that's coming for Hines. A car," he said carefully, "is taking me to the airfield on the Downs, where the VSTOL will pick me up." Something told him not to say what car, or where. He might need it later, if everything went wrong and he had to get her away.

Anwar took the maglev and walked out of Gateway alone, across Marine Parade and into Regency Square. Obvious symbolism, but it was now October. Everything seemed a little colder and greyer.

Regency Square had a small Green at its centre, with eighteenth-century town houses overlooking it. They were quite grand houses, three or four stories, with black wrought-iron balconies and railings. Some had external spiral staircases.

There was an underground car park on the Green, with private lock-up garages. He went down into it and saw the car he had ordered. It was in one of the private lockups, behind bars like a beast in a cage.

It was a replica Shelby Cobra. Not with the original 427 cubic inch petrol engine, of course, but four computer-synchronised electric motors, one for each wheel, charged by a jet turbine. Twelve hundred bhp (three hundred per motor) and four wheel drive. Its paint was simple matt black, not one of the fashionable kinetic or pseudoliving surfaces; that would have been wrong for a Cobra.

But otherwise, it was thoroughly modern. The jet turbine was variable-cycle for optimum power and fuel efficiency. It took air through the car's front grille, mixed it with biomass-derived jatropha oil fuel, and used the resulting controlled explosion as a constant charge to the four electric motors. It didn't need storage batteries. The body was ultra lightweight ceramics and plastics, so there was a huge power-to-weight ratio. It would easily out-accelerate and outcorner the original Shelby Cobra which raced at le Mans in the early 1960s—and most current cars too.

Modern high-performance cars were stunningly beautiful, almost unearthly, and filled with similar technology to that of the Cobra, but the Cobra was different. Although its shape was designed over a century ago, it had a quality of timelessness. It was simultaneously ugly and beautiful. Squat, muscular, and brutish, with a low crouching stance and hugely flared wheel-arches. The shape of the grille, like a snarling mouth, made it look like it was saying Fuck You to the world. A genuine original, like the ginger cat.

These days, replicas were a strong subculture choice. Some people, like Anwar, preferred them to their modern rivals, for many different lifestyle reasons. For Anwar, it was the tension between outside and inside: old on the surface, brilliant and cutting-edge underneath.

He inserted a finger in the orifice concealed in its flank. After checking his DNA it unlocked for him. Arden Bierce had dealt with its programming and specification and delivery with her usual precision. He sat in it and allowed himself a moment to take it in. Considering what it had cost, the interior was quite spartan. Almost industrial, with lots of exposed oiled metal. Two things were very close to his heart, and he knew it was impossible they could ever come together, unless there really were infinite alternate universes: Doctor Johnson and the Shelby Cobra. He tried to imagine the former, riding as a fractious and querulous passenger in the latter.

The car didn't have the wet-throated roar of the 1960s V8 original. When he told it to start and it recognized his voice (another piece of Arden Bierce's attention to detail) the four electric motors merely hummed. Microseconds later the jet turbine fired up, but that too was almost silent: a soft, throbbing whine.

The drive from here to the airfield would take a matter of minutes: a few miles of countryside, past the spectacular gash in the Downs known as Devil's Dyke. (He'd noticed it on the drive from the airfield to Brighton when he'd first arrived, and following his habit of bestowing private nicknames, he'd called it Lucifer's Lesbian.) At the airfield they'd lock the car away somewhere securely (Arden Bierce again) and the VSTOL would probably already be waiting, hovering politely a couple of inches above the ground.

But it wouldn't have arrived just yet. It was about 6,500 miles from Kuala Lumpur to Brighton: a flight of less than ninety minutes, including acceleration and landing, and it was nearly an hour ago that Arden Bierce had told him she'd send it. So he sat back in the Cobra smelling the leather and oil and metal of its interior, listening to the thrumming of 2060s technology inside its 1960s body.

Time, he thought, a few minutes later. He drove the Cobra—it fitted him as well, and felt as right, as one of his expensive tailored suits—out of the underground car park, out of Regency Square, and out of Brighton; towards the airfield, and Kuala Lumpur, and Rafiq.

SEVEN: OCTOBER 1 - 6, 2060

1

"This is still your mission," Rafiq told Anwar. "My concern is the summit, not her. And no, I'm not sending others, it'd make us look weak and she isn't important enough. So when we're through here, you should go back to her. You're all she's got."

Anwar picked up and echoed Rafiq's unusually direct tone. "And if I'm killed and she's killed, it's only a below-average Consultant and an Archbishop and a UN summit; the first two aren't crippling losses, and there will always be more summits. If their target was you or Secretary-General Zaitsev, it might be different. But neither of you are their targets. Not this time."

"Yes, I know what Gaetano told you about this being part of something bigger. We'll come to that. I said I'm not taking you off this mission, and I'm not. But frankly I wish you'd take yourself off it. Some of the others would do better."

A word like Frankly *isn't one you* use much, *even when you're faking.* "Then why didn't you pick them? At least seven or eight of the other eighteen score higher than me."

"Sixteen," Arden Bierce corrected him.

Before Anwar could reply, Rafiq's wristcom buzzed. "Excuse me," he murmured.

The Cobra had taken Anwar north out of Brighton, past Devil's Dyke, to the small airfield on the Downs where the VSTOL was waiting. The Cobra's speed was merely tremendous, but the VSTOL's was unearthly, covering 6,500 miles in well under ninety minutes with no apparent effort. It did something with ions that made air thinner in front than behind, pulling it into a frictionless vacuum perpetually dancing in front of it. And its powerplant used low/medium-temperature superconductors, a technology which when perfected would be close to perpetual motion. Its design, and what powered it, were the product and property of UNEX. Rafiq had been investing in such things for years, to the unease of the UN's major members.

Arden Bierce was waiting for him on the lawn in front of Fallingwater. He felt a huge relief on seeing her; it seemed like he'd been around Olivia for weeks, not just a couple of days. But from the moment he entered Rafiq's office, Anwar had been struck by his change of manner. Such directness was almost unheard-of for Rafiq; coming from anyone else it would have seemed like a sign of strain.

Rafiq was still speaking into his wristcom. Anwar could have ramped up his senses to hear the other half of the conversation, but didn't, out of courtesy. It wasn't necessary anyway.

"No, Mr. Secretary-General, I won't budge. UNESCO has enjoyed a comfort zone, on public money, for too long. What they do is important but they'll do it on my terms, and in accordance with my performance goals." Rafiq paused, listening to Zaitsev's reply, then laughed; not his usual quiet laugh, but something louder and more unpleasant. "Vote of no confidence? Your predecessors tried that and failed. So will you."

He flicked his wristcom shut and turned back to Anwar, switching attention instantly; there was no grimace or shrug or other unspoken comment on the last call.

Anwar, too, resumed instantly. "You said she isn't important. That she's not your concern."

"I meant it, Anwar; she's appalling. You wouldn't believe how she negotiated with me for the venue."

"Yes I would. I know what she's like," Anwar said. "But what she stands for *is* your concern. If it isn't, it ought to be."

"Alright, then I *didn't* mean it. It was just said for effect. Don't take it at face value."

"I'd be ill-advised, now," Anwar replied, "to take anything you say at face value."

"You mean about your mission and Levin's being connected? I genuinely didn't know when I assigned you. I know now, but I didn't then."

Genuinely. Like Frankly. *If you're adding words like that to your vocabulary, and if you need to use them with people like me rather than the media, you're in trouble.*

Rafiq's skill at working people close-up meant he usually got more from a face to face meeting than they did. And *he* had called for this meeting, immediately after studying Anwar's reports; to review, he said, the identity of those who'd killed Asika and Levin and apparently threatened Olivia. But Anwar sensed that Rafiq wasn't scanning him as closely as usual; and he'd made unguarded remarks, and used words loosely.

It was unthinkable that Rafiq, of all people, could be preoccupied: Rafiq, whose reputation was that he'd never give whoever was in front of him anything less than his undivided attention, no matter what other things concerned him at the time. *Maybe UNESCO is more serious than he's letting on. No, he has situations like that every day. It's something else. Miles was preoccupied with something too, the last time I saw him alive, here at Fallingwater.*

"They're like you," Rafiq said suddenly. "Like The Dead—they have their real identity, and their identity in the world. They come into the world and go back out of it. Like you, in and out. I could be one of them. Or Arden, or Zaitsev. Or Gaetano.

Everyone you know, you could re-interpret all they've said and done as being one of them."

Even his syntax isn't quite as polished as usual. "I know *you* could be one of them. You'd be perfect. The damage you could do before anyone found you out...And no," Anwar's voice hardened, "they're not like The Dead. Arden made that mistake. They're more like Black Dawn. A cell, but with trillions and with a network of corporations and subsidiaries and proxies and cutouts. You must have reached that conclusion yourself."

Rafiq gazed closely at Anwar. Anwar held his gaze.

"A play within a play, Anwar. Shift the world-picture just one notch, and there's a parallel world. Theirs."

He noticed Rafiq had started calling him by his first name. He'd never done it before. *And he* is *preoccupied. He's trying to cover it up by being louder and less formal and more direct.*

Along one wall of Rafiq's office was a floor-to-ceiling array of screens, carrying news and current affairs feeds. The sound was muted, but they listened to it for a couple of minutes, in preference to the silence which had started to lengthen between them. Rochester had sparked off a debate about the New Anglicans: whether they should be hosting the summit, whether they were getting above themselves, whether they should be more of a Church and less of a corporation or a political movement. But the New Anglicans were already countering it; their PR machine was as formidable as the rest of their organisation, and Olivia's five years had given them huge popular support. Rochester might put them on the back foot for a moment, but no more.

"Conventional political parties," said Rafiq, "detest fundamentalists, but they won't confront them openly. The New Anglicans will, and do—Olivia saw that niche in the market. So maybe we're getting ahead of ourselves. Maybe it isn't the

New Anglicans' founders. Maybe this is all a double or triple bluff, and it's really the fundamentalists. What do you think?"

"No," Anwar said. "They don't have the imagination, or the resources. She was telling the truth about that, at least."

"And we'd know," Arden Bierce added. "We have people there."

"Very well," Rafiq said. "Then the working hypothesis is the founders. In my briefing I said they don't like her because she's taken the Church away from them. She and Gaetano told you that too. And," he went on, as Anwar started to reply, "I know, not the Bilderbergers and the rest, but a cell operating through them indirectly. Shall we call them The Cell? We can't keep referring to them as the ones who set up the New Anglicans, are threatening Olivia, and killed Asika and Levin."

"Yes, The Cell is fine." *I prefer White Dusk, but I don't share my private nicknames.*

"Then let's consider what she told you, or told Gaetano to tell you. That line about 0.5 percent owning 40 percent is hardly new. Here's another one: over half of the hundred biggest economies in the world aren't even countries—they're corporate bodies."

"So?"

"So the 0.5 percent aren't the same people. There's been an explosion of individual wealth, and corporate wealth: Russia, China, India, Brazil, Indonesia. And others, undercutting China and India in costs—just as China and India once undercut America and Europe and Japan, even though those three are still very wealthy. So if there's a cell, the members might come from further afield than the original founders. And if the members have changed, the motives have changed. Is that what she meant?"

"Possibly," Anwar said. "But there's more. Something she isn't telling me. Something quite specific. Almost a detail, but it could blow everything else away."

Rafiq looked at him curiously for a moment, then said, "Maybe. But since you don't presently know what it is, we can't process it. In the meantime, let's stay with who they are."

"No," said Anwar. "Forget who they are and focus on where they are."

"Intelligence haven't found them yet."

"So blitz it. Throw masses of stuff against the wall. Check all the known mercenaries and ex-Special Forces with profiles like Carne and Hines, and question them until you..."

"Find who recruited them?" said Arden Bierce. "We've already questioned dozens. So far we've found five who were recruited like Carne and Hines—indirectly, through multiple layers and proxies."

This is new. "And was your questioning any better than mine?"

She paused. "I'm sorry, Anwar. I know Miles was your friend. They said he'd been annihilated, and when Chulo was sent to find him, he was annihilated too. They even used similar phrases: 'What our employers did to Asika. And what they did to Levin, which was worse. And Levin's face, when he realised he couldn't defend himself. There wasn't enough left of him to make into an exhibit like the one they'd made of Asika.'"

Anwar was silent for a few moments, then asked carefully, "Are they still alive?"

"No. They all died like Carne and Hines. Autopsies showed the same crude enhancements as Carne. Nothing like yours, and even less like whatever killed Levin and Asika. And, before you ask, we're tracing back the manufacture of the enhancements."

"That's an obvious direction, so they'll throw all their countermeasures into it."

"Then try another direction," Rafiq said. "How do you think Hines knew about your questioning of Carne?"

"One of Olivia's people? Not all of them are loyal."

"How did he know it in such detail?"

"Microbot listeners?" As soon as he said it, and even before he saw Rafiq smile derisively—another unusual mannerism, for him—Anwar knew it was a lame answer. Microbot listeners were pseudo-insects, devices used regularly by the UN, by governments, and by large corporate bodies like the New Anglicans. They were known technology, and there were reliable ways of detecting and neutralising them.

"Fine, not microbots," Anwar went on hurriedly. "A listener of some kind, but different. That's something you can work on."

"Oh, you think? Well, we'd better do that. Arden, will you make a note?" Anwar was startled. Of all the weapons in Rafiq's considerable arsenal, Anwar had never heard him resort to sarcasm.

"We've already found them," Arden explained quietly. "Nanobot implants, molecule-sized, located in the inner ear. Able to listen and transmit. Carne had one; so did the five we questioned. They're quite sophisticated devices."

"But if they don't do enhancements very well..."

"Not organic enhancements, like yours. It doesn't mean they don't do other things very well."

Hines said that, or something like it. But it isn't what he meant. "Can you trace them back?"

"Not easily. Molecules don't have serial numbers."

"Those other enhancements—the ones you found in Carne..."

"Yes, we've started tracing them. There were smaller and smaller components and sub-assemblies, subcontracted downwards and downwards, until the people who finally made them were tiny one- or two-person machine shops, and the components they made were so small they had no idea what they were; and when we worked back upwards there were proxies and dead-ends and dummy corporations. We've been doing that," she added, "since I got your account of Hines' questioning."

Anwar stayed silent. He'd started thinking again of Levin.

"Does nothing else occur to you?" Rafiq asked him.

"Not at the moment."

"Can't you do better than that?"

Levin used to say things like that, but mockingly. Not in that tone. "Why don't you just tell me what should have occurred to me?"

"How about what they've done? I don't mean about killing Consultants and threatening Archbishops, I mean what they've done strategically. They set up the New Anglican Church in 2025 and ran it, indirectly, through its founders. They work in long cycles and they aren't part of the usual landscape. So we must find what pattern they're working to, and then go back over years and search for what fits it. For what else they've done."

"Isn't that more your territory than mine?"

"Yes, but I thought you might have suggested we research it... And their network of corporations and proxies and financial holdings and subcontracting, we must unravel it and trace it back. That's my territory too. But whatever they're sending for her, whether it's still on its way or already at Brighton: that's your territory."

"I know."

"And are you sure nothing else occurs to you?"

"If it does, I'll call you. From Brighton."

Rafiq's voice softened. "Remember, Anwar. They've got something that kills Consultants. Carne's enhancements were crude, but they would be. If they had an advanced version of *you*, they wouldn't let us see it. You do realize that, don't you?"

"Of course I do."

"Because Arden believes it was a single opponent that did that to Chulo. Probably to Miles too. Whoever they are, if they have something that can do that...I know, I'm repeating myself, but I offered you help or a way out and you won't take either. So I think we're done here." *And I feel you're going to your death. I don't think I'll see you again.*

They stood and shook hands.

Anwar saw Rafiq's mouth open to speak, and could tell from its shape that the back of his tongue was against the roof of his mouth, about to form the hard G in Good Luck. He didn't say it. Instead he said, "I'll see you again, when all this is finished."

"I'll walk back to the VSTOL with you," Arden said.

"That extraordinary car..." she began, as they walked across the parkland in front of Fallingwater.

"You can only get them in England, from a specialist company in Surrey. I've always wanted a Cobra. Perhaps, when this mission is over, I'll have it shipped back here."

"Perhaps," she said.

"Rafiq didn't seem like his usual self."

"He isn't," she said, and, "Anwar, if you want, we could..."

"Don't, Arden, don't finish what you were going to say."

"You're involved elsewhere, aren't you?"

"No!" he said, too loudly.

When they reached the VSTOL, which was hovering politely a couple of inches above the lawn where a marquee had stood ten years ago, he added, "Really, I'm not. She's poison. Whatever she stands for publicly, inside she's poison."

"Protesting too much? Be careful, Anwar. Not just of what they send to kill her, but of her."

She shook his hand, and remained holding it for a moment. A door melted open in the VSTOL's silvered flank. He stepped inside, and it melted shut behind him. The VSTOL lifted silently into the Kuala Lumpur night. It was 10:10 p.m. local time, on October 1.

"He was a waste of time," Rafiq told Arden, later. "He gave me nothing. Why didn't he mention the link with Marek? I gave him at least three opportunities, and he missed them all."

She said nothing.

"He's not good enough," he said, unwittingly echoing Olivia. "I should have sent someone better. Why did I pick him for this mission anyway?"

Still she said nothing.

"I really don't care about her, Arden. Better if they don't kill her, but if they do it isn't the end of the world."

"Isn't it?"

"Of course not. It would be sensational, and public, and would throw everything into chaos. But I'd back myself to be better than *them* in picking my way through the wreckage."

"Do you think," she asked him, "the Secretary-General will go to war with you over UNESCO?"

"He'll try, but a no-confidence vote will fail. I have the voting covered." He paused, and added, "I'm proud of UNEX. It works. It delivers on schedule and on budget. But it's unelected; it could turn into a monster. That's what he'll argue in the General Assembly. He'll lose, but he does have a point."

"Maybe it works because it's unelected."

"Maybe...Arden, about Anwar. I gave him at least three openings to mention Marek and he missed them all. He knew, from you, that Marek's the common factor in Levin's and Asika's deaths, but he didn't mention it."

"He's only a Consultant. He's not good at the Before and After."

"He was a waste of time. He gave me nothing. I thought I'd shaken him when I started acting like I was in trouble, but it didn't work. Wasn't my acting convincing enough?"

"Yes," Arden said. "It convinced me."

He glanced at her sharply, but did not reply.

It was in his nature to think ahead, in long cycles. When the time came, he wanted his successor to be a member of his personal staff, rather than an outsider. Arden Bierce was a possible contender, but not the leading one. She wasn't ruthless enough, though she had other qualities: intelligence, interpersonal skills, motivation. And something else, her empathy.

"And it wasn't all acting," she added. "If it was, he'd have spotted it. He's still a Consultant."

Rafiq was well aware of her empathy, her instinct for what made people tick. She wasn't like him—subtle, labyrinthine, always holding something back—but her empathy was a quality even he couldn't match, either genuinely or by faking. Maybe she could do his job with the aid of that empathy, but she wouldn't do it like him. She couldn't manipulate people, or cheat them, or ruin or sacrifice them. No, people like Zaitsev and Olivia would eat her alive. And yet...

2

Something was in Anwar's blood. He didn't let it surface during the flight back from Kuala Lumpur, which he spent reclining in a contour chair in the VSTOL's lounge, watching the play of shapes and colours moving just under the silvered surfaces of the walls. He didn't let it surface when the VSTOL arrived without event and ahead of time at the small private airfield on the Downs—a measly collection of buildings, made to look even more so by the presence of the VSTOL and, when he released it from its lockup, the Cobra. There were only a few people there, most of them under contract to the UN; they nodded politely but avoided conversation.

He didn't let it surface as he drove slowly from the airfield, south towards Brighton, and stopped at the edge of Devil's Dyke. *Lucifer's Lesbian.* He knew he'd be driving the Cobra past this vaginal gash in the landscape at least once more after today. How fast, and whether alone or pursued, would depend on how the mission ended.

Kuala Lumpur was seven hours ahead of Brighton. He'd left Fallingwater at 10:10 p.m. and landed back at the airfield at 4:30 p.m. Brighton time, 11:30 p.m. in Kuala Lumpur. It was now nearly 5:00 p.m. on October 1: not yet wintry, but grey and chilly. It had rained earlier in the day, and the air was still damp. Back in Kuala Lumpur, October 1 would just be tipping over into October 2. He sat in the Cobra, gazed down along the length of Devil's Dyke, and let what was in him surface.

Uncertainty. The meeting with Rafiq was unsatisfactory and unsettling, and compounded the uncertainty which was dogging him. He wanted to hit back at it, but was uncertain how to. He wanted to find these unnamed enemies, and he wanted them all to have just one throat, so he could give it a Verb.

He thought about what Arden had almost offered him. She was intelligent and beautiful and had an instinctive rapport that made people feel comfortable around her. Within the bounds of her job she even showed something like sensitivity. But he couldn't have taken her offer, because she was a colleague. And, more importantly, because he couldn't have known where it would lead. Whether it would entail baggage.

Olivia was different: less obviously attractive, and sex with her was sudden and sodden, impersonal and opportunistic, erupting between periods when she barely noticed him. But it carried no baggage, and it was simple and tidy afterwards. Literally in/out, like his missions used to be. Before this one.

He thought about his family, and what it would be like to walk once more along Ridge Boulevard, past the big brownstone house where he'd grown up. His family was still living there. They believed him dead, but didn't know he'd become one of The Dead. Even if they knew, they wouldn't have recognised him.

Kuala Lumpur had been his home for years, and he'd been in Brighton for only a couple of days; but going back to meet Rafiq made him feel like Kuala Lumpur, not Brighton, was the interruption. He'd expected Rafiq would manipulate him the way he usually did, and felt uneasy when Rafiq didn't. In fact Rafiq seemed almost to be struggling, a thought which troubled Anwar; another part of his comfort zone peeling away.

This won't be decided by Rafiq in Fallingwater, but by me in Brighton. Whatever they're sending to kill her, I'm all she's got. That meant that if Rafiq wasn't acting, if he really was struggling, Anwar needed help elsewhere. There was only one place.

Gaetano was competent, but had his limits; among other things, he was obsessive—a quality Anwar recognised and shared. Most Consultants were obsessive to varying degrees, although two of the best weren't: Levin (flamboyant, confident) and Asika (settled, comfortable with himself). But that was academic now. Being dead trumped being obsessive.

I'm only a Consultant, he thought, unwittingly echoing Arden Bierce. *I only do missions, I don't do the Before and After.* But Gaetano did, and was very good at it. Among the New Anglicans he was the only possible ally, at least until the summit. *Maybe I should take a leap now, tell him everything Rafiq said. Or most of it. But I won't tell him about this car.* And working with Gaetano was still only a partial answer. It didn't address the uncertainty.

Or the other matter, the whatever-it-was that she hadn't told him, the possibly small and specific thing which might overturn everything else. Had she told Gaetano? Had Gaetano kept it from him? He tried to park it all for a few minutes, so he could sit in the Cobra and breathe in the smell of its leather and oiled metal surfaces, and the smell of the damp earth and grass outside. Maybe, if he stopped consciously trying to solve it, a solution would come unbidden.

Devil's Dyke was hardly the Grand Canyon, but still impressive: a mile long, three hundred feet deep, the largest dry valley in Britain. Clumps of trees and bushes dotted its slopes. The remains of an old Victorian funicular railway ran up the steep sides of its northern end, and there were other traces of its history as a tourist attraction: rotting concrete pylons which had once supported an Edwardian cablecar.

A few cars went past as he sat there, some of them slowing to look at the Cobra. Light was fading. He heard the buzzing of insects, the calls of rooks and starlings flying inland to roost before night set in, and the songs of finches and linnets in the trees. He'd read somewhere that birds weren't singing when daylight dimmed, they were screaming: screaming because they didn't know the dark would ever end. Chaos seethed under every serene surface: the grassy slopes where small chitinous things ate or were eaten, the silver and white interiors of the New Anglicans, even the impeccable quiet control of Rafiq. He thought of the figure in Munch's *The Scream*, clamping its hands to its head under a red streaky bacon-rasher sky while all the world screamed its underlying chaos.

Chaos was normally anathema to him; he liked comfort zones, places where everything was just so. But now he had the germ of an idea, and it involved the deliberate creation of chaos. A particular kind of chaos that came from doing something unexpected and which would give him, at last, the initiative.

He considered it from all angles, and it seemed viable. It was almost worthy of Olivia: she did it all the time, leaving uproar and mess behind her, on her way to somewhere else. With her, doing the unexpected was natural. With him it would be acting, but he could still do it. He'd already done it once, on a smaller scale, when he'd changed his usual fighting style against Gaetano's people in the Cathedral.

And maybe it wouldn't entirely be acting. *Maybe this is what I really am, inside.* He'd never had a mission like this. *Look at what it's making me do.* He'd always studied the differences between outside and inside in other people, never in himself.

Time. He fired up the Cobra's motors and turbine, and drove swiftly back through the gloom and traffic thrombosis, to Brighton and the summit, Gaetano and Olivia.

He put the Cobra back behind the bars of its cage in the underground lockup. He strode across Regency Square, across Marine Parade, and past the huge Patel vehicles still parked outside the entrance to the New West Pier. He strode through the security checks—as far as they could tell, he was still unarmed and still had an identity—and into the concourse at Gateway, where he took a maglev to Cathedral. He strode through the Garden, through the reception of the New Grand, and into Gaetano's office.

He gave Gaetano an exact, word-for-word account of the meeting with Rafiq, omitting only the references to the number and names of Consultants, and the conversation with Arden as he boarded the VSTOL. He spoke quickly and precisely, and with an unexpected energy. In less than half a day he'd travelled 13,000 miles to and from a difficult meeting, but he didn't look or feel tired. He felt fresher now than he'd felt at Kuala Lumpur, because his idea still looked viable.

"So," he finished, "Rafiq was a waste of time. He gave me nothing. For the first time since I've known him, I think he was struggling."

Gaetano had listened calmly to Anwar's account of the meeting, even when it touched on some of Rafiq's stranger remarks. He listened no less calmly to Anwar's assessment of Rafiq. After a moment he said quietly, "We're struggling too, unless we work together. You know I've already made that decision."

"So have I, now. That's why I came here and told you all this. I think we're all she's got."

"And you still think there's something she hasn't told you. You said to Rafiq that it was something specific, but it could overturn everything."

Good, he thought, you zeroed in on *that*. "Gaetano—" It was the first time Anwar had used his name. Somehow it conferred a new and different identity. "—I need to be sure of this. The briefing you gave me: you left nothing out?"

"Nothing."

"Not even some detail she mentioned which didn't seem worth repeating?"

"I said, Nothing."

Anwar needed only the briefest of scans to ensure Gaetano wasn't acting. "Then I know what to do next. We must go to the Conference Centre. I want to see the Signing Room. I want you to bring at least ten of your people, ones you can trust, and I want them armed. I want Proskar and Bayard kept away. And I want the Patel contractors there too, the ones who've been working there. And I want *her* kept away, by force if necessary. And I want..."

3

Anwar and Gaetano walked swiftly through the Conference Centre. One by one, they were joined by the people Gaetano had urgently summoned—his security staff, the Patel contractors, the Patel site manager. Their varying states of dress reflected the urgency of the summons: drop everything, Gaetano had told them, and come here *now*.

The ragtag procession, increasing in size as it went, made its way through the huge main interior space of the Conference Centre with its clean swooping lines, white and silver walls, and citrus air. The Conference Centre was even bigger inside than the Cathedral, because there was no full upper floor, only a mezzanine: a balcony running round the entire circumference, with doors leading off. Anwar, Gaetano, and the others made their way up the wide staircase to the mezzanine, and through a set of pale wood double doors which opened into the large room set aside for the signing ceremony.

Anwar stood there silently for a few moments, waiting for stragglers to arrive; it was the first time he'd seen the Signing Room, and he studied it carefully.

The room was about fifty feet wide by sixty feet long. One end was effectively a stage-set for the signing ceremony. There were expanses of wood panelling: exact matches of the 1960s-style teak and mahogany panelling from the UNHQ Press Suites in New York. They covered the walls in the direction where they would be facing the cameras, which would all be massed at the other end of the room. The rebuilt area had been calculated exactly from the camera angles and lines of sight. The rest of the room was unchanged. There was an abrupt division between the newly-built replica panelling and the original curving white and silver walls. It was curious, seeing two such different styles in one space. Levin wouldn't have liked it.

The wood panelling stood three to four feet proud of the original walls, as the room's natural shape was curved and organic and the UN wanted to give the impression, where the panelling had been fitted, of a conventional rectangular space. The contractors had done it carefully and very well, Anwar concluded, with no detail missed. It was immaculate and very convincing.

He continued to admire it (and, being who he was, also to record it) as the final latecomers arrived. They were all there now, the people he'd asked Gaetano to summon: ten of Gaetano's staff, carrying sidearms and rapidfire rifles, which they held rather self-consciously; the nine Patel contractors who'd worked round the clock for the last three weeks in this room to create the painstaking illusion of a Press Suite; and nineteen more Patel contractors who'd worked on board the vehicles parked at Gateway, pre-assembling and disassembling panels and material so it could all be carried unnoticed to the Conference Centre, as Olivia had insisted. The final latecomer was the Patel site manager, a large beefy man who'd been dragged out of another meeting and who burst in dramatically, glaring. The Patel people shot glances at Anwar and Gaetano, and asked each other and Gaetano's staff what this was about. Nobody knew, and the conversation gradually died to a murmur; then to silence.

"Tear it down," Anwar said.

"What?" the site manager shouted.

"I want it pulled apart, all of it, and then I want it rebuilt while I'm watching."

There was uproar. Anwar used it to turn to Gaetano. "Starting now," he said above the noise around them, "I'll stay here twenty-four-seven while they work on it. I want at least five of your people here, also twenty-four-seven and armed like now, until they finish work. After they finish work I want three of them here, round the clock, until the summit starts."

He was hoping to find, buried in the walls, the entity or device they'd sent to kill her. But even if he didn't, it would put him on the front foot. Give him the initiative. And it would ensure that even if it hadn't already been buried there, it wouldn't be buried there before the summit.

"Can we talk this over privately?" Gaetano whispered. "I understand the reasons but I'd like to discuss the scale, and I don't want us to be overheard if we have differences."

"No," Anwar said. "I'm not leaving this room until the work is completed. Even if it takes days." The uproar was continuing unabated. Anwar took Gaetano to one side and continued. "This isn't negotiable. Whatever they're sending for her, it'll be concealed in these new walls. If it's an advanced version of me, it could have got past security in the same way I could. If it's some kind of mechanism, it could be disassembled, brought in piece by piece, and reassembled."

The uproar intensified. The Patel contractors were now arguing furiously with Gaetano's staff—quite unreasonably, since Gaetano's staff had also only just been summoned there and were no wiser than anyone else.

The site manager finally pushed through the melee and located Anwar and Gaetano where they'd moved to one side. "It's taken three weeks," he shouted at Anwar, "THREE WEEKS, to do this work, and you want it torn down? We've got less than twelve days to do it again!"

"You've got a lot less than twelve days," Anwar said. "I want it done in six."

The site manager turned to Gaetano, whose face he at least recognised, in the hope that he might mediate. "We had to get exact replicas of the panelling from New York. Grain, texture, density, all had to be matched exactly. We can't do that again, not in twelve days! Certainly not in six days!"

"Then bring in more people," Anwar said, before Gaetano could reply. "Work them round the clock. Just throw people and money at it."

"But..."

"And screw the texture and density and grain. As long as it's teak and mahogany, that'll do. Get it from ordinary timber merchants in Brighton." Anwar left him red-faced and apoplectic, and turned back to Gaetano. "I want her orders cancelled. No disguising workers as tourists, or disguising material as luggage and bringing it here in small amounts. There isn't time. Bring in workers and materials openly. Load everything on the maglevs. If it won't fit on the maglevs, bring it to the Pier by sea or helicopter."

"But..."

"You must convince her. She's not to come anywhere near this room until it's rebuilt, and until I say so."

"She'll be..."

"I don't care if she'll be furious, tell her I'm quitting if she enters this room before I say so. I'm staying here for as long as it takes them to rebuild it. I'll watch everything they do. I want food and drink brought in here, and I want you to bring it personally. And I want a bucket. And I want at least five of your people, armed, here all the time until the work is completed. And I want your deputies Bayard and Proskar kept away. And I want *her* kept away. And I want..."

So his stay in the Signing Room began.

He wouldn't take food from anyone other than Gaetano. He had screens wheeled in from the Pier hospital and arranged so they curtained off a small area at the far wall where he used the bucket regularly and copiously. He refused any change of clothes. He stayed unshaven and unwashed, with stale breath and body odour—a condition of such total novelty to him that he privately catalogued its development. And through it all his expensively tailored suit still kept its shape impeccably despite his dirtiness. Elegant container, foul contents, he mused, picking at one of his favourite themes.

He almost revelled in it. All his life he'd never been anything less than immaculate. But in all his life he'd never done anything as unpredictable, as Olivia-like, as this. He was learning things from this mission: how to do the unexpected, how to take the initiative, even how to tear down and replace wooden wall panels.

On the first day he watched them start work. They decided to uncover a small area first, no more than ten feet square, to test their techniques before tackling the main area. He watched them rip out the old wooden panels, revealing the structures underneath: layers of plaster and, underneath the plaster, a latticework of carbon-ceramic laths. The laths had been fixed to the original walls with polymers which, although immensely strong, could be removed by the application of contra-polymers so they left no mark on the walls. As the first panels started to be torn away, he motioned to Gaetano's men to have their guns ready. Nothing was there so far. The rubble and dust and debris mounted.

Then, the layers under the panelling were also ripped out: plaster, laths, back to the original silver and white surface. The first small area of the original wall was uncovered. The room's shape was curved and the panelling was designed to create, at that end of the room, the impression of a regular rectangular space.

They paused. Nothing was there but the original walls. Anwar let out a breath and retired to the curtained alcove holding his bucket, where he called Gaetano and reminded him to double-check the Patel employees. Then he called Arden Bierce and told her to do the same. His priority was to find whatever (if anything) was hidden in the Signing Room, but his next priority was to find who put it there, how, and on whose orders.

The Patel contractors started on the main area of panelling. As the hours passed more of them joined the work, partly because the operation was becoming more frantic, and partly because Anwar's cancellation of Olivia's orders made it possible. Anwar observed them minutely. More teak and mahogany panelling was brought in from local timber yards to replace the panels that would be torn out. Anwar couldn't tell the difference in grain or texture or density, and didn't care.

After two days he had a visit from Bayard.

"I told Gaetano not to let you come here."

"He doesn't know," Bayard replied. "I came on my own initiative. You know about initiative now, don't you? At least, a bit more than you did before."

There was some more of this. Bayard mocked him like Levin used to, but without the underlying friendship. They had to raise their voices above the noise of the Patel contractors. There were more of them than yesterday.

"...and you wouldn't believe," Bayard continued, "how furious she is at being kept out of here. But Gaetano kept his word. A couple of times, he even threatened to restrain her physically. Imagine, in her own Cathedral..."

"That's enough," Anwar snapped.

"...and all her orders cancelled. She was incandescent. Almost converted her mass to energy."

"I said, that's enough. Just go."

"Alright, I'm leaving...But honestly, the mayhem and confusion you've caused. I'd have done it much better. If you want to know how you should have done it, no further than me."

He sauntered out, aware that Anwar was trying unsuccessfully to think of a one-line rejoinder. As with Levin, Anwar would only think of one later, when it didn't count.

The contractors carried on. The rubble and debris mounted. The dust thickened. The bucket filled, and was emptied.

After three days he had a visit from Proskar. This time, protocol was observed. Anwar got a call on his wristcom from Gaetano to say he'd given Proskar permission to see him.

"I told you he's not to come here. I don't trust him."

"I do," Gaetano snapped back. "And he wants to speak to you."

Proskar had never mocked him like Bayard, had never said or done anything questionable, but Anwar still couldn't get past his resemblance to Marek. When Proskar arrived, they again had to raise their voices above the noise and activity of the Patel contractors. It didn't make for much nuance of expression.

"I came here," Proskar began, "because..."

"Your collarbone healed yet?"

"Still healing. And your knife-wound?"

"Healed...You're skillful with a knife," Anwar murmured. "It's a Marek type of weapon, a knife."

"I'm sorry, what did you say?"

"Come into my office, we can't hear ourselves think out here." He took Proskar to the screened-off alcove he had rigged in a far corner of the Signing Room, where he kept his bucket. The alcove stank, as did Anwar.

"I said you're good with a knife."

"It's my speciality, that's all. Look, I came here because..."

"I said it's a Marek type of weapon, a knife."

"I heard you. *That's* why I came here. My resemblance to Marek. I know you think he's me."

Anwar said nothing.

After a while, Proskar added, "And about knives: there's no record of Marek having any close combat skills, with knives or anything else."

"He wasn't bad with bombs and guns."

"I said close combat."

"So you did. You know about him, do you?"

"Yes, after years of having to prove I'm not him. I've learnt so much about Marek that at times I thought I was turning into him."

"I want you gone."

"*What?*"

"I know you've convinced others you're not Marek, but I can't get over your physical resemblance."

"If I was Marek, would I still choose to look like this?"

"A reasonable question if you're not, and a clever one if you are."

"Would I keep my hands like this?" He waved them in front of Anwar's face. Large, spadelike hands, with long and slender fingers. "Who else has hands like this?"

Anwar said nothing.

"Look, I came here in good faith. I know you're concerned about my identity, but I can *prove* I'm not Marek. There's endless proof. Do you want me to take you through it?"

"I'm tempted," Anwar said, "to kill you here and now. You may be innocent..."

"I never said I was innocent. I said I'm not Marek."

"...but I'm still tempted to play the percentages and kill you anyway."

"This is the only job I've ever had that really amounted to anything. Before I came here I was just freelance muscle, doing things I wasn't proud of for people I didn't much like. Then Gaetano took me in and I got to do something worthwhile. I've served him and the Archbishop for five years. I'd go and die for either of them."

"Don't die, just go. I want you gone."

"Didn't you hear what I said? This is everything I am."

"You've had five good years. Don't try for six."

"Why are you doing this?"

"To protect *her*. If you're loyal to her, you don't want me watching you when I should be watching her. And I would be watching you, because I can't be sure you aren't Marek. I'd never leave you alone. Better for her, and you, if you were gone."

Proskar went to reply, then changed his mind and walked quietly out. Anwar was left looking at the walls, where still, after three days, nothing had been found.

But his initiative continued to buoy him. He'd never have done that with Proskar before. He'd only decided to do it while they were talking. But it made sense. Whatever they were sending for her, if it wasn't in the Signing Room yet, it wouldn't get there now. If it was a person, it might already be walking among them. Proskar wasn't the only possibility, but he was the easiest to remove. Privately Anwar thought Proskar was worth ten of Bayard, but he couldn't get over the resemblance to Marek. After all the evidence to the contrary, he still wanted to stick with his instincts.

Proskar, after this, would probably slip quietly away. Gaetano would just have to make do without him.

This mission, he thought. When he'd first come here the New Anglicans hadn't known what to make of him, and they suspected he didn't know what to make of himself either. Then he'd found out about taking initiatives and creating chaos, and they still didn't know what to make of him.

He still didn't know what to make of himself either, but he knew that he wasn't quite the same.

Another day passed. More of the panelling was ripped out, and still nothing was found behind it. The plaster and the carbon-ceramic laths holding the panelling were also ripped out. Contra-polymers were applied to the adhesive holding the laths to the original walls, and it relaxed its huge grip and dissolved away as though it had never been there. The original walls were unmarked.

Anwar's abrupt decision to abandon exact matches for the wood panelling had provoked uproar among Zaitsev's staff at the UN in New York, but Gaetano dealt with it and made sure it didn't reach Anwar—who, even if he'd known, would have ignored it.

The bucket got filled and was emptied. Food came and was eaten. Gaetano's five armed people started to look a little excessive, even to Anwar. They were also starting to look irritated. Gaetano was getting worried at the distraction. Each time he brought food, he reminded Anwar that the summit was getting closer and these people should be on other duties. Anwar wouldn't budge.

The panelling and plaster and laths were now completely ripped out, and nothing had been found behind them. The whole Signing Room was now back to its original curving shape. The walls were pristine: white and silver and gleaming. Even the dust didn't seem to settle on their surface, though it settled everywhere else. Anwar finally and grudgingly admitted there was nothing to find. It still didn't detract from his feeling of having the initiative.

He ordered the Patel contractors to start fitting the new panelling. He told Gaetano over his wristcom that he now needed only three security staff while the new wood was being fitted. But they should be armed, and should stay there round the clock until the summit.

"How much longer will you be staying there?" Gaetano asked him.

"Until I see them complete the new panelling." It occurred to him to ask something he should have asked before. "How are your preparations for the summit?"

"Satisfactory. But the Archbishop is getting difficult."

"About the summit?"

"No. About being kept away from the Signing Room. And," Gaetano's voice sounded uneasy, "about you. You've been in there four days, and she intended to see you the instant you got back from Rafiq. She doesn't usually go more than a day without..."

"Why not one of your people? Or you?"

"Not me, we don't do that... and she laughed when I suggested the others. Normally she has no trouble in fixing herself up, often just this side of rape, but she wasn't interested this time."

Anwar felt a stirring of unease. "Keep her away from here."

"I've already impressed on her the need to keep away."

Anwar stayed to watch them finish. They did what they'd done before to fit the earlier panelling. They made a new latticework of laths which they fixed by polymer against the silver and white of the walls, extending out in regular rectangular shapes. On this they put a layer of plaster. Anwar was fascinated by the skill of those making the laths and applying the plaster: accurate without much apparent measuring, quick without much apparent hurrying.

And then, after another day, the new panelling was done. There was mess and dust on the floor and in the air, and a smell of sawn wood and wet plaster. The room still had to be cleaned and prepped. By early evening he was still there, smelly and unshaven, when he got another call from Gaetano.

"I hear you're finished in there."

"Just about. I'm going for a shower and cleanup."

"No you're not. She wants to see you. Now. In the Boardroom."

JUNE 2061

This is Olivia's fourth Sunday, and fourth Evensong, at Rochester Cathedral. Not her fourth consecutive Sunday, because she has missed last week's. If she gets to like somewhere enough to go regularly, as she does with Rochester, she usually misses one service after three or four visits—a simple precaution, in case the congregation start noticing her.

So, her fourth Sunday out of five. And, like each preceding one, it is a warm, copper-toned summer evening. But her precaution hasn't worked. Out here in the Cathedral precincts, where refectory tables have been set out for coffee after the service, a couple of them have already sought to make eye contact.

And then there are the ones hunting her. Instinctively she feels that they're getting closer, and that this may be her last Evensong at Rochester. A pity: she likes it here and has felt almost settled. Currently she works at a secondhand bookshop in the High Street. It is a lowly job but it reminds her of Anwar. He used to like old books. He'd have dealt easily with those hunting her, but he isn't here anymore. He's long gone.

She knows about Churches and how they work, but the Old Anglicans puzzle her. What they deal in—simple companionship—gives them no apparent gain or advantage. It doesn't readily translate into a business model. The Old Anglicans continue as always on their gentle decline, while the New Anglicans get more and more powerful.

She decides as usual not to stay for coffee but to walk back along the High Street to her flat. But Michael Taber, the Dean of Rochester Cathedral—he'd taken this evening's service—goes up to her. She's seen and heard enough of him to know that he's charming and patrician but also, underneath, very smart.

He flashes his smile. "Won't you stay for coffee, Ms.—?"

She sees he's also switched on his I'm Listening expression in preparation for her reply. She doesn't want to be drawn into a conversation, especially not with him, so she answers hastily, "Taylor. Olive Taylor. Thank you, but I can't stop, I have to go now." She almost adds, "Because my cat's waiting for me," but just manages not to. She shudders inwardly; at least she's avoided giving him that clue.

But it doesn't matter. Taber studies her as she walks hurriedly away. He is thinking about her. Olive, Olivia. And Sarto means Tailor. It can't be. It can't be.

EIGHT: OCTOBER 6, 2060

The pale wood door of the Boardroom stood impassively before him. Kicking it down, he decided, would be too theatrical, so he merely opened it (though without knocking) and strode in.

She was standing in the middle of the room, waiting for him. Gaetano stood behind her and to one side. She was wearing a long velvet dress in her usual style, this one in dark blue. He took in the fitted bodice almost painted over her slender upper body, and the long voluminous skirt that he somehow found more arousing than a short tight one. The front of his trousers started to tent.

"This pantomime!" she spat. "You've taken five days out of our summit preparations! You've openly cancelled my orders! In my Cathedral! And," pointing behind her at Gaetano, "do you know what he *did* to me when I tried to get into that damn room?"

Anwar glanced at Gaetano, who remained expressionless. "I don't know. Or care."

"Have you any idea what stories we've had to tell the media? And at the end of it all, you got us nothing. You had us check the Patel people, yet again, and we got nothing. You spent five days in the Signing Room while they tore it apart, and you got nothing. You gave us five days of disruption, five days of the media laughing at us and Zaitsev's people screaming at us, and you haven't got shit. I was right about you the first time, you're a—"

"Don't call me a fucking autistic retard. I didn't like it the first time you said it. If you say it again, I might forget who I am."

"When did you last remember who you are?"

He looked at her, long enough for her to look away. Then she gathered herself, stared back at him, and said, "Oh no, you do not do that to me. You do not stare me down reproachfully."

"I remember who I am," he said quietly. "I'm the thing you rented for your protection. I may not be enough, because you haven't told me enough about who's trying to kill you; but I'm all you've got."

She didn't reply, but neither did she look away; she wouldn't be stared down.

"And I remember who you are," he went on. "You stand for things I admire, but inside you're ugly." He looked her up and down. "A velvet bag of shit."

He heard Gaetano stifle a gasp.

She continued to return his gaze, but addressed Gaetano. "The retard speaks out for itself. What's happened to it? It seems to have changed."

"And," Anwar continued, as if she hadn't spoken, "in the Signing Room I was..."

"Yes, yes, I get that. You were trying to find what they're sending to kill me."

"And I made sure..."

"Yes, I get that too. You made sure it isn't there yet, and you can make sure it won't be there before the summit. But you didn't *ask* anyone. You camped out in the Signing Room while they ripped it to pieces and caused five days of fucking chaos and you didn't *ask* anyone!"

"Would you have asked anyone?"

"Of course not."

"Exactly. I did what you do every day: leave people running around in your wake, clearing up after you."

Again, without leaving his eyes, she spoke to Gaetano. "Hear that? It identifies with me. With my methods. Just because for once it does something a bit decisive, it thinks it's turning into me."

He threw out a hand, spread into a Verb configuration, at her throat. It stopped maybe a tenth of an inch before touching her. He was frighteningly fast. If he'd wanted to, he could have completed the blow and left her headless before Gaetano had even started to move. Before she had even started to register the shock she was now registering.

Molecules had rearranged to harden his fingers into striking surfaces. He allowed himself to brush her throat lightly, then withdrew his hand. He'd put his hands all over her before, over parts much more private than her throat, but this touch was different. It caused something between them to shift.

"That's how easy it would be for me to put an end to this mission, and this conversation, and you. And the people I'm supposed to be protecting you from have apparently got something that kills people like me. And still you won't tell me the truth about them."

She seemed to be having trouble breathing. He turned to Gaetano, shrugged an apology, and turned back to her.

"You see, I really don't buy what you've told me. Not all of it. These people who threaten you, they're serious enough for you to get Rafiq to give you a Consultant, but not serious enough for you to tell me everything about them. Who, where, and why. All I've got is conspiracy theories. A cell of mega-rich movers and shakers operating indirectly through the founders, passing you handwritten notes. The rest of it, you just hint at. Almost coyly, like it's some second virginity you might let me have one day."

He paused, glanced again at Gaetano, and continued. He still spoke quietly, but his voice took on an edge.

"And there's something else you haven't told me. Not world-picture stuff about the founders, but something quite specific. A final detail which overturns everything else. I know it's there. *What is it?*"

"I never said..." She stopped, caught her breath, and began again. "I never said anything about some final detail."

"No, you didn't. That was me."

"Then you're putting words in my mouth."

"No. Of all the things I'd like to put in your mouth..."

She looked up at him, as if reminded of something she'd forgotten. An instant of scalding attention, then she turned to Gaetano. "Leave us," she said hoarsely.

Gaetano was almost relieved to do so. He didn't know what he'd been doing there in the first place.

As the door closed behind Gaetano, they faced each other.

"You still haven't answered my question. After we've done here, I'll ask you again."

"After we've done here, I'll give you an answer."

They started circling.

"I should get showered and cleaned up first."

"No you shouldn't. I want it now."

"I haven't shaved or washed," he told her, "in five days. Or cleaned my teeth, or changed my clothes." They were only token objections. He was surprised at how much he'd been looking forward to returning to his routine. Nothing else with her was simple or uncomplicated, but sex was.

"Yes," she said, "you smell like shit. The suit still looks good, though."

"You get what you pay for," he said, lifting her onto the table. He pulled up her skirt, carefully and tidily. She was wearing silk knickers which, with equal care, he pulled down and left around her knees; an encumbrance, but the essence was to disarrange, not denude.

She waited, patiently but uninterested, while he did all this, even while he made some final adjustments of her skirt upwards and her knickers downwards; then, after pausing to admire his handiwork, he entered her. That was his part done, and now she began hers, taking him inside her voraciously. Such particular intimacies, to a normal couple, might have meant something; but Anwar and Olivia were neither normal nor a couple. It was an arrangement, simple and self-contained, where each party did what he or she wanted, without regard for the feelings of the other. Masturbation for two.

By now she was well into her part. Where he'd been painstaking and obsessive, she was greedy. After five days, greedier than ever. For a moment he felt she'd never let him out again, at least not the way he'd come in. Eventually she did, but only to go another time, and another.

Who was it she was taking into herself like this? Not a real person but a device, a designer dildo. And who was it that he was entering like this? Not a real person but a container, into which he was pumping his contents. It suited both of them perfectly: only a Consultant would have the constitution and stamina to match *her* appetites.

Afterwards, they sat at opposing places on the table. She smoothed down her skirt; so careful had he been in his preliminaries that it looked no tidier rearranged than it had been when he'd pulled it up.

She usually looked at him without noticing, or noticed him only in passing, and he realised he'd been doing the same to her. But now he noticed. Her face looked drawn, as if she too had spent the last five days in the Signing Room. There was a feverishness in her stare and a downturn, accentuated by lines, at the corners of her mouth. A sort of desperation about her. Arden never looked like this.

"Not enough," she said hoarsely.

He hoisted her up on the table again, and was about to restart his ritual, but she stopped him. "No. You prefer it naked, don't you?"

Surprised, he nodded. They started undressing.

*Of all the things I'd like to put in your mouth...*He did put it in her mouth. Then her hands. And then her vagina, and that surprised him, because this time she took it less greedily. *She's trying to share*, he thought incredulously. She was clumsy at it because it was alien to her, and it made him feel embarrassed; and also uneasy, at the apparent shift from their previous routine.

"Don't do that again," he said afterwards. "It didn't work."

"The other way wasn't enough."

"That way was too much."

She looked away. Then she gathered herself, like she'd done when he tried to stare her down. "I said it wasn't *enough!* Go again. It's not enough any more."

Like the Reith Lecture, he thought, a small animal baring its teeth. But none of the attacks in the Reith Lecture had unsettled her like this. Not even the one on her life.

They went again, and it still didn't work. *Still trying to share,* and she still wasn't much good at it—her reciprocal movements were clumsy and unsynchronised to his, and she didn't pick up quickly enough on what he liked her doing. He preferred it when she didn't care what he liked. This way gave him nothing. He didn't think to wonder what she might have wanted from it, only that gave *him* nothing. It didn't work and it wasn't the same. Something had shifted.

He stood up abruptly, and started dressing. After watching for a while the play of his almost nonhuman musculature, she too started dressing.

"What's this about?" he asked, trying to keep the irritation out of his voice.

"What do you..."

"Don't say, 'What do you mean.' You know what I mean. Why isn't it enough? Why does it have to be different?"

"Something you said in Brighton, about if I hated people less and understood them more."

"What has that got to do with what happened here? I was talking about fundamentalists, about how you treat your enemies."

"You were talking about how I treat everyone. I can deal with media and mass audiences, but not with individual people, whether they're enemies or friends. I've never noticed them. I've never had a relationship that works both ways, not with any of them. So..."

"So you decided to practice on *me*?"

"Not practice. Start."

He laughed out loud. "Start a *relationship,* with a *Consultant*?"

"Don't flatter yourself, not that kind of relationship." She hurried on, conscious that she'd immediately backed down at the first sign of derision, and was now fighting only for her fallback position. "And I have to start with someone. And I got Rafiq to send you here, and I never really stopped to notice you. And when I asked you things about yourself, I'd forget your answers even before you finished speaking. And—" She was conscious of too many Ands, as if she was scrambling for anything she could find. She took a breath and began again. "—And you'd be only the first. I have to start somewhere." She knew how lame it sounded, and added "After you I could go on to real people." She'd meant it to cover her retreat, but it sounded worse; gratuitous, and ugly.

He stopped laughing. "Then skip the part with me and go straight to real people, because *this* didn't work. It was embarrassing."

He wasn't merely embarrassed, he was burning with embarrassment. It was knotting his stomach. A woman in her thirties trying to learn the elements of courtship, of pleasing a partner. *Sucking me into herself.* Or, if he believed her fall-back position, trying to learn how to notice and value people. Either way she had years to make up, and he couldn't see beyond mid-October.

He strode over to the full-length Boardroom window. The early evening view of the Brighton foreshore and the i-360 Tower was beguiling as always, but he wasn't really looking at it; only turning his back on her.

This mission had threatened to overturn his life, and he'd staved that off by the change that had come over him since meeting Rafiq—the change that had made him take decisive action and let others do the worrying and pick up the pieces. And now that change, and her reaction to it, was in turn threatening to overturn his life. The same threat, from another direction.

"You're different since you've come back," she said, and immediately knew how fatuous it sounded; she'd only said it to avoid saying other things. When he didn't reply, she added, "Was it your meeting with Rafiq?"

"Yes."

"What happened there? Tell me about it."

He told her. As with Gaetano, he omitted references to the names and number of Consultants, and left out the conversation with Arden Bierce, but he was grateful to be able to retreat into the detail. It stopped him saying other things.

"Well," she said when he'd finished, "it checks out."

"What checks out?"

"Gaetano told me all that yesterday, and his account was almost exactly the same as yours. He practices—" she hurried over the word "—eidetic techniques. He works very hard at it."

He would, Anwar thought. *Not like me, I was made. He has to work at it.* And he'd work with quiet persistence and thoroughness. With near-obsessiveness. He'd make a good

Consultant. In fact, maybe he was. Another labyrynthine move of Rafiq's? A secret twentieth Consultant, unknown to the others? *No, now a secret nineteenth. No, eighteenth.*

He turned away from the window and faced her. "You said you'd answer my question about that final detail."

"You started this. You shouldn't have said that to me in Brighton. If Rafiq had sent someone else, I'd never have heard it."

"Answer my question."

"And you should go and get cleaned up. And I must go, too. I have an organisation to run, and a summit in seven days. And I need to eat." She looked at him. "Alone."

"My question."

"I'm sorry. I can't answer it."

"You *said...*"

"I can't. But if we survive this, you'll know why I can't."

2

He walked through the early evening, across the Garden from the Cathedral to the New Grand. He walked through the lobby and up to his suite. He shaved, cleaned his teeth, took a long shower, and changed his clothes. It took him over an hour to clean off the last five days, particularly the last hour of the fifth day.

His book, the replica of the Chalmers-Bridgewater edition of Shakespeare's Sonnets, was on his bed where he'd left it. He picked it up and held it in his hands. He thought, *I've only really known two women, and in the space of five days I've refused them both. I had to. One's a colleague, and the other's an obscenity. And a threat.*

Relationships could kill you, he knew, or at least rape you. Being that close to someone was a kind of violation. They'd suck you dry, or touch parts of you nobody else should be allowed to touch. But he wished he hadn't laughed out loud at her. What she'd said was embarrassing, but laughing out loud was worse.

He looked at the book for a moment longer, then did something he'd normally have thought impossible: he tore out a page.

It was the page with Sonnet 116. He ringed the first four lines, and wrote *I want you to have this. A.* His handwriting was a neat italic, done with an old-fashioned fountain pen. Hers, he remembered from random documents where he'd glimpsed her annotations, was large and untidy, with strong loops and vertical downstrokes, done with any old pen which happened to be at hand.

He'd often thought that getting to know someone's handwriting was one of the opening stages of intimacy. But that was appropriate only for simple sexual relationships or complicated loving ones, or perhaps for close friendships. He sensed that the first had ended and knew that the other two would never begin.

He went up to the next floor. He walked past the door leading to her apartments, nodding politely to the guard (not Proskar this time), and on to Gaetano's office.

Gaetano looked tired, but stood as he entered and greeted him courteously. The office was tidy as always, but in the last five days it had become crowded. Several monitor screens had been added, some free-standing and some fixed to the walls. They showed readouts and status reports for various aspects of the summit preparations. The first members of the delegations would start arriving tomorrow—not VIPs but support staff, and not in New Grand suites but in smaller hotels in Brighton. Anwar recalled the exhaustive and painstaking description Gaetano had given him of his, Gaetano's, involvement in the security for the summit: a huge edifice, for which he was solely responsible. *Meatslab or not, he's there by his own efforts. Me, I was just made. Enough. I must stop telling myself that. It's his problem, and he knows what he's doing. I've got other concerns.*

"I'm sorry," he said to Gaetano, "what did you say?"

"I said something changed tonight between you and her. I didn't like it."

"Neither did I." But neither of them felt disposed to elaborate. After a brief but uncomfortable silence, Anwar went on. "And what was all that about, speaking to me through you, and calling me It? Has she ever done that before?"

"No. I didn't like that either. And when you made that play of striking at her..."

"Yes, I'm sorry about that."

"I couldn't see any other way you could shut her up. You seemed to know what you were doing."

Thanks, Anwar thought, but didn't say. It would have sounded like over-egging the pudding. His working relationship with Gaetano was satisfactory, but not exactly comfortable, and delicately balanced.

Another silence ensued, which Gaetano broke. "What's that bit of paper you're holding?"

"Something I want to her to see. Will you take me to her apartments?"

"She won't be there, she's in meetings."

"I know. I'd like to leave it for her. On her bed."

"On her *bed?*"

"I'll explain when we get there. Will you take me?"

Never look surprised, was one of the maxims from his training. When he saw her bedroom for the first time he managed to mask his surprise, but only just. The one interior, on the whole of the New West Pier, that wasn't pearlescent white and silver. And what it was, was even more surprising than what it wasn't.

It was like the bedroom of an upmarket whore: deep-pile carpet and shot-silk wallhangings, deep-buttoned velvet upholstery and satin sheets, all in voluptuous dark purples and blues and reds, the colours of her dresses. And her untidiness was daubed over it like slogans: an unmade bed, clothes left over chairs and on the floor, chocolate wrappers strewn everywhere, and scraps of paper with notes scribbled in her large handwriting with its loops and downstrokes.

Her ginger cat was there too, fixing him with a baleful amber glare and hissing furiously. "Yes," he agreed, "and Fuck You too."

They'd walked through some of her other rooms—reception, library, office, sitting room, dining room—to get here, and all were exactly like rooms everywhere else on the New West Pier. It was as though this was her last personal refuge. He felt like he shouldn't have seen it.

Anwar gave the page to Gaetano, who read it and handed it back. Carefully, Anwar put it on her bed; then, in case it got lost amid the tumble of unmade bedclothes, he put it on her pillow.

"I don't like this, it's wrong," Gaetano said.

"It's only a gesture."

"I warned you before: don't read too much into how she behaves with you."

"I'm not. Particularly after tonight."

"I think you are. That Shakespeare quote is hardly ambiguous."

"Ambiguous is exactly what it is."

"Then I've got another quote, just for you. 'The verb To Love is hard to conjugate. The past isn't simple, the present isn't indicative, the future is very conditional.' I read books too."

Or perhaps just quotation dictionaries. "Yes, Cocteau knew he was being clever when he wrote that, but in this case it's irrelevant. I've got another quote too: Velvet Bag of Shit. That's what I think of her, Gaetano, that and nothing else. I'll protect her because it's what my mission says and I don't walk away from missions, but otherwise..."

"Then why," Gaetano asked, "put *that* on her bed?"

"Because it might remind her of something I said in Brighton, just before I showed her that page in my book and watched her read those lines."

"You've torn a page out of a *book* for her?"

"Yes."

When he'd recovered from what seemed like genuine surprise, Gaetano said, "I'll warn you again, don't imagine things she didn't intend. She's no good at relationships."

"Neither am I."

"So what did you say to her in Brighton?"

"Something about hating people less and understanding them more. It's one of the few times she's actually noticed me."

"Is that where she got this idea for an Outreach Foundation?"

"Yes. I was talking about how she treats her political and religious enemies, but she widened it into building relationships... Relax, I don't mean those kinds of relationships, and I don't mean with me." He gave Gaetano only her fallback position; not her primary one, which he'd laughed into nonexistence. "Relationships generally. She said she wants to start noticing people and valuing them. God knows, I had no idea that what I said would lead to that."

"I don't like it. If you harm her..."

"I know. You said all that before. I haven't forgotten."

3

Early evening in Brighton was early morning in Kuala
Lumpur; the beginning of the following day. Arden Bierce had
been working through the night.

She'd been reading and re-reading transcripts: of Anwar's
questioning of Carne and Hines, of her own questioning of
the five others like Carne and Hines, of Anwar's conversations
with Olivia and Gaetano, and of her report to Rafiq given from
Opatija as she stood over Asika's remains. Something was in
there, hiding in plain sight.

In the villa at Opatija, she'd hoped that Asika had been
killed by a swarm of opponents and not a single opponent. But
a single opponent was what she sensed then and still felt now.

Even Levin couldn't have done that to Asika without suffering damage himself. In fact Levin couldn't have done it at
all, because Asika was better. And it was academic anyway,
because Levin was as dead as Asika. Carne and Hines had
told Anwar, and five others like Carne and Hines had told her:
Levin died first, then Asika. But what they'd done to Levin
was worse. There wasn't even enough of him left to make a
corpse. And they all remembered his face, when he realised
he couldn't defend himself. *So what have they got that kills
Consultants? How and where did they make it, or create it?*

She had originally joined UN Intelligence as a field officer.
She proved effective, not because she was particularly ruthless
but because she understood people instinctively, whether colleagues or opponents. With colleagues, she established good
working relationships and sensed what they needed from her.
With opponents, she sensed what made them tick and how
they'd act or react.

UN Intelligence was a source from which Rafiq drew many
of his personal staff, and she was quickly promoted. She was

the obvious choice for her present role, as the staff member with responsibility for The Dead. Only she could instinctively know what made *them* tick. Or Rafiq, who was even more impenetrable.

But after the meeting with Anwar, she wasn't so sure about Rafiq. The meeting still worried her. Rafiq had told her beforehand how he would play it, how he would try to tease ideas out of Anwar by pretending to be struggling to understand these new opponents. She was unconvinced then, and remained unconvinced now, about how much he was acting. She sensed something in him which, in anyone else, might almost have amounted to uncertainty.

She'd never met Olivia del Sarto, or spoken to her directly, but she knew all about her. Why weren't she and Rafiq closer? They stood for similar things. They should be natural allies. She was about to park that question for later, but then thought, *Didn't Anwar ask him that too?*

Anwar. She rarely made errors of judgement, but her near-offer to him after the meeting was an error. Not a crucial one, but she wished she hadn't made it. Or maybe it wasn't an error, and her instincts were correct. It had made Anwar tell her, by the strength of his denial, how Olivia was sucking him into herself.

She normally ran relationships with Consultants by giving them space, by not crowding them. She always felt that she needed to find Anwar some extra space, for the way he worried about his lack of ability compared to some of the others. And for his obsessiveness, his insularity (he was solitary but not lonely), and his need for routine and a comfort zone, all of which were now being torn to pieces by this mission as it got more complicated and far-reaching than even Rafiq had suspected.

Or maybe Rafiq was still holding something back. It wouldn't be the first time. Surely he'd have picked someone other than Anwar, if he'd known how this mission would turn out. *Unless he knew something else about it. And Rafiq knows everything. Doesn't he?*

Anwar had told Rafiq of a detail that he sensed and that bothered him, a final detail that might overturn everything. She had also felt something, first at Opatija and again more recently, when it almost surfaced in Anwar's questioning of Carne and Hines, and her own questioning of the others like them. She didn't yet know what it was, or even if it was the same thing Anwar had sensed. But she felt that it, too, might overturn everything, and she would work until she found it.

Her style of work was careful and reflective and thorough, like that of Anwar. But she had something he'd never had: her empathy, her instinctive feeling for people. Though she suspected, because of how this mission was turning on him, that he might acquire it.

Or it might acquire him.

4

Anwar left the New Grand and walked back across the Garden to the Cathedral. Early evening was turning into night, and the night air carried the astringent scent of witch hazel to counterpoint the smells of damp earth and grass.

He entered the Cathedral. It was almost empty, with just a few worshippers in the pews. He only needed a glance, and an assessment of their positions and postures, to confirm that they were worshippers and nothing more. The Cathedral air was cool and still, with the usual hint of citrus.

He walked to the front of the pews, in the space before the altar where he'd fought Bayard and Proskar and six others, and where she'd ridiculed him. He looked up at the silver cross on the altar. Like all New Anglican crosses it was plain and unadorned, with no figure of Jesus nailed to it. A cross, not a crucifix.

He felt a movement in the air, and ramped up his senses. He knew, before he turned around, that she had entered and was walking towards him. The air she displaced was her shape.

He didn't know how to greet her after what had happened between them. But she solved it for him, to the surprise of the few worshippers.

"Fucking autistic retard."

"Velvet bag of shit," he replied.

They sounded like he and Levin had once sounded, greeting each other. *Muslim filth. Jewish scum.*

"About what you left for me," she said. "I liked reading it again. But you tore a page out of a *book*."

"Yes."

"Nobody's ever done something like that for me, except maybe Gaetano."

"Tell me, why do the New Anglicans only have plain crosses and not crucifixes?"

He was steering her away from what happened in the Boardroom by getting her to talk about what she knew best. That suited her, too.

"We don't do guilt and pain and misery, that's for the Catholics. We do affirmation and aspiration. We don't deny that they nailed Jesus to a cross, but we don't need to wallow in it."

"But you do have images of him. I've seen them."

"Yes. Replicas of the statues in Lisbon and Rio, Cristo Rei and Cristo Redentor. Jesus with arms outstretched, offering benediction. Not only benediction, but encouragement. Even urging. *Be all you can be, for me.* Those are my words," she added proudly. "I wrote them."

"Yes, I can hear your voice in them. Even more than His."

If his remark had any subsurface meaning she didn't notice it, and she continued the direction of their conversation. It kept them on surer ground.

"I'm proud of the New Anglicans. We're rich and powerful and assertive. As much a corporation as a church, but a properly-run corporation. We pay all our taxes. We declare all our salaries. We declare all our investments."

"And," he said, remembering their dinner, "you declare all your costs. Have your finance people given you an amended operating statement yet?"

She didn't hear his question. She was in full flow. "You know, Archbishop was a title I inherited five years ago, but it doesn't sound right now. In a few years, when the New Anglicans are a finished product, I might change my title. To CEO. Or—" she glanced at him "—Controller-General."

Or, he thought, *Archbitch.* The word was already in his store of privately-invented names, like Meatslabs and Lucifer's Lesbian and Levin's Levities. They were all rather anal-retentive: a reflection of how much time he spent alone, adding building-blocks to his interior world. A world that was ordered and comfortable, and about to collapse.

"You know," she said, "you've made yourself ridiculous here. No one would ever say so, not to your face, but they're laughing behind your back."

"You mean because I shut myself in the Signing Room?"

"Yes."

"But you know why I did that." This was more safe ground, and it suited him. Operational detail. "We've made sure there's nothing of theirs in there. The signing ceremony is scheduled for October 23. So if that was their preferred option, it's gone."

"So it could be any time."

"Yes. But you said they wanted it live and in public at the summit. So any time during the nine days commencing

October 15." When she didn't reply, he hurriedly added, "But it was their *preferred* option. This one will be..."

"Less preferred. But earlier. Look, I was wrong, let's not waste those few days. Let's go back to how it was."

"Do you mean that?"

"Yes. Let's go back to just fucking each other senseless, and each of us takes what we want from it." She watched him as he visibly lightened. It was as though a weight was slipping off him. She added, "I mean it. No relationships, just relations."

"I'd like nothing more," he said, then added, as the relief spread through him, "but not here in front of the altar?"

"I can find somewhere better."

Later, in her bedroom, they went back to how it was. This time she raised her bottom slightly to assist him in pulling down her underwear. He didn't seem to notice consciously, though he was aware that his preliminaries worked a little better. She knew how he liked her passive during this part, so he could enjoy doing his part slowly and artistically.

It was a minor embellishment which might, indirectly, help her. Just a detail, and later she'd add others. Build empathy in careful penny pieces. Not all in one lump, as she'd tried so clumsily and embarrassingly before. The next detail— the thought came to her quite suddenly—could be to find a replacement for his book.

"Retard," she murmured afterwards.

"Bag of shit," he replied, and they went again.

How many times have we gone tonight? she thought. *He's like a pistol. As one chamber's spent the next one comes around. And keeps coming.*

She was learning empathy, though her version of it, unlike Arden's, didn't come naturally. And—because of who she was— there was something oblique and sinuous about it. Starting a relationship with him by accommodating his embarrassment at the idea of a relationship. Sharing with him his wish not to treat sex as something to be shared.

She would work at it, carefully and quietly. Not her usual style of working, but it was worth it. He was obsessive and strange, potent and vulnerable, but he was the only one with a chance of protecting her. That, at least, was the obvious reason to draw her to him, but that—she told herself over and over until she almost believed it—wasn't the only one. There was something else.

Empathy had found her, and it would find him. And—the admission frightened her—she wanted it to find him. Nobody else would do.

NINE: OCTOBER 7 - 10, 2060

1

The delegations for the summit started to arrive on October 7. They were minor officials and support staff, put up in hotels all over Brighton. The VIPs—political leaders and senior staff—would not arrive until two or three days before the summit. The most important would be put up in the New Grand, the others in the more prestigious hotels along Marine Parade. Their suites were being made ready.

Yuri Zaitsev, the UN Secretary-General, would also be taking a suite in the New Grand. He was due to arrive on the evening of October 14, when he and Olivia would co-host a reception to mark the opening of the summit.

The first administrative and housekeeping matters had begun. They were the first of a multitude: agenda headings, translations, dietary requirements, transport, media relations, religious observance. The New Anglicans' staff had foreseen them and prepared for them, and addressed them with their usual efficiency.

As well as the host of security issues associated with the summit, Gaetano was attending to something else.

Proskar had gone.

"Do you know anything about that?" he asked Anwar.

Aware that Gaetano was not likely to ask questions to which he didn't have answers, Anwar said, "Yes. I told him in the Signing Room that I couldn't be sure his resemblance to Marek was only on the surface..."

"You've been through that again and again, with me and with Kuala Lumpur."

"...and that he should go."

Gaetano seemed about to erupt, to shout obvious things like *He reports to me, not you!* But he controlled it, and when he eventually spoke, his voice was quiet. "I'm glad at least that you gave me a straight answer, because he left a note. It says that after what you told him, he wouldn't be coming back."

"Sounds rather theatrical."

"Not theatrical. I've known him for five years, and I have a bad feeling. I don't think I'll see him again."

Anwar shrugged, but didn't answer.

"His early life," Gaetano went on, trying to ignore Anwar's manner, "was chaotic. Like mine. He always said that when he joined us he found..."

"A comfort zone?"

"Do you know what you've done?"

"Removed an uncertainty."

"Removed my closest colleague, and my deputy. I needed him for the summit, and you've driven him away!"

"You're overstating."

"You've done one thing that seemed right since you've been back from UNEX, or at least one thing that *she* half-admitted might be right, but it gives you no licence to talk like that. Listen to yourself. You and I have to work together."

"You're still overstating."

"I'll have him found and brought back."

"Then," said Anwar over his shoulder as he left Gaetano's office, "you and I might have to have an accounting."

"Yes," Gaetano whispered at the closing door, "we might."

Olivia knew the four lines by heart, but still preferred to read them rather than recite them.

Let me not to the marriage of true minds

Admit impediments. Love is not love
Which alters when it alteration finds,
Or bends with the remover to remove.

Each time she read them, the lines turned themselves inside out and presented another face to her. One of the faces was uncomfortably close to The Detail. Maybe Anwar already suspected it, when he tore that page out of his book for her. Maybe Shakespeare did too. *Always ambiguous and multilayered, Shakespeare. Like the bastard of Rafiq and a Consultant.*

She could have got her staff to search for a replacement book, but she didn't. She searched personally, through dozens of antiquarian book dealers' websites. One of the websites might even have been Anwar's. She'd never know; most small business proprietors retained anonymity, and she had no idea of Anwar's trading name.

She remembered exactly what he'd told her about his book, though: a replica of the Chalmers-Bridgewater edition of the Sonnets. Odd, because she hadn't always noticed what he was saying. Then she remembered that that would have been after he'd said that thing to her in Brighton. She'd started to notice him a bit more after that.

Eventually she found a copy, ordered it, and had it express-couriered to her. It arrived in hours. On the inside title page she added an inscription *You mistimed. O.* Her writing wasn't like Anwar's, but large and upright with flourishes. She'd written it with a cheap marker pen that happened to be the first one within reach. The ink started to bleed into the weave of the paper almost before she'd finished writing, and she thought, *Fuck, I should've got a proper pen*; then it stopped, and what she'd written remained legible.

She'd go to his suite, on the floor below her apartments, and leave it on his pillow. No, that was too obvious. She'd give it to him personally. No, that was even more obvious. She'd ask Gaetano to give it to him. There was always Gaetano.

Fuck, she thought again, *these details. Why does everything have to be just so?* While he'd been doing decisive things and made her mock him about almost turning into her, she was getting obsessive and almost turning into him.

Maybe literally, she thought sourly. *He's already pumped enough of himself inside me.*

Anwar started to feel worse and worse about Proskar. He rehearsed uncomfortably to himself how he might try admitting to Gaetano that he'd behaved hastily and gone for an easy target; but Gaetano had already said as much, and admitting it to him wouldn't do much practical good. The only thing that would, would be to find him. He could do something about that: he'd ask Arden to put UN Intelligence on it. But then, he thought, *What if I was right about him, against all the odds, and I actually* invited *Marek back?* Rather apt that Marek came from Croatia: vampires' victims, it was said, had to *invite* them in.

But he knew he hadn't done himself any credit in the last exchange with Gaetano, whereas Gaetano had; he'd shown control and restraint. And the next time they met, the following day, Gaetano showed exactly the same qualities and behaved as though nothing had happened between them. Anwar remarked on it, saying he was glad they could put other differences aside.

"We have to," Gaetano said. "The summit's getting closer. The preparations are mounting and I can't afford to have baggage between us. But that isn't why I asked to see you." He handed Anwar the book. "She wanted me to give you this."

Anwar looked at it, saw the title and the spine and the cover and the binding, and went cold. *She could have left it on my pillow, or given it to me personally, but that would give away what she intended. I know what she intended.*

She'd have had to trawl through innumerable dealers to find this. He knew, because he'd had to, to find his copy. And here she was, taking time to think of something that mattered to him, taking time—her own time—to get it. To get a toe in the door. To establish something they'd share. She'd thought to start a relationship, and he thought he'd laughed the idea out of existence, but she wasn't afraid of his laughter. She wasn't afraid of anything, and she'd never back down and never give up.

She'd just come back, again and again, each time more oblique and sinuous than the last. He should have remembered that about her.

Relationship. He spoke the word to himself, stressing the second syllable, and it tasted like copper in his mouth. His life was turning inside out. There was a rushing in his ears, which he remembered reading somewhere was what you heard when you started to die.

Relationship.

He knew she was working on him. Sucking him into her. It would overturn his life, but his life was half overturned already. He half wanted it to continue, but sensed that she'd be worse, for him, than whatever they'd send for her.

Then he saw her inscription, and smiled without humour.

Several large corporations had a presence on the Cathedral Complex of the New West Pier—usually a boardroom and adjoining CEO suite. It was prestigious to have Board meetings, or to do entertaining or lobbying, at one of Europe's premier business addresses. As a matter of course, Gaetano had had the companies on the New West Pier checked—maybe some of them were part of, or had links to, the founders or The Cell. He'd found nothing, but he got Anwar to ask Arden to do a deeper check. She called back with the results, but first he briefed her on the events of the last few days.

From the wall of his suite, her projected image registered not only surprise, but genuine shock. "You tore a page out of a *book* for her?"

"Yes. And what about the results of your checks?"

Arden had found that years earlier Proskar did some freelance security work for a subsidiary of one of the Pier companies; neither that company nor its associates showed any traceable links to the Cell or the founders, and the security work was low-grade and short-lived. He'd been dismissed. His life really was chaotic then.

"And," she said, "he's now entered Croatia."

"You know where to reach him?"

"No. He entered Croatia, then completely disappeared."

"Just like..."

"Yes. Just like Marek used to do. If I was to find, despite all our checking and all the evidence, that you were right about him all along..." She made a face. "I need that like I need a third nostril."

Anwar looked sharply at her image. She was half-joking, probably three-quarters joking, but it was not her usual kind of phrase.

Then she said, "We both have a lot to do," and ended the call.

2

Arban Proskar was travelling legally on a genuine passport. He entered Croatia on October 8, and disappeared on October 9.

Also on October 9, late at night, Kiril Horvath turned his flatbed Land Rover onto the road that led out of Opatija, past the Villa Angiolina and up into the foothills of the Mount

Ucka national park. Horvath was an illegal hunter; he hunted brown bears. They weren't as big as grizzlies, but they were still very big: the biggest wild predators in the Croatian highlands, or anywhere in Europe. Conservation measures had rescued them from near-extinction, but they were still very rare.

Horvath hunted not with bullets but with tranquiliser darts, fired by special low-recoil, low-impact guns with night sights and laser target designation. He'd always hated the idea of killing wild animals for sport; he hunted brown bears to capture them and sell them. He sold only to zoos and wildlife parks, or sometimes to conservation foundations who were prepared to bend the rules, and he made a reasonable (but still strictly illegal) profit. He could have made a lot more if he sold them to circuses for entertainment or to Asian dealers who milked their glands for medicines and aphrodisiacs, but he had no time for either; he thought they were scarcely better than those who killed for sport.

He liked brown bears, and he knew a lot about them: where to find them at night, especially at this time of the year when they were getting sluggish and fat in the leadup to hibernation. He only targeted males, preferably younger males because the fully-grown ones would be impossible to manhandle onto his vehicle's flatbed, even with lifting gear. He wouldn't take females in case they had dependent cubs.

He was average build and thirtyish, with a reticent but not unfriendly manner. He was a farmer, and like most farmers in Croatia he hadn't been doing well for some time. Farming was like no other business. Each year you had to invest everything—all your capital, everything you had—in the next year. He had a young family, and the strain was beginning to tell on him. His bear-catching hadn't made him a fortune, but it provided enough to top up his farm income.

What he did was illegal, but other people supplemented their earnings in more unpleasant ways. He worked on his farm during the week but every Saturday he used his old Land Rover to go up into the Mount Ucka hills, past the villa where he'd heard some strange things had happened, and higher up into the mountains. It had been a regular, and moderately successful, routine: every Saturday from September through to mid-November. He'd been doing it for the last two years. This late on a Saturday night there was no traffic. Those who weren't at home were in town, not up here in the forested hills.

But tonight was different. Nobody had followed him out of Opatija on this road, but now something was behind him, closing rapidly: a big lumbering black truck, unlit and unmarked. It couldn't be the police, they'd have lit up the night and had sirens blaring, and they didn't travel in vehicles like that. It must have been parked offroad and pulled out to follow him as he drove past, which at first seemed frightening, though on reflection he had little to feel frightened about. They could be drug dealers or gangsters, but he had no involvements with either and wasn't so rich that anyone would try robbery. Not a gambling creditor or a jealous husband, either; his life wasn't that interesting.

By now it had caught him up and was tailgating him.

He shrugged. He'd been an army driver during his military service—quite a good one—and his Land Rover, though aging, was in good condition and was more agile than any truck. And he didn't like being tailgated. He was approaching a series of uphill bends he knew well, where he'd be able to out-accelerate and outcorner the truck. He dropped a gear and floored the accelerator, and left it wallowing far behind and downhill.

Except that he didn't. It was still there.

It negotiated the uphill bends expertly, even more expertly than he'd done, and kept coming. They came to a straighter, more level stretch of road and it still kept coming. *Who's driving that? And what do they want with me?* Nothing, apparently, because to his amazement the truck moved out to overtake, cut in front of him like a sports car, and ran him neatly off the road. Then it hurtled past, still unlit, and away up into the hills.

He should have been angry but instead he was puzzled. This wasn't a road-rage incident, it was too precise for that. The truck had done just enough to force him off the road without making him crash or overturn. As it sped past, he saw it had no license plates. The cab was too dark and too high to see who was driving, but whoever it was, was very good.

He gunned his engine and followed it. The road wound further up into the dark forested hills, and the truck slowed. He saw it turn into the driveway of the villa, and he drove past and drew to a halt a little way further on. He turned in his seat and looked back down the road at the villa.

He could hear the rustlings and drippings of the night forest, which was unusual because those noises should have been drowned by the noises made by the people who'd jumped down from the truck and were manhandling something out of the back; but they worked very quietly, and very quickly. There were four of them. It was too dark for him to make out their faces, and in any case they seemed to be wearing something like balaclavas or ski masks, but they were all larger than average and moved with a rehearsed athleticism. In just a few minutes they'd taken a large rectangular container out of the back of the truck and set it down on its end in the middle of the villa's driveway, about halfway between the road and the front door. Then, apparently without speaking, they climbed back into the truck. It backed out of the driveway and headed down the road towards Opatija, quickly but not as quickly as when he'd first encountered it. It was still unlit.

He reversed back to the opening of the driveway, stopped, and lowered a window. Now he was on his own the forest noises should have sounded louder, but they didn't; that was how quiet those four had been.

It was as if they'd chosen him as a witness. As if it was all an act, and they were waiting for him so they could perform it.

They hadn't threatened him—even when they'd forced him off the road it was done with a strange precision and lack of emotion. As if they just wanted him to see them, then they'd leave him to call it in. Which meant they might know things about him. Like the fact that he made this journey regularly, and what the journey was about. And that he'd still call in what he'd seen, even though it would mean having to explain what he was doing up here.

The villa was familiar to him from newscasts and previous journeys: low, white, with the dark verticals of cypresses looming in the shadows behind it. And, in the middle of the driveway, the container. Standing on its end. It was large, dark, rectangular, and featureless. It reminded him of the monolith in that old movie whose name he could never remember. He stared at it, and felt that it stared back at him.

The authorities were smarter than Horvath gave them credit for. They knew about his Saturday night drives into the mountains, but they knew also about his farm and his family and his financial difficulties. Some time ago they'd decided that as long as he dealt only with zoos and wildlife parks they'd turn a blind eye. All of which meant that Horvath, when he decided to call it in, would be an ideal witness.

He flicked open his wristcom.

3

Arden was told less than an hour after Horvath had called the local police. It was five in the morning of October 10 in Kuala Lumpur, about midnight on October 9 in Croatia.

She called Rafiq. He listened as carefully to her as she had listened to the UN Embassy attache who'd called her. Once Horvath had told the local police they'd acted quickly, notifying the UN because it concerned the villa, and deploying their own military to surround the villa—but not, she asked them, to attempt to open the container until she arrived.

Rafiq made a hasty call—not enough time, he told her drily, to write a letter—and arranged for a Consultant to go with her. Eve Monash arrived just as the VSTOL on the lawn in front of Fallingwater was ready to lift off.

Monash was about Arden's age, but with a tall rangy build and a habit of not wasting words. She would have had the normal dislike of bodyguard duties, though she said nothing about that, or indeed about anything much, during the flight. She'd probably decided to stretch the point this time; Arden was, after all, the staff member responsible to Rafiq for the Consultancy, which made it almost like guarding Rafiq himself.

Eve Monash was one of the higher-rated Consultants, Arden knew, probably among the top four or five. *Top two or three now.*

The villa was owned by a Croatian banker who was sufficiently rich and well-connected to sidestep local planning regulations and get his house built on national park land. Then he'd fallen on hard times and rented it to a property company, from where it was sublet and assigned and disappeared into corporate networks which—so far—the Croatian authorities hadn't unravelled. Once the flurry of activity following the discovery of Asika's remains had died down, the villa was no longer guarded. Not even the police Do Not Cross tapes remained. It stayed empty and dark, until now.

For the second time she saw it from above, lit with arclights and surrounded by police and military and their vehicles. The VSTOL landed on the main drive. A door rippled open and she stepped out, followed by Eve Monash.

"Wait," Arden told the VSTOL, "but don't hover. I may be some time."

The flight from Fallingwater to the villa had taken just under an hour. It was approaching one in the morning of October 10, local time. Horvath had seen the truck unloading here about 10:30 p.m. on October 9. A few hours after Arban Proskar had entered Croatia and disappeared.

She looked at the container. It stood there insolently and looked back at her. It was about twelve feet tall, standing on its end.

The villa itself was dark and empty. It sported fresh sets of Do Not Cross tapes over its door and windows. As far as anyone could tell it hadn't been entered, and Horvath's own account tallied with this. But if the villa was dark and empty, the driveway and grounds were anything but. The whole area shivered in the cold arc-light blaze and boiled with people: local police, forensics, and military. Especially military.

Horvath had readily agreed to wait for Arden and give her his account personally, although it had already been relayed to her. She liked him. He was about average height and weight, early or maybe middle thirties. His face was open and pleasant, but there was an air of competence about him and his account was precise and unadorned. She asked a few questions and thanked him, and he got in his old Land Rover and drove away through the cordon of miltary vehicles and back to his family.

During the flight out, Arden had called Anwar in Brighton and briefed him. He in turn briefed Gaetano. They would be waiting for her call.

Most of the Croatian military were Special Forces. They had an assortment of weapons trained on the container, but stayed in a semicircle well clear of it. She'd learnt, during the flight, that it had proved impervious to all attempts to scan its interior. It was inert; no electronic or other emissions. Nothing had been heard moving inside it. Its surface was dark rough wood, but there would be an inner lining of something, probably lead and altered carbon, to prevent scanning.

It had no visible locks, but a series of simple clamps along its top edge and a series of hinges along its bottom edge. When the clamps were released they would (unless they were booby-trapped) enable the entire front section to fall open and the contents to tumble out. As though it was intended for someone to open it without knowing what was inside.

It was twelve feet tall and five feet wide, easily big enough to contain a human, living or dead; or something much bigger than a human. She thought of Arban Proskar's abrupt disappearance, and thought also of Chulo Asika's remains and of whatever had killed him.

Container and contents. I'm turning into Anwar.

She called Rafiq. After a short pause, he said, "Open it."

"Stand back with the others," Eve Monash told her. "I'll do this." It amounted to more words than she'd addressed to Arden during the whole of the flight.

Eve Monash spoke briefly to the Special Forces commander. A ladder was brought for her. She approached the container and leant the ladder against its side. She glanced back at Arden, then climbed the ladder and reached the container's top edge. She leaned sideways out from the ladder and ran her hands across the clamps. She released the first one.

Arden's wristcom buzzed. It was UN Intelligence. She signalled Eve Monash to pause, and flipped it open.

"It's about Proskar," a voice said. "Bad news. We know what happened to him."

"Tell me," she said, and the voice told her. "I'll call you back," she said, and signalled Eve Monash to continue.

The first clamp slid back easily. The container did nothing. One by one, Eve Monash released the others. They too slid back easily. She held on to the top edge.

"All done," she called back to Arden.

"Whatever comes out of there..." Arden began.

"I know. I'll let it fall open, jump down and cover you."

"No. Refasten one of the top clamps, then jump down and shoot off the clamp."

She did, very quickly, landing in a crouch in front of Arden with her gun already levelled. She fired, once.

The top clamp shattered. The front section of the container fell open, hitting the driveway with a crash. Cold vapour erupted out of the dark interior, and something else erupted out in its wake.

Anwar and Gaetano were in Gaetano's office. They'd been there for an hour, and there was an uncomfortable silence between them. It was 1:00 a.m. on October 10 in Brighton, 2:00 a.m. in Croatia. Noises from the Brighton foreshore floated over the two miles of sea. There were still plenty of lights there, and the i-360 Tower was still in operation.

Anwar's wristcom buzzed, and Arden announced herself. There was something strange about her voice, and she'd blanked her screen.

"Say that again?" Anwar asked.

"It tumbled out of the container. A dead body. Been kept in cold storage. Forensics have done all the preliminary checks— DNA, dentition, retinas, fingerprints—and it's unmistakeable." She hesitated, and went on. "Features are unmistakeable too: the build, the hands."

Gaetano rounded on Anwar. "So you really did it! I said I didn't think I'd see him again. We will have an accounting, Anwar."

"No," Arden said, "it wasn't Proskar's body..."

Anwar froze.

"...it was Parvin Marek's. And he's been dead for at least three years."

TEN: OCTOBER 10 - 14, 2060

Olivia was given the news about Marek as soon as Anwar got it, in the early morning of October 10. Her reaction was quiet, almost uninterested. It was, of course, a story from the past that had no reason to concern her as personally as it concerned Rafiq or anyone else from UNEX. But she told Anwar, after a short pause, "I need to be sure you'll stay until the summit's over."

"I already told you—"

"Tell me again."

"Yes. I'll stay."

"Until the summit's over."

"*Yes*. You know I won't walk out on a mission."

"I'm taking tonight's Evensong service in the Cathedral. I want you there. I'm giving the sermon."

The news spread like wildfire: she was actually taking a service. She hardly ever took services, at least not routine ones like Evensong.

The media attention was huge. Reporters packed the Cathedral. Someone (Olivia herself, or the New Anglicans' PR people) had told them it would be her biggest public statement since the Room For God broadcast. The Cathedral filled up. Gaetano and several of his staff were placed strategically, and Anwar had chosen an aisle seat in the pews, five rows from the front.

She wasn't known for observing details of ceremony and ritual, and half the congregation (the media half) were hoping for her to slip up somewhere and give them some good footage. She didn't, though. She took the service impeccably.

The choir was singing the evening's first psalm. She recognised the words from other Evensongs at other churches. The New Anglicans had regular Evensongs. She'd seen to that after the one she attended at Rochester Cathedral five years ago. She remembered meeting Michael Taber there. A nice man, and also very smart. She'd seen him only a few days earlier on her banks of screens, when Rochester Cathedral was occupied.

For he shall deliver thee from the snare of the hunter.
He shall defend thee under his wings,
And thou shalt be safe...

October had turned cold and grey. No copper evening sunlight. A biting wind, a choppy pewter sea. The effect of the cold evening light on the Cathedral's white and silver interior, the plain pale wood, the altar with its plain silver cross on which no figure was nailed, was to turn it colder.

Lord, now lettest thou thy servant depart in peace...

The words of the Nunc Dimittis always sounded like they should be the closing words, but they weren't; there were some responses and collects, and then a brief silence during which the noises from Brighton's foreshore could be dimly heard as she walked up to deliver her sermon. The New Anglicans didn't do pulpits; she simply stood, a small figure in a dark red velvet dress, in the space before the altar where Anwar had fought Bayard and Proskar and six others, and where she'd ridiculed him. And where he'd met her on October 6. She spoke without notes.

"These last few days, I've found an unexpected companion. Someone who's shown me some unexpected things.

This companion told me recently I should hate our enemies less and understand them more."

Anwar felt a thrill go through him.

"I was walking along the seafront, past those arches between here and the Palace Pier, and past some arcades with games. There was one where things popped up and you had to knock them down with a rubber mallet, only for others to pop up, also to be knocked down. My companion asked 'Remind you of fundamentalists?'"

There was a faint ripple of laughter in the congregation.

"Yes, that's how I should have reacted, but I didn't. I went into a rant about fundamentalists everywhere. Filth, I called them, and scum. 'I hate their beliefs,' I said, 'more than I love mine.' My companion said, 'If you hated them less and understood them more, maybe even more people would support you. Including some of them.'"

She looked around the Cathedral. The sounds of the Brighton foreshore and the gulls and the sea, which had been waiting outside for just such a moment, crept into the Cathedral as she stopped speaking.

She knew exactly where Anwar was sitting and carefully avoided looking in his direction when she went on. "That was important for me. More important than my companion suspected. It's come back to me several times since. And for several different reasons, some of which I'll share with you this evening."

But only some, Anwar silently prayed, *and nothing which gives any clues about me.*

"I've seen injustice and suffering and it should make me compassionate, but it doesn't. It makes me furious. My first instinct isn't to comfort the victims but to strike at the perpetrators. I'm an Archbishop, but compassion doesn't come easily to me. Hatred comes easier.

"Which brings me to our enemies. You know what I call them. Batoth'Daa: the Back to the Dark Ages Alliance. I hated all of them, leaders and followers; followers because they're weak and stupid, leaders because they make use of weakness and stupidity. But my companion's remark made me look again at the followers.

"So to everyone who's ever been duped or brainwashed or bullied into these ghastly fundamentalist cults, we'll offer something new: an Outreach Foundation. It'll be like everything else we do, businesslike and properly funded. And it'll offer something better. Dignity. Self-esteem. Purpose. Not superstition and guilt and blind obedience—they can get those from any of our competitors.

"But if they don't take it, then they'll have what I still offer their leaders: my hatred."

There was a murmur around the Cathedral. She'd said it with relish.

"Yes, you heard me. Hatred. We can't love everyone. We can't make heaven on earth. We can't make everything perfect, but we can make some things better."

She sounds so much like Rafiq, Anwar thought. *Why haven't they ever got into bed, either politically or literally?*

"And we must make them better, because we may be all there is. We exploit space, but we've stopped exploring it. Is it because we think that nothing's out there? We've turned inwards. Maybe there really is nothing except us. And God."

This is new. They've never heard her say things like this. Where's she going?

"Maybe we really are alone as a species. Often enough we're alone as individuals. Think about our relationships: the line where an individual ends and a couple begins. A secret can mark that line. If one half has a secret they can't share, maybe they should never become a couple. Maybe it would be better if they both stayed alone."

There was a puzzled murmur from the congregation, and she didn't elaborate. But for Anwar, it struck a chord. A cold and sickening one. He knew exactly what she meant. He'd said it to her himself, when she almost offered him something real and he rejected it. Not only rejected it, but laughed it into nonexistence. *What have I done?*

And later, when she gave him that book, he'd sensed she was again moving in and he'd felt a copper tang of fear. He felt it now, but a different fear: the fear that he was wrong. *What have I done?*

"Stayed alone," she repeated softly, as if talking to herself. "Individual identity. It should be the last line, the one never crossed. The place where the soul lives. But I've seen it invaded..."

Even Anwar didn't understand that reference. Maybe he wasn't the only one here to whom she was addressing cryptic remarks.

She shook her head violently, as if to clear it.

"Our society is capable of great things. Technology hasn't cured all our problems, but it has solved the food and fuel shortages that people feared fifty years ago would bury us. And yet, there's always the thread of selfishness and self-obsession. While we work to solve the remaining problems, like the water rights that are why the UN is coming here, we see everywhere, on every screen, advertisements showing people putting things in their mouths."

Again, a surprised murmur. Again, she didn't elaborate. And again, Anwar was the only person in the Cathedral who knew what she meant.

Anwar, when he was Rashad, was fascinated by advertisements. His classmates talked about their favourite programmes, but he preferred the advertisements. An unconscious commentary on society. Have you ever thought, he asked repeatedly, how many of them show people putting things in their mouths? Burgers, chocolate, pies, lividly-coloured drinks? People putting things in their mouths: a logo for our society. His classmates chewed their burgers and stared at him, open-mouthed and uncomprehending.

Just like tonight's congregation. They probably think she's veering all over the place, but there's no mistake. She's been waiting to say this as long as I've thought it.

"Yes, the New Anglicans are a political movement. We've had to be, because established politics has too often chosen to appease fundamentalism rather than challenge it. Yes, the New Anglicans are a corporation. We've had to be, because having a better way than the Dark Ages isn't enough unless you have the wealth and organisation to put it out there and make it work. And *yes,* the New Anglicans are a Church! More than ever. So we'll reach out to the bullied and disenfranchised and marginalised and brainwashed, and bring them into the light where they can question anything and everything, including us, because we aren't infallible. We don't promise to make everything good. But we do promise to make some things better.

"I may not always be out here, in front of you, but God is always out there. And you know what *our* God wants from you. Not worship, but ambition. Remake youselves! Take *Him* into *you!*"

2

After the service she left quickly, going through a small door behind the altar. Gaetano stood there to prevent anyone following. People and press remained in the Cathedral for some time, milling around and discussing her sermon—the parts they understood, and the parts they didn't.

One by one, wristcoms were flipped open and journalists started calling in their reports. A few went outside to call, hunching their shoulders against the cold—the wind from the sea had become more biting as evening turned into night—but most preferred to stay in the relative warmth of the Cathedral. Anwar, wandering dazedly among them, thought they were speaking in tongues.

Their reaction to her sermon was mixed. They didn't know if her tone was optimism or despair. And they were puzzled about some of her references: relationships, for example, and people putting things in their mouths.

Along with the puzzlement Anwar heard annoyance and even scorn. Her sermon had been pitched as her most significant public statement since the Reith Lecture, and most reporters thought that, well, frankly it was nothing of the sort. The Outreach Foundation was significant, but hardly on a par with the huge policy and strategic initiatives she'd taken with Room For God. And many New Anglicans, below Olivia's level, were already doing similar things, albeit informally and piecemeal.

Some of them were doubly annoyed because they'd expected her to say more about the summit, in view of everything that had happened in the last few days—her sudden cancelled meetings, rumours of rows with Zaitsev over the Signing Room, and the strange occupation of Rochester Cathedral with the failed ultimatum. More than once he heard the phrase "the Troubled Summit."

And then, there was the Companion. That prompted a feeding frenzy. Who was it? Had she got one of The Dead, maybe there ahead of the summit to protect Zaitsev? He even heard someone likening the Companion to Shakespeare's Dark Lady, but perhaps with the roles reversed. It was only a passing remark, and wasn't picked up by anyone else. It didn't even make it to that journalist's channel. Some fat subeditor, between uncomprehending mouthfuls of burger, took it out.

And finally, her closing remark about not always being here. Some of them took it to be just an expression, but others wondered if it hinted at an attempt on her life. Most of them, however, tied it in with her suddenly-cancelled meetings, and wondered what was going on. Was she planning to leave the New Anglicans?

All these elements were enough to make the sermon a good story, but it didn't get automatic top ranking. It was upstaged on most channels by the brief but breaking news about the discovery of Parvin Marek's remains—which, by now, had been rushed back to Kuala Lumpur and definitively identified. It was an old story, but now it had returned strangely, and prompted speculation about the effect it might have on the families of Marek's victims. And on Laurens Rafiq.

3

When he'd heard enough, Anwar walked up to the door behind the altar. Gaetano was still there.

"What did you make of that?" Anwar asked him.

"It sounded like Goodbye."

"Where is she?"

"She went into the Garden."

Anwar passed through the door and out of the Cathedral. He found her standing under a spreading laburnum tree. The Garden was darkening, and wind rushed through the shrubbery. Noises from the Brighton foreshore across two miles of ocean—music, people, traffic, laughter—made an unsuitable counterpoint to the weather, and to his mood.

A couple of Gaetano's people were standing nearby, but when she saw him she waved them away. He took off his jacket and offered it. She draped it over her shoulders.

He began "I think I was wrong—"

"Didn't you hear me in there? You've won. You can have your comfort zone, I won't violate it. And I won't try to trick you, or suck you in. So that's my part of the deal, and your part, which you've already told me you'll honour, is to stay for the summit. For the whole of the summit."

"Why are you talking like this?"

"It all kicks off in four days. October 14, the eve-of-summit reception. Then October 15 for nine days or however long it lasts. Are we still agreed?"

"Is this because of the news about Marek?"

"They were saving Marek for later, but something made them decide to reveal him now. They're still active. You stopped their plans for the Signing Room, but they're still coming for me."

"That book you gave me. You went out and looked for it yourself, didn't you? Not your staff, but you."

"Yes."

"Nobody's done anything like that for me before, except maybe Arden."

"Who? Oh yes, her...Well, you tore a page out of your book, and nobody's done anything like that for me. Not even Gaetano. But they're both gestures and they both belong in the past."

He wanted to argue, but couldn't find the right words. Her sermon, the part of it intended for him, had hit him like one of his Verbs. He saw her differently. He was beginning to think he understood her.

"What if I was wrong?"

But she wasn't listening. She had already decided she understood him. "Your obsession about—what do you call it?—The Detail. That's in the past too. If we both survive this I'll tell you. But it'll wipe out what you think you feel for me..."

"How do you know what I think?"

"Because you're looking gormless. God knows what you'd have said if I hadn't interrupted you...And it'll wipe out everything I'd planned for getting closer to you, some of which I'd almost believed would work. But it won't, not with a Consultant. You were right about that. So you've won and I'll leave you alone."

He didn't reply.

"Oh, come on. We can still do the fucking if you want, that doesn't mean anything. We'll each take what we want from it."

"You said that once before."

"This time I mean it."

"You said that once before too. Why are you talking like this?"

"Because you're starting to sound as gormless as you look. I understand you better now. You changed after your meeting with Rafiq, but only on the surface. Underneath you've still got the same one-person comfort zone. And that's just you, I haven't even started about me."

He didn't reply.

"Too much keeping us apart, Anwar. On both sides. Think about it. *Me?* And a *Consultant?* You were right the first time. That train's left the station."

"Maybe it hasn't arrived yet."

"Don't be crass. It's gone. Like I wrote in your book, you mistimed."

"It doesn't have to be like that."

"Yes it does. Listen to yourself. You're in denial. When your head's in the sand, you know what you're talking through."

Again he didn't reply.

"Why do you think I promised to tell you The Detail afterwards? Because we won't be here afterwards. You *really* mistimed. When I thought I wanted you, you were scared to commit. Now you think you want me, but in a few days we won't be here. Even you can't defend me against what they'll send. It will kill you, Anwar! Rafiq knows that. That's why he's left you here on your own. He's saving his best Consultants, however many there are, for when they come for him. He's next, and he knows it."

A noise behind made him whirl round, and both of them gasped. Gaetano was coming towards them, and with him was Arban Proskar.

4

Back at Fallingwater, Arden briefed Rafiq about events at the villa.

UN Intelligence had told her that what happened to Proskar was bad news because, to them, it was. They'd missed him. They traced his entry into Croatia easily enough, as he was travelling openly on his passport, but because of the way he'd left Brighton they expected him to go into Zagreb, where his flight had landed, or on to Dubrovnik; he had family in both cities. They didn't expect him to leave Croatia directly after entering; but that was what he did, slipping over the border into Slovenia, where he used his passport to get a flight back to Britain. For UN Intelligence it was an almost unheard-of error, though his change of mind was a genuine act of impulse. As his plane touched down at Dubrovnik he'd simply decided that he shouldn't walk out on her.

Rafiq's usual courtesy almost slipped during all this. He had trouble concealing his boredom, since it was all academic now. She'd previously told him that the examinations carried out exhaustively on Marek's body at Kuala Lumpur confirmed conclusively the findings of the field examinations carried out at the villa at Opatija. Beyond any doubt it was Parvin Marek, and beyond any doubt he'd been dead, and kept in cold storage, for at least three years. Carefully-worded news releases were already breaking in the media.

While he gazed at Arden, Rafiq saw a number of scenes passing behind his eyes; scenes from ten years ago which he couldn't repeat to her, but didn't need to.

"I know what you're feeling," she told him, and immediately regretted how empty it sounded. For once, her famous empathy had deserted her.

"I was going to tell you," he said, "to let me have an hour privately with the body so I could do things to it. No," he waved down her reply, "it was only a passing thought. Get forensics to take the body. And get *them* to do things to it."

"They already have," she reminded him. "I told you earlier."

"And the families of his other victims? They've been contacted?"

"Yes, all of them. I told you that earlier too."

"Thank you."

5

Olivia rushed past Anwar to Proskar. She took both his hands—those unusual hands—in hers. "Thank you for coming back."

"I couldn't walk out on you, Archbishop."

She kept his hands in hers. "I missed you. And," cocking her head back at Anwar, "*he* has something to say to you."

"I owe you an apology," Anwar said. "And however I word it, it's going to sound inadequate."

"I'm just glad to be back," Proskar said awkwardly. "Let's leave it, we have a lot of work to do."

Olivia still hadn't released his hands. They dwarfed hers. "Are you finally sure," she asked Anwar, "that he isn't Marek? Maybe Arden what's-her-name isn't what she seems. Maybe she switched the bodies. Proskar could be the one getting cut up in Kuala Lumpur while here, before us, we have the real Parvin Marek."

Laughing, the three of them walked away and left him in the Garden. He heard her call back to him over her shoulder, "You mistimed, Anwar."

He thought about her sermon. He'd thought of little else. What she said about her meanness of nature. She didn't do compassion, she preferred to strike at perpetrators rather than comfort victims. Anwar, despite his physical prowess, had never behaved with any particular meanness towards any opponent. He'd just done what was necessary. *There,* he thought, *there's an example of how we could fit together, how we could become more than the total of our individual parts.*

He was still in denial. *Before,* he told himself, *there was nobody. Now, there's nobody else.* He walked over to where she'd dropped his jacket. He picked it up, dusted it carefully down, and put it back on. *"Now, there's nobody else?"* he thought. *"Now, there's nobody else?"*

When you're in denial, you tell yourself ridiculous things. When your head's in the sand, you know what you're talking through. He started laughing at himself, the way he'd laughed at her.

ELEVEN: THE SUMMIT, COMMENCING OCTOBER 15, 2060

1

By October 14, all the delegates had arrived. The New Anglicans had, as expected, attended efficiently to all their needs: dietary, religious, administrative, communications, PR, transport. And security. The huge and complicated security network of which Gaetano was the central part had, like some old brass mechanism, juddered into motion, got up to optimum speed, and was now moving smoothly.

The eve-of-summit reception began in the Conference Centre at 9:00 p.m. on October 14. There was a brief opening address by Olivia. She was smart enough not to over-egg it, or to slip in commercials for the New Anglicans. Her remarks amounted to no more than *Welcome, glad you could come, we're just the hosts but we wish you well, enjoy tonight's gathering.*

She wore her usual long velvet dress. This one was dark green. Anwar found it arousing, but he preferred her in dark red, or purple, or dark blue. *Green,* he thought, *doesn't suit her quite as well.* He still caught himself having thoughts like that.

The security regime he'd agreed on with Gaetano was fully operational. It had been so since he last spoke to her in the Garden, a conversation whose aftertaste wouldn't leave him. At any time she had at least three of Gaetano's staff with her, chosen by Anwar at random each day from Gaetano's "trusted" list. Anwar was also around her for at least twelve hours a day—at services, meetings, press conferences, wherever she went. He hardly let her out of his sight. Only when he slept was he not in her immediate vicinity; and even then he primed himself, catlike, to sleep for the minimum time.

And his parameters had narrowed. Not Who, or Why, or even How, but just Where and When. Who and Why no longer concerned him. He'd got all he'd ever get out of her. Only Where and When mattered now. In a society adept at retro replicas and concealed motives and manufactured identities, Who and Why were the most complicated of the five questions. He didn't have time for them, not anymore.

Anwar moved carefully among and through the delegates, always in Olivia's vicinity without being obviously so. He stayed alone, but kept moving with an expression on his face as though he'd just left one conversation and was on his way to join another. He listened carefully to the smalltalk around him but didn't participate. The way he felt, he'd probably insult or offend anyone who spoke to him.

Something was in his blood and wouldn't let him alone. *Her,* obviously, but he didn't let it affect his watchfulness. Or his obsessiveness.

Yuri Zaitsev was due to join the reception at 10:00, but he didn't arrive until 11:30. He'd been delayed by the debate in the UN General Assembly on Rafiq's running of UNESCO, and the vote of no confidence in Rafiq that he, Zaitsev, had initiated. Rafiq's UNESCO policy was carried by a large majority, and the no-confidence vote was defeated by an even larger one. It didn't put Zaitsev in an ideal frame of mind. He thought he'd covered enough angles on the voting, but Rafiq had covered more, and covered them better. In such things, Yuri Zaitsev wasn't even remotely in the same league as Rafiq.

Zaitsev was furious and mortified, but did his best to conceal it and to make an impressive entrance. He acknowledged the many courtesies, sincere and ironic, which came his way and set about working the room. The reception would go on a little later than intended, but not so late that it would affect the summit.

It was now one minute past midnight on October 15.

A large open area in the Conference Centre, between seating and stage, had been cleared by the removal of the first few rows of seating. Drinks and food were served by circulating waiters, and from tables set up on the stage. The various adjoining rooms on the ground floor of the auditorium (for use during the summit as breakout spaces, subsidiary meeting rooms, and coffee lounges) also had their own food and drink. The huge white and silver auditorium, the walls and ceiling a combination of swooping organic shapes, looked like a replica of the New West Pier seen from inside.

The mezzanine running round the upper levels of the auditorium was now a minstrels' gallery. A string quartet played there, softly and discreetly. The rooms leading off the mezzanine (including the Signing Room) were closed but would be open when the summit began, making more areas for breakout meetings and informal discussions—except for the Signing Room, which would stay shut until the signing ceremony (if any) at the end of the summit. It was still guarded inside: there were never less than three security people in there at any time. Their stay in the room was less conspicuous, less noisy, and more hygienic than Anwar's had been.

Some delegates had gone upstairs to listen more closely to the music, and were leaning over the handrail of the mezzanine balcony, looking down on the main reception. Considering the size of the space and the numbers present, it was fairly quiet. Conversations were animated but not loud. And everywhere, as always, there was the discreet scent of citrus. After a while, Anwar thought as he continued circulating, you got to think that citrus was what white and silver smelt like. Or that white and silver were the colour of citrus.

The Conference Centre didn't look anything like it would look at 10:00 the following morning, when the opening speeches would be made and the summit would commence. The reception should have ended at midnight, but in view of Zaitsev's late arrival it would go on for an hour or so. The New Anglicans had foreseen the delay and prepared for it; their staff would reinstate the front rows of seating, check computers and audio-visual, set up catering and put the whole auditorium into full conference mode before 10:00 a.m.

Extra staff had been recruited to deal with administration, catering, transport, and communications. All of them were checked by Gaetano's people, and double-checked by UN intelligence—a condition of Rafiq's, which (unlike some of his other conditions, when the venue was negotiated) met with no opposition from Olivia.

Anwar continued listening to the smalltalk. He heard a few people repeat the old stories about Olivia having driven a ferociously hard bargain when negotiating for the venue, and Rafiq having hated negotiating with her. Strange, when they should be allies. Arden had said that. So had he, Anwar, to Rafiq. *"I know what she's like. But what she stands for is your concern. If it isn't, it ought to be."*

Also, and more interestingly, he heard references to the New Anglicans, to their rapid growth and most un-Churchlike style, and to their extraordinary New West Pier and Cathedral and Conference Centre. Some delegates hadn't been to Brighton before, and were learning from those who had about its various eccentricities.

Olivia was working the room, discreetly putting over, to a few selected individuals, the commercials for the New Anglicans which she'd been careful to keep out of her welcome speech. Zaitsev and the other VIP participants were also working the room, but from their particular standpoints of what they wanted from the summit: re-establishing contacts, opening new channels, beginning threads they'd pursue later.

The VIPs' and senior delegates' security people—Meatslabs of varying proficiency—stood around and, for the benefit of anyone watching them, looked watchful. Gaetano and his people covered the space much less obviously and much more intelligently. Several of them were joining in the small talk. Anwar liked the way they worked.

Anwar continued circulating. He had an electronic ID badge, as did everybody present. His one said he was a middle-ranking member of Gaetano's staff. Ironically, the surname was Khan—Yusuf Khan, an IT specialist and a man of roughly similar appearance and build, in case anyone cared to check.

Although he tended always to plan for the worst outcome, Anwar didn't expect anything to kick off at the reception. The reception wasn't public, and wasn't being broadcast live. The opening ceremony tomorrow would be, and he'd be covering all vectors and lines of sight which, by now, he knew intimately.

He knew Gaetano would be increasingly occupied with the summit, and since the Garden they'd hardly spoken. Their agreed security regime meant he'd become increasingly occupied with Olivia, though they too had hardly spoken. They both knew they'd moved into the final phase, where he was simply her bodyguard and nothing more.

He hadn't come to terms with her rejection, or his own feelings. But he couldn't decide if either, or both, or neither, were real. He parked it. If she'd been a desk or a chair, or Rafiq himself, the logistics of protecting her would be just the same, and he'd attend to them just as obsessively.

"Mr. Khan?"

Anwar didn't jump at the mention of his original name, or even when he turned round and found himself facing Zaitsev.

"Mr....Yusuf Khan, is it?"

Anwar had never actually met Zaitsev before, and had only seen him from a distance at various functions. He was unprepossessing: jowly and flat-faced, heavily built almost to the point of obesity, though the drape of his expensive suit concealed some of it. Close up, his skin was pock-marked and stubbled. He was one of those people, Anwar thought, who always looked unshaven no matter how much they shaved.

Zaitsev knew about Anwar, or thought he did. Not in detail, or by name, but he suspected Rafiq had sent a Consultant. He'd seen Consultants before—not much, but often enough to suspect Anwar was one. He drew him aside to a more private corner.

"It's an honour to meet you, Mr. Secretary-General," Anwar lied.

"You're one of Rafiq's creatures, aren't you?"

"I'm what my badge says I am, Mr. Secretary-General."

"You look like one of Rafiq's creatures. Are you here to protect my life?"

"I don't know Mr. Rafiq personally," said Anwar, truthfully. "But your life is of no concern to me."

"That's discourteous. You should show more respect for my office. Unlike your owner, I'm democratically elected."

"Yes, this evening you must have a heightened appreciation of the value of voting."

Seeing Zaitsev's expression, two of his retinue of Meatslabs moved closer. They were quite impressive. They would have dwarfed even Levin.

Olivia moved in quickly and extricated him. "Come on, Mr. Khan, you mustn't monopolise the Secretary-General's time..."

Anwar did almost jump then, to hear *her* using his original name.

The music continued, as did the low murmur of conversation. The string quartet played baroque chamber music. In deference to the delegates it should perhaps have been traditional African or Asian music, but no cultural offence was intended or taken. Chamber music was appropriate for the reception. It didn't intrude on the ambience. More traditional regional music would be played during the next few days at the summit's various social events.

Later, as the reception was drawing comfortably to a close, one of Zaitsev's Meatslabs came up to Anwar.

"I don't know what that was about, but you irritated the Secretary-General. Don't do it again. Or I'll tear off your penis, dip it in relish, and make you eat it."

"What kind of relish?"

Anwar watched the chest swelling and nostrils dilating. The chest filled most of his immediate field of vision. He thought, *If he slugs me, I'll just have to take it. I mustn't disable him, not here in front of everyone, that would be stupid.* But the Meatslab's mood subsided and he stalked off. Sometimes Anwar could encourage people to do that, by particular tricks of eye contact and body language that sent out strong warning signs. He'd tried to avoid doing it here, to stay consistent with his temporary identity. *Or maybe I didn't avoid it, and that's why he left so quickly. Or maybe...*

Midnight had come and gone. It was now October 15, the first day of the summit.

He and Olivia had only nine days left together. Maybe less than nine days. Maybe a lot less. Things were coming to a climax, but also coming to an end.

2

October 15 was moving round the earth. When it reached Brighton, it had already been in Kuala Lumpur for seven hours.

Rafiq, surrounded by unseen security, walked through the park in front of Fallingwater. He was smoking, which occasionally he did at the start of a particularly significant day. He rarely smoked more than once a day, but Arden Bierce still faintly disapproved; yet she still carried a lighter in case he forgot his.

She came up to him.

"What are you doing, smoking a cigarette?"

"By the rules of linguistics, that question's unanswerable."

She felt like rolling her eyes. Then she thought of all that had happened in the last few hours, particularly the news about Marek. She couldn't imagine the effect it must have had on him.

She tried to change to a subject he might find a bit more congenial. "The Secretary-General turned up late for the eve-of-summit reception in Brighton. Late, and in a bad mood. You really did a job on him."

"Yes, I think he's back in his cage for a while. But he's not as stupid as he looks."

"Or as clever as he thinks."

Rafiq smiled an acknowledgement. "Still, you shouldn't have had to tell me twice about Marek's autopsy, or the press releases, or contacting the families. I should have been on top of those things, but when I heard his body was found..."

"It's understandable."

"No it isn't. In this job, the first rule is that nothing ever lets up. Do you remember the day my family was killed?"

"Of course I do."

"There was a General Assembly debate that evening; one of Zaitsev's predecessors, attacking my restructuring of one of the agencies. I don't even remember which one. But the debate wasn't postponed. Just like yesterday's wasn't."

"Yes. But you won both of them. You outlasted the man who initiated that debate, and you'll outlast the man who initiated this one."

It was exactly the right thing to say, at exactly the right time. She always did that. She was a settled person, comfortable with herself, and she made Rafiq feel comfortable.

"When I eventually retire, which won't be yet, you'll be one of the contenders to take over. But not one of the leading contenders. Do you know why?"

"Tell me."

"You're not ruthless or ambitious enough. But what you are is good with people. They like your company."

"Why are you telling me this, Mr. Rafiq?"

"Because it might explain what I say next. I like your company too. I'd like us to meet, socially. Have dinner or go to the theatre or something. It's time I had a companion."

"Are you saying you'd like an attachment?"

"Well...yes. But to start, just your company."

"I didn't see that coming."

"I hadn't planned to ask you. I mean, I had, but I'd been putting it off. And now Marek's definitely dead, maybe I can move on."

She didn't reply.

"So, can we just start seeing each other?"

She paused. "I'd like to park it for a while."

"Why?"

"Well, first there's Anwar."

"Anwar won't..."

"Won't survive the summit?"

"I was going to say won't even notice, because of Olivia, but yes, I'm afraid he won't survive. And neither will Olivia. They've got maybe nine days together."

"If they're together," she said.

"Yes, it seems he never stops calling you about that. First she'd like a relationship, then not. Then he'd like one, then not. They've both got their heads up their asses." He found himself fighting a temptation to add *Up their own, not each other's*. He had little time for either of them. He'd never taken to Olivia, for some reason. And Anwar's obsessions, private dark imaginings, and anal-retentive interior world were starting to get tiresome. They reminded Rafiq of what he'd once become, ten years ago. *Abbas. It should be Abyss.*

She was silent. Thinking that their relationship, if it happened and if that was the right word for it, might be as ambiguous as Anwar and Olivia's.

Rafiq might almost have heard her thoughts. "It doesn't have to be a full-blown attachment, if that makes you uneasy. And it doesn't have to be physical, though I'd like it if it was. It's been a long time...Now I know for certain Marek's dead, it's time to move on. My family died ten years ago. I'd like to find someone."

"I understand."

"You said *first* there's Anwar. Was there anything else?"

With Rafiq, she knew, you had to examine your words minutely, because he'd be examining them minutely too. And your inflections and body language. In that way he was like a Consultant, but he did it naturally. Like her empathy, it was a gift he'd always had.

"Was there anything else?" he repeated.

"I'm taller than you," she said, straightfaced. "And you smoke."

"Most people are taller than me. My wife was. And I didn't smoke while she was alive."

She was silent again.

"So what do you think?"

"It can't start until after the summit. Anwar needs my full attention. Also..."

"Yes?"

"Are you holding something back about Anwar's mission?"

"I always hold things back. But about his mission, no." He looked directly into her eyes when he said it; but he was good at doing that. *The most important thing is sincerity. If you can fake that, you can fake anything.* Still, she believed him, on balance. Her empathy against his labyrinthine cunning, and on balance she believed him.

"There's something about his mission that's worrying me," she said. "I can't quite find it yet."

"Like Anwar and his Detail. Remember him going on about it when he came here?"

"He goes on about it to me, too. Almost as much as he goes on about *her*. I don't think that my Detail is the same as his, but it's there somewhere. I will find it."

For once, he was silent.

"And," she added, "there's something else."

"Another Detail?"

"Maybe. When I said park it, I meant only that. I didn't mean abandon it or forget it." She looked directly into his eyes. "I'll help Anwar through this, if I can. But when it's over, you and I have unfinished business. Laurens."

3

The opening ceremony began at exactly 10:00 a.m. It was large-scale and well attended. In addition to the delegates there were august non-participants and well-wishers like the British Prime Minister and Foreign Secretary, the Mayor of Brighton, and the Old Anglicans' Archbishops of Canterbury and Rochester. And their entourages, including a security complement for each. It was a huge arrangement of interlocking and interfacing mechanisms that Gaetano somehow contrived to keep moving. Anwar hadn't seen him or spoken to him much during the last few days.

There was also a large media presence, not only in the Conference Centre but also at Gateway, to cover the VIPs as they arrived. Paths were cleared for them, but the Pier was not closed to the public. Tourists and sightseers still milled around as usual, as did the people who worked in the Pier's business district. One maglev was set aside for the summit participants, and paths were cordoned off where they disembarked for the delegates to walk through the Garden, or the squares and piazzas of the business district, on their way to the Conference Centre.

All the major UN members were present. Countries not directly involved in water rights disputes sent ministers or senior civil servants. Those directly involved—sometimes to the extent of being at war with each other—sent heads of state.

The delegates and other participants were seated in the main auditorium, facing the stage on which the top table was set. The people who would usually occupy the top table during the proceedings were Zaitsev and five others. Zaitsev would be chairing the summit. The others were the members of the committee responsible for drafting the Agenda—a mixture of retired diplomats, senior civil servants and UN officials. For the opening ceremony they were joined by Olivia.

She again gave a short, non-political opening address. "Welcome. We're proud to be your hosts, and we hope you'll find the arrangements work well and assist your deliberations. We wish you every success. It would be nice to look back on this summit and think that we helped to make it productive."

Zaitsev gave a rather more fulsome opening address. Anwar recognized many of the phrases from Rafiq's briefing; Zaitsev must have picked them up in conversation with Rafiq. He used them without attribution, of course.

"Thirty years ago, this summit would have been about fossil fuels—oil, gas, maybe coal and shale. Thirty years ago, fossil fuels were limited. They still are. But now we have alternative energy sources, and we've made them commercially viable: wind, sun, tides, high-atmosphere turbulence, nuclear fusion, hydrogen cells, even continental drift. So we've come to Brighton, to this magnificent venue, not to talk about energy sources, but about something much more basic. Something ever-present, but ever-scarce where it's most needed: water."

Zaitsev's voice was more suited to oratory than conversation. In conversation it sounded harsh and rasping. In oratory it was deep and modulated, slightly tremulous with manly but restrained emotion at the important bits. A better actor than Rafiq.

"Some of the UN member states represented here have been at war over water rights. Some still are. It's inconceivable to me that we could be on the way to making energy shortages a thing of the past, while water shortages are still a thing of the present. It's inconceivable to me that people are dying over a substance which is more abundant in the world than fossil fuels ever were. With your help and goodwill, we'll leave here nearer to a solution than when we arrived."

Anwar found himself joining in the applause, and grudgingly admitted that Zaitsev was good. Cleverer than he looked. But the ultimate success of this summit would be decided not by what was said here, but by what was done later by Rafiq.

Rafiq couldn't have matched Zaitsev's oratory, but he would never need to. As clever as Zaitsev might be, Rafiq was cleverer still, distancing himself by professing to deal only with executive matters, not policy. He used Zaitsev, or whoever else was Secretary-General at the time, as a human shield. The media would often try to draw him out on matters of policy, but without success. Political matters, he would intone virtuously, and monotonously, are not the province of the unelected executive arm.

I first got that briefing, Anwar thought, *about two weeks ago. It seems longer than that.* He was annoyed at his readiness to join in the applause. All Zaitsev had done was to retail, in a slightly better voice, content he'd picked up from Rafiq.

Anwar would have liked to do an immersion hologram, like the ones he did in his teens, with them all naked.

Especially Zaitsev. Somewhere in the deep interior darkness of Zaitsev's capacious trousers, a pair of large buttocks lurked like a couple of conjoined cave bears. *Oh for an immersion hologram,* he thought, *to bring them walloping and wobbling into the daylight.*

4

She hadn't seen it coming, but when it was out in the open she knew it was right. Rafiq was right for her, and she for him. They had a new life waiting.

Rafiq had gone off to meetings, leaving Arden in the parkland in front of Fallingwater. What they had spoken of was pivotal. Whatever would take place between them was on hold until after the summit, but then it would resume. She'd make sure of it. And then the detail would kick in.

Her life would change. She'd have to leave the UN, and hand over to someone else; it would be unprofessional to continue working with Rafiq if they became more than colleagues. As she knew they would.

A move to another part of UNEX, or even the wider UN, wouldn't work. She'd have to find a new career, which wouldn't be difficult with her CV, but at this point she couldn't imagine herself anywhere else. And she couldn't imagine leaving before her own part in this was finished. She wouldn't need to leave immediately after the summit concluded. However it turned out, there would be time to finish her work before the media got wind that she and Rafiq were an item.

Which meant she had a bit longer than Anwar to find what worried her about his mission. *No, that's stupid.* So stupid she almost laughed out loud. She *had* to find it in nine days or less, because Anwar *had* to be told what it was before they made their move.

They. Them. She couldn't bring herself to call them The Cell; it sounded theatrical, though it was probably accurate. Anwar was right about that: they could only operate on such a scale, over such a long time, if they operated as a cell. Like Black Dawn, but with apparently limitless resources. And an inbuilt sense of timing. They knew exactly when to emerge and when to go back.

Except this time. Maybe Anwar's rather gauche sojourn in the Signing Room had made them change their timing. Otherwise they wouldn't have revealed what happened to Marek. She felt they'd been planning to play that card during the summit, as a final massive misdirection before they moved for Olivia, and something had made them play it early.

They stayed enigmatic, wrapped in the stuff of conspiracy theories. It magnified their threat. They'd even invented the concept of Conspiracy Theory, made it an urban myth—like Rafiq did, on a smaller scale, with his Tournament rumours. Made it the province of cranks. Marginalised it. And amplified it at the same time.

They only emerged once or twice in a lifetime, to give history a nudge. Other than that, they existed, but didn't *do*. They weren't part of anybody's landscape, or anybody's living memory. They were part of the long slow circling of history. Individuals lived and died and were replaced, but goals remained. Individuals were traceable and vulnerable; goals, if part of a long game, weren't.

Like Anwar, they came out of their comfort zone, struck, and went back. But they followed different ends and used different means. In a world pervaded by electronic comms, they simply used handwriting and bits of paper, and made themselves untraceable. *Laurens does the same, of course,* she thought, *but he does it for reasons of style. He has a singular sense of style.*

And they used Special Forces, but only for low-grade wet work. They didn't have the UN's techniques of physical and neurological enhancement, so they couldn't make them into rivals of The Dead. Not the ones she and Anwar had questioned, certainly.

But they had something that had killed Levin and Asika.

And that summarised all that she knew about them. The last point might yield something, but hadn't so far, and otherwise there wasn't much more she could usefully learn. So she parked it, and considered other routes: what they did, and who they employed to do it.

Nine days or less.

5

Anwar recalled what Rafiq once told him. The more established major members—the Americans and Chinese and Europeans—liked to think of the UN as a corporation, with themselves as shareholders. "They're wrong," he said. "My part, the unelected part, is like a corporation. But Zaitsev's part, the political part, isn't. It's just a microcosm of the world, with all the world's history and hatreds and differences. Those things don't go away just because you put them into a General Assembly." Or into a summit, like this one.

The most powerful UN members were currently America, China, Europe, Brazil, Indonesia, and India. Russia and Japan were now less important, politically and economically: Japanese manufacturing and electronics had been overtaken by China and India, and Russian natural resources were worth less now that new energy sources were becoming viable. Russia still remained a Security Council member, but the new energy geopolitics might eventually change even that. Middle Eastern countries were less important for the same reason.

After the opening ceremony, the real business commenced and fault lines already began to appear. Olivia stayed to listen, and so, therefore, did Anwar. He sat a few rows back from her, absorbing lines of sight and possible angles of attack. He sensed from voice inflections and body language that things weren't going well, but he didn't listen closely to the words: only enough to know that the early objections were not about detailed Agenda items, but about the Agenda's very existence.

Other honorary guests and worthies who came for the ceremony gradually left, not wishing to be associated with the process of real business and real disagreements. But, to their credit, the two Archbishops from the Old Anglicans did stay on for an hour or so. They adjourned with Olivia afterwards for a private meeting in one of the adjoining rooms leading off from the main auditorium. Anwar waited discreetly at a distance, covering the door and listening to the discord between the delegates.

Gaetano's briefing to Anwar was as thorough as one of Rafiq's. It included the latest version of the Agenda. Anwar had studied it carefully. It set out to define policies and codes of conduct—not diverting or damming rivers to deny water downstream, reforestation to ensure rainwater didn't run off uselessly, no dumping of untreated waste, desalination technology, and much more. It aimed to identify and define what it termed Guiding Principles which, when agreed, could be applied to the several current disputes, and even wars, between some of the members present.

The Agenda was a document that had been negotiated almost as fiercely as water rights themselves. And, only a few hours into the first day, it was unravelling.

6

Parvin Marek had been theirs. Their instrument.

He was a freak of nature. Normal family, ordinary upbringing, average accomplishments. Averagely gregarious. No special talents or failings. Not bullied or sexually abused. Then, in his twenties, a dark light switched on inside him. It made him brilliant and monstrous. Nihilism was his religion.

Arden had no detailed proof that he'd been one of theirs at the time of Black Dawn, but all her instincts suggested it. His particular role had probably been to destabilise Balkan politics, or to provide misdirection while they destabilised politics in more important areas. He was notable only because his agenda and philosophy were unlike anyone else's. That would have been his value to them. He didn't kill as many people as other terrorists, particularly the religiously-motivated ones, but he killed them more unexpectedly.

And he went back. At the UN Embassy in Zagreb, with passers-by. At Fallingwater, with Rafiq's family. He went back, shot them in the head to make sure they were dead. *How could you survive that, Laurens, and still come back here?*

But that was as far as that particular route took her. Interesting historically, but Marek was dead.

She considered their other instruments.

Richard Carne was one of their minor functionaries. One of many. He'd been in London to address the Johnsonian Society. Only a short trip from there to Brighton. He wouldn't have been privy to his employers' detailed plans for Olivia, but possibly he'd heard something—enough to make him want to take a stroll round the famous New West Pier. Maybe he just wanted to see the Cathedral and Conference Centre where it would happen. He wasn't doing detailed planning; those he worked for would have done that long ago. Maybe this was just idle curiosity, and genuine coincidence.

Or was it? Maybe they'd sent Carne deliberately. Or maybe they'd known he'd go to Brighton anyway. Either way, they'd known Anwar would want to question him personally, and they'd known Carne would defeat Anwar in the questioning. Not just defeat him, but leave him reeling.

She'd studied exhaustively what Carne had told Anwar. Hines had told him similar things. So had the five like Carne and Hines who she'd questioned. But, even though she hadn't been present, there was something about Carne's questioning to which she needed to return. *Park it for now. It might surface when I stop looking for it.*

At the end of the first day, Anwar was with Olivia in her bedroom. He slept there now, and would do until the summit was over. The day before the summit began, he had decided to go to full close-protection mode.

"I'll take the sofa," he told her. "Don't worry about these chocolate wrappers, I'll move them."

She didn't answer.

"And the bits of paper. And the discarded clothes."

Fuck you the ginger cat meaowed from somewhere underneath the sofa.

"You know, I always imagined you more with a Siamese cat."

"Why?" she asked, reluctantly. She'd have preferred to avoid conversations with him about anything except security matters.

"A better fashion accessory. Similar shape and similar eye colour."

She said nothing, which was what she should have done the first time.

Fuck you the ginger cat meaowed again.

Zaitsev's suite, like Anwar's, was on the floor below. Zaitsev's security people were there constantly, in shifts. Anwar's temporary identity would have made it plausible for him to be visiting her bedroom; her reputation for coming on to any male within reach of her pheromones was well known. But Anwar, after the brush with Zaitsev and his minders at the reception, preferred not to be seen there.

He didn't like her bedroom. The untidiness. And the dark voluptuous colours, which he liked on her dresses, but which were overpowering and intrusive as decor. He'd come to like the customary silver and white, and this was the only interior on the New West Pier—at least the only New Anglican interior—that didn't have those colours.

He watched her sleeping. As usual, when she'd finished with sex or when (as he now knew) she had nobody else in bed with her, she fell asleep quickly and slept soundly. Her appetite for sleep, like her appetites for food and sex, came on suddenly and overwhelmingly, to the exclusion of everything else.

She isn't real, he thought bitterly. Her appetites. Her mood swings. Her initial failure to notice him. Then she did. Then she wanted an involvement but maybe didn't, then she didn't but maybe did.

He wasn't real either. His motives changed in response to hers, always the opposite and (like hers) maybe secretly containing the reverse of the opposite. Containers and contents. But his motives, he could explain. They were the products of his obsessiveness and self-absorption, which in turn were the products of his occupation. How could he explain hers? He couldn't. She wasn't real.

7

The summit droned on. It was the second day, October 16. The proceedings should have belonged in an atmosphere of dark wood and dust motes, not in this huge white-and-silver space with curving pearlescent walls and cool citrus air and perfect acoustics. It really was a very good venue. It got cooler and fresher and more pleasant as the proceedings got more contentious.

Olivia stayed to the first coffee break, then discreetly left. So did Anwar. She went across the Garden, into the Cathedral, and up to the Boardroom where she attended a series of routine meetings. So did Anwar.

The meetings in the Boardroom were beginning to drag, and Anwar made a decision.

Olivia was surrounded by colleagues and her normal guard of three trusted people in addition to Anwar. Proskar—who, at last, Anwar had learnt could also be trusted—had entered, not as a guard but as a participant in the meeting.

Anwar made eye contact, mouthed, "Thirty minutes," and raised an eyebrow. She nodded.

He went back to the Conference Centre. The summit didn't sound like it was going any better than when he'd last been there, but he wasn't presently concerned with the summit. He managed to sidle through the main auditorium relatively unnoticed and mounted the staircase to the mezzanine. He walked along it, trailing his arm along the balcony rail, until he came to the Signing Room doors, which he opened and entered.

There were three of Gaetano's staff, a woman and two men. They were heavily armed. They were sufficiently awake to train their weapons quickly and easily on the opening doors, though they'd probably been hours doing absolutely nothing. The Signing Room was pristine and undisturbed. The fake wall panelling looked as out of place, against the original curving silver and white walls, as it always did. But nothing had happened; no disturbances, no intrusions.

Their conversation with Anwar was lively and polite. Such monotonous duties, even in shifts, might have made them casual or resentful or careless, but they were none of these things. Anwar had never seen any traditional Meatslab tendencies among Gaetano's people. They were never sloppy.

It was the second day of the summit. Anwar had visited the Signing Room on the first day, and planned to visit it on the third and fourth and beyond, at least once a day. It meant he'd be leaving *her* for a few minutes, but he'd have to do it. The Signing Room had a special resonance for him. Although, the way the summit was going, it might not be needed.

Six thousand miles and seven hours away, Arden Bierce was about to call Anwar and ask for another eidetic account of his questioning of Carne. She didn't. Not because he wouldn't be able to do it, but because she wouldn't learn any more. There was nothing he'd left out the first time. It wasn't a matter of finding something he'd overlooked. Anwar remembered everything and overlooked nothing: that was how he'd been made. This was about interpreting what he'd remembered, and that was her territory, and she'd have to go over it again and again. Until then, she couldn't go to Anwar. Not during the summit.

She tutted irritably; not something she did often. *Keep looking for it,* she told herself, *until it finds you.*

8

The summit moved on to its third day, October 17. Olivia only attended the morning session for a few minutes, and so, consequently, did Anwar.

It was descending into chaos. The breakout sessions for mediation weren't working. Members were adopting extreme positions. Nobody was prepared to take a decisive first step until everybody else was. The usual standoff, which he'd heard Olivia describe contemptuously as, "I won't put anything right until you put everything else right." It struck a chord with him. It was the same attitude he'd often heard Rafiq describe in equally contemptuous terms. They both stood for its opposite: making some things better while you can.

The detail of it was something Anwar would normally have found absorbing, but he blanked it out. He'd also have found the delegates absorbing, but he blanked them out too. Africans, Asians, Latin Americans, Eastern Europeans. All at a strange economic and political cusp which in time would make America and Europe irrelevant. Maybe even China and India.

But the delegates weren't within his compass. They weren't what he was looking for. Or guarding her from. If they were, Gaetano would have found out and would have told him. He had to trust Gaetano to watch the known people, all checked and double-checked, and Gaetano had to trust him to look for the others, either unknown, or known but with something inside them that hadn't been seen before.

There were hundreds of faces and names, each with a profile detailing individual history, background, and minutiae of behaviour. He carried them all in his memory. Nothing, so far. He was used to analysing microscopic deviations from normality, and hadn't seen any yet. It was beginning to worry him. Days were piling up, with no sign of any move against her. He had the abilities (maybe) to stop it when it came, but not the temperament to wait when it didn't come. He didn't like things so open-ended.

He was pleased when she left and returned to the Boardroom, allowing him to follow her out discreetly.

Back in the Boardroom she took a succession of internal meetings on the Outreach Foundation. This time Anwar, who'd parked himself in one of the adjoining rooms—the one where he'd questioned Carne—did listen. He found it absorbing. It proceeded smoothly and efficiently, closing point after point, steadily building a whole corporate edifice. The senior New Anglican officials impressed Anwar almost as much as Olivia herself. Even her Finance Director, whose unwise attempt to slip something past her he still remembered, was smart and well-prepared. They all were.

He'd long ago ceased wondering whether the New Anglicans were a Church, a corporation, a political move-ment, a gangland syndicate, or a mix of all four. Today the answer was obvious. Today, they were in full corporate mode. It contrasted starkly to the summit, just across the Garden.

The Outreach Foundation was rapidly taking on life and shape. *And all because I made that remark to her in Brighton.*

Olivia visited the auditorium briefly on the afternoon of October 17, and Anwar managed to check the Signing Room, where he found everything in order. The summit was any-thing but in order. The impasse had gone on all morning and threatened to go on all afternoon.

Zaitsev tried desperately to bring it back on line. The reception for that evening was moved to the following day, and replaced with an all-night session. It broke up at 4:00 a.m. without any significant progress. Two members were on the verge of walking out, and Zaitsev managed—just—to persuade them to stay. But he was looking and sounding ragged, and the atmosphere was foul.

October 18, day four of the summit, was no better. After the failed all-night session, the atmosphere hadn't improved. It was in stark contrast to what was going on all around the Conference Centre.

The New West Pier had been deliberately kept open to the public and to normal business. There were sightseers in the Garden, worshippers in the Cathedral, people coming and going in the business quarter, coffees and meals being served in restaurants in the piazzas. And everywhere there were media. The contrast between the summit and the rest of the New West Pier, where there was business as usual, was not lost on them. After the bright opening ceremony, the Troubled Summit phrase began to resurface.

Zaitsev was clearly floundering and the media, like their oceanic counterparts, detected him thrashing around and zeroed in. Some of them, perhaps rather spitefully, recalled the collapse of his attempt to get a vote of no confidence in Rafiq at the General Assembly, and compared it to the imminent collapse of the summit. Zaitsev, they were saying, was the new slang for Collapse.

But if most of the negative media comment was centred on Zaitsev, Olivia wasn't immune either. Although there was praise for the New Anglicans' venue and facilities and organisation, there was renewed speculation about her position. Especially after her puzzling and ambiguous Evensong sermon.

Anwar looked around the auditorium. The usual three people were covering her, but the angles and distances weren't ideal for him to leave her while he checked the Signing Room. So he suggested she should go with him.

"I must check with Gaetano," she said. "He told me not to go there until the Signing."

"He's busy. And," Anwar added drily, "I think he'd give you special dispensation this time."

A couple of days ago he would have worried about being seen so much around her, but it didn't matter now. Zaitsev's security had already noticed and had raised it with Gaetano, whose explanation—ironically—was No, he isn't security, he's just her current sexual partner. They'd probably check, but it didn't matter. The end time was approaching.

They entered the Signing Room. She greeted the three security people there—two women and a man this time—and looked around her.

"I really don't like the two styles together," she said.

"Neither do I."

"It's spotless now. It was full of dust and muck for five days, they told me. And you were here all that time."

He glanced at her.

"Can we," she said, "move over to the far end?" (It was the end where he'd kept his bucket, but he didn't tell her.)

"Of course. Why?"

"There's something I need to say to you privately. I've been thinking about it for a long time."

He felt a stirring, which died abruptly at what she said next.

"If I really felt anything for you, I'd let you go now and give you a chance to survive. In fact, I do feel something—guilt at dragging you into this. So, you can go if you want."

"You're speaking to the gallery. You know I won't go." He added, "All the things you fight for are things I believe in. I should be proud to protect you, but I'm not. Not particularly. That may be you or me, or both of us, I don't know."

She said nothing.

"But I won't walk away."

On the evening of October 18, the social function postponed from the previous night took place. Like the eve-of-summit reception, it was held in the Conference Centre. This time, however, the media were allowed in.

The music was a compilation of old African recordings: mostly Congolese Rumba, with artists like Awilo Longomba and Koffi Olomide. The style was Big Band, with jazz and

Cuban influences: trumpets, saxophones, drums (Western and African), keyboards, and guitars. Joyous, affirming music, upbeat and foot-tapping and infectious.

But it was out of place with the mood of the evening. The summit was collapsing.

Tucked into the middle of the compilation was a song called Ebale Ya Zaire, written by Simaro Lutumba. There was the same big band lineup, but this time it alternated with a solo voice and a single guitar. The singer was Sam Mangwana. His voice was distinctive and wistful. Anwar spoke several languages fluently, but had only a working knowledge of Lingala—enough, however, to identify the words.

The deep river changes its course with the seasons...

Anwar almost laughed out loud. Someone with a sense of irony had put this compilation together. Water rights disputes often arose because one state dammed or diverted a river, stopping water from reaching states downriver. They would claim that they weren't deliberately diverting the river, that it changed course naturally with the changing seasons. And more irony—this song wasn't about just any river, but the deepest in the world, and one of the largest: the River Zaire.

And, later in the song, two other lines:

The one you reject, is the one who ends up loving you the most.

The one you run away from, chases after you the most...

Love. It probably didn't exist, but if it did, it came and went with a deliberate perversity of timing. Like a lighthouse beam switching on and off. On when ships weren't in danger of being wrecked, off when they were.

Anwar didn't laugh at that.

Olivia was there, circulating. A few people came on to her. She wasn't interested. One of them, a tall grey-haired man in elegant robes, was more persistent than the others. When she didn't respond, he made small talk for a few minutes and then took his leave courteously.

"Who was that?" Anwar asked her.

"The Foreign Minister of the United Federation of Congo and Kinshasa."

United Federation of Congo and Kinshasa. In Lingala it made perfect sense, but in French, the old colonial language, the initials were unfortunate.

"You should introduce him to the President of Vietnam. *The Heart of Darkness* meets *Apocalypse Now.*"

"I don't understand...Oh, your old books again."

9

Arden was working late at Fallingwater. The rest of Rafiq's staff had gone. Rafiq came out of his inner office and walked over to her.

"You're working too late to be effective," he told her. "Give it a rest."

"I can't. I have until October 23, maybe less, to find whatever it is. I have to find it. It might be something Anwar needs."

By unspoken agreement neither of them had mentioned, or would mention, what took place between them until after the summit. Rafiq paused before he spoke next.

"You have a lot less than that. The summit will finish early."

"Yes. The Troubled Summit. It's already collapsing."

"No, it'll finish early because it will succeed. Unexpectedly. There will be a breakthrough."

She glanced up at him sharply. "What are you up to, Laurens?"

"What I'm usually up to. What I get paid for. You've got maybe three or four days. Arden."

Olivia attended the summit's morning session on its fifth day, October 19. Anwar was there too, at a discreet distance. The proceedings were only a few minutes old and the previous days' hostilities were already being fully resumed. The atmosphere was rancid.

Then something strange happened.

Olivia and Anwar were sitting in the auditorium, with the main body of delegates and participants. Zaitsev as usual was at the top table on the stage, chairing the morning's proceedings along with the members of the committee who had drafted the now increasingly beleaguered Agenda. Zaitsev's security people were placed at strategic points—all the obvious ones Anwar would think of looking for—around the stage and auditorium. Suddenly one of them strode quickly onto the stage and towards Zaitsev. He wasn't the one with whom Anwar had exchanged words at the reception. This one was bigger.

For a moment Anwar had a surreal feeling that Zaitsev was about to be assassinated by one of his own people. But the Meatslab walked rapidly over, went to whisper something in Zaitsev's ear, thought better of it in view of the mikes and cameras trained on the stage from all angles, and used hand gestures—more like semaphore, given his size—to ask to borrow his pen. Zaitsev passed it to him, but he couldn't make it open. Patiently, Zaitsev indicated the button on the side of the pen's barrel, and did sign language with his thumb to demonstrate how to open it. Then he had to ask Zaitsev for some paper, and the dumb show was in danger of repeating itself until one of the others at the top table passed him a notebook. He scribbled something and handed it to Zaitsev. Zaitsev stared at it for what seemed like a long time, then got up and announced he had to leave for a few minutes. He got one of the others on the top table to chair the proceedings while he was away, and then walked rapidly off the stage and out of the auditorium.

He returned an hour later. He looked shockingly different. Either devastated or exultant, but obviously consumed by something that wasn't consuming him when he left. He waved away requests for him to resume the Chair, and sat silent and rigid while the fractious proceedings continued to get more fractious. He was actually trembling.

What was that *about?* Anwar asked himself. Even he couldn't read Zaitsev's body language or voice inflections reliably. One of the very few occasions when he couldn't. But he knew one person who might know.

"It was a call from Rafiq," Gaetano told him. Olivia had left the summit, with Anwar in tow, to attend another Outreach meeting in the Boardroom. Anwar had got her to stop in the piazza in front of the Conference Centre so he could call Gaetano.

"And," Gaetano continued, "I understand it was followed by a flurry of calls between Rafiq's staff and Zaitsev's. They're still going on now. And no," he said, anticipating Anwar's next question, " I don't know the substance of the calls, any more than you do. But something is changing. Very quickly."

"Gaetano," Olivia said, into Anwar's wristcom, "tell them to put the Outreach meeting on hold. I'm going back to the summit."

Zaitsev sat for a few minutes, still visibly trembling. Eventually he told the acting Chairman (a retired UN diplomat) that he was ready to resume the Chair.

The auditorium was silent.

"The Agenda..." Zaitsev began, then stopped. His voice was high-pitched and feverish. He cleared his throat, and began again. "The Agenda of this summit was agreed after hours of preparatory negotiation. It contains," he was now reading from the Preamble, "detailed proposals, painstakingly computer-modelled and costed, to establish Guiding Principles and codes of conduct to address all water resources disputes—damming, diverting, forestation, and other matters—plus detailed schedules for individual discussions between those most affected, coming back to collective discussions when the individual discussions have borne fruit..."

There was more, and he read it all. It was a typical UN document: logical, rational, with infinite possibilities for subsequent spin, and leaving enough room to cobble something together for the signing. He read it slowly and magisterially, to the annoyance of the delegates who, having argued about it for five days, already knew it quite well enough.

"So: the Agenda." Theatrically, he held it up between thumb and forefinger, and brandished it.

"And you know what we're going to do with it? Tear it up."

He proceeded to do so, scattering pieces on the stage.

"Tear it up. Throw it away. All of it. I have something better."

10

After the uproar died down, the summit got into the particulars of what Zaitsev had for them. Then the uproar began again, but this time in a different tone.

When the summit broke for lunch at midday on October 19, Olivia returned with Anwar to her bedroom. They'd said nothing to each other since leaving the Conference Centre, and didn't now. They didn't know where to begin.

She switched on the newscasts.

"...this morning's developments at Brighton. UN Secretary-General Zaitsev left the summit abruptly, and returned an hour later. Whatever happened in that hour inspired him to take the summit down a new and quite unexpected road. Some say it could make history. This commentator would still counsel a degree of caution, as some consequential details remain to be settled. But it is, without doubt, an extraordinary development. The summit looked to be on the point of collapse. Now it looks to be on the point of achieving something far beyond the Agenda, which Zaitsev rather theatrically tore up, live on stage, before outlining his new initiative."

"Seems to have taken everyone by surprise," she said.

"Including Zaitsev."

"What?"

"Switch to one of the science channels. See what they say."

She did. There was a studio discussion going on between two people, probably environmental journalists drafted to cover the developments.

"...so this is a risk, but an intelligently calculated risk," one of them was saying. He had the complexion and facial mobility of a waxwork, and wore a brown suit whose cut made Anwar wince almost as much as its colour. "Zaitsev will be getting the UN to invest money and technology in this venture. But the money and technology both come originally from UNEX. Ironic, no?"

"Absolutely. I wonder if Rafiq would still have released the technology if Zaitsev had won that no-confidence vote a few days ago?" The answering speaker looked like a TV evangelist: bouffant hair, smooth complexion, perfect teeth, expansive smile.

"I think," said Brown Suit, "that our colleagues in the news channels would say that Rafiq knew exactly how that vote was going to go. But what about this UNEX technology?"

"Ah," said the TV evangelist, "that's even more interesting. There are the energy sources, of course. Rafiq's been committing UNEX for years to making new energy sources viable. Not just those Zaitsev mentioned in his opening address: wind, tides, fusion. That's old hat." The evangelist sat forward, eyes greedy. "It's those wonderful aircraft that UNEX has, the VSTOLs. Those beautiful silver planes that are so much better than everyone else's. They use superconductors. That's the future, right there, and Rafiq is going to let us see inside his magic shop!"

The voices droned on. Anwar got up and walked out onto Olivia's balcony. After checking she was still within his line of sight, he turned and looked out, back towards the seafront. He could see and hear celebrations: fireworks, horns sounding, and the i-360 Tower shining its night illuminations, still bright even at midday. News travelled fast. Nothing had been signed yet, of course, but there was plenty to celebrate. A UN summit, for the first time, was about to embark on something genuinely radical and different, and it would be good for Brighton.

"It would be nice to look back on this summit," she'd said, "and think that we helped to make it productive."

He stayed out on her balcony for a while longer. The weather was chilly and the sea was gunmetal blue, but there was some sharp pale sunlight of the kind you sometimes get in October. He would have continued to stay there, but she called to him from inside.

"Come and listen to this."

She'd switched back to one of the main news channels. Zaitsev was being interviewed by a well-known current-affairs journalist. She looked like a politician's mistress: young enough to be jailbait, pneumatic enough to be a scaled-up Barbie. Amanda Mapplethorpe, said the badge that had carried her smiling through several layers of security.

"Yes, we made good progress this morning," Zaitsev was telling her. To say he looked pleased would have been an understatement. He looked as though he could hardly contain himself, though he kept his words and voice carefully statesmanlike. "I hope we can agree on the broad principles this afternoon and then move on to draft a Statement of Intent. We should have it ready for signing sometime tomorrow."

Anwar and Olivia exchanged glances, but said nothing.

Tomorrow, Anwar thought. *So when will they make their move?* Although he knew it wouldn't have any practical value, he closed the glass doors to her balcony and pulled the curtains. They continued watching the interview.

"So, Mr. Secretary-General," asked Barbie, "are you satisfied the technology is reliable?"

"Oh yes, it's all part of the UN's long-term development programme."

"Then why hasn't it been made available before?"

"Excuse me?"

"You said, 'It's inconceivable to me that we could be on the way to making energy shortages a thing of the past, while water shortages are still a thing of the present.'" She did a passable imitation of Zaitsev's diction and style. "So why hasn't it been made available before?"

Zaitsev smiled indulgently. "It's a fair point, and you're right to raise it. The same question was asked this morning at the summit. And answered. The technology we'll make available didn't suddenly spring fully-formed from nowhere. The UN has been developing it carefully over years."

"Don't you mean UNEX?" Barbie asked, politely.

Anwar wondered if anyone without enhanced vision would have noticed the there-and-gone-again tightening on Zaitsev's face. "Yes, UNEX. That's where the developmental and operational work is done. And the political climate hasn't been receptive in the past. Now, though, it's very different. Everything has come together."

Barbie looked skeptical, but said nothing. Zaitsev went on smoothly.

"We've broken the mold. We have the technology ready, and a business model to put it to work. Neither of them were available before. The technology, you've heard about. But the business model is the real story."

He paused for effect, and perhaps to permit himself a long up-and-down look at Barbie, before continuing.

"The technology will be licensed free of charge to UN members involved in water rights disputes or suffering water shortages—if they sign up to the Agenda codes on damming and diversion, reforestation and replanting. But the Agenda codes, which once seemed essential, are now only a subset. We're starting a project which will eventually render them unnecessary."

"Licensing free of charge? Sounds like you're giving a lot away."

"Not giving, Amanda: *investing*." Zaitsev modulated his voice to match perfectly the gravitas of his words, but Anwar heard what was underneath the voice. Publicly Zaitsev was the hero, and he was loving it; but he was doing Rafiq's bidding. Rafiq's call that morning must have left him eviscerated.

"We're investing," Zaitsev went on, "in a project that will deal a decisive blow to these water shortages. We're going to create water grids. Like individual countries have electricity grids, but these won't only span individual countries. They'll cover entire sub-continents. They'll need massive pipelines and pumps, and massive amounts of energy. They'll source and distribute fresh water from streams and rivers and lakes and underground aquifers. They'll take years to build and plan, but they'll employ thousands and they'll change the face of the planet! And they'll always be associated with what we did here, this morning..."

Anwar blanked out the rest.

It seemed like a gamble for Rafiq, but Anwar knew it wasn't. A calculated risk, maybe, but not a gamble. Rafiq would already be investing in the next generation of technology. Perhaps even the one after that. He'd never give away anything he couldn't afford to give. *He always plays long.*

Anwar laughed softly to himself.

"What's amusing you?" Olivia asked.

"This whole breakthrough," he said. "Good news, of course, but everyone's so surprised. It took everyone unawares. Especially Zaitsev, who's now announcing it to a startled world like he already knew all about it."

"What do you mean?"

"At ten this morning, he knew no more about it than you or me. He knew no more about it than your cat. But you know who *did* know about it, don't you?"

"Rafiq."

Anwar nodded, and again laughed softly to himself.

The summit had started a process that would move the UN closer to what Rafiq always wanted it to be: a power in itself, a State among an association of States. A State with its own assets and resources and property, capable of entering into treaties with others, individually or collectively. The UN, through UNEX, would act like a State of similar power to any one of the five or six major members. It could even, at strategic times, give them a nudge.

Anwar thought, *Rafiq, you clever bastard. All this and you've said nothing. You didn't even need to come here.*

On the face of it, Zaitsev would get the immediate credit. But below the face of it, in those dark labyrinths where real politics was done, the real players would know who was the prime mover. Rafiq's power would grow considerably behind the scenes, which was exactly where he wanted it to grow.

11

The main auditorium of the Conference Centre seemed unchanged on the surface: the same clean citrus air, the same swooping white and silver interior. But after the lunchtime feeding frenzy of the media, and the individual closed-door discussions where members at war with each other had examined the new initiatives from all angles and found they were still viable, there was a subsurface buzz. A feeling of euphoria and anticipation which Zaitsev, although taking care to look and sound statesmanlike, did nothing to dispel. He said nothing openly to claim credit, of course, but it was there in his posture and the timbre of his voice and his whole demeanour. He sat at the top table on the stage, still with a slight trembling, which he had probably cultivated to hint at his restrained but deeply felt emotion at making history. He spoke with a slight hoarseness which he had also probably cultivated, to hint at long and intense behind-the-scenes negotiations to bring this breakthrough to the world. A better actor than Rafiq.

"We've been fortunate," he pronounced, "to have worked together on what promises to be a new way forward. What we'll sign will necessarily be an outline only. A Statement of Intent. It will describe the big picture, but a *different* big picture. It will need networks of treaties, commercial agreements, and contracts to be negotiated as a result, but this will set the overall direction. This is genuinely different.

"It's a better-than-expected outcome. A breakthrough. The Statement of Intent will be substantive, not cobbled together.

The signing will take place earlier than we all expected. All the meetings and negotiations under the old Agenda are out of the window. The Statement of Intent can, we think, given the goodwill we've all shown so far, be drawn up relatively quickly. That will be our goal this afternoon: to finalise it, and get it formally signed and adopted tomorrow. Then, all the treaties, commercial agreements, and contracts needed to implement it can follow. Perhaps," he added, as though it had only just occurred to him, "if the Archbishop agrees, some of them can be done in this marvellous venue which will now have such good associations for us."

Olivia nodded graciously as some delegates turned towards her, and returned their smiles and words of thanks. But she was scared, and Anwar saw it. *She might have less time to live.* They exchanged a glance which, to anyone around them but not to themselves, was unreadable.

They walked back together through the Garden, through the lobby of the New Grand, and up to her apartments without exchanging a word. Only when they got into the main living room did they speak.

"Our last night in each other's company." She made it a statement, not a question, and was careful with the words. Not "together," but "in each other's company."

"Yes," Anwar agreed. "Our last night, whatever happens."

It was their own private statement of intent.

While they sat together in her apartment, the drafting in the summit went on. It was going well, as they verified from time to time by listening to news channels or the live feed from the Conference Centre.

The media circus, which was already huge, got bigger. Some of the worthies who had attended the opening ceremony and left early when problems appeared, were wheeled out by news channels to make statesmanlike pronouncements.

Other heads of state, who hadn't initially gone to the summit but were now quick to be associated with it, were similarly wheeled out. Anwar knew a similar frenzy would be roiling in state intelligence and science agencies the world over, as everyone would be hungry to get access to Rafiq's toys.

Anwar switched back to the live feed and listened to Zaitsev as he luxuriated. The Statement of Intent had been successfully drafted, as expected, and would be formally signed tomorrow at 10:00 a.m. in the Signing Room.

Without actually saying so, Zaitsev was using the outcome to erase his humiliation over the voting in the General Assembly. At one point someone rather mischievously suggested just that. "A fair question," he said graciously, "but no."

An accurate question. "A chance to erase your humiliation" would be exactly how Rafiq sold it to him, Anwar thought. Of course, Zaitsev wasn't stupid enough to buy something that wouldn't work, and Rafiq wouldn't sell him something that wouldn't work. Rafiq had made sure over the years to do all that research on the technology and all that work on the business model, so that when a time came that was right, all of it *would* work. He always played long. *You really are a clever bastard. It's always the same when you put these intricate plans together. You get what you want, and you make something better.*

Olivia, who'd also been listening, asked, "Did Rafiq really foresee all this?"

Anwar hardly thought it worth an answer, and she didn't press for one.

Outside it was getting darker. The sky was now the same gunmetal colour as the sea. Celebrations continued along the Brighton seafront, as at midday, but now the horns and music and beach party noises carried more sharply over the evening air, and the lights were brighter in the gathering dark. From

Zaitsev's suite on the floor below—Anwar's floor, where his suite stood empty—came sounds of celebration.

Also, he could now hear waves. And seagulls. The noises from the sea had been something he'd previously blanked out, but now he was ramping up his senses for the coming night.

He waited until Olivia was asleep. As usual, when she had nobody in bed with her, she fell asleep quickly and slept soundly. When he was satisfied she was deeply asleep, he went out into the main living room of her suite. He left her bedroom door open.

He called Gaetano. "I won't be able to check the Signing Room tonight. Have you checked it?"

"Yes. It's secure. I'll check it again, last thing tonight."

"Thanks. Talking of last things..."

"Yes?"

"This is their endgame. Between now and the signing, they must move for her. So put your people outside her suite in the positions we discussed. I'll be in here with her, and I won't be sleeping. Come for us with your people at 9:00 tomorrow, in the formation we agreed, and escort us to the Conference Centre. If nothing happens there, put them in the agreed positions in the Signing Room and along the mezzanine. And be there yourself. I'll take it from there."

They *had* to move before the signing. He would stay awake all night. Not a problem: he could blank out his sleep requirement for a short period, say a day or two. And right now, he couldn't see further ahead than a day or two.

He left the doors to her balcony open, and the lights off. Now that the endgame had been reached, it became simpler: just throw people at it. He knew Gaetano would have people on other balconies. On the roof. On adjoining roofs. On the corridors, this one and the ones below.

But not in her apartment. If anything came for her, he wanted to be alone with it.

He stayed awake all night, and nothing happened and nothing came. It was about 8:00 a.m. Two hours to the signing. He made a quick check-in call to Gaetano, confirmed Olivia was still asleep, and put in a call to Arden Bierce. *Maybe my last one to her,* a voice inside him said. *Don't be morbid,* another voice replied. *Or self-indulgent,* a third one added.

"Still nothing," he told Arden. "They didn't move for her throughout the summit. They didn't move during the night. It must come today. They want it live and public, and everyone will have gone tomorrow."

"What about your Detail? The one she wouldn't tell you?"

"I've left it. No time, not any more."

"There's something I should tell you..." She was going to tell him about Rafiq and herself, but stopped as she realised how wrong it would be at this time.

"Something you should tell me?"

"Not tell you, ask you." She was floundering, uncharacteristically.

"Ask me what?"

She cast around desperately. "Something," she blurted, "about what Carne said to you. No," her voice shook as she realised this was what she'd been looking for, "about the *way* he said it."

"You weren't there."

"I know, but your account covered everything as if I was. Why do you think we give you all eidetic memories? It was the *way* he said it! Dammit, Anwar. I'll call you later."

When she flicked her wristcom shut, she was shaking. This was pivotal. There really *was* something, and she'd only thought of it when she'd been trying to avoid telling him about Rafiq and he'd been pressing her and now she *had* to chase it down and would there be time? He only had about two hours until the signing, and if they were still going to move for her then this—whatever it was—might be something he needed to know. She *had* to chase it down.

Anwar went into Olivia's bedroom. She was still sleeping. The act of watching her sleeping, and the act of waking her, which he'd do in a moment, could in different contexts both be acts of intimacy. But not in this context. Her face was small and sharp-featured against the bulk of her pillow. Far from ugly, but not beautiful like Arden's, either. It didn't matter now. Her face carried too many associations for him to bother about its aesthetics.

You've shown me more double meanings, he thought, *more things under the surface, in the last three weeks than I've seen in the rest of my life. I don't know if love exists, but I've listed all the pros and cons about you and I think it must. Nothing else seems to fit.*

She moved slightly, but didn't wake.

And now it's academic. We both mistimed. Whatever happens today, whether I protect you or not, the mission will finish and we won't see each other again.

He reached down and shook her shoulder to wake her. "Time," he said.

12

Anwar and Olivia left the New Grand at 8:55 a.m. on October 20. Gaetano was with them. They walked through piazzas and gardens to the Conference Centre. Anwar wore his light grey linen blend suit and dark grey woven-silk shirt from his first day at Brighton. Olivia, coincidentally, wore the dark red velvet dress she'd worn when she first greeted him.

It had to be coincidental, because they no longer dressed or undressed in each other's presence.

Anwar also wore his Yusuf Khan badge, though it was probably too near the end to worry about details of identity.

Anwar and Olivia said nothing to each other while they walked. There wasn't much to say, not now. The weather was like yesterday: cold, but sharp and clear, with pale sunlight. The sea was calm. Not so much placid, perhaps, as unconcerned. Gulls swooped and soared gracefully around the Pier. There was something wistful and sad in their calls, redolent of savage lonely shores; but also, if you listened a little differently, something like a cruel cackling laughter.

For the walk, Anwar briefly ramped up his senses to check where everyone was. It seemed like there was just the three of them, but Anwar saw (and heard, *and* smelt—that was one of the irritations of sense-heightening) Gaetano's people all around, covering them discreetly. *Must be most of his staff today,* he thought. Proskar and others he recognised, but he didn't see Bayard; he hadn't seen him for a few days.

"You won't see him here," Gaetano said, when Anwar asked. "I wasn't sure of him."

Anwar reduced his senses to normal for the rest of their walk. He never liked heightening them for too long; people might infer, from his behaviour, what he was.

They entered the Conference Centre. The main auditorium, and the wide staircase up to the mezzanine, and the mezzanine itself, were already crowded with people not able to get into the Signing Room: junior delegates, support staff, broadcasters from minor channels. The big screen in the main auditorium would show a live feed of the signing.

They walked along the mezzanine, Olivia trailing her hand along the balcony rail. They went through the pale wood double doors and entered the Signing Room at 9:01 a.m. The signing was scheduled for 10:00, but already the room was starting to fill.

Once through the double doors they came immediately, on their left, to the panelled area mocked up to look like a UN Press Suite. The rest of the room, which was about sixty feet long by fifty wide, stretched away to the right, and still had the original curving walls of white and silver.

In the panelled area to the left was the top table. It held Zaitsev and three others, the senior politicians who'd drafted the Statement yesterday. Olivia, in deference to her position as host, also had a place there. She took it, leaving Anwar and Gaetano in the main body of the room. Anwar stayed in the middle, near to the top table, and Gaetano moved to the wall. Other security people—Gaetano's, and those of the delegates—had already taken up positions.

Olivia sat quietly at the top table, next to Zaitsev. Her expression was unreadable. Anwar made brief eye contact with Zaitsev (A to Z, he thought irrelevantly) but neither of them said anything.

The Signing Room was large, but not large enough for all the summit delegates. Only the delegation heads—usually political leaders or senior ministers, with their security people—were allowed in; many of them were now standing in the main area of the room. At exactly 10:00 a.m., Zaitsev would formally read out a communiqué incorporating the Statement of Intent. The heads of delegations would then come up and sign in the alphabetical order of their countries' names.

Anwar saw Zaitsev's array of Meatslabs: the one who'd threatened to tear off his penis, the one who couldn't operate the button on Zaitsev's pen, and some others. The one who'd threatened to tear off his penis sauntered up to him.

"Hello, Yusuf. Glad I let you keep your prick? I understand it's *her* property these days. Good fuck, is she?"

Anwar smiled but didn't answer.

To him, and he suspected most of those present, the pan-elling didn't look any different. It covered the walls in the direction where it faced the cameras, which were massed at the other end of the room with mikes and lighting and reporters.

Every time he'd been in this room he noticed the same thing: the jarring division between the newly-built replica panelling and the original curving white and silver walls. He'd always thought it looked ridiculous. He couldn't imagine two interior styles which so completely contradicted each other. Levin would have mocked both of them unmercifully.

It wouldn't show on the broadcasts, though. The cameras were angled so that the panelled area would fill their entire picture. The wood panelling stood three to four feet proud of the original walls, as the room's natural shape was curved and organic and the panelling was meant to look like a conven-tional rectangular space. The contractors had done it carefully and very well the first time, and equally well the second time after Anwar ordered it ripped out. But it still seemed a lot of trouble. Just for a theatre set.

Anwar tried to stare through it. He'd been there while it was actually being fitted, and armed guards had been there ever since, so he knew nothing was behind it. Yet he still ramped up his senses in the hope that he might see or smell or hear something there. He didn't, though he saw and smelt and heard rather more than he wanted of the other people crowding the room.

They wore a mixture of modern clothes and traditional robes and he saw the microscopic texture and weave of the fabrics, the tiny dust motes in their interstices. And smelt them, though they'd all been painstakingly laundered and pressed for the occasion. Their colours were different when seen microscopically, because colours didn't really exist, they were only selective light filters.

And the textures of their faces, in unforgiving close-up: minute tips of embedded stubble despite careful shaving, or traceries of cracks in makeup carefully applied for the occasion. Hair smelling stale despite careful shampooing. Body odours, bad breath, sweat, and subcutaneous grease despite careful morning toiletries. Snatches of conversation, normally indistinguishable in the background murmur, now each one a separate and distinct thread, some benign and some embarrassing. Sexual liaisons were a regular feature of most summits and conferences, and often had more far-reaching results than the formal business itself.

This was how The Dead could step outside the world and perceive it as nobody else could: by ramping up their senses, for surveillance or combat. Sights and sounds and smells crowded Anwar. Each one was separate and distinct, and each one was already matched, in his memory, to a name and a face and a profile and an identity. More information than he wanted or needed. He powered down his senses, and saw and heard and smelt what everyone else did. The cool pleasant citrus air returned to his nostrils and the individual conversations sank into the background murmur.

It was now only a few minutes before 10:00, and the Signing Room was full. Delegates crowded into the main part, standing. Occasionally, spotting a photo opportunity, Zaitsev would smile or wave at someone, glancing to camera as he did so.

The media were at the back of the room, the other end from the panelled theatre set. Quite close, Anwar remembered, to where he'd put his bucket during his stay there. Cameras, mikes, lights were all angled towards the top table and the illusion of rectangular panelling behind it.

At one minute to 10:00 the top table party nodded to each other, and the room fell silent. Zaitsev took a deep breath and, exactly as 10:00 came around, smiled and began.

"Welcome," he said. "It's an unexpected path that has brought us here. A few days ago the path we'd chosen seemed impassable. Then we took another, and we've arrived at a place none of us would have thought possible."

Humility, not triumphalism. A mere messenger, carrying something of greater import than his mere self. But Anwar noted the careful modulation of the voice, and the slight contrivance of the near-rhyming of Impassable and Possible. Still a good actor.

He continued, "You all know what happened yesterday: the new direction we took, and the Statement of Intent to confirm that new direction and our unanimous commitment to it. If you'll permit me" (*who's going to forbid you?* Anwar thought) "I'll read out the summit's official communiqué."

He cleared his throat; looked around the room portentously; and began.

"The following communiqué on the United Nations summit on Water Rights was issued today, October 20, 2060.

"The United Nations summit on Water Rights was convened by the Secretary-General and was held at the Conference Centre, New West Pier, Brighton from October 15 to October 19, 2060. Delegates unanimously agreed that the previously published Agenda should be set aside, and the following Statement of Intent was adopted by all those present:

"Brighton, October 20, 2060. We the undersigned—"

An explosion of dust and fragments, a tearing and rending of structural members, and the wall burst open. Not the wood-panel theatre-set wall whose construction Anwar had witnessed, but the original pearlescent white wall at the other end of the room.

Arden at last knew what she was looking for. But she hadn't found it yet, and there wasn't *time*. It was buried somewhere in Anwar's questioning of Carne: not the transcript, that was just words on a screen, but the recording of his verbal report. It was probably some chance remark, maybe even an aside,

which had slipped past her unnoticed. Anwar's memory enabled him to reproduce not only the words, but the way Carne
had spoken them.

She'd been playing it back for nearly two hours, since he
last called her. Nothing. She played it back again, and there
it was.

Carne's voice was copied exactly by Anwar: not just every
word, but the inflection of every word. It was almost mimicry.
That's what she should have listened for. Not the words, but
one word. And how Carne had said it.

"They annihilated Levin. Then Rafiq sent Asika, and
they annihilated him too." *They annihilated Levin* (strong
emphasis on the second syllable) *then they annihilated Asika*
(no emphasis). As if it meant something different, something
less than they'd done to Levin. Consistent with "there wasn't
enough left of Levin..."

Annihilate: Destroy completely. Reduce to nonexistence.
Nullify or render void. Eradicate, erase, exterminate; extin-
guish, kill, obliterate.

"...what our employers did to Asika. And what they did to
Levin, which was worse. And Levin's *face,* when he realised
he couldn't defend himself. There wasn't enough left of him to
make into an exhibit, like the one they'd made of Asika."

The one they'd made in that villa in Opatija.

What was done to Asika was merely physical. What was
done to Levin was spiritual. Deeper, more absolute.

"*Fuck.*" She occasionally swore mildly, but she'd never
spoken *that* word before. It felt strange, forming her lips over
the *f* and her palate and tongue over the *ck*.

At last she'd found it. Hiding in plain sight, and she hadn't
seen; or in plain hearing, and she hadn't heard. She'd only
found it when she'd lied to Anwar to avoid telling him about
Rafiq and herself, and now there was no *time*.

She flicked open her wristcom.

Anwar moved to the centre of the suddenly-emptying Signing Room, to stand between *her* and what had burst out of the far wall.

It was Levin. Except it wasn't, anymore.

Levin would have greeted him with *Muslim Filth*. Levin would have had some clever one-liners to which Anwar would have thought up rejoinders too late. Levin wouldn't have had a face like an unmoving theatrical mask, or eyes like dead, brilliant jewels.

Ridiculously, his wristcom buzzed. He cancelled it.

Levin wore a shirt and trousers of silver-grey, and thin gloves of the same material. Maybe woven monofilament. Or maybe a similar composition to Rafiq's VSTOLs, which always seemed quietly indestructible.

They both ramped up their senses, and went to full combat mode. This time Anwar ignored the microscopic weave of fabrics or the particle-level building-blocks of colours or the body odours beneath perfumes, and funnelled everything towards Levin.

A kind of relativity: time and thought moved normally for them, but for everyone around them they were a flicker.

The Patel contractors hadn't only built the fake wood-panelled wall, they'd built a replica of the original pearlescent wall. A perfect, seamless replica. At the other end of the room. Levin was already there when Anwar ordered the old panelling ripped out. *Already there, in the wall three feet away, when I was crapping in my bucket.*

Broadcasters, camera crews and delegates were crowded at the far end. When Levin burst out he didn't just scatter them, he killed them. He was so fast that nobody got in a shot, except Gaetano. He hit Levin once in the throat, normally a killing shot, but Levin didn't notice.

With his senses ramped up for combat, Anwar saw all this in what for him was normal time. Relativity: everyone else in the room, except Levin, was wallowing in treacle-time. Screaming in deep bass notes. Thinking at geological speed. Or dead.

Two of Zaitsev's guards were moving in strange animated slow motion to cover him. The other three, moving with equal strangeness, went to face Levin in the centre of the room but he killed them without breaking step as he hurtled—flickered—towards Olivia at the top table. Everyone assumed the target was Zaitsev, who was now pushed under the table and covered by his two remaining guards. Olivia was standing behind the table, her mouth open in an O that seemed too big for her face.

Anwar moved—slowly in his time, a blur in theirs—to the centre of the room to stand between them.

He faced Levin, and saw what they'd done to him.

He knew it instinctively, not in detail. They'd taken his identity, and left him as a *thing*. He'd always been bigger, younger, stronger, faster, more skilful, than Anwar. Now he was more so, and a monster. A killing machine. Maybe what had once powered his mind was now redirected into his body. *Details later. No time.*

Remembering Gaetano's throat shot, he aimed his best Verb at Levin's throat. Levin didn't notice, and broke Anwar's collarbone. In full combat mode Anwar's resetting processes worked faster, but would still be too slow. He hit Levin with two more Verbs, and Levin broke three of Anwar's ribs and re-broke his collarbone. Then his left upper arm.

Simple maths: a few seconds, and he'd be strewn like Chulo Asika over the floor of that villa in Croatia. Levin could break 90 percent of his major bones before 10 percent of them could reset. Anwar kept hitting at the throat. Nothing else was exposed, or vulnerable. No time for elegant moves from his training, he'd be killed.

"They an*nih*ilated Levin," Anwar's memory helpfully replayed, "then Rafiq sent Asika, and they annihilated him too."

Yes, Asika. I'm being broken up like Chulo. Levin wasn't going to kill him with one blow, though he could probably have done so, but to annihilate him piece by piece.

"Jewish scum," he whispered, hoping ridiculously that Levin might remember and hesitate, but there was no reply. Levin couldn't speak anymore. Or, Anwar guessed, even form thoughts that might become speech. Everything was gone. A container was all that remained.

Normal time for him and Levin, heightened time for everyone else, which meant they blurred and flickered. Anwar kept landing Verbs, and Levin kept not noticing, and Anwar kept getting parts of himself broken, and broken again before they'd had time to reset. He blanked out the physical pain, that was easy, but he couldn't blank out the spiritual shock.

"...And Levin's *face*," his memory replayed, "when he realised he couldn't defend himself. There wasn't enough left of him to..."

Spiritual. Worse than physical obliteration, it was spiritual. They'd taken everything he was. His identity. His soul. And remade him as a thing. It would burn out and die soon through operating at such a heightened level, but that didn't matter. Olivia would die sooner. And they could always steal another Consultant and make another thing. They seemed to be good at it.

Another Verb. He was good at Verbs. Open hand to the throat, fingers locally hardened, perfectly executed. It didn't work. Wasn't noticed. More Verbs, and more, and each one brought damage to him without him doing any of his own. His right forearm was broken, and his left upper arm was still resetting, too slowly. He ignored both, and willed them to keep functioning, because for the first time in his life, he had someone to fight for.

It didn't matter what he felt for her, or didn't feel, or whether any feelings were real or could have a future. Just to be fighting to *protect* someone, not to abduct someone or sabotage something, felt strange. And this time he was fighting a real opponent, one that outclassed him, and he was fighting not to disable but to kill. That felt strange too. *She* did it all the time, faced real danger and bared her teeth at it, but he'd never had to.

He looked back at her, but she was focused on Levin, and there was the strangest expression on her face. Almost of recognition, or understanding. She hadn't moved from the table. Levin was now closer to her, and the only reason he hadn't already reached her was that he'd paused to destroy Anwar piece by piece.

More Verbs. He had nothing else to try. Nothing else was vulnerable. Levin didn't seem to notice. But all those Verbs, more than he'd landed in his previous missions put together, and Gaetano's throat shot, had to have some effect sometime.

Then Levin executed a classically elegant move, the only one either of them had done. It was a mighty swivelling roundhouse kick—a Circumnavigator, Consultants rather preciously renamed it—which didn't only break bones, but did something worse. It hit under Anwar's heart and ruptured his major cardiac muscles. He went flying through the doors of the Signing Room and out onto the mezzanine. He could feel the start of cardiogenic shock, and again the sound of water rushing in his ears which he'd once read—*where did I read that?*—was the sound you heard when you started to die.

Somehow he managed to get up. He stood shakily on the mezzanine, looking back through the pale wood double doors into the room where Levin was moving—slowly for him, a blur to everyone else—for Olivia.

Gaetano and others were getting off shots. Levin didn't notice. Whoever made him probably didn't care about gunshots: they'd made Levin into a thing that had only one job to do and could then expire. When you had trillions, you could afford to make things and throw them away.

"Shoot for the neck! Shoot for the throat!" Anwar shouted, but he was shouting out of heightened time to people still floundering in treacle time, and they didn't hear. Relativity, not of light, but sound. Most of them missed, anyway. Levin was too fast.

Olivia still stood at the table. Levin could have turned to her and finished her, but instead came out onto the mezzanine to finish Anwar. She was his prime target, but he had time and advantage, and to finish his secondary target would take only moments. Even at heightened time.

Anwar willed his heart not to go into shock, not yet, because he'd decided to gamble. Whoever did this to Levin probably knew about Anwar by now, about his mediocre ratings and cautiousness. But that was then. Brighton had changed him. *And I have someone to fight for.*

He was standing on the mezzanine, his back to the balcony, when Levin came for him.

Anwar gambled: a *tomoe nage*. If he mistimed he'd die, but he was dying anyway.

Levin hurtled towards him. Anwar took Levin's neck in his hands, placed a foot in his stomach—so much of what he was using was broken and hadn't reset properly—and rolled backwards. Not a classically-executed stomach throw, but not mistimed either, with Anwar holding onto Levin's neck as Levin flew over him. Over the edge of the mezzanine, smashing the balcony railing.

Anwar landed on his back with his hands still locked around Levin's neck. He didn't let go. Levin hung over the edge of the mezzanine, dangling by the neck from Anwar's outstretched arms, with bits of smashed balcony crashing to the auditorium below. He kept trying to break Anwar's forearms, or break Anwar's hands and fingers, but they were already broken and Anwar wouldn't let go. He felt the neck *snap*—there was a rightness about it, like when you were hammering a post into the ground and there was a moment when it settled—and he still wouldn't let go. He felt Levin's legs and arms and body dancing, like someone on the end of a noose.

Even after the snap, Levin continued trying to smash Anwar's forearms or break his fingers, then subsided. Anwar kept holding onto him. Levin's feces and urine poured down into the auditorium, brown and yellow against white and silver. He'd been still for a long time, but Anwar held on to him for longer. Then he let go, and Levin dropped to the floor of the main auditorium below.

Most of the cameras had been smashed and most of the broadcasters killed, but not all. It was still going out, live and worldwide.

Anwar said, "Goodbye, old friend."

Heightened time ended with Anwar's stomach throw. Everyone still alive saw Levin die in normal time, but only another Consultant could have seen the rest of it. To everyone else it was a few seconds' blur. The rubble and dust from where Levin had burst out of the far wall was still settling, even after Levin died. Some of those he'd killed as he burst out and hurtled towards Olivia were still falling.

This strange relativity was why Anwar felt like he'd been laying on his back, with his broken arms still lolling over the edge of the mezzanine, for whole minutes after Levin had gone. Then, as his senses powered down, he realised that people were no longer moving at the speed of continental drift but were actually moving quickly, in fact very quickly, to gather round him.

Olivia was one of the first. She knelt down to say something to him, but then Gaetano ran up and embraced her. She pushed him away and pointed down at Levin's body in the auditorium. Anwar heard her calmly telling Gaetano, "Go back and kill it. Make sure it's dead. Shoot it, in the head." Then he became unconscious.

13

Even before Anwar had finished killing Levin, Rafiq had dispatched a VSTOL to Brighton. Arden Bierce was in it, among others.

At 11:00 a.m. on October 20 Anwar was taken to the hospital on the New West Pier. They put him in the room where, coincidentally, he'd questioned Taylor Hines a few days ago, and where Hines had died. The hospital was small, but very well-equipped and well-staffed; even more so, while the summit was on.

He hadn't regained consciousness. He was so quiet and still in the hospital bed that he might not have been there. Sometimes, coming and going in his room, they talked about him as if he wasn't.

"Why aren't you doing anything?" Olivia demanded of the hospital's Director.

"UNEX asked us not to. They're sending a medical team and they want to attend to him in private."

"But surely..."

"Archbishop, they expressly asked us not to look at him."

"Why?"

"Because they don't want anyone to know what Consultants are like inside. And in view of what he did for you..."

"Yes, yes, alright. But I'm not leaving this room."

"You can tell them."

"I'm telling you. Last time I looked, you were still Director of this hospital. "

She sat by Anwar's bedside, her body language giving every indication that she was not to be moved or trifled with. He woke once, briefly, and sank back without seeming to see or recognise her.

By 12:20 p.m., a VSTOL had landed on the pad at the end of the New West Pier. The UNEX medical team disembarked and strode into Anwar's hospital room. Olivia didn't move. The UNEX doctors shot her irritated glances, but said nothing and started unpacking their equipment.

Arden walked in behind the doctors. It was the first time she and Olivia had met or spoken directly.

"Archbishop, the doctors will need you to leave when they finish these preliminaries and start the main treatment."

"Why?"

"They'll be doing deepscan procedures. Projecting holograms of Anwar's internal structure. They can't risk anyone seeing it. I'm sorry." When Olivia said nothing, Arden added, "Depending on what they find, it should take about three hours. After that, you're welcome to return."

"You're on my ground here. You don't tell me when to come or go."

"Consultants don't get medical treatment in front of outsiders. There are no exceptions. Don't you want him treated here, as quickly as possible?"

"Don't be ridiculous. If he survived *that,* in the Signing Room..."

"Archbishop, they will not treat him in front of you. If you won't leave they'll just take him back to Kuala Lumpur and treat him there, or inflight." She paused, and knew instinctively what to say. Don't persist with No, offer something Olivia couldn't get unless she said Yes. "Don't make them take him away. Let them treat him here. Then you can say goodbye to him properly."

They made eye contact, and Olivia nodded. On her way out, she said, "Please let me know when the treatment is finished. I want to come back straightaway."

"Of course."

They worked on him. They'd done this before. They were entirely dispassionate, like technicians.

Within a few minutes they'd completed the preliminaries and started the deepscanning. A life-sized hologram of his entire structure, his bones and muscles and internal organs, was projected onto the air at the foot of his bed. They studied it at different depths and from different angles. It stood there like his soul, recently gone from his body. The doctors gave it their full attention and ignored his real body.

They projected local magnifications from the hologram of those major bones that had been broken by Levin: ribs, clavicle, radius, ulna, tibia, fibula, metacarpals, phalanges. And his sternum, which together with his upper ribs had been shattered by Levin's mighty kick on the way to its main target, his heart.

The texture of the bones, in such high close-up, was granular and fibrous, particularly at the open edges where they'd sheared. The breaks, on images so big they looked like pieces of furniture, were spectacular. But they were resetting and regenerating as expected, and surgery wouldn't be needed on them; just time.

The magnifications of bones retracted back into the hologram, and it turned itself inside out and projected another magnification, this time so enlarged it filled most of the room. It was Anwar's heart, where they expected to find more serious damage; they'd magnified it so much it almost made the room into an immersion hologram whose workmanship Anwar, if he'd been conscious, would have admired.

It wasn't a human heart. It was denser and heavier and had much larger muscles, formed in a much more intricate pattern over its surface. But it was organic: no mechanical or electronic components.

They studied the damage done by Levin's mighty Circumnavigator kick, and decided it needed closer examination. They ramped up the magnification, as Anwar might have ramped up his senses, and the perspective changed. The image enlarged until it assumed the dimensions of the room's floor and walls and ceiling. The doctors walked through it and around it, conversing quietly.

The muscles were torn by the pressure waves of the kick, as the doctors expected, but they needed to know the extent of the damage. The transverse dark and light striations on the muscles, normally regular, were turned almost into graffiti by the concussion. The surface of Anwar's heart was damaged structurally like the white and silver wall Levin had burst out of, but this damage was done by Levin bursting in, not out. Eventually they concluded that it wouldn't heal as quickly as the bones; regeneration of all that torn muscle tissue would be much slower and more complicated. It might take all of another day.

This was how they made Consultants. A few seconds more in the Signing Room and Anwar would have died like Asika. But a few seconds *after* Levin had died Anwar's molecular defences, always first to the scene of any trauma, had begun working. By the time the doctors reached him, resetting and regeneration and healing were proceeding as expected.

The UNEX doctors concluded their deepscan, and Anwar's hologram disappeared. They'd been told en route that a Consultant had been seriously injured, so they'd come prepared for extensive surgery, and they were lazily relieved that it wouldn't be necessary. They formally handed him back to the hospital with instructions about mild sedation and food and drink intake. They departed at 2:45 p.m. on October 20, taking Levin's body with them in the VSTOL.

Arden had decided to stay for the two to three days it would take for Anwar to reach something like full recovery. She called Olivia, and left the room as she entered.

After a couple of hours Anwar started to slip in and out of unconsciousness, and each time he woke he'd see Olivia there. Standing guard ridiculously in his hospital room like (he remembered) he'd stood guard ridiculously in the Signing

Room. Every time he woke she was there. Maybe she'd brought a bucket.

Many of the broadcasters in the Signing Room died, but not all of them. Enough survived to make sure the events were seen worldwide and live. The news channels treated it as a failed attempt on Zaitsev's life.

Mass killing at UN summit in Brighton.

Battle of The Dead.

Nineteen killed in attempted assassination of UN Secretary-General Zaitsev.

Nineteen killed, but very few injured. Anyone not near to Levin when he burst out of the wall lived. The others, if he touched them, died.

With so much coverage, a slow-motion analysis of Anwar's combat with Levin was inevitable. Rafiq knew better than to try to suppress it, though he refused to make any public comment on it. It was broadcast extensively and analysed by an assortment of retired military people. There were headlines like *Who were they?* and *Battle of The Dead* and *Do we need things like this?* Rafiq knew that inquiries would be inevitable, and was fighting on several fronts to ensure they stayed private.

Zaitsev managed to hold things together politically. His remark about "this marvellous venue that will now have such good associations for us" was expected to come back and bite him, but it didn't. His tone was restrained, dignified, and exactly right. He kept to a simple message, not descending into hasty speculation about who was responsible or why they'd done it. And certainly not about whether the target was anyone other than him.

"This was a summit on water rights. Vitally important, yes, but not an explosive subject like political or ethnic or religious persecution. Not something for which any of the participants would expect to be killed. Just water rights. Civil engineering ideas. Ways to make water so readily available that people don't have to fight over it, or die for the lack of it. A ground-breaking and imaginative business model. And a political and financial model to match. The summit succeeded, better than any of us expected. Let's hold to that, and work as we agreed to implement it. Anything less would be a discourtesy to those who died, and to their families and colleagues."

Even to Anwar, who heard snatches of this during a brief waking spell, it didn't sound like all of it was acting. Some, maybe, but not all. And yet, all that Zaitsev would get from it would be to survive a summit most people didn't expect him to survive. Rafiq, who wasn't even there, would get a massive increase in UNEX's future status and would get to make some things better in the process. *What a piece of work!* Anwar thought, and went back to sleep.

He woke on the morning of October 21 feeling pretty good. His night's sleep had been dreamless and relaxing. He'd expected it to be more troubled.

Olivia was sitting at his bedside. He managed to close his eyes before she noticed he'd opened them, and to pretend sleep for a few minutes until Arden came in.

"Archbishop, please take a rest. You've been here all night. I'll sit with him for a while. I'll call you if there's any change."

"Thank you," Olivia said, and actually smiled. Even she felt comfortable around Arden. Most people did.

Anwar, as the door closed behind Olivia and without opening his eyes, said, "What did they do to him?"

"Anwar, I'm so..."

His eyes snapped open. "I know. But tell me what they did to him!"

"You probably guessed some of it. They..."

"Wait. This was your Detail, right?"

"Yes. I called you too late...When they abducted him, we think they didn't have the time or the ability to reverse-engineer his enhancements, so they rewired him to take away his personal identity. To make him use his abilities only in response to their orders. And everything was channelled into his physical abilities. Everything else, personality and memories and judgement and constraints, they wiped out."

"Like taking his soul."

"Yes. They turned him loose on Asika, then put him into the wall and made him go to near death to conserve energy while he waited. Then they turned him on full blast to kill her and you."

Anwar said, "They should just have kept him as Levin. I'd never have beaten him then....Do you know exactly how they rewired him?"

"No, because Gaetano emptied a gun into his head. But we'll find it eventually. His body's gone to Kuala Lumpur for autopsy."

"We're shipping so many bodies from here to Kuala Lumpur we should start an airline. Maybe call it Air Abbas."

"How about Dead Air?"

Anwar laughed, for the first time in days. He felt some residual pain in his sternum and upper ribs.

"The Patel people. They're the real surprise."

"Yes," she said, "and we're tracking them. There were nine in the original party. They were helped by Olivia's insistence that they should work away from public view. She didn't want her Conference Centre looking like they had the builders in."

"Gaetano checked them, and so did you. How did they beat the checks?"

"We'll know that when we find them. Maybe techniques like those they used on Levin. Also, the misdirection of sending people like Carne and Hines didn't help, and—" she paused "—neither did your obsession with Proskar."

Anwar smiled bleakly. *Not to mention my obsession with Olivia. The Detail. Not the one Arden found, but the one I'm still looking for. Unfinished business.* "The best plans are always simple. Hiding in plain sight. They made a replica of the original wall at the other end of the room, and put Levin behind it, while they were shut in there building the panelled wall. The panelling was such a major piece of work, especially when I made them tear it down and remake it, that nobody would think they'd built another fake wall elsewhere. I didn't." *Usually I look for pockets of darkness, but I missed that one.* "And I'd already told Gaetano how I'd be able to stay undetected if they got me in there."

He remembered his conversation with Gaetano. Quite detailed and precise, given that they hadn't then known or trusted each other very much. *I'd go to near-death. Hibernation. No body-heat detectors would find me: surface temperature would be the same as my immediate surroundings. No heartbeat or breath detectors would find me: pulse and breathing would be almost nonexistent, and random. No scanners or imagers or DNA detectors would find me: my body would echo the texture and shape of its immediate surroundings.*

And then, an electronic signal to activate. From the next room or the next continent. A single pulse. Two targets, Olivia primary, Anwar secondary (because Anwar, though outclassed, was still the only one there who might be able to do something). Simple: two faces, kill both.

"Yes," Arden said, as though she'd heard what Anwar had been thinking. "Their primary objective was to kill Olivia publicly. But also, as a bonus, to kill a Consultant publicly, the way they had Levin kill Asika privately. Not quickly, but piece by piece, limb by limb. To send a message, live and worldwide: total functional annihilation. Of a Consultant, by a Consultant."

"*Who are they*, Arden?"

"Laurens is already fighting back. He knows more about them."

"Laurens?" In two syllables she'd told him what she'd tried to hide earlier. "You and Rafiq. I didn't see that coming."

"Neither did I. But it feels right."

"Yes, I think it will work...what's he found out?" He was assessing it like a chemical or mechanical process, the way he'd repeatedly (and unsuccessfully) tried to assess himself and Olivia.

"Thank you for your good wishes." Her deadpan expression took any sarcasm out of the remark.

"Sorry. What's he found out?"

"They miscalculated. About how you had changed, how you survived Levin, and how Laurens had engineered the summit outcome. And something else, that made them reveal Marek's body earlier than they wanted."

They don't do bodies as well as we do. But they do other things better.

"Well, they're his problem now. But I think they're going to find they've never had an opponent like him before."

He stayed there for most of October 21, alternating between waking and sleep. Still unexpectedly dreamless and deep sleep.

Arden was still there when he woke. It was late afternoon on October 21.

"I don't think Rafiq expected me to survive. But he always does. He gets the girl, and he gets what he wanted from the summit. I still don't know why he picked me for this. Do you?"

"No. He told me he didn't know himself, and I think I believe him. But..."

Her voice trailed off, and he didn't attempt to fill the silence that grew between them.

"Anwar," she said suddenly, "I'm so sorry about Levin! About what they did to him!"

"I did my grieving for him at the right time. It wasn't Levin I fought. He really did die days before."

"When you faced him, how did you do it? Where did it come from?"

"You didn't think I could do it?"

"Of course I didn't! Remember what I do for a living, Anwar. If Chulo was killed, I couldn't see how you could..."

"What do you think Chulo felt when Levin was breaking him piece by piece? Not fear, the training would cover that. Pain? The training should cover that too, but none of us has taken damage like that before. I expected pain, but I willed it to go away and I willed the broken parts to go on working. But only part of that was the training. Maybe it was because I had someone to fight for."

"So did Chulo. His family."

"His family weren't there and they weren't being directly threatened, and he knew their feelings for him. *She* was present and she was directly threatened, but her feelings, I don't know. So I thought I had an answer to your question but I don't. I don't know where it came from."

She didn't reply. She usually knew when to say nothing.

"I've been doing sums, Arden. Addition and subtraction. Nineteen of us originally, then we started to say, 'Eighteen, or is it Seventeen?' Then gradually we started saying Seventeen. It wasn't then, when we started saying it, but it is now.

"Before I came here I'd only killed one person, and that was accidentally. I've now killed four. One accidentally, two indirectly through botching up their questioning, and one directly and deliberately. I've never entered any combat before where I was wishing and intending to kill an opponent. I've never had to."

She still didn't reply.

"Go back to Fallingwater, Arden. I have unfinished business here."

"Unfinished business?"

"We found *your* Detail, and it's dealt with. For now. You still have to find how they got to Levin and how they remade him, but that's for you.

"Now I need to find *her* Detail. I almost saw it for a moment, right after Levin died, but it's gone. Would you believe that? For once, *I* can't remember something!"

"You will."

"I'll see you back at Fallingwater. Please have one of those VSTOLs at the airfield, ready. I'll drive out there in a day or two."

The VSTOL that brought her, and took the doctors away, had returned and was already waiting for her on the Pier's landing pad; hovering politely, as always, an inch or two above the surface. Arden Bierce left.

He lay there, doing nothing. He thought, *she* was here all night. Why? Because she hadn't expected either of them would survive, and now they had, and she wanted to be sure he hadn't seen The Detail? Or maybe just because she wanted to help him recover. Sometimes pick the simpler explanation.

He slipped into another unexpectedly dreamless and relaxing sleep. When he woke it was the evening of October 21.

He knew he was getting better because he started taking stock of his hospital room. Spotless, white and silver, like everywhere except *her* bedroom. The window looked out to sea, not back towards the Brighton foreshore or over the spires and domes of the Pier's Cathedral complex. The sea was featureless, dark grey.

The hospital was located in part of a Pavilion-style building on the edge of the Pier and near its end, so emergency planes could land nearby. He saw gulls from his window. Their sheer numbers, and their messy opportunistic feeding, made them almost vermin. But they were beautiful when they flew, graceful and most un-verminlike as they slid down the air or soared on it. Their slender white shapes would have graced any New Anglican interior. Sometimes, maybe the surface and not the inside *was* what counted.

Gaetano visited. Anwar felt the same kind of relativity he'd felt in the Signing Room. They spoke to each other out of different frames of reference. They communicated only obliquely, across different universes. Remarks that were mundane or conventional or well-meant in Gaetano's universe were charged with menace and double-meaning when they travelled across the room to Anwar's.

"If anyone threatens her...Can never repay...Most important person in the world to me...She'll always owe..."

And vice-versa, from Anwar's universe to Gaetano's.

"Not over yet...I owe her too...Still some details... Unfinished business."

And, as the door closed behind Gaetano, Anwar kept thinking, *You went back. You shot him in the head, to make sure he was dead.*

On the night of October 21, the first dream came. He was alone in the room. Olivia, who seemed to have evolved a shift pattern, left a gap in her shift, and the dream slid in softly, visiting him when she wasn't.

Maybe it was the accumulated trauma, hitting him at last. What should have been the final part of the dream, the part where he learned The Detail, came first and most easily. The Detail walked up to him, showed itself to him...and swirled coquettishly away.

The parts which should have come first, leading to the climax where the Detail appeared, now crept in. He recalled bits of his past life and waited patiently for them to go away because they were irrelevant. He recalled snatches of conversations with Arden and Gaetano, his five days in the Signing Room, his meetings with *her,* and waited patiently for them to go away because they were irrelevant. But they wouldn't go until they repeated themselves.

Snatches of words. And his inner obsessions, the themes shaped by his solitude, slid between and through and over the words, leaving a silver surface slime that glistened on them and illuminated them. Containers and contents. Surface and substance. Outside and inside. Private names, immersion holograms, books. Theatre Masks. Identity Soul Body. Containers Contents.

Levin. Her almost-recognition/almost-understanding. But, "Go back and kill it. Make sure it's dead. Shoot it, in the head."

Gaetano went back. Anwar heard him empty his gun, shot after shot after shot.

Make sure it's dead, shoot it in the head. Make sure it's dead, shoot it in the head..

If they'd done that to Levin, they...

They don't do bodies, but...

He saw The Detail again. Not Arden's Detail, that was dealt with for now, but *hers.* It walked up to him again, then swirled coquettishly away. Again.

He woke in the early morning of October 22. He knew the dream had come because it had left him exhausted; but he couldn't remember it.

Olivia was there, sitting at his bedside. *Wants to know if I've seen it yet? Or wants to help me recover?* He pretended to fall asleep to avoid talking to her, then pretence became reality. He woke a little later to find her touching his shoulder.

"I have to go for a few hours" she said. "Appointments I've been putting off. I do have..."

"An organisation to run," he completed for her. "That's alright, I'll see you later."

She smiled briefly and left, and he promptly fell asleep again.

The dream returned. But this time, like Levin bursting out of the wall, it returned as a monster.

Random phrases he'd heard since coming to Brighton, dancing in front of his face. Then swirling coquettishly away. If the phrases had been *her*, they'd be suggestively moving their meanings under the surface of their words like *she* suggestively moved her bottom under her long voluminous skirt as she turned away from him. She'd been good at turning away.

He couldn't take his attention off the words, just as he couldn't take his gaze off *her* when she moved like that, pretending she didn't notice him. Some of the words he remembered just as words. They floated to the surface, spoke themselves as they were spoken, and sank back. Offer and Acceptance. Muslim filth. Jewish scum.

And then they came back, with music. With his dream-memory of the Congolese big band music he'd heard a few days ago, distorted by the random subconscious tides of his dream into something less pleasant: minor key, not major, with blaring dissonant brass and singers' voices, not melodious but harsh and mocking like seagulls'. The music massaged the words, stressing alternate syllables regularly and masturbating them until their rhythms and inflexions and cadences spilled out.

Offer and Acceptance, Offer and Acceptance,
Muslim filth, Jewish scum.
Offer and Acceptance, The Dead fight in silence,
Muslim filth, Jewish scum.

"I'm Miles ahead of you, Anwar." *Yes you were, even in reaching death. Hear that, Miles? I've got a good rejoinder at last!*

"Goodbye, old friend."
Go back and kill it. Make sure it's dead.
Shoot it in the head, in the head, in the head.

Reith Lecture. Room For God. Small sharp-featured figure on his screen.
Her life's amounted to something. Never backing down.
Her life's amounted to something. Never backing down.
A small animal, baring its teeth, and never backing down.

Greed, for food and sex.
Where does she put that food, where does she put that sperm?
Better than the best prostitutes.
In and out, with no baggage. Sex and nothing more.
In and out, with no baggage. Sex and nothing more.
In and out, with no baggage. Better than a whore.

Old greeting Muslim filth Jewish scum.
Post-Levin, Velvet bag of shit Fucking autistic retard.
I needed the best, and Rafiq sent me you. A fucking autistic retard!
I needed the best, and Rafiq sent me you. A fucking autistic retard!
"Say that again, I'll forget who I am."
"When did you last remember who you are?"

"It does something a bit decisive, and thinks it's turning into me."
"It does something a bit decisive, and thinks it's turning into me."

"Something you haven't told me. A final detail that over-turns everything else."
The Detail. The Dead. The Detail.

Hate my opponents less, and understand them more.
Hate my opponents less, and understand them more.
Better than the most expensive whore.

The music paused. The words continued, sounding naked.

"I may not always be out *here*, in front of you, but God is always out *there*."
"What did you make of that?" / "It sounded like Goodbye."

She isn't real. Appetites moodswings. Didn't notice me then she did. Wanted involvement but maybe didn't. Then she didn't but maybe did. And me, the same but in reverse. Action and reaction. Not love. Not even companionship. Only action and reaction, making one of us the other's opposite.
My feelings the opposite of hers, and (like hers) containing the opposite of that opposite. Containers and contents.

The music began again.
The one you run away from, chases after you the most...
Love came and went with deliberate perversity of timing. *Deliberate.* Like a lighthouse beam switching on and off. On when ships weren't in danger of being wrecked, off when they were.
You mistimed.

Shot him dead, twice in the head.
Go back and kill it. Make sure it's dead.
In Zagreb Marek went back. Shot dead two people who he noticed were still alive. At Fallingwater Marek went back. Shot dead a boy who he noticed was still alive.

Go back and kill it. Make sure it's dead.
Shoot it in the head, in the head, in the head.
Gaetano went back. Anwar heard him, shot after shot after shot.

You've shown me double meanings and things under the surface.
You've shown me double meanings and things under the surface.
I don't know if love exists but nothing else fits.
I've listed all the pros and cons and nothing else fits.

Sonnet 116 fits. The marriage of true minds. As usual, *he* got it right.

And now it's academic: we both mistimed.
And now it's academic: we both mistimed.
Today, whatever happens, the mission is finished.
The mission is finished, the mission is finished,
And we won't see each other again.

The dream showed him October 20, when he'd reached down and touched her shoulder to wake her. "Time," he said.
He woke, and cried out. He knew The Detail.

14

He woke to an empty room. She hadn't returned yet. And he knew The Detail.
He cried out, his soul tearing like his heart muscles had torn, his heart breaking like his bones had broken. He knew The Detail, and it didn't swirl away. He wanted it to, but it wouldn't.

She thought it would die with her. *She didn't think either of us would survive.*

It was mid-morning on October 22, the day before the summit was originally planned to end. He hadn't completely recovered, but he was well enough to do what came next.

In the wardrobe in the hospital room were the clothes he'd worn on October 20: the grey linen blend suit and woven silk shirt and underwear and socks, all variously pressed and cleaned and washed and hung up or stored in drawers, neatly and tidily. His shoes, soft leather loafers, were polished and stowed in the wardrobe.

He showered and shaved, then dressed. He walked out of the room to the hospital reception desk. "I'm discharging myself," he told the receptionist.

"Mr. Abbas! Are you..."

"I'm quite well, thank you. Please call the Director and thank him for his attention. If he needs to contact me I'll be in my suite at the New Grand."

"I'll tell him. So will you be leaving us, Mr. Abbas?"

"The hospital, right now. The Pier, soon."

He walked out of the hospital onto a small piazza at the edge of the Pier, overlooking the sea. It was the view he'd seen from his hospital room, looking out to sea rather than back towards the foreshore. The day was grey, cold and windy. The sea was the colour he remembered from the day he'd arrived at Brighton: pewter, like his shirt. He stood for a moment watching the gulls, and listening to their cries. Then he turned and strode away, through the Garden and past the Conference Centre and back towards the New Grand.

All of the paraphernalia of the summit had gone, cleared up as tidily as if it, and the summit, had never existed. The Pier was still busy, though: there were people who worked in the business quarter, tourists and casual visitors, and a group of New Anglican staff who greeted him politely. He recognised one of them as Yusuf Khan, the IT specialist whose identity he'd briefly borrowed, and two others as Olivia's personal staff.

"Hello, Mr. Abbas. Are you well enough to be walking in this weather?"

"I'm fine, thanks. I've just left the hospital, and I'm going back to my suite to sort some things out."

"So you're leaving us?"

"Soon."

The sheer ordinariness of the conversation made him realise all the things it *didn't* contain, all the things he now knew but couldn't say. He wanted to cry out, even more intensely than he'd cried out for Levin, but he stayed silent. That would come later, back in his suite. Until then, he had to keep it contained. *Containers and Contents. Containers are hardware. Contents are software.* Usually software would be more important than hardware. But if the contents of a container are liquid or gas or powder, the container will shape them.

Her contradictory signals towards him, her strange Evensong sermon, were all part of what was happening to her. How had she held it together so long?

Somehow he made it back to the New Grand without showing externally what he was feeling inside. He strode through the lobby, nodding politely to the reception staff. Then into the lift and along the corridor and into his suite, where he waited until he heard the expected knock on his door.

She was wearing the dark red dress.

"I heard from the hospital and from some of my staff that you're leaving soon, so I wanted to..."

"Say goodbye? Yes, I did too."

She walked past him into his suite and turned to face him.

"If you hadn't come here," he continued, "I'd have stopped off at your apartment on my way out." He closed the door softly. "You knew I'd find it, didn't you?"

"Of course."

"You thought your Detail would die with you. You didn't think either of us would survive."

"I didn't expect to live past tomorrow. And you, in the Signing Room! Where did you find..."

"Find the ability to win? I don't know. Maybe it was having someone to fight for."

"Do you know all of it?"

"I think so," Anwar said. "Let's try, and you can tell me if any of the details aren't quite right..."

She smiled. "Always obsessive. Not just about The Detail, but about details."

He clicked his tongue in annoyance. "Of course I am! It'll be one of the last things we talk about. I want to get it right, it's important...So. To begin with, they abducted you before you were Archbishop. Is that right?"

"Yes."

"I thought so. They're good at abducting people. They're not good with bodies, but they're good with minds. Look at what they did to Levin."

"Was that his name?"

"You recognised what they did to him. I saw you, in the Signing Room. But with you, they did something more."

She said nothing. Her dark violet eyes, which always seemed to see everything and which wouldn't be stared down by anyone, did not leave his face.

"Shall I tell you?" he asked.

"Oh, for God's sake! All this playacting, the show of annoyance and the lead-up questions, are because you know what it is but you're afraid to actually say it!"

"Yes, I am. Now."

"Then," her voice became quieter, "I'll say it. When they abducted Levin they wiped his identity and left him a monster. A killing machine.

"When they abducted me they wiped my identity and put another one inside me: Parvin Marek. Then they set me up to lead what was then their creation, the New Anglican Church. Unfortunately for them, it didn't work out like that, for reasons I'll tell you later because this *is* the last thing we'll talk about. Is that what you were going to say but couldn't?"

"Yes."

"So when did you know?"

"I didn't, until the Signing Room. Until after my friend Levin died. Because of what you told Gaetano. *You remembered about going back.*"

She looked at him quizzically.

"*You went back.* Marek would always go back. He'd go back to make sure, and he'd shoot someone who was wounded and helpless. A passerby outside the UN Embassy in Zagreb. Rafiq's seven-year-old-son. No," he said, as she started to speak, "this isn't just for Rafiq. Rafiq said, 'Marek killed far more people than just my family. For all of them, this is unfinished business.' I can't leave it unfinished."

"Body and mind. Hardware and software. Container and contents. It seemed obvious to them, when they did it, that the mind was the most important. But it wasn't, it was the container! I didn't change into Marek. Marek changed into me."

"*You went back.*"

"You don't need to do this. Marek changed into me, and I wanted to love you."

"*Wanted?*"

"Love's more intimate than just intimacy. Friendship and companionship grow out of it, over the years. Nothing could grow out of what we did together, Anwar."

"You were right, it does overturn everything." He paused, and added, "How did they do it to you?"

"Does it matter?"

"I'd rather talk about that than what you just said. And yes, it does matter. It's the last thing. I need to tell Rafiq. They must have other Marek identities stored somewhere."

"Wouldn't matter. They'd all seep..."

"I still need to know. Are they organic or electronic?"

"Both. They converted his brain patterns to algorithms, billions of them, stored as electronic programs. Then they converted them again to something organic, like a virus."

"Why?"

"To insert them into a living brain that had been wiped of its last identity and needed billions more protocols to reorder itself. It spread and grew, like they intended. Lots of empty space to spread and grow into. But they didn't know it would seep."

"Seep?"

"Souls aren't the same as software, and bodies aren't the same as hardware. You can't just transcribe or transplant them like computer components. They interact. They seep into each other. One becomes stronger, and it isn't the one you'd think."

"So Marek isn't gone. They've got his identity encoded in some electronic or bionic storage device somewhere."

"Yes. And if they put it in someone else, the same thing will happen. That's the thing about taking an identity. You put it in another body, and the other body eventually shapes it like a glass shapes the water inside it. It can look quite beautiful... Of course, that didn't suit *them*. I was supposed to be their creature, run the Church for their ends."

"Why did they want Marek?"

"The Church was their counter to religious fundamentalism. Marek was political and secular. And an organisational genius. He thought strategically and played long. All points of similarity to Rafiq, and Rafiq would be their next target."

She paused. "I still have the name I had before, but I don't remember what it felt like to be me before. I made the Church do what I wanted, not what they wanted. When they looked into my eyes and realized Marek wasn't in control anymore, they decided to kill me."

"But *you went back.*"

"Do you want to stop saying that, and think of something better?"

"All right. How about this? How much of you is still Marek?"

"The dying part."

"Can you prove that?"

"Why, you want to complain that all this time you've been fucking a woman who's also partly a forty-two-year-old man?"

"Not fucking. That was just the means. Loving was the end."

"Yes," she laughed, "the end. Do you know what it's like, having a dying conjoined identity in your mind? Dying but not quite dead? All these years, I couldn't quite kill it, but I kept it in a state of dying."

"I can't leave it unfinished. I *can't,* Olivia."

He wasn't an Othello person, he was a Lear and Hamlet person. Lear and Hamlet ripped the soul out of him, Othello just made him uncomfortable. That scene where Othello towered over Desdemona before killing her and chanted, ridiculously, 'It is the cause, it is the cause, my soul...' as if chanting something monstrously wrong would somehow make it right. That was what he was doing now. Different words, but still just as wrong, and still just as inevitable. He had to do it. His feelings screamed its wrongness, but everything else inside him, everything he was, ridiculously chanted its rightness.

Time. He towered over her in cold perfection. Looked directly into her eyes. "I love you," he said, and executed a perfect Verb. He turned away before she fell, in two separate impacts, and before her blood started pumping.

Outside the door of his suite he encountered the ginger cat. Its eyes were amber and wide, and for once it didn't seem able to meow Fuck You. He had never been in combat with a cat before, but he found a pressure point easily enough, just behind its ear. It would be out for at least three hours. He went back to the suite, got a soft leather holdall from his wardrobe, put the cat inside, and took it with him. He didn't know why he did it. From now on, he didn't think he'd know why he did anything.

He took the maglev to Gateway, left the New West Pier, and walked across Marine Parade to the underground car park in Regency Square where the Cobra would be waiting.

15

He thought, *The Two Of Her. Two people, one of them my beginning and the other my end. What have I done?*

Scarcely aware of what he was doing, he'd taken the Cobra from its underground lockup. He was now driving it out of Brighton, perhaps for the last time. It was early afternoon on October 22, but damp and murky enough to be early evening. Traffic out of Brighton was heavy and slow and bad-tempered, labouring under a sky that was the same colour as the wet pavements.

The last words he said to her were I Love You. He'd never said that to anyone before, and he'd never say it again.

She was the love of his life, and the hate of his life. Bloodpoison.

Neither of them was perfect: sharp features and strange appetites and vicious combativeness on one side, hook nose and introspection and obsessiveness on the other, self-absorption on both. Once he'd thought they might make a couple, with their imperfections as complementary echoes, but *she* was right. "Friendship or companionship could never grow out of what we did together."

Whereas with Rafiq and Arden, it would. Sweltering sex to begin with, then over the years it would settle into a measured pace. Maybe even children. He liked the idea of them having children.

He was passing the heavy Victorian wrought-iron boundaries of Brighton Station on his right. The traffic hadn't got any quicker, and wouldn't for some time, so he was able to peer in and see the white and silver maglevs inside. Like those on the Pier.

Everything comes back there eventually.

They put Marek in her, expecting that his soul would control her body. But her body controlled his soul, though at times only just. How had she held it together all this time? When would he ever again meet anyone even remotely like her? *I won't. I can't ever come back from this. Mentally I'm finished, and Rafiq will know that. Rafiq knows everything.*

He had to stop this relentless spot-picking. He needed to focus on unrelated things. Anything that would take his mind somewhere else. The Cobra, for instance. He'd always wanted a Cobra. It looked like no other car ever made, right on the cusp of ugliness and beauty. Its power wasn't much in evidence in this foul traffic, but he'd open it up when he got further out of Brighton.

Thinking about the Cobra didn't work, though. He felt as empty as if his own identity had been wiped, and there was nothing put into him to fill it.

And then he thought of something.

They put Marek's identity into her mind after wiping her mind clear of hers, and hers came back and shoved Marek's aside. Does that mean the soul, or the identity, resides in the body and not the brain? No, that couldn't be. But maybe, however good they were at this, they weren't good enough. *You can never completely wipe a soul away.* Some residual traces will always remain, and they'll always grow back. Like grass will always grow back through concrete buildings, if the buildings are left empty for long enough. Makes you wonder where the soul really resides.

For a moment he felt comforted and even slightly optimistic at the thought. Then he remembered what he'd done, and realised he was whistling in the dark. No, it doesn't make you wonder where the soul really resides. It might sound more poetic if the body's microscopic building blocks, its cells or its atoms, have some residual memory of the original identity. But, more likely, *they* just weren't as good at wiping identities as they thought they were.

And it leaves me no better than I was when I left the Pier. Consultants aren't alone. Consultants who kill the only two people who ever meant anything to them, they're alone.

By now he'd reached the Seven Dials district of Brighton, on the way out towards the Downs. The traffic was still heavy, but he expected it to thin out soon.

He was driving past the Al Quds Mosque, the new one built on the site of the old one, when he noticed a car following him. It was a Ferrari Octavian—low, wide, with an almost alien beauty, like one of Rafiq's VSTOLs. He noticed the car because it had been expertly weaving its way through the traffic and was getting closer. It was about five cars behind him now.

Its colour was distinctive, too. It wasn't the usual rather vulgar Ferrari orange-red, but a beautiful deep dark red. Like her dress. By now it was only three cars behind him, and he could make out Gaetano's face behind the windshield. He'd never talked about cars with Gaetano before, but a Ferrari Octavian would seem about right for him. As fast as the Cobra. Maybe even faster. Certainly more conventionally beautiful.

Gradually, coming out of Seven Dials, the traffic thinned. The buildings lining either side of the road were less densely packed, and the road itself was faster and wider. *Time.* Anwar floored the accelerator, and the Cobra did what it had always been designed for, both in its original incarnation and in its replica form.

The car chase that followed was something whose irony wasn't lost on Anwar, and probably wasn't on Gaetano either: it was a repeat of the Cobra-Ferrari Wars at Le Mans in the 1960s, though this one lasted only a fraction of the time. The Ferrari was at least as fast as the Cobra, and Gaetano was a driver of almost equal ability to Anwar. He couldn't quite catch Anwar, but Anwar couldn't quite lose him either.

In this fashion, though only for a few short miles, the two cars hurtled out of Brighton in the direction of the Downs. Then Anwar thought, *Why do I need to lose him?* He slammed on the brakes, downshifted the gears, and did a handbrake turn, so the Cobra was facing the Ferrari as it came round a bend.

He'd stopped right on the edge of Devil's Dyke. In the small car park overlooking its northern slopes. He smelt the damp earth and grass, the same smell from before.

They both got out of their cars and walked slowly towards each other. *I always knew I'd come back here before I left Brighton. I never thought it would be like this.*

"I'm done here," he said to Gaetano. "I'm going to the Downs to pick up a VSTOL back to Rafiq. You should go back too. We don't need this."

"I can't," Gaetano said. "Not now." There was something wrong about his voice, something thick and choked. He made an odd, swift movement inside his jacket.

"Don't go for the gun," Anwar said. "Or the knife. I'd be quicker."

"Then..."

"Not combat, either. I'd win. And it'd be an anticlimax after the Signing Room."

Why did you do it? Gaetano's eyes were red-rimmed. Anwar knew what she'd meant to him, but he couldn't for the life of him imagine Gaetano actually shedding tears.

"I can't tell you. And you wouldn't believe me anyway. Go back now. This belongs to another time."

"I'll hunt you down," Gaetano said quietly. "For the rest of my life, and yours. I'll never stop. I will find you."

"I know you will. But it won't be me."

JUNE 2061

She knows Gaetano is coming. Now. This evening. It will be either here in her flat, or in Rochester Cathedral. She doesn't want it to be in the Cathedral.

She decides she won't go there tonight. She'll miss Evensong.

And Gaetano isn't the only one getting closer. There's also Michael Taber. She remembers her conversation with him after last week's Evensong, and thinks wryly, He's too clever. Surely Deans of Cathedrals aren't supposed to be like that. Only people in positions like Rafiq are supposed to be like that.

Rafiq. *She thinks of her meeting with him, at Fallingwater, on October 22, 2060.*

"I've done your bidding. I completed the mission. I avenged your family. Now I want out of the Consultancy, and I want you to do this last thing for me."

"Are you sure about this, Anwar?"

"Yes. I can't remain as I am."

"We can make you look like her on the surface, but you won't *be* her."

"Surface will be enough."

Rafiq paused, and considered yet again. The whole idea was so insane he kept going over and over it, trying to find reasons for refusing. *Psychologically he's blown to pieces. He's no use to me now, he'll never recover from what he's done. We've put a fortune into him, but sometimes with Consultants you just have to take the hit and let them go. Like Adeola*

Chukwu, when she became Adeola Chukwu-Asika. Also, he was never really one of the top ones, even now. And...what he said. I owe him.

"Our surgeons will brief you fully, but I can give you some of the details."

"Please. I'm good at details."

"They can't make you exactly her size: too many major bones to shorten. You'll be a little taller than she was, but the resemblance will still be close. Your enhancements will be reduced. You'll keep some of your abilities, but not enough to face people like Gaetano. The surgery will take weeks, and so will the physiological and psychological adjustments. And we can't give you her mind, or soul, or identity. That's gone, Anwar. We only do bodies."

"I understand."

"Do you? Or do you really think that looking like her will somehow make you turn into her?"

"No. I don't think that."

"Then why do you want this?"

"So I can go to churches she went to, looking like her. Walk in places she walked, looking like her. Walk in her world for a while, rather than live without her in mine." He wasn't consciously paraphrasing Jim Weatherly's old song, but he recognised the words when he spoke them. They fitted.

She has left the front door of her flat open so she can hear them when they enter the hall and walk up the stairs. She expects there will be more than one. Gaetano, certainly, and perhaps Proskar and two or three others.

She is still shabbily dressed. Her cheap blue jeans are faded and frayed. Her blonde hair is lank and greasy, not coiffed and swirled to hide the sharpness of the features Rafiq's surgeons have recreated so closely.

And all this time she hasn't been able to bring herself to wear a skirt or dress. Anwar has been remade to look like

Olivia. *Does that mean Anwar could get an erection if he stood in front of a mirror and looked at his remade body? He could, if the remaking hadn't been so thorough, and if he still had a penis. But Rafiq's surgeons have thoughtfully given him a clitoris.*

Anwar is long gone. *She knows she has to keep thinking of him in the third person. And Olivia, too. She's neither, and both. She doesn't know where her identity resides.*

Or where she resides. She has been drifting from one seedy flat to another, from Evensongs at one church to another, but she has always wanted Rochester Cathedral to be her final destination. She remembers that Olivia liked it, and liked the quiet understated companionship of the Old Anglicans. She remembers that Olivia told Anwar that, once.

The irony isn't lost on her. The ones who wanted Olivia dead, the ones Anwar had fought and defeated, are now satisfied. The ones who loved Olivia, who fought alongside Anwar to protect her, are the ones coming for her this evening. Or coming for me, whoever I am.

She thinks, how would Anwar feel about all this? He'd loved a woman who'd been abducted and force-fed the soul of a man—an unspeakable man—and the man's soul started to revert back to the woman's. And now Anwar is a man's soul inhabiting the surgically-replicated body of that woman, and knowing, because the body is only a replica, that he'll never turn into her.

She knows exactly how Gaetano will feel, though. Gaetano will kill someone who looks like Olivia, knowing she isn't the real Olivia. Maybe the real Olivia wasn't what Anwar had killed, either. Or maybe she was. Parvin Marek had died, or had been dying, inside her.

Which makes her recall another irony. Marek, who'd murdered Rafiq's family, was also part of Olivia when Olivia was persuading Rafiq to give her someone to protect her life.

She doesn't want to go down that road anymore, so it's almost a relief when, at last, she hears the door to the hall downstairs being softly but precisely forced open. .

"Time," she says to the ginger cat. It has been standing in her open doorway. It looks back at her, its amber eyes huge and expressionless. "Go. They'll probably take you back to Brighton with them."

The ginger cat walks out through her open doorway. It pauses to look back at her over its shoulder and meows Fuck You. It is not, and never has been, fooled by her appearance.

She sits in an old stained armchair and waits for them. She hears them entering the hall downstairs and hears their voices (Gaetano's and Proskar's, among others) greeting the ginger cat.

In her bedroom, on the pillow, is the page Anwar once tore out of his book, the page with the first four lines of Sonnet 116. On the floor by the side of her chair she has placed Olivia's book, the one Olivia gave Anwar and which Anwar took with him along with her cat. She has left it open at the title page, with Olivia's inscription in large untidy writing.

You mistimed.

She considers putting Anwar's torn-out page on top of Olivia's spread-open book, but decides the symbolism is rather obvious. And there isn't time. She can hear them walking up the stairs.

Author photograph by Gemma Shaw

John Love spent most of his working life in the music industry. He was Managing Director of PPL, the world's largest record industry copyright organization. He also ran Ocean, a large music venue in Hackney, East London.

He lives just outside London in northwest Kent with his wife and cats (currently two, but they have had as many as six). They have two grown-up children.

Apart from his family, London, and cats, his favorite things include books and book collecting, cars and driving, football and Tottenham Hostpur, old movies, and music. Science fiction books were among the first he can remember reading, and he thinks they will probably be among the last.

Evensong is John Love's second novel. His first, *Faith*, was published by Night Shade Books in 2012.